Raavan

Amish is a 1974-born, IIM (Kolkata)-educated banker-turned-author. The success of his debut book, *The Immortals of Meluha* (Book 1 of the Shiva Trilogy), encouraged him to give up his career in financial services to focus on writing. Besides being an author, he is also an Indian-government diplomat, a host for TV documentaries, and a film producer.

Amish is passionate about history, mythology and philosophy, finding beauty and meaning in all world religions. His books have sold more than 7 million copies and have been translated into over 20 languages. His Shiva Trilogy is the fastest-selling and his Ram Chandra Series the second-fastest-selling book series in Indian publishing history. You can connect with Amish here:

- www.facebook.com/authoramish
- www.instagram.com/authoramish
- www.twitter.com/authoramish

Celebrating
30 Years of Publishing
in India

Other Titles by Amish

SHIVA TRILOGY

The fastest-selling book series in the history of Indian publishing

The Immortals of Meluha (Book 1 of the Trilogy)

The Secret of the Nagas (Book 2 of the Trilogy)

The Oath of the Vayuputras (Book 3 of the Trilogy)

RAM CHANDRA SERIES

The second-fastest-selling book series in the history of Indian publishing

Ram – Scion of Ikshvaku (Book 1 of the Series)

Sita – Warrior of Mithila (Book 2 of the Series)

War of Lanka (Book 4 of the Series)

INDIC CHRONICLES

Legend of Suheldev

NON-FICTION

Immortal India: Young Country, Timeless Civilisation

Dharma: Decoding the Epics for a Meaningful Life

Idols: Unearthing the Power of Murti Puja

'{Amish's} writings have generated immense curiosity about India's rich past and culture.'

– Narendra Modi
(Honourable Prime Minister of India)

'{Amish's} writing introduces the youth to ancient value systems while pricking and satisfying their curiosity …'

– Sri Sri Ravi Shankar
(Spiritual Leader and Founder, Art of Living Foundation)

'{Amish's writing is} riveting, absorbing and informative.'

– Amitabh Bachchan
(Actor and Living Legend)

'Amish is one of India's greatest storytellers, creative, imaginative, so you have to turn the page.'

– Lord Jeffrey Archer
(One of the highest-selling authors of all time)

'{Amish's writing is} a fine blend of history and myth … gripping and unputdownable.'

– BBC

'Thoughtful and deep, Amish, more than any author, represents the New India.'

– Vir Sanghvi
(Senior Journalist and Columnist)

'{Amish} is an extraordinary gift to the world from India. He has done a great service by taking ancient myths and giving them relevance in modern times.'

– Deepak Chopra
(World-renowned Spiritual Guru & Bestselling Author)

www.authoramish.com

'{Amish is} one of the most original thinkers of his generation.'
– *Arnab Goswami*
(Senior Journalist & MD, Republic TV)

'Amish has a fine eye for detail and a compelling narrative style.'
– *Dr. Shashi Tharoor*
(Member of Parliament & Author)

'{Amish has} a deeply thoughtful mind with an unusual, original, and fascinating view of the past.'
– *Shekhar Gupta*
(Senior Journalist & Columnist)

'To understand the New India, you need to read Amish.'
– *Swapan Dasgupta*
(Member of Parliament & Senior Journalist)

'Through all of Amish's books flows a current of liberal progressive ideology: about gender, about caste, about discrimination of any kind... He is the only Indian bestselling writer with true philosophical depth – his books are all backed by tremendous research and deep thought.'
– *Sandipan Deb*
(Senior Journalist & Editorial Director, Swarajya)

'Amish's influence goes beyond his books, his books go beyond literature, his literature is steeped in philosophy, which is anchored in bhakti, which powers his love for India.'
– *Gautam Chikermane*
(Senior Journalist & Author)

'Amish is a literary phenomenon.'

– *Anil Dharker*
(Senior Journalist & Author)

www.authoramish.com

Raavan
Enemy of Aryavarta

Book 3
of the
Ram Chandra Series

Amish

HarperCollins *Publishers* India

www.authoramish.com

First published in 2019

This edition published in India by HarperCollins *Publishers* 2023
4th Floor, Tower A, Building No. 10, Phase II, DLF Cyber City,
Gurugram, Haryana – 122002
www.harpercollins.co.in

2 4 6 8 10 9 7 5 3 1

P-ISBN: 978-93-5699-820-9
E-ISBN: 978-93-5699-821-6

Typeset by Jojy Philip, New Delhi 110 015

Printed and bound at
Thomson Press (India) Ltd

Om Namah Shivāya
The universe bows to Lord Shiva.
I bow to Lord Shiva.

To You,

I was drowning,
In Grief, in Anger, in Depression.
You have pulled me into the open air of Peace,
If only for a little while,
By merely listening to my words.

And it is not Mere Words when I say,
That you will always have my quiet gratitude,
You will always have my silent love.

'When extraordinary good fortune of overwhelming
Glory comes to a person,
Retreating misfortune increases the power
of its Sorrows.'
— Kalhana, in *Rajatarangini*

Who among you wants to be great?
Who among you wants to lose all chance at happiness?
Is this Glory even worth it?

I am Raavan.
I want it all.
I want fame. I want power. I want wealth.
I want complete triumph.
Even if my Glory walks side by side with my Sorrow.

India, 3400 BCE

List of Important Characters and Tribes

Akampana: A smuggler; one of Raavan's closest aides

Arishtanemi: Military chief of the Malayaputras; right-hand man of Vishwamitra

Ashwapati: King of the northwestern kingdom of Kekaya; father of Kaikeyi and a loyal ally of Dashrath

Bharat: Ram's half-brother; son of Dashrath and Kaikeyi

Dashrath: Chakravarti king of Kosala and emperor of the Sapt Sindhu; father of Ram, Bharat, Lakshman and Shatrughan

Hanuman: A Naga and a member of the Vayuputra tribe

Indrajit: Son of Raavan and Mandodari

Janak: King of Mithila; father of Sita

Jatayu: A captain of the Malayaputra tribe; Naga friend of Sita and Ram

Kaikesi: Rishi Vishrava's first wife; mother of Raavan and Kumbhakarna

Khara: A captain in the Lankan army; Samichi's lover

Krakachabahu: The governor of Chilika

Kubaer: The chief-trader of Lanka

Kumbhakarna: Raavan's brother; also a Naga

Kushadhwaj: King of Sankashya; younger brother of Janak

Lakshman: One of the twin sons of Dashrath; Ram's half-brother

Malayaputras: The tribe left behind by Lord Parshu Ram, the sixth Vishnu

Mandodari: Wife of Raavan

Mara: An independent assassin for hire

Mareech: Kaikesi's brother; Raavan and Kumbhakarna's uncle; one of Raavan's closest aides

Nagas: Human beings born with deformities

Prithvi: A businessman in the village of Todee

Raavan: Son of Rishi Vishrava; brother of Kumbhakarna; half-brother of Vibhishan and Shurpanakha

Ram: Son of Emperor Dashrath and his eldest wife Kaushalya; eldest of four brothers; later married to Sita

Samichi: Police and protocol chief of Mithila; Khara's lover

Shatrughan: Twin brother of Lakshman; son of Dashrath and Sumitra; Ram's half-brother

Shochikesh: The landlord of Todee village

Shurpanakha: Half-sister of Raavan

Sita: Daughter of King Janak and Queen Sunaina of Mithila; also the prime minister of Mithila; later married to Ram

Sukarman: A resident of Todee village; Shochikesh's son

Vali: The king of Kishkindha

Vashishtha: Raj guru, the royal priest of Ayodhya; teacher of the four Ayodhya princes

Vayuputras: The tribe left behind by Lord Rudra, the previous Mahadev

Vedavati: A resident of Todee village; Prithvi's wife

Vibhishan: Half-brother of Raavan

Vishrava: A revered rishi; the father of Raavan, Kumbhakarna, Vibhishan and Shurpanakha

Vishwamitra: Chief of the Malayaputras; also temporary guru of Ram and Lakshman

Note on the Narrative Structure

Thank you for picking up this book and giving me the most important thing you can share: your time.

I know many of you have been patiently waiting for the release of the third part of the Ram Chandra series. My sincere apologies for the delay, and I hope the book will live up to your expectations.

Some of you may wonder why I decided to change the name of the book from *Raavan – Orphan of Aryavarta* to *Raavan – Enemy of Aryavarta*. Let me explain. While writing Raavan's story, I realised a few things about the man. Right from when he was a child, Raavan raged against the circumstances he found himself in. He was very much a man in charge of his destiny. Initially, I felt Raavan had been cast aside by his motherland and was thus, in a sense, an orphan. But as the story unfolded in my mind, I felt the decisions that took him away from his motherland were deliberate. He *chose* to be the enemy rather than being cast into the role of the orphan.

As some of you know, I have been inspired by a storytelling technique called hyperlink, which some call the multilinear narrative. In such a narrative, there are many characters; and a connection brings them all together. The three main characters in the Ram Chandra series are Ram, Sita and Raavan. Each character has life experiences, which mould who they are, and each has their own adventure and riveting backstory. Finally, their stories converge with the kidnapping of Sita.

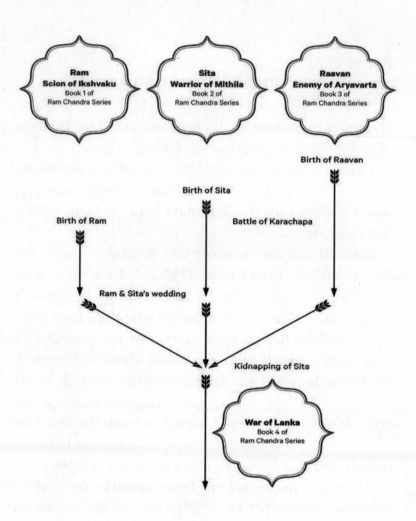

So while the first book explored the tale of Ram, the second the story of Sita, the third burrows into the life of Raavan, before all three stories merge from the fourth book onwards into a single story. It is important to remember that Raavan is much older than both Sita and Ram. In fact Ram is born on the day that Raavan fights a decisive battle—against Ram's father Emperor Dashrath! This book, therefore, goes further back in time, before the birth of the other principal characters—Sita and Ram.

I knew that writing three books, in a multilinear narrative, would be a complicated and time-consuming affair, but I must confess, it was thoroughly exciting. I hope it is as rewarding and thrilling an experience for you as it was for me. Understanding Ram, Sita and Raavan as characters helped me inhabit their worlds and explore the maze of plots and stories that illuminate this great epic. I feel truly blessed for this.

Since I was following a multilinear narrative, I left clues in the first book (***Ram – Scion of Ikshvaku***) as well as the second (***Sita – Warrior of Mithila***), which tie up with the stories in the third. There are surprises and twists in store for you here, and many to follow!

I hope you enjoy reading ***Raavan – Enemy of Aryavarta***. Do tell me what you think of it, by sending me messages on my Facebook, Instagram, or Twitter accounts given below.

Love,
Amish

www.facebook.com/authoramish
www.instagram.com/authoramish
www.twitter.com/authoramish

Acknowledgements

The acknowledgements written below were composed when the book was published in 2019. I must also acknowledge those that are publishing this edition of **Raavan – Enemy of Aryavarta** *The team at HarperCollins: Swati, Shabnam, Akriti, Gokul, Vikas, Rahul, and Udayan, led by the brilliant Ananth. Looking forward to this new journey with them.*

***

It has been a terrible two years. I have been cursed with more grief and suffering in this benighted period, than what I had experienced in my entire life before. Sometimes I felt that the structure of my entire life was collapsing. But it did not. I survived. The building still stands. This book worked like a keystone. And the ones I acknowledge below, have been my buttresses; for they have held me together.

My God, Lord Shiva. He has really tested me these last two years. I hope He will make it a little bit easier now.

The two men I have admired most in my life, men of old-world values, courage, and honour; my father-in-law Manoj Vyas and my brother-in-law Himanshu Roy. They are both up in heaven now, looking at me. I hope I can make them proud.

Neel, my 10-year-old son; and you will pardon this father's emotionality when I say, 'My boy is the best there ever was and ever will be!'

Bhavna, my sister; Anish and Ashish, my brothers, for all their inputs to the story. As always, they read the first draft. Their views, support, affection, and encouragement are invaluable.

The rest of my family: Usha, Vinay, Shernaz, Meeta, Preeti, Donetta, Smita, Anuj, Ruta for their consistent faith and love. And I must acknowledge the contribution of the next generation of my family towards my happiness: Mitansh, Daniel, Aiden, Keya, Anika and Ashna.

Gautam, the CEO of my publisher Westland, and Karthika and Sanghamitra, my editors. If there are people outside of my family, who are the closest to this project, it is this trio. They are an unbeatable mix of capability, politeness and grace. Here's hoping for a long innings together. The rest of the brilliant team at Westland: Anand, Abhijeet, Ankit, Arunima, Barani, Christina, Deepthi, Dhaval, Divya, Jaisankar, Jayanthi, Krishnakumar, Kuldeep, Madhu, Mustafa, Naveen, Neha, Nidhi, Preeti, Raju, Sanyog, Sateesh, Satish, Shatrughan, Srivats, Sudha, Vipin, Vishwajyoti and many others. They are the best team in the publishing business.

Aman, Vijay, Prerna, Seema, and the rest of my colleagues at my office. They take care of my business work which gives me enough free time to write.

Hemal, Neha, Candida, Hitesh, Parth, Vinit, Natashaa, Prakash, Anuj, and the rest of the Oktobuzz team, who have designed the cover for the book, and done a fantastic job at it. They have also made the trailer and helped manage many of the social media activities for the book. A brilliant, creative, and committed agency.

Mayank, Shreyaa, Sarojini, Deepika, Naresh, Marvi, Sneha, Simran, Kirti, Priyanka, Vishaal, Danish and the Moe's Art team, who have driven media relations and marketing alliances for the book. They are more than an agency, they are advisors.

Satya and his team who have shot the new author photos that have been used on the inside cover of this book. He made a rather ordinary subject look better.

Caleb, Kshitij, Sandeep, Rohini, Dharav, Heena and their respective teams who support my work with their business, legal and marketing advice.

Mrunalini, a brilliant Sanskrit scholar, who works with me on research. My discussions with her are enlightening. What I learn from her helps me develop many theories which go into the books.

Aditya, a passionate reader of my books, who has now become a friend and a fact-checker.

And last, but certainly not the least, you, the reader. I know this book has been delayed a lot. My sincere apologies for this. Life just took me away from writing. But it did bring me back. And I will not falter from here on. Thank you for your patience, love and support.

Chapter 1

3400 BCE, Salsette Island, west coast of India

The man screamed in agony. He knew his end was near. He wouldn't have to bear this pain much longer. But he had to hold on to the secret till then. He had to. Just a little longer.

He steeled himself and repeated the chant endlessly in his mind. A chant that held immense power. A chant sacred to all in his tribe: the tribe of the Malayaputras.

Jai Shri Rudra… Jai Parshu Ram… Jai Shri Rudra… Jai Parshu Ram.

Glory to Lord Rudra. Glory to Lord Parshu Ram.   ·

He closed his eyes, focusing on the mantra. Trying to forget his present surroundings.

Give me strength, Lords. Give me strength.

His nemesis stood over him, preparing to inflict yet another wound. But before he could strike, he was pulled back roughly. By a woman.

She whispered in an angry, guttural voice, 'Khara, this is not working.'

Khara, a platoon commander in the Lankan armed forces, turned towards Samichi, his childhood love. Until a few years back, Samichi had been the acting prime minister of Mithila, a small kingdom in north India. But she had since abandoned her post and was focused on finding the whereabouts of the person who had appointed her. The princess she had once served: Sita.

'This Malayaputra is a tough nut,' Khara whispered. 'He won't break. We have to find the information some other way.'

'There is no time!'

Samichi's whisper was rough in its urgency. Khara knew she was right. The man on the rack was their best possible source of information for now. Only he could tell them where Sita, her husband Ram, his brother Lakshman, and the sixteen Malayaputra soldiers accompanying them were hiding. Khara also knew how important it was to extract this information. It was their chance to get back into the good books of Samichi's *true lord*. The one she called *Iraiva*—Raavan, the king of Lanka.

'I am trying, but he will not last much longer like this,' Khara said in a low voice, trying to mask his disappointment. 'I don't think he'll talk.'

'Let me try.'

Before Khara could respond, Samichi strode up to the table where the Malayaputra lay shackled. She yanked off his dhoti and threw it aside. She then wrenched his langot away, leaving the poor man completely exposed and moaning in shame.

Even Khara seemed horrified. 'Samichi, this is—'

Samichi shot him a sharp look and he fell silent. Even torturers had a code of conduct. At least in India. But clearly, Samichi had no qualms about flouting it.

The Malayaputra's eyes were wide open in panic. Almost as if he could anticipate the pain that was to follow.

Samichi picked up a sickle lying nearby. It was dangerously sharp on one side, serrated on the other. A cruel design crafted to inflict maximum pain. She moved towards the torture rack, the sickle in her hand. She held it up, felt its sharp edge, letting it prick her finger and draw blood. 'You will talk. Trust me. You will talk,' she snarled as she poised the sickle between the Malayaputra's legs. Dangerously close.

She moved the sickle slowly, deliberately. It sliced through the soft epidermis and cut deeper. Deeper into the scrotum. Inflicting the maximum pain possible at a point that had an almost sadistic concentration of nerve endings.

The Malayaputra screamed.

He cried, he pleaded for it to stop.

It wasn't his Gods he cried to. This was beyond them now. He was calling out to his mother.

Khara knew then. The Malayaputra would talk. It was only a matter of time. He would break. And he would talk.

—ऋॐI—

Raavan and his younger brother Kumbhakarna sat comfortably inside the Pushpak Vimaan, the legendary flying vehicle, as it flew over the dense jungle.

The king of Lanka was quiet, his body tense. He clutched his pendant tightly—the pendant that always hung from a gold chain around his neck. It was made of the bones of two human fingers, the phalanges of which were carefully fastened with gold links.

Many Indians believed in the existence of tribes of demonic warriors that adorned themselves with relics from the bodies of their bravest adversaries. In doing so, they were said to transfer to themselves the strength of the dead men. The Lankan soldiers, thoroughly loyal to Raavan, believed and propagated the legend that the pendant around his neck was made from the remains of an archenemy's hand. Only Kumbhakarna knew the truth. Only he knew what it meant when Raavan held the pendant tight, the way he was gripping it now.

Leaving his elder brother to his silent ruminations, Kumbhakarna looked around the Pushpak Vimaan. The gargantuan flying vehicle was shaped like a cone that gently tapered upwards. Its many portholes, close to the base, were sealed with thick glass, but the metallic window shades had been drawn back. The diffused light of the early morning sun streamed in, lighting up the interiors. Though the vehicle was reasonably soundproof, the loud sound of the main rotor at the top of the vimaan could be heard. Added to that was the noise of the many smaller rotors, close to the base of the aircraft, which helped control the directional and lateral movements of the flying machine.

The craft's interiors, while spacious and comfortable, were done in a simple, minimalist style. As Kumbhakarna looked up, his eyes fell on the only embellishment inside the vimaan—a large painting of a single rudraaksh, near the inner summit of the vimaan. A brown, elliptical seed, the rudraaksh literally meant the 'teardrop of Rudra'. All those who were loyal to the *God of Gods*, the *Mahadev*, Lord Rudra, wore threaded rudraaksh seeds on their body or placed it in their puja rooms. The painting depicted a particular type of rudraaksh that had a single groove running across it. The original, much smaller seed, which was the model for the painting, was known as an *ekmukhi*. A rare kind of rudraaksh, it was difficult to find and extremely expensive. A specimen impaled on a gold thread was kept in Raavan's private temple in his palace.

Apart from the painting, the vimaan was mostly bare—more of a military vehicle than one designed for luxury. Because it placed function over form, it was able to accommodate more than a hundred passengers.

Kumbhakarna noticed with satisfaction that the soldiers sat silently, in disciplined arcs that fanned out across the vimaan. They had just finished eating. Fed and rested, they were ready for action. It was a matter of a few hours before they would descend on Salsette Island. There, Kumbhakarna had been told, Samichi awaited them with crucial information about the exiled Ayodhya royals—Ram, Sita, his wife, Lakshman, his younger brother—and their band of Malayaputra supporters.

The Lankan soldiers believed they were on their way to avenge the insult to their mighty king's sister, Shurpanakha, who had been injured by Prince Lakshman. While cosmetic surgery would take away the physical marks of the injury to her nose, the metaphorical loss of face could only be avenged with blood. The soldiers knew that. They understood that.

But few of them stopped to wonder exactly what Princess Shurpanakha and Prince Vibhishan, the younger half-siblings of Raavan, had been doing so far away, deep in the Dandakaranya, with the exiled and relatively powerless royals of Ayodhya.

'They are complete idiots,' said Raavan gruffly, keeping his voice low. A curtain draped on an overhanging rod partially screened Raavan's and Kumbhakarna's chairs from the rest. 'I should never have trusted them with this mission.'

After a botched encounter and the resultant skirmish with Ram and the others, Vibhishan had taken Shurpanakha and the Lankan soldiers on a quick march back to Salsette, on the west coast of India. From there, led by Raavan's son Indrajit, they had taken a ship back to Lanka. Upon hearing of their failed mission, Raavan had left his capital city immediately, with as many soldiers as could be accommodated in the Pushpak Vimaan.

Kumbhakarna took a deep breath and looked at his elder brother. 'It's in the past now, Dada,' he said.

'Such fools! Vibhishan and Shurpanakha have taken after their stupid barbarian mother. They can't even handle a simple job.'

Raavan and Kumbhakarna were the sons of Rishi Vishrava and his first wife, Kaikesi. Vibhishan and Shurpanakha were also the sage's children, but by his second wife, Crataeis, a Greek princess from the island of Knossos in the Mediterranean Sea. Raavan abhorred his half-siblings, but had been forced to accept them, by his mother, after their father's death.

'Every family has its idiots, Dada,' said Kumbhakarna with a smile, trying to calm his brother down. 'But they're still family.'

'I should have listened to you. I should never have sent them.'

'Forget it, Dada.'

'Sometimes I feel like—'

'We'll handle it, Dada,' Kumbhakarna interrupted him. 'We'll kidnap the Vishnu, and the Malayaputras will be left with no choice but to give us what we want. What we need.'

Raavan took his brother's hand. 'I've given you nothing but trouble, Kumbha. Thank you for always sticking by me.'

'No, Dada. I am the one who has given you nothing but trouble since my birth. I am alive because of you. And I will die for you,' Kumbhakarna said, his voice edged with emotion.

'Nonsense! You will not die anytime soon. Not for me. Not for anybody. You will die of old age, many many years from now, when you have bedded every woman you want to and drunk as much wine as your heart desires!'

Kumbhakarna, who had been celibate and a teetotaller for several years now, laughed. 'You do enough of that for both of us, Dada!'

—ᚱᛟᛁ—

Strong winds buffeted the Pushpak Vimaan. The vehicle lurched and juddered, like a toy in the hands of a giant demonic child. The rain was coming down hard. They watched it fall in sheets, past the thick glass of the portholes.

'By the great Lord Rudra, it can't be my fate to die in a stupid air crash.'

Raavan double-checked the body grip that held him securely in his chair. As did Kumbhakarna. These grips had been specially designed to evenly distribute the force of restraint over the torso of the seated passengers. Even their thighs were restrained.

The Lankan soldiers, meanwhile, had attached themselves to the standard grips fixed to the floor and walls of the vimaan. Most of them were managing to keep calm, and the contents of their stomach within. Some of them, however, being first-time travellers in the vimaan, were vomiting copiously.

Kumbhakarna turned to Raavan. 'It's an unseasonal storm.'

'You think?' said Raavan, grinning. Nothing brought out his competitive spirit like adversity.

Kumbhakarna turned to look at the four pilots, who were struggling with the levers, trying to direct the craft against the wind with the sheer force of their bodies against the controls.

'Not too hard!' shouted Kumbhakarna, making his voice carry over the howling wind. 'If the levers break, we are done for.'

All four men turned towards Kumbhakarna, who was probably the best vimaan pilot alive.

'Don't fight the wind so hard that the controls break,' ordered Kumbhakarna. 'Let it flow. But not too loose either. Just keep the vimaan upright and we'll be fine.'

As the pilots gave the levers some slack, the vimaan lurched and swung even more vigorously.

'Are you trying to make me throw up?' asked Raavan, grimacing.

'Puking never killed anyone,' said Kumbhakarna. 'But an air crash would do the job most efficiently.'

Raavan scowled, took a deep breath, and closed his eyes. He gripped his hand brace even tighter.

'Plus, there is a positive side to this storm,' said Kumbhakarna. 'These loud winds will drown out the noise of the rotors. We'll have the element of surprise on our side when we attack them.'

Raavan opened his eyes and looked at Kumbhakarna, his eyebrows furrowed. 'Are you crazy? We outnumber them five to one. We don't need an element of surprise. We just need to land safely.'

———॥१८॥———

The battle was short and decisive.

There were no Lankan casualties. All the Malayaputras, save their captain Jatayu, and two of his soldiers, were dead or critically injured. But Ram, Lakshman and Sita were missing.

While Kumbhakarna set about organising the efforts to find the trio, Raavan stood staring at a Malayaputra soldier who lay flat on his back on the ground. The man was still alive, but barely. Moving rapidly towards his death with every raspy breath.

Thick blood was pooling around his body, soaking into the wet mud and discolouring the green grass. The vastus muscles on his thighs had been slashed through. Almost down to the bone. Blood gushed out in torrents from the many severed arteries.

Raavan stared. As always, he was fascinated by the sight of a slow death.

He could hear Kumbhakarna.

'Jatayu is a traitor. He was one of us before he defected to the Malayaputras. I don't care what you do to him. Get the information, Khara.'

'Yes, Lord Kumbhakarna,' said Khara. He sounded relieved. Samichi and he had proven their worth, with information and muscle. He saluted and marched away towards his quarry.

Raavan focused on the dying Malayaputra. He was losing blood fast. It seemed to be spurting out from what appeared to be a small incision on his abdomen. But Raavan could see that the wound was deep. The kidneys, liver, stomach, had all been cut through. The man's body was twitching and shivering as the blood drained out of it.

Kumbhakarna's words pierced his consciousness again.

'I want seven teams. Two men in each team. Spread out. They can't have gone far. If you find the princes, or the princess, do not engage. One of you should come back and inform us while the other continues to track them.'

Raavan's attention was still on the Malayaputra. His left eye had been gouged out. Perhaps by a Lankan soldier wearing hidden tiger claws on his hand. The partially severed eyeball hung out of the eye socket, held tenuously by the optic nerve. Blood dripped weakly from the bloody, discoloured white ball.

The Malayaputra's mouth was open, his chest heaving. Trying to swallow air and pump oxygen through his body. Desperately trying to stay alive.

Why does the soul insist on hanging on to the body until the absolute last minute? Even when death is clearly the better alternative?

'Dada.' Kumbhakarna's voice broke his reverie. Raavan raised a hand for silence and his brother obeyed. Raavan looked on as the Malayaputra's life slowly ebbed away. His breathing grew more and more ragged. The harder he breathed, the more quickly the blood flowed out of his numerous wounds.

Let go ...

Finally, there was a deep convulsion. The last, shallow breath escaped out of the dying man's mouth. For a moment, all was still. He lay with his eyes wide open, as if in panic. Both fists clenched tight. Toes bent at an ungainly angle. Body rigid.

And then, slowly, he went limp.

A few moments passed before Raavan turned away from the corpse in front of him. 'You were saying?' he asked Kumbhakarna.

'They can't have gone far,' said Kumbhakarna. 'Khara will get the information out of Jatayu soon. We'll find the Vishnu. We'll get her alive.'

'What about Ram and Lakshman?'

'We'll do our best not to hurt them. And make them think that this is revenge for what was done to Shurpanakha. Do you want to go back to the vimaan and wait?'

Raavan shook his head. *No.*

—र्ठI—

'Let me see Sita,' said Raavan.

'Dada, there's no time. King Ram and Prince Lakshman are close by, they might reach soon. I don't want to be forced to kill them. This is perfect. We've got the Vishnu, and Ayodhya's so-called king has not been injured. Let's leave now. You can see her once we are back in the vimaan.'

The Lankans were in a small clearing where the Malayaputras had set up their temporary camp. They were surrounded by dense forest, with almost nothing visible beyond the tree line. Kumbhakarna was understandably eager to leave before the princes arrived on the spot.

Raavan nodded, and started walking towards the vimaan. His advance guard marched ahead, while Kumbhakarna strode alongside. The main body of soldiers followed, bearing the stretcher that carried a bound and unconscious Sita. The rear guard brought up the end.

Knowing that Ram and Lakshman were free and armed, the Lankans were on their guard. They did not want to be surprised by a hail of arrows.

Periodically, a voice sounded in the distance. Getting louder, and closer, with every repetition.

'Sitaaaaaaa!'

It was Ram, the eldest son of the late King Dashrath of Ayodhya. Since Ayodhya was the supreme power in the region, Dashrath was also the emperor of the *Sapt Sindhu*, the *Land of the Seven Rivers*. When Ram was banished for fourteen years for the unauthorised use of a *daivi astra*, a *divine weapon*, during the Battle of Mithila, Dashrath had nominated Bharat to be the crown prince instead. However, when it was time for Bharat to be crowned emperor after Dashrath's passing, he had, against all expectations, placed Ram's slippers on the throne and begun ruling the empire as his elder brother's representative.

Technically then, despite being in exile, Ram was the reigning king of Ayodhya and the emperor of the Sapt Sindhu. In absentia. Even though he had never formally been crowned king. Treaty obligations on other kingdoms within the Sapt Sindhu would be triggered if he was hurt or killed. These kingdoms would then be forced to mobilise for war against those who had harmed their emperor. And Raavan knew Lanka could not afford a war. Not right now.

But there was no such obligation with regard to the wife of the emperor.

The anguished voice was heard again. 'Sitaaaaaaa…'

Raavan turned towards Kumbhakarna. 'What do you think he'll do? Can he rally the armies of the Sapt Sindhu?'

Kumbhakarna, surprisingly sprightly despite his massive size, kept pace alongside Raavan. He said thoughtfully, 'It depends on how we play it. There are many who oppose Ram and his family in the Sapt Sindhu. If we can make it known that Sita was kidnapped to avenge the attack on Shurpanakha, it will give the kingdoms that don't want to go to war an excuse to back out. Also, there are no treaty obligations that refer to the eventuality of any Ayodhya royal, other than the emperor, being hurt. So they are not treaty-bound to march just because we've kidnapped the emperor's wife. Those who want to stay away can choose to stay away. I don't think he'll be able to rally a large army.'

'So those idiots, Shurpanakha and Vibhishan, have proved to be of some use after all.'

'Useful idiots,' offered Kumbhakarna, with a twinkle in his eye.

'Hey, I have the copyright on that term!' said Raavan, laughing and playfully slapping Kumbhakarna's massive belly.

The brothers had reached the Pushpak Vimaan and now quickly stepped in.

The soldiers followed and started taking their positions inside the craft. Raavan and Kumbhakarna were soon bracing themselves in preparation for take-off. The doors of the vimaan closed slowly with a hydraulic hiss.

'She's a fighter!' said Kumbhakarna with an appreciative grin, nodding in Sita's direction. The Lankan soldiers hovered around her, fastening straps around her unconscious body.

It had been a struggle to capture the brave warrior princess.

Thirty days had passed since the botched encounter between Shurpanakha and the princes, and the Ayodhyan royals had eased their guard, presuming that the Lankans had lost track of them. That day, they had decided to step out and get themselves a proper meal. Sita had gone to cut banana leaves with a Malayaputra soldier called Makrant. Ram and Lakshman had gone hunting in a separate direction.

The two Lankan soldiers who had discovered Sita had managed to kill Makrant, but were, in turn, killed by Sita. She had then stolen to the devastated Malayaputra camp and picked off several Lankans from behind the tree line, using a bow and a quiverful of arrows very effectively, moving quickly from one hiding place to another. But she had not been able to get to either Raavan or Kumbhakarna, who had been sealed off behind protective flanks of Lankan soldiers. Finally, she had been forced to come forward to save her loyal follower, Captain Jatayu. It was then that she was overpowered and rendered unconscious with a toxin, before being tied up and hauled to the vimaan.

'The Malayaputras believe she is the Vishnu,' said Raavan, laughing softly. 'She'd better be a good fighter!'

According to an ancient Indian tradition, towering leaders, the greatest among greats, who could become the propagators of goodness and harbingers of a new way of life, were recognised with the title 'Vishnu'. There had been six Vishnus till now, and the tribe of the Malayaputras had been founded by the sixth Vishnu, Lord Parshu Ram. Now the Malayaputras had recognised a seventh, one who would establish a new way of life in India: Sita. And Raavan had just kidnapped her.

The soldiers around Sita dispersed and returned to their positions.

She lay there, safely strapped onto the stretcher, some twenty feet away from Raavan. Her angvastram was drawn over her body, and the straps were tight across her torso and legs. Her eyes were closed. Saliva trickled out of the corner of her mouth. A large quantity of a very strong toxin had been used to render her unconscious.

For the first time in their lives, Raavan and Kumbhakarna saw Sita's face.

Raavan felt his breath stop. He sat immobile, heart paralysed. Eyes glued to her face.

To Sita's regal, strong, beautiful face.

Chapter 2

Fifty-six years earlier, the ashram of Guru Vishrava, close to Indraprastha, India

For a four-year-old, Raavan was quite sure and steady in his movements.

The precocious child was Rishi Vishrava's son. The celebrated rishi had married late, when he was over seventy years of age. Though you couldn't tell by looking at him: the magical anti-ageing Somras he drank regularly kept him looking youthful. In his long career spanning many decades, Rishi Vishrava had made a name for himself as a great scientist and spiritual guru. In fact, he was considered to be among the greatest intellectuals of his generation.

Being the son of such a distinguished rishi, the weight of expectations rested heavily on Raavan's young shoulders. But it appeared he would not disappoint. Even at this early age, he had a fearsome intellect. It seemed to all who met him that the child would someday surpass even the vast achievements of his illustrious father.

But the universe has a way of balancing things. With the positive comes the negative.

As the sun set on the far horizon, Raavan patiently tied the fragile legs of the hare he had trapped to two small wooden stumps sticking up from the ground. The creature struggled frantically as the boy pinned it down with his knee and pulled the ropes taut. It lay there with its limbs splayed, underside and chest exposed to the sky. The little boy was satisfied. He could begin work now.

Raavan had dissected another hare the previous day. Studied its muscles, ligaments and bones in detail, while it was still breathing. He had been keen to reach the beating heart. But the hare, having suffered enough already, died before he could cut through the sternal ribs. Its heart had stopped by the time Raavan got to it.

Today, he intended to go straight for the animal's heart.

The hare was still struggling, its long ears twitching ferociously. Normally, hares are quiet animals, but this one was clearly in a state of panic. For good reason.

Raavan checked the sharpness of his knife with the tip of his forefinger. It drew some blood. He sucked at his forefinger as he looked at the hare. He smiled.

The excitement he felt, the rapid beating of his heart, took away the dull ache in his navel. An ache that was perennial.

He used his left hand to steady his prey. Then he held the knife over the animal, the tip pointed at its chest.

Just as he was about to make the incision, he sensed a presence near him. He looked up.

The Kanyakumari.

In many parts of India, there was a tradition of venerating the *Kanyakumari*, literally the *Virgin Goddess*. It was believed that the Mother Goddess resided, temporarily, within the bodies of certain chosen young girls. These girls were worshipped as living Goddesses. People came to them for advice and prophecies—they counted even kings and queens among their followers—until they reached puberty, at which time, it was believed, the Goddess moved into the body of another pre-pubescent girl.

There were many Kanyakumari temples in India. This particular Kanyakumari who stood in front of Raavan was from Vaidyanath, in eastern India.

She was on her way back to Vaidyanath after a pilgrimage to the holy Amarnath cave in Kashmir, and had stopped at Rishi Vishrava's ashram. The holy cave, buried under snow for most of the year, housed a great lingam made of ice. It was believed that this cave was where the first Mahadev had unveiled the secrets of life and creation.

The Kanyakumari's entourage had returned from the pilgrimage with their souls energised but their bodies exhausted. The Goddess had decided to stay for a few weeks in Rishi Vishrava's ashram by the river Yamuna, before continuing on her journey to Vaidyanath.

The rishi had welcomed her visit as a blessed opportunity to speak to the Goddess and expand his understanding of the spiritual world. Despite his best efforts, however, the Kanyakumari had kept to herself and spent little time with him or the many inhabitants of his ashram.

But that had only added to the natural magnetism and aura of the living Goddess. Even Raavan, usually preoccupied in his own world, had stared at her every chance he got, fascinated.

He looked up at her now, transfixed, knife poised in mid-air.

The Kanyakumari stood in front of him, her expression tranquil. There was no trace of the anger or disgust that

Raavan was used to seeing whenever anyone from the ashram caught him at his 'scientific' experiments. Nor was there any sign of sorrow or pity in her eyes. There was nothing. No expression at all.

She just stood there, as if she were an idol made of stone—distant yet awe-inspiring. A girl no older than eight or nine. Wheat-complexioned, with high cheekbones and a small, sharp nose. Long black hair tied in a braid. Black eyes, wide-set, with almost creaseless eyelids. Dressed in a red dhoti, blouse and angvastram. She had the look of the mountain people from the Himalayas.

Raavan instinctively checked the cummerbund tied around his waist, on top of his dhoti. It was in place, covering his navel. His secret was safe. Then he remembered the hideous pockmarks on his face, the legacy of the pox he had suffered as a baby. Perhaps for the first time in his life, he felt self-conscious about his appearance.

He shook his head to get the thought out of his mind.

'*Devi* Ka… Kanyakumari,' he whispered, letting the knife drop to the ground. His eyes were fixed on the *Goddess*.

The Kanyakumari stepped forward without a word, her expression unchanged. She bent down and picked up the knife. With quick, efficient movements, she cut the restraints on the wretched hare.

She then picked it up and gently kissed it on the head. The hare was quiet in her hands, its panic forgotten. The voiceless animal seemed to know that it was safe again.

For a fleeting moment, Raavan thought he saw the Kanyakumari's eyes light up with love. Then the mask came back on.

She put the hare down and the animal bounded away.

The Kanyakumari looked again at Raavan and returned the knife to him.

Her face remained impassive.

Without saying a word, she turned and walked away.

Not for the first time since she had arrived at the ashram, Raavan wondered what the Kanyakumari's birth-name had been, before she was recognised as a living Goddess.

—ऱॊI—

Raavan had slipped out of the house as soon as his mother, Kaikesi, fell asleep. He moved quickly towards his destination.

He was seven years old now. And already renowned in many ashrams, besides that of his father's, as a brilliant child with a formidable intellect. He had started his training in the martial arts as well, and was already showing great promise. As if that wasn't enough, he had a keen ear for music too. His favourites were the stringed instruments, especially the magnificent Rudra Veena. It was only a few months since he had started learning to play the veena, but he was already in love with it.

The Rudra Veena was named after the previous Mahadev, Lord Rudra, whom Raavan worshipped with a passion. The instrument was considered to be among the most difficult to play. He had been told that to master it required years of practice—each time he heard this, he drove himself harder, for how could Raavan be any less than the best?

As he walked quickly through the darkness, Raavan's mind was on the contest that had been arranged for the following morning, against a musician called Dagar. A young and already well-known Rudra Veena player, Dagar was visiting Rishi Vishrava's ashram.

Though it was only a friendly competition, Raavan had no desire to lose.

He thought again of the first time he had beheld the instrument of his choice. He had felt a deep reverence as he touched the rounded teak-wood fingerboard fixed on two large resonators: they were made of dried and hollowed out gourds, he had been told. On both ends of the tubular body were woodcarvings of peacocks, known to be the favourite birds of Lord Rudra. Twenty-two straight wooden frets were fixed to the fingerboard with wax and there were three separate bridges.

This most dramatic of instruments had eight strings— four main and three drone strings on one side of the player and one drone string on the other. All the strings were wound around the eight friction pegs on the tuning head.

During that first lesson, Raavan had watched as the older students sat on the floor and settled the veena with one gourd over the shoulder. Some of them rested it on their left knee. That was when he had realised that the instrument was customised for the person who handled it; there was no question of one-size-fits-all.

Anyone who has observed the structure of the Rudra Veena knows that it is an extremely complex instrument to understand, let alone play. Wire plectrums worn on the index and middle fingers of the right hand are used to pluck the main strings, while the drone strings are played with the nail of the little finger. The strings have to be manipulated with the left hand from beneath the horizontal neck, made more difficult by the fact that the right hand ends up blocking the drone string on the side.

But what truly separates the Rudra Veena from other stringed instruments is the dramatically higher quality of resonance, which is due to the two large gourds attached to its ends. The frequency and strength of the resonance have a significant impact on the tonal quality and the music.

Damage the gourds. Damage the resonance. Damage the music.

Raavan quietly slipped into the small hut where he knew the musical instruments were kept. Dagar's veena was there too. Musicians were known to worship their instruments every night and morning. It seemed Dagar was no different. Puja flowers and burnt incense sticks lay at the base of his Rudra Veena.

Raavan sniggered to himself.

Dagar's prayers will not be answered tonight.

He worked quickly, without a sound. First, he slipped the cloth cover off the instrument. Then he unscrewed the gourd on the left and felt its insides. Polished and smooth. He took out a metallic wrench from the pouch tied to his waist and used it to begin scratching the insides of the gourd.

Dagar would not be immediately able to make out that the resonance was not right, not even while tuning his instrument the next day. He would realise it only when playing the raga during the competition. By which time, it would be too late.

Raavan kept glancing towards the door as he worked. He couldn't think of a single excuse to offer if someone were to walk in just now. But there was no time to worry about that. He focused his energies on the task at hand.

The morning of the competition dawned clear and blue-skied. Much to the surprise of the ashram's inhabitants, the Kanyakumari of Vaidyanath was back amongst them. It had been a good three years since her previous visit. This time, she was on her way to Takshasheela, the famed university-town in north-west India, along with her entourage. And Rishi Vishrava's peaceful ashram had proved to be an ideal resting point.

With the Kanyakumari as a witness, the two musicians began playing. The contest didn't last long. Dagar's damaged veena ensured that he gave up barely ten minutes into his performance, and his younger opponent was declared the winner.

But Vishrava knew his son well.

He dragged Raavan to their frugal hut immediately after the competition.

'What did you do?' he hissed, closing the door behind them so no one could overhear the conversation.

'Nothing!' said Raavan defiantly, his head barely reaching up to his father's chest, his eyes blazing. 'I was just better than that idiot whom you like to favour.'

'Mind your tongue,' said Vishrava, his fists clenched with anger. 'Dagar is one of the finest young Rudra Veena players of this modern age.'

'Not fine enough to beat me,' Raavan scoffed.

'The Kanyakumari is here. How can I allow any subterfuge in her presence?'

Raavan didn't know what the word meant. 'Subter*what*?'

Kaikesi, who was standing behind them, spoke up in a gentle voice. 'Vishrava, if you feel that Raavan is guilty of deceit, please publicly announce Dagar as the winner. Raavan will understand. Perhaps the Kanyakumari herself can—'

Raavan cut in. 'But your husband is guilty of deceit too. He has been lying since the time of my birth. Why doesn't he tell the Kanyakumari about that? Why doesn't he tell everyone the truth about me?'

The old sage raised his hand in anger.

'Please don't!' pleaded Kaikesi, rushing up and throwing her arms around her son. 'You have to stop hitting him. It's wrong... please...'

'Silence! This is all your fault. I am suffering due to your karma. Your bad karma has infected his navel! And his mind!' Vishrava's voice was bitter.

'Hey!' said Raavan angrily. 'Don't talk to her. Talk to me.'

Enraged, Vishrava pushed Kaikesi aside and lunged at Raavan. He slapped the boy hard on his cheek. The seven-year-old went flying across the room. Kaikesi shrieked and ran to shield her son.

Vishrava looked at the boy lying on the ground. Raavan's cummerbund had come undone, revealing a small purple outgrowth from his navel—his birth deformity. Proof that he was a Naga. All across India, people believed that birth deformities were the consequence of a cursed soul, of bad karma carrying over from the previous birth. And such blighted people were called Nagas.

Vishrava spoke with barely disguised disgust. 'Cover that thing!' He glared at his wife. 'Your son will destroy my name.'

Raavan pushed his mother's protective hand away. 'Yes, I will. Because everyone knows I am better than you in every way.'

'Arrogant brat! Lord Indra has bestowed his gifts on the wrong person,' growled Vishrava as he turned to leave.

'Yes, go away! Get lost! I don't need you!' Raavan shouted, struggling to keep his voice level despite the tears that threatened to well up.

The ever-present ache in his navel intensified. Growing in ferocity.

—ॐ—

Raavan was sitting by the side of the mighty Yamuna River, not far from his father's ashram. His cheek still burned, though the tears had long dried up.

He was staring at the ground, a magnifying glass in his hand. With great care, he focused the rays of the sun into a powerful band of light, burning the little ants that scurried about. He was breathing hard, raw anger still pulsating in every vein. His navel throbbed, the centre of constant pain.

The fragrance reached him first. He felt his breath catch.

He turned his head and saw her.

The Kanyakumari.

His body froze, the magnifying glass still in his hand. Burnt and shrivelled ants lay near his feet. The sun's concentrated rays singed the grass.

The Kanyakumari's expression remained calm. No sign of disgust. Nor anger.

She stepped closer and took the glass from Raavan's hand.

'You can be better than this.'

Raavan did not say anything. His mouth was suddenly dry. The long-held breath escaped in a sigh.

The Kanyakumari smiled slightly. An ethereal smile. The smile of a living Goddess.

She pointed towards the ashram, where the music competition had taken place in the morning. 'You can be better than that too.'

Raavan felt his lips move. But no words came out. His mind was blank. Unable to construct even simple thoughts and words.

His heart had picked up pace. He noticed that the ache in his navel had magically disappeared. For a few moments.

'At least try,' said the Kanyakumari.

She turned and walked away.

—र्ठI—

'You would have won anyway,' Dagar said, smiling.

It was past sunset. Most of the ashram's residents were back in their huts. Raavan had come to see Dagar, bringing with him the holy lotus garland he had won earlier in the day. Reluctantly, his eyes unable to meet Dagar's, he had mumbled a confession. The older contestant had responded graciously.

Dagar, like most others present at the event, had suspected that something was not right with his instrument. He had examined the veena after the competition and quickly identified the problem. But he couldn't bring himself to be angry. Raavan was a child, after all.

Raavan did not say anything. He stood with his head bowed. Thinking of the Kanyakumari. She was to leave the next morning.

The sixteen-year-old Dagar, standing head and shoulders over the younger boy, ruffled his hair. 'You have talent. Use that to win. You don't need to do anything underhand.'

Raavan nodded silently. He didn't like his hair being ruffled by anyone.

Except her... he would do anything to get her to ruffle his hair.

'And don't worry,' said Dagar, with a smile. 'My veena is being repaired. No permanent damage done.'

Raavan let out a long breath. He had expected the ache in his navel to disappear. But it hadn't.

'And you can keep this,' said Dagar, returning the lotus garland to him.

Raavan grabbed it. And ran back home.

Chapter 3

Two years passed. Raavan turned nine. Every day, he strove consciously to keep the Kanyakumari's words alive within him. *You can be better,* he often reminded himself. Very rarely did he do anything without considering what her reaction to it might be. And it appeared to be working. He got along more easily with the people in the ashram; some actually seemed to like him.

He had also started covering his navel with a cummerbund when he was at home. He knew it embarrassed his father that his son was a Naga, and he had been trying his best for the past two years to not aggravate the situation.

As a result, the fights with his father had reduced.

So had the pain. It was still there. But so mild that Raavan sometimes forgot about the growth on his navel.

Then, one day, Rishi Vishrava left the ashram for a long journey westward. To the island of Knossos in the Mediterranean Sea. The king of Knossos had expressed a desire to meet the eminent rishi, and Vishrava had decided to accept the invitation.

A few weeks after his departure, Kaikesi discovered that she was pregnant. She considered sending a messenger after the rishi, asking him to turn back. But then decided against it. She would surprise him on his return.

Also, truth be told, the thought weighed heavily on her mind: *What if the second child turned out to be a Naga too?*

Unaware of his mother's misgivings, Raavan was excited about the arrival of a younger sibling. He hung around his mother constantly, taking care of her and making sure she had everything she needed. Until, finally, the day arrived.

A wet nurse was attending to Kaikesi inside the house. Raavan waited outside, eagerly pacing up and down, almost like an anxious father-to-be. Waiting for news.

Many of the ashram's residents waited with him. But it was a long labour. Twelve hours had already passed. Slowly, people began returning to their huts, until only Raavan and Kaikesi's elder brother Mareech were left. Mareech had arrived several days earlier, to help his sister through her pregnancy in Rishi Vishrava's absence.

After some time, even Mareech decided to call it a night. 'I'm going to sleep, Raavan. So should you. The midwife will call us. I've given her strict instructions.'

Raavan shook his head. Wild horses couldn't drag him away.

'All right,' said Mareech, getting up. 'I'll be next door. You are to come and fetch me as soon as the midwife calls. Is that clear?'

'Yes.'

'As soon as you hear anything, call me immediately.'

'I heard you the first time, Uncle.'

Mareech laughed softly and ruffled Raavan's hair.

Raavan jerked his head back and looked at his uncle in irritation. Mareech laughed even louder and raised both hands in mock apology. 'Sorry... sorry!'

Chuckling to himself, he turned and walked away, and Raavan set his hair back in place. Neatly.

Now all alone, the young boy looked up at the starless sky. The tiny sliver of a new moon struggled to push the darkness away. Lamps had been lit around the open courtyard in front of the hut, creating tiny enclaves of light.

As he stared into the darkness, he thought he saw shadows lurking in the distance. The breeze picked up, the sound of it somehow eerie. Like ghost whispers. The nine-year-old shivered. The pain at the centre of his body returned. His navel throbbed in fear.

He folded his hands together in prayer and began chanting the *Maha Mrityunjay* mantra. *The great chant of the Conqueror of Death.* Dedicated to the Mahadev, the God of Gods. Lord Rudra.

As he repeated it, over and over again, he felt the fear disappear. Slowly. Leaving his muscles relaxed. His heartbeat slower.

The pain in his navel quietened once again.

He looked into the darkness with renewed confidence.

Who will fight me? Come on! Who will fight me?

Lord Rudra is with me.

Strangely, his navel began hurting again.

He began chanting even more fervently.

Suddenly, a loud scream resounded through the night. 'Raavan!'

It was Kaikesi.

Raavan sprang up and ran towards the hut.

'Raavan!'

He could hear the sound of a baby crying.

'Raavan!'

His mother's cry was more urgent this time.

Raavan flung the door open and rushed into the hut.

It was dark inside. Only a few lamps threw shadows across the floor. His mother was still on the bed. Weak. Struggling to get up. Tears pouring down her cheeks.

The midwife was holding the baby. Rather, she was dangling it by one leg. It was a boy. Raavan noticed that the baby was quite large for a new-born. As he took in the scene in front of him, he realised to his horror that she was about to smash the baby's head on the ground.

'Stop!' he screamed, dashing forward and drawing his short sword in one quick motion.

The midwife froze as she felt the blade against her abdomen.

'Hand over my brother, now!' Raavan said, his voice hoarse.

'You don't know what you are doing! I am saving your mother! I am saving you!' the midwife screeched.

It was only then that Raavan noticed the outgrowths on the baby's ears. The strange lumps made his ears look like pots. There were outgrowths on his shoulders too, like two tiny extra arms. The new-born was unusually hirsute. And he was howling.

Raavan pressed the sword against her skin, puncturing it. 'I said, hand him over.'

'You don't understand. He has to die. He is cursed. He is deformed. He is a Naga.'

'If he dies, so will you.'

The midwife hesitated, resisting the pressure of the sword that threatened to pierce her abdomen. She wondered if she could survive a stab wound if a physician attended to her immediately.

'You will not survive this,' snarled Raavan, as if reading her mind. 'My sword is long enough to cut through your abdomen and slice your spinal cord. I have practised on animals. Even human bodies. No doctor will be able to save you. Just give me my baby brother and I'll let you go.'

The midwife was in a dilemma. She had her orders, and she was expected to follow them. But she didn't want to die as a consequence. She knew of Raavan's experiments. She knew he was good with a blade. Everyone knew.

Raavan pushed closer. 'Give. Him. To. Me.'

The midwife looked at the furious expression on his face with a sense of foreboding. She had seen it before, this bloodlust. On the faces of warriors. People who killed. Sometimes, simply because they enjoyed it.

And then she noticed.

Raavan's cummerbund had come undone. His navel was visible, and the ugly outgrowth. Proof that he, too, was a Naga.

The shocked woman stood rooted to the spot.

She could hear people gathering outside. They would support her. They knew what they had to do.

There was no reason for her to die. She thrust the baby into Raavan's arms and rushed out.

—ᚱᛞI—

Raavan could hear the angry voices outside. Arguments. People screaming about order. Ethics. Morals.

The door of the hut was closed. But there was no lock on it. Anyone could barge in at any moment.

He tried to control his breathing, his body tense. He gripped his sword tightly. Ready to kill anyone who entered. He looked back at his baby brother. Safe in his mother's arms. Suckling at her breast contentedly. Unaware of the danger they were in.

His mother's face, though, was a picture of terror.

'What are we to do, Raavan?' asked Kaikesi.

Raavan didn't answer. His alert eyes were glued to the door, ready to attack anyone who dared to try and harm his loved ones.

Suddenly, the door swung open and Mareech rushed in. His sword was drawn. Blood dripped from its edge.

Kaikesi moaned in fear and hugged her baby to her chest. She pleaded with her *elder brother*, '*Dada*, please! Don't kill us!'

The baby pulled back from his mother and started crying again.

Raavan stepped in front of Mareech. Brandishing his sword. His voice surprisingly calm. 'You will have to fight me first.'

Mareech shot him an impatient look. 'Shut up, Raavan!' He turned to his sister. 'What's wrong with you, Kaikesi? I am your brother! Why would I kill you?'

Kaikesi looked at him, confused.

Without wasting any more time, Mareech yanked a cloth bag off a hook on the wall. And threw it towards Raavan. 'Two minutes. Pack whatever you need for your brother and mother.'

The boy stood unmoving. Baffled.

'Now!' shouted Mareech.

Raavan snapped back to reality. He pushed his sword back into its scabbard and picked up the bag, rushing to obey his uncle.

Mareech turned to Kaikesi. 'Get up! We have to leave!'

Within a few minutes, they were outside the hut. Raavan had the cloth bag slung over his shoulder. His baby brother was secure in his mother's arms, the palm of her right hand supporting the new-born's neck.

The residents of the ashram were gathered in front of the hut. Angry faces, torches in their hands.

Three bodies lay on the ground. Cut down by Mareech's sword.

Mareech himself stood in front of his sister and her children, brandishing his sword at the crowd. The ashram's residents mostly comprised intellectuals and artists. Good at social boycotts. Good at verbal violence. Good at mob violence as well. But unequipped to handle a trained warrior.

'Stay back,' Mareech growled.

Slowly, he edged towards the stables, sword aloft. His eyes still on the crowd. Quickly, he helped his sister mount a horse. Raavan was soon seated on another. In a flash, Mareech opened the gates wide and vaulted on to his own horse.

And they galloped out of the ashram.

—ॐ—

The group had been riding for hours. Eastwards. The sun was already up, and rising higher and higher.

'Please, Dada,' pleaded Kaikesi. 'We have to stop. I can't carry on like this.'

'No' was the simple answer from a grim-looking Mareech. 'Please!'

Mareech bent and whipped Kaikesi's horse, sending it cantering again.

—र०I—

It was almost noon by the time they sat down to rest.

Mareech didn't think much of the tracking and fighting skills of the ashram's residents. But better safe than sorry, he had said, each time Kaikesi begged him to slow down.

They were in the Gangetic plains, where the thick alluvial soil and low, rocky terrain made it easy for someone to track them. They had changed directions often. Riding through streams. Moving through flooded fields. Doing all that was necessary to avoid being hunted down.

The three horses were safely tethered and Kaikesi was resting against a tree, suckling her infant. Mareech had left Raavan on guard while he went foraging for food.

He was soon back with two rabbits. In the bag over his shoulder were some roots and berries.

They cooked and ate the food quickly.

'Twenty minutes of rest,' said Mareech. 'Then we ride out again.'

'Dada,' said a tired Kaikesi. 'I think we've left them far behind. Why don't we stay here for a little while?'

'No. It's safer to move on to Kannauj. Our family is there. They will protect us.'

Kaikesi nodded.

Mareech looked at Raavan, noticing he had not touched his food. 'Eat up, son.'

'I'm not hungry.'

'I don't care whether you are hungry or not. Do you want to protect your mother and brother? Then, you need to be strong. And for that, you have to eat.'

Raavan started to protest.

'Just eat, Raavan,' said Kaikesi.

Raavan looked at his mother, then turned back to his food and started eating.

'I don't understand how the ashram people can do this,' Kaikesi said. 'I am the wife of their preceptor. We are the family of their guru. How dare they!'

Mareech glared at his sister. 'Are you trying to play dumb, Kaikesi? Or are you in denial?'

'What do you mean?'

'Do you really think they made this decision on their own?'

'What are you insinuating, Dada?'

'It's clear as daylight. They were following instructions!'

Kaikesi shook her head in disbelief. 'No, it can't be. He left before learning of my pregnancy.'

'It was him. He suspected this might happen, so he left instructions. Those people were simply carrying out orders.'

'I refuse to believe it.'

'Refusing to believe the truth doesn't make it any less true. We had heard about it in Kannauj. Why do you think I came to stay with you at the ashram?'

Kaikesi kept shaking her head. 'No, no. It can't be true.'

Raavan spoke up. 'My father ordered them to kill us?'

Mareech looked at Raavan and then back at Kaikesi. He had forgotten the boy's presence in the exchange with his sister.

'I asked you something,' said Raavan.

'Kaikesi?' Mareech said helplessly.

'Uncle, did my father order our killing?' asked Raavan.

'Kaikesi…' Mareech repeated.

His sister remained silent. Still shaking her head. Tears rolled down her cheeks.

'Uncle…'

Mareech turned to Raavan. 'You have to take care of your family now. You may as well know the truth.'

Raavan kept quiet. His fists clenched tight. He knew the answer already. But he wanted to hear it.

'From what little I know, he didn't order your death or your mother's,' said Mareech. 'But he did order the killing of your brother, in case he turned out to be a Naga.'

Raavan drew in a sharp breath. Anger and grief clouded his mind. He looked at his brother, sleeping peacefully in his mother's lap. The two short extra limbs at the top of his shoulders moved slightly in his sleep. The rest of his body was motionless.

Raavan bent and picked up his infant brother. He cradled him in his arms, his eyes radiating love. 'Nothing will happen to you. Nobody will hurt you. Not as long as I am alive.'

Over his head, Mareech and Kaikesi looked at each other, nonplussed and, at the same time, overcome. Mareech touched the boy's shoulder sympathetically, but Raavan shrugged the comforting hand away and continued to croon to the baby.

Chapter 4

Two days had passed since Mareech had helped Kaikesi and her sons escape from Vishrava's ashram. They were camped in a clearing in the jungle for the night, the horses tied in a circle around the camp.

It was the third day of the waxing moon. With the dense jungle cover and the night-time fog, visibility was reduced to barely a few feet. So Mareech set about lighting a small fire. Not just for heat, but also for safety.

He sat hunched over a flat wooden board that had a notch cut into its surface. The fireboard. In his hands he held a long slender piece of wood, which spun when he rubbed his palms together. Patiently, he got the wooden spindle into the notch. Waiting for the glowing black dust, like smouldering coal, to collect. It was a primitive and time-consuming method, but their only option in the jungle.

As he waited, Mareech's eyes fell on the dark outlines of his sister and her infant son. They appeared to be sleeping, fatigued after the day's journey. The baby, only a few days old, had a name now: Kumbhakarna—the one with pot-shaped ears. It was Raavan who had suggested it and Kaikesi and Mareech had instantly agreed.

Mareech looked at Raavan, who sat close to him. The nine-year-old's knife was out of its scabbard. Mareech tried to get a look at Raavan's face.

Were his eyes closed?

He was about to scold Raavan and order him to help with the fire, when the boy brought down his knife in a flash. There was a loud screech. Mareech stared at him, stunned. It was too dark for him to be certain, but it appeared his nephew had just pinned down a hare with his knife.

Very few people could shoot arrows unguided by vision. Even fewer could throw knives based on sound alone. But to stab a fast-moving animal like a hare, based only on sound, was unheard of.

Mareech looked at Raavan in awe, his mouth slightly open. Then he turned his attention back to where the smouldering dust had started collecting on the fireboard. Quickly, he slid the dust onto the small pile of tinder he had collected. Then he blew on it gently, till the tinder caught fire. One by one, he transferred the flame to the logs he had arranged beside the burning tinder. Soon there was a roaring fire in the centre of the small clearing.

The fire taken care of, Mareech turned to Raavan. The boy had begun skinning the hare's hind legs. With a start, Mareech noticed the animal was still alive. Making frantic, yet weak sounds, like an agonised pleading. In the light of the fire, Mareech could also see Raavan's expression.

A chill ran up his spine.

He got up, and in one fluid move, pulled out his own knife, took the hare from Raavan and stabbed it in the heart. He held the blade there for a few moments, till the hare stopped moving. Then he handed it back to Raavan. 'This animal has done nothing to you.'

Raavan stared at Mareech, his face devoid of expression. After a long, still moment, he turned back to the hare and started skinning it again. Mareech walked over to where his bag lay and pulled out some dried meat. He began heating it over the flame, using a slim, sharpened rod as a skewer.

'Uncle.'

Mareech looked up.

'I didn't thank you,' said Raavan.

'There's no need for that.'

'Yes, there is. Thank you. I will remember your kindness. I will remember your loyalty.'

Mareech smiled at the nine-year-old who spoke like an adult. And went back to heating the meat.

If only the night would pass quickly, and the dawn arrive soon. For the next day, they would finally be home, in Kannauj.

—ॐI—

The ancient city of Kannauj had blessed many Indians with a great deal.

Situated on the banks of the holy Ganga, the city had been a great centre of manufacturing, especially of fine cloth, as far back as anyone could remember. It was known for its production of equally fine perfumes. It had also long been a centre of debate, research and shared knowledge, and was the heartland of the Kanyakubj Brahmins, a community of illustrious, if impoverished intellectuals. The joke among the Kanyakubjas was that Saraswati, the Goddess of Knowledge, was very kind towards them, while Lakshmi, the Goddess of Prosperity and Wealth, was wont to ignore them altogether.

As a seat of learning, the city was home to many of the finest thinkers and philosophers of the time, including the celebrated Rishi Vishwamitra, who had been born into the royal family of Kannauj. But it turned out to be not so understanding when it came to the weary band of runaways that showed up at its gates, seeking sanctuary.

Kaikesi and Mareech's parents, it transpired, had decided that it was best to excommunicate their daughter as soon as they heard that she had given birth to a Naga child. By this time, the well-kept secret of Raavan's identity had also been revealed. And, of course, everyone knew that it was Kaikesi's fault. After all, the revered Rishi Vishrava could not be responsible for the bad karma that gave birth to their Naga offspring.

Even those who sympathised with Kaikesi's plight had no inclination, or will, to take on their community or their elders.

Within a day of reaching Kannauj, the four of them found themselves outside the city once again, on the banks of the holy Ganga, wondering where they could go.

'What do we do now?' asked Kaikesi.

Mareech looked away at the river, his mind seething with anger. He couldn't believe that his family had turned its back on them. Even those who had initially supported his decision to go to Vishrava's ashram to protect his sister had changed their tune. They'd had the temerity to tell him, 'We didn't expect Kaikesi to actually give birth to a Naga! How could we have expected that?'

'Dada,' Kaikesi said again, 'what is to become of us?'

'I don't know, Kaikesi!' said Mareech. 'I don't know!'

Raavan had been using a smooth stone to sharpen the blade of his knife. He looked up and said, 'I do. Let's go further east. Let's go to Vaidyanath.'

'Vaidyanath?' asked Mareech, surprised. 'What's in Vaidyanath?'

The Kanyakumari, thought Raavan. But, for some reason, he didn't want to say it aloud. He started sharpening his knife again. 'I know who's not there: my father.'

Mareech kept quiet.

'Let's travel eastwards, towards the rising sun. Some light of wisdom may dawn on us as well.'

'You made that line up yourself?' Mareech asked, impressed.

Raavan glanced at him superciliously. 'No, I read it somewhere. You should try reading too, Uncle. It's a good habit.'

Mareech rolled his eyes and looked away. *Pesky kid.*

—— ॐ ——

They found lodgings in a charitable guesthouse in a small village, a short distance from the famous Vaidyanath temple. Vaidyanath was famed for its physicians, and Kaikesi lost no time in taking Kumbhakarna to one, to see if the outgrowths on his shoulders and ears could be removed. The doctor, however, advised against it. There was too much vascularity in the outgrowths, too many blood vessels, and removing them surgically could lead to the death of the child, he said. In any case, Kumbhakarna seemed like a happy baby whose outgrowths, unusually, did not cause him pain. It was best that he learn to live with them.

Kaikesi was deeply disappointed. So was Raavan. But the reason for his disappointment was different. Not that he spoke of it to anyone.

The next morning, at the crack of dawn, they left for the main Vaidyanath temple. It would soon be time for the morning aarti, the public offering of devotion to the Mahadev, Lord Rudra.

The Vaidyanath temple was, in effect, a huge complex of many temples, set in the middle of a dense jungle. There were temples dedicated to the previous Vishnus, to the many Goddesses who protected India, to Lord Indra, Lord Varun, Lord Agni, and others. Of course, the largest temple was dedicated to Lord Rudra. The Mahadev. The God of Gods.

The temple complex was separated from the flood-prone Mayurakshi by marshlands and flood-plains that sponged the excess waters of the tempestuous river during the monsoon season, thus keeping the temples safe. Several species of medicinal herbs and roots grew in the swamp, making the small temple-town a treasure trove of medicines for the treatment of most diseases. In fact, its name derived from this: Vaidyanath, the Lord of the Medicine Men.

The main temple of Vaidyanath was shaped like a giant lotus. It had an uncomplicated but enormous core, with a hall, the sanctum sanctorum, and a spire built of stone and mortar, following the standards prescribed in the Aagama architectural texts. The main spire shot up a massive fifty metres from a fifteen-metre base. On top of the base, a hundred and eight wooden 'petals' had been affixed—an architectural triumph. Each petal was four times the size of a full-grown man. Made from the wood of robust sal trees, among the best hardwoods anywhere in the world, each petal had been further hardened through a process of chemical treatment and painted with a pink dye. They were laid out on four levels, one above the other, to create a gargantuan lotus flower that encompassed the core of the temple. The main spire was painted yellow and grew out of the centre of this lotus like a giant pistil. The base was coloured green, to signify the stem of the lotus. The elongated base was hollow and functioned as a tunnel-shaped entry into the temple.

It was almost surreal. And deeply symbolic.

The lotus was a flower that retained its fragrance and beauty even while growing in slush and dirty water. It posed a silent challenge to the humans who visited the temple, to be true to their dharma even if those around them were not. The number of petals—one hundred and eight—was significant too. The people of India, the followers of the dharmic way, attached a huge significance to the number. They believed that it was a divine number repeated again and again in the structure of the universe. The diameter of the sun was a hundred and eight times the diameter of the earth. The average distance from the sun to the earth was a hundred and eight times the diameter of the sun. The average distance of the moon from the earth was a hundred and eight times the diameter of the moon. There were several other examples of this number appearing almost magically in the universe. Over time, it had been incorporated into many rituals. For instance, it was recommended that a mantra be chanted a hundred and eight times.

At the far end of the temple, in the sanctum sanctorum, was a life-size idol of Lord Rudra. The Lord sat cross-legged, like a yogi, his eyes closed in concentration. Right behind him was a massive three-metre high lingam-yoni—an ancient depiction of the One God. The lingam was in the shape of half an egg, and some ancients believed that it represented the Brahmanda, or the Cosmic Egg, which allowed creation to coalesce. Others believed that it was a representation of masculine energy and potential. At the base of the lingam was a yoni, often translated as 'womb', but literally the 'origin' or 'source'; a symbol of feminine energy and potential. The union of the lingam and the yoni represented creation, a result of the partnership between the masculine and the feminine, an alliance between passive Space and active Time from which all life, indeed all creation, originated.

Outside the sanctum sanctorum, in the centre of the lotus-shaped temple, was the main gathering hall for devotees.

By the time Raavan and his family reached the temple, they had little time to admire either its beauty or symbolism. The aarti had already begun in the main hall. And it was spectacular.

Thirty massive drums were placed sideways on large stands positioned throughout the hall. Big, burly men holding drumsticks the size of their own arms stood beside them, pounding the drums repeatedly.

Dhoom-Dhoom-danaa-Dhoom-Dhoom-danaa.

The beat and the rhythm pulsated through Raavan's body. He could feel the waves of sound in his bones. And like everyone else in this throng of Lord Rudra's devotees, he too was compelled to dance to the tune. Even Kumbhakarna, the little baby, shook his arms excitedly.

Dhoom-Dhoom-danaa-Dhoom-Dhoom-danaa.

Dhoom-Dhoom-danaa-Dhoom-Dhoom-danaa.

As the music gained in tempo, male and female devotees surged across the hall, towards the two-hundred-odd bells that hung from different points. They began ringing them now. In perfect harmony.

Then, in a low voice, the devout, in tune with each other, began chanting a simple disyllabic word. A word of immense power.

'Maha… dev!'

'Maha… dev!'

'Maha… dev!'

As the chanting gained momentum, the voices grew louder and louder. In ecstatic devotion to the Mahadev. The Greatest God. The God of Gods. Lord Rudra himself.

The drums kept pace with the chanting.

Dhoom-Dhoom-danaa-Dhoom-Dhoom-danaa.

Dhoom-Dhoom-danaa-Dhoom-Dhoom-danaa.

Raavan looked around him. For the first time in his life, he experienced the sheer joy of being a part of something bigger than himself. He was a devotee of Lord Rudra. They all were. And there was no differentiation here. None at all. Rich men danced next to their visibly poor compatriots. Students pirouetted next to their teachers. People with deformities chanted beside soldiers blessed with formidably fit bodies. Purist priests danced with hedonist aghoras. Women danced with men and transgender people. Children with their parents. People of all denominations and castes. Indians and non-Indians.

No differentiation.

Freedom.

Freedom from judgement. Freedom from expectations. Freedom from right and wrong. Freedom from Gods and Demons. Freedom to be oneself. And revel in the union with Lord Rudra.

Dhoom-Dhoom-danaa-Dhoom-Dhoom-danaa.

'Maha… dev!'

Dhoom-Dhoom-danaa-Dhoom-Dhoom-danaa.

'Maha… dev!'

The aarti ended on a high, with a wild, throaty cry that echoed through all of Vaidyanath.

'Jai Shri Rudra!'

Glory to Lord Rudra.

As though on cue, the drums and the bells fell silent. Only the echoes remained, lingering in the hushed silence of a deep and blissful devotion.

The aarti had lasted no more than five minutes. But it gave the joy of a lifetime to all those who were present there. Raavan glanced around him. There was ecstasy on every face. He looked at his uncle Mareech and his mother Kaikesi. Tears of joy were flowing down their cheeks. Raavan felt his own cheeks and was surprised to find them moist.

He whispered to himself, 'Jai Shri Rudra!'

Loud voices were suddenly heard from the crowd.

'Kanyakumari!'

'Kanyakumari!'

At the end of the aarti, it was customary for the Kanyakumari to perform the first traditional puja, the *Rudrabhishek* of the lingam-yoni. The Virgin Goddess had come forward to fulfil her duty.

Everybody looked up. Craning their necks. Balancing on their toes to look beyond those in front of them. All keen to catch a glimpse of their living Goddess.

But not Raavan. He kept his eyes on the ground. His fists clenched tight.

'Is this a new Kanyakumari?' asked Kaikesi.

Mareech glanced at his sister before turning back to look at the Kanyakumari, his hands held together in devotion. 'Yes. I am told the previous Kanyakumari got her first period a few months ago. She has moved on and a new Kanyakumari has been recognised.'

Kaikesi swayed gently, rocking baby Kumbhakarna back to sleep. 'I've always wondered what happens to them afterwards. Where do they go? What do they do?'

Mareech shrugged. 'I don't know. Maybe they go back to their villages once they are not Kanyakumaris anymore. But how can anyone find them? Very few even know their original birth-names.'

Raavan raised his head and stared at the new Kanyakumari. Hatred flashed in his eyes.

For a brief, insane moment, he considered lunging forward and striking her dead. That would get rid of her forever. But he banished the thought as quickly as it had occurred to him. It was pointless. They would simply recognise another girl-child as the Kanyakumari. *His* Kanyakumari was not coming back. He didn't know where she was. He didn't even know her real name.

He knew almost nothing. All he remembered were her words. Her voice. And her face.

Her angelic face was burnt into his mind. A face that made all the pain go away.

The thought he had been avoiding finally burst through to his consciousness. He was never going to see her again. She was gone from his life. Forever.

He felt his breath constricting. As though he was suffocating.

He took his mother's hand. 'We have to go.'

'What? Why? The Kanyakumari—'
'You can ask for her blessings tomorrow. Let's go.'
Raavan turned and walked away.

Chapter 5

'Leave?' asked Mareech, surprised. 'Why?'

Mareech, Kaikesi, Raavan and Kumbhakarna were back in their small room in the guesthouse.

Raavan's voice was calm. 'I had hoped we could find a cure for Kumbhakarna here. But the doctors have told us there is not much they can do. So there's no point in hanging around anymore.'

'But we didn't come here only to find a cure for Kumbhakarna. It's a safe place, at least for some time.'

'I don't want to just be safe. I want to achieve something. I can't do that here.'

Mareech sighed, a little irritated with this precocious young boy. 'Raavan, you are nine years old. You are a child. Just take it easy and let the adults—'

'I am not a child,' said Raavan firmly, interrupting Mareech. 'I am the eldest male in my family. I have responsibilities.'

Mareech tried hard to supress a smile. 'All right, great elder, tell me, which place do you think would be better than Vaidyanath? There is a tradition of selfless charity here. Your mother and brother can live on the free food and lodging that's provided at this guesthouse. How will you feed them if we go elsewhere?'

'I have read of great ports to the east which trade with lands like Bali and Malay. We could go there. We could work there.'

'Raavan, don't assume that it will be easy to find—'

'I have already decided, Uncle,' said Raavan. 'I have spoken to maa as well. The question is, what do you want to do?'

Mareech looked at his sister in surprise. He didn't know that she had already acquiesced to Raavan's demand. The look on Kaikesi's face was a mixture of helplessness and resignation. Many years later, Mareech would remember this as the first of many surrenders. The moment when his relationship with Raavan changed. The moment Raavan went from being his young nephew to his future lord and commander.

'All right,' he said. 'Let's go further east.'

—१६I—

It had been four years since Raavan and his family moved east, to a small town on the shore of the Chilika lake.

Chilika was a vast lagoon, among the largest in the world, extending over more than 1,000 sq km, north-east to south-west, on India's eastern coast. Some of the major distributaries of the mighty Mahanadi River, such as the Daya and Luna rivers, drained their waters into the lake. Fifty other minor rivers fed the Chilika besides. During the monsoon, the heavy downpour caused the lake to swell even more.

A first-time visitor to the kingdom of Kalinga, settled around the delta of the Mahanadi, could be forgiven for assuming that the fertile land, abundance of fresh water and a regular bountiful monsoon were responsible for its immense prosperity. In reality, while agriculture was indeed a munificent source of the kingdom's riches, its overflowing coffers were the result of brisk trade with other regions, near and far.

And the centre of this trade was the Chilika lake.

Given its dimensions, Chilika allowed for the construction of several ports along its shores. The deep draught of the lake meant even the biggest seafaring ships could sail into it comfortably. Several islands in the lake, most of them close to its seaward side, served as minor ports for smaller ships, thus dividing the heavy traffic of vessels. Most crucially, the lake's eastern boundaries, which separated it from the Eastern Sea, were marked by a series of sand flats. These worked as breakwaters to stop the stormy sea from intruding into Chilika, making the lake waters a calm refuge for ships. Two openings in these sand flats, the broader one at the northern end and a narrow one at the southern end, allowed ships to sail into the lake. Furthermore, from Chilika, one could sail up the Mahanadi to the kingdom of South Kosala and then travel northwards into the heartlands of the Sapt Sindhu.

Chilika provided a safe and secure harbour, and afforded easy access to a rich hinterland. In fact, the richest hinterland in the world.

At any point in time, there were at least a few hundred ships, large and small, anchored in the lake. And a smaller number of ships waiting to berth. Cargo was constantly being loaded or taken off vessels. Traders could be heard negotiating aggressively, while Customs officials tried to extract the tax revenues due to the state. Sailors were routinely spotted making their way to the shore, on their day off, looking for wine and women. Tavern owners and women tried their best to attract as many sailors as possible. Meanwhile, soldiers on duty worked to maintain some semblance of order amidst the chaos.

What made Chilika a favourite among traders was that, unlike in other parts of India, trading activities were not unduly restricted here.

Over the past few decades, in many parts of the Sapt Sindhu, ordinary people as well as the ruling families had turned against the trading caste of Vaishyas on account of what was perceived to be large-scale corruption. Severe restrictions had been placed on trading activities. Traders needed licenses at every stage, and these had to be procured from non-Vaishya administrators. As it turned out, far from ending corruption, an element of bribery—large amounts at that—was added to the process. On top of that, the administrators, in their arrogance, did not think they were doing anything wrong in leeching bribes from the traders. They looked at it as a way of punishing the 'thieves'.

Of course, any wise person would know that to blame an entire community for the faults of a few was to take an extremely myopic view of things. Every society needs entrepreneurs and merchants as much as it needs intellectuals, warriors and artisans. And an imbalance in the structure, favouring a particular class, ends up creating problems. Unfortunately, there was a shortage of wisdom in the ruling class in the Sapt Sindhu and the trading community continued to be persecuted.

Eventually, traders from across the Sapt Sindhu got together under the leadership of Kubaer, the wily businessman-ruler of Lanka. Kubaer struck a deal with the emperor of the Sapt Sindhu, and its subordinate kingdoms, by which he took over all their trading activities and paid the empire a large share of the profits. However, this did nothing to make the traders' lives easier. Kubaer's method of maximising his profits was to squeeze their margins. By allying with him, the traders, it turned out, had merely jumped from the frying pan into the fire.

The only kingdom in the Sapt Sindhu that had refused to join up with Kubaer so far was Kalinga. Therefore, while trading had become difficult in most parts of the country, it had intensified in Chilika. The port was under the control of the king of Kalinga, who ruled from his capital, Cuttack, over eighty kilometres north of the lake. 'Cuttack' literally meant military cantonment or royal camp, the name resonant of the warrior past of the Kalingans. But over many centuries, the people there had grown into a non-violent and peace-loving community, whose interests lay in trading and in cultural and intellectual pursuits. This also made the Kalinga kings relatively liberal in their approach to the vexed issue of state controls. As a result, several Vaishya families chose to settle in Kalinga and ply their trade there.

But things were slowly changing. The anti-Vaishya mood in the rest of the country had begun to seep through to Kalinga. Everyone wanted to ingratiate themselves with Dashrath, the powerful king of Ayodhya, who was also the emperor and overlord of the Sapt Sindhu. And it was well known that the mood in Ayodhya was anti-Vaishya. Furthermore, the mighty kingdom of South Kosala, in the upper parts of the Mahanadi, not far from Kalinga, had recently forged a strong alliance with Ayodhya through marriage. Princess Kaushalya had become the first wife of Emperor Dashrath.

Influenced by its powerful relatives, South Kosala too had started placing severe restrictions on trade. Kalinga, sensing the shift in its immediate neighbourhood, had started realigning itself too. A Naharin administrator from the lands to the north-west of Babylon, in Mesopotamia, was brought in as the governor of Chilika to 'discipline' the wayward traders. Nobody knew the man's original name, but he had taken on an Indian one: Krakachabahu, the one with 'arms like a saw'. Regrettably, his style of administration was as repugnant as his name. However, the Kalinga king, far away in his capital city, left Krakachabahu to run Chilika by himself.

Soon, traders in Kalinga began suffering the same tax terrorism and countless regulations that their fellow traders endured in the other kingdoms of the Sapt Sindhu. If they couldn't do business even in Chilika, where could they? Despondent, some decided to give up trading altogether, but the majority laboured on, for it was the only profession they had any experience in. However, the feeling was gathering strength that they had to look for ways to bypass Krakachabahu's oppressive restrictions.

It wasn't long, then, before smuggled goods began to find their way from the Sapt Sindhu to the outside world. There was very little that Indians required from foreign lands since they had plenty of home-grown produce to live on. Even if something was smuggled in, it could get confiscated in any of the kingdoms of the Sapt Sindhu if it lacked the customary permits. Understandably then, the smuggling market was geared more towards exports. The Sapt Sindhu produced many goods that the world wanted. Smuggling them out became a convenient way to avoid hefty export duties and make good profits.

A three-tier smuggling system evolved over time. The first tier involved transporting manufactured products from different kingdoms in the Sapt Sindhu to Chilika. This was relatively simple because many of these goods could easily be mixed with legal exports. It was also the least risky—and the least profitable—of the tiers. The second-tier operators used small cutter-boats to run the gauntlet of Krakachabahu's tax-boats in Chilika before escaping into the sea, either undetected or after bribing the Customs officers. The third tier came into effect in the Eastern Sea, where large seafaring ships, anchored many nautical miles south of Chilika and hidden among other ships waiting to sail into harbour, picked up goods from the cutter-boats and sailed off into distant foreign lands.

Now, the second tier clearly constituted the riskiest part of the operation. And yet, since it was mainly done by young smugglers in small boats, who were desperate to make ends meet, the cream of the profits was skimmed by the third tier: the owners of the large seafaring ships. They negotiated prices down by playing one against the other, while they themselves charged the full and legal, duty-paid price in foreign markets like Arabia, Malay or Cambodia.

When they had first moved here, Raavan and Mareech had taken up employment as dock workers. They survived the hard toil for some time, but eventually, encouraged by the opportunities on offer, Raavan had hired a small cutter-boat and progressed to second-tier smuggling. He had quickly made a name for himself as a smart lad and a talented sailor who was willing to take risks and sneak out goods in the most adverse conditions. It was not a surprise, therefore, when he was approached by a smuggler called Akampana, who specialised in the third tier.

Normally, smugglers in the third tier were capable seafarers, raking in huge profits. Akampana, however, was a bit of a misfit in that category. His was among the least profitable third-tier operations. He was notorious for delaying payments to his crew or not paying them at all. It had reached a point where men simply refused to work for him. But he did have a major asset—his own ship. A large one. One that was capable of sailing on the high seas.

The only way a smuggler in the second tier could graduate to the profitable third tier was by owning or working on a seafaring ship. Knowing this, Raavan agreed to meet Akampana.

The next day, Raavan and Mareech, along with their regular crew of five cutthroats, sailed out in their cutter-boat to a small, hidden lagoon south of Chilika, where Akampana's house was located.

Raavan ordered his crew to row the boat close to Akampana's ship, which was anchored not too far from the shore.

'By the great Lord Varun,' exclaimed Mareech, invoking the name of the God of Water and the Seas in his surprise. 'Does this Akampana not do any maintenance work on his ship at all?'

One of the ways to classify ships was by the number of masts they possessed. Most seafaring ships that came to Chilika had three masts. So did Akampana's. But the sorry state of the vessel was quite obvious. The rigging, including the sails, looked worn and incapable of drawing wind effectively. In fact, the sails hadn't even been furled up to prevent damage from sudden gusts of wind, which were quite common in the area. The masts were clearly in desperate need of fresh woodwork. The crow's nest on top of the main mast had most of its floorboards missing. The tar on the ship's hull, crucial for keeping the vessel waterproof and preventing leakages, needed recoating.

'I thought Akampana's ship had a reputation for speed,' Raavan said, equally surprised.

'So did I,' said Mareech. 'Are you sure you want to work with this man?'

Raavan stared at the ship, lost in thought. Then, abruptly, he threw his angvastram aside. 'Stay here.'

'What are you doing?' asked Mareech.

Before he could finish, Raavan had slipped into the water and was swimming towards the ship. When he got to it, he stopped and floated alongside, carefully examining the hull. He then dived underwater to look at the part just below water. He came back up and swam the length of the ship, this time not just looking at it but feeling it with his fingers, disappearing underwater and coming up every few minutes to take a breath before going back in again. On Mareech's orders, the cutter-boat followed, circling the ship and keeping abreast of Raavan.

When Raavan finally swam up to the surface and climbed onto the boat, Mareech looked at him questioningly.

'There's something odd about this ship,' said Raavan.

'What?'

'Not one barnacle. Not one mussel. No shipworms. The hull is as smooth as it must have been on the day it was made.'

Biofouling was a hazard as old as sailing itself. The wooden base of ships provided a ready breeding ground for barnacles and other sea creatures. They clung to the wet surface, multiplying and growing to cover much of the hull below water. Some ships were so badly infested that it was impossible to even see the wooden surface below the waterline.

These bumpy masses of barnacles drastically reduced the speed of a ship. Another peril was the infestation of shipworms, a type of clam that grew as long as two feet. These creatures bored holes into the wooden hull, causing slow, long-term damage. It was with good reason that they were called the termites of the sea. Raavan had never seen a seafaring ship, the hull of which was *not* infested with these creatures. But Akampana's ship was, strangely, completely devoid of them.

Raavan knew that the best way to clean the hull was in a dry dock where the ships were rested on a dry platform so that workers could scrape off the sea creatures and repair or replace the wood. But it was impossible for smugglers to get access to a dry dock. So what they usually did was careen the ship—essentially, ground it on a beach at high tide and turn it on its side. This allowed the hull to come up above the water so that it could be cleaned, and the old wood repaired or replaced.

As if on cue, Mareech spoke up. 'Maybe they careened the ship and cleaned the hull?'

Raavan shook his head. 'Uncle, if Akampana hasn't had the sense to tie up the sails to prevent accidental damage, do you think he would have gone to the trouble, and the expense, of careening the ship?'

Mareech nodded. 'Valid point.'

Raavan considered the facts before him. With no biofouling, Akampana's ship could travel at nearly twice the speed of other ships. A huge competitive advantage.

He made up his mind.

—₹७I—

'I cannot pay all of you a salary,' said Akampana, 'but I can give you a small share of the profits that we make.'

Raavan and Mareech had left their motley team at a distance, out of earshot. It would make negotiation easier. The three men sat on wooden chairs in an unkempt garden that had clearly seen better days. In the same compound stood Akampana's large, crumbling mansion. The house was located not far from the shore, so Akampana's ship was clearly visible from where they were seated.

As soon as Mareech heard what Akampana was offering, he looked askance at Raavan, waiting for his nephew to refuse the ridiculous offer. But Raavan remained silent, his expression inscrutable.

Akampana, a slim man of average height, shifted uneasily. He touched his forehead, unknowingly smudging the *tilak,* the *long, black mark* drawn across it. Finally he broke the silence.

'Listen,' he said, 'we can work out something for living expenses but—'

An angry female voice interrupted him. 'What the hell is going on here?'

They turned to see a tall, sharp-featured woman marching towards them.

'Are you trying to hire a crew again, Akampana?' asked the woman, her exasperation evident to everyone.

Akampana was visibly nervous. 'We have to do some business to earn money, dear wife. These people—'

'Business? You don't know how to do business! You keep making losses. I am not giving you any more money. I am not selling any more of my jewellery. Just sell that damned ship!'

'No, but—'

'You are a moron!' shouted the woman. 'You will be better off if you realise that and stay within your limits.'

'But we need—'

'No buts! Just sell that cursed ship! I could have gone with Krakachabahu, you know that. He was interested in me. I rejected the affections of the governor of Chilika and stuck by you. But I have had enough of your foolishness. Just sell that ship!'

Akampana looked away in embarrassment. But his silence only appeared to infuriate his wife further. Her tone became even more aggressive. 'What is the matter with you? You know I am speaking the truth, right?'

'Of course,' simpered Akampana. 'How could I think otherwise, dear wife?'

The woman shook her head, glared at Raavan and Mareech, then turned and stomped off.

Akampana watched the retreating back of his wife, an expression of intense loathing on his face. Then he checked himself, conscious of being in company. He cleared his throat and turned to Mareech, a weak smile on his face. It was Mareech's turn to look away, embarrassed.

But Raavan didn't seem affected at all. 'Here's what we'll do,' he said, as if they hadn't been interrupted. 'We'll take the ship, repair it at our own cost, and start sailing it. You are welcome to join us if you wish. And the profits will be shared, ninety–ten.'

Akampana brightened. 'Ninety seems fair.'

Raavan regarded Akampana with lazy nonchalance. 'Ninety for me. Ten for you.'

'What? But... but it's my ship.'

Raavan got up. 'And it can continue to rot here.'

'Listen, I don't—'

'And I'll also take care of your wife for you.'

Even Mareech, who had got used to his thirteen-year-old nephew's ruthless ways over the last few years, looked at Raavan in shock.

Akampana glanced nervously in the direction his wife had gone, and then at Raavan. 'What... what do you mean?'

'I'll do what you are too scared to even think about.'

Akampana swallowed visibly. But it was obvious from his expression that he was interested.

'It's a deal,' said Raavan firmly.

Chapter 6

In the two years since Raavan, now fifteen, had taken over Akampana's ship, he had already turned it into a hugely profitable enterprise. After repairing the ship, he had run many successful smuggling missions, supplying goods far and wide, and raking in revenues.

Since the north Indian ports were becoming more and more resistant to free and easy trade, Lanka had emerged as one of the most dynamic entrepôts in the Indian Ocean rim. Raavan had made frequent trips to the island in the past twelve months. On one of these, he had discovered that Kubaer, the trader-king of Lanka, was his guru-brother—a disciple of his father, Vishrava. But this was not something Raavan mentioned to anyone in Lanka. He didn't want any help from his father—not from the person, not even from the name.

As his business grew, Raavan decided to make the main port of Lanka, Gokarna—literally, the cow's ear—his base. The city was conveniently located in the north-east of the island. It had a natural harbour, with a deep bay and land jutting out on the seaward side, acting as natural breakwaters. It was in a position, therefore, to receive and safely anchor ships during any season in the year. A crucial advantage.

The *Mahaweli* Ganga, the longest river in Lanka, flowed into the Gokarna bay at its southern end. This was useful, for it offered a navigable channel for ships to sail deep into the heartland of the island. The river had been named many years ago by Guru Vishwamitra—the chief of the Malayaputra tribe, which had been left behind by the previous Vishnu, Lord Parshu Ram. Perhaps the venerable rishi wished to honour the river that flowed beside his own hometown, Kannauj, by naming this one the *Great Sandy* Ganga.

Guru Vishwamitra was held in high esteem in Lanka, not only because he was a great rishi, but also because he had helped settle the island and turn it from a rural backwater into one of the powerhouses on the Indian Ocean trade routes. There was a time when Lanka was only known for being the surviving part of the great submerged land of Sangamtamil— one of the two antediluvian fatherlands of Vedic India. People used to travel from across the Indian subcontinent to pray at the ruins of the ancient temples built by their forefathers. But all that had changed. Now, they came here to grow rich. And most of those who had arrived recently were from Kalinga.

As things stood, most Lankans were happy with Kubaer's rule. And the trader-king and his people continued to accord the greatest respect to Vishwamitra. For it was he who had, more than a century ago, helped King Trishanku Kaashyap establish the great Lankan capital city of Sigiriya, and while very few mourned the deposition of the increasingly unpopular monarch some years later, Vishwamitra remained dear to them.

Raavan had never travelled inland to Sigiriya, which was a hundred kilometres south-west of Gokarna. He had, however, purchased a beautiful house in Gokarna, close to the great Koneshwaram temple, dedicated to Lord Rudra.

It had been built in ancient times, on a promontory off the northern part of the bay that jutted out into the Indian Ocean. Kaikesi visited the temple every day, with the six-year-old Kumbhakarna in tow. Raavan's little brother was still too young to be sailing with him.

On that particular day, Kaikesi was visiting the Koneshwaram temple with a sense of purpose. She knew that Vishwamitra was in the city, en route to Sigiriya. Many years ago, she had met both Vishwamitra and his right-hand man Arishtanemi, at Vishrava's ashram. While the meeting with Vishwamitra had been all too brief, she had spent considerable time with Arishtanemi and had even started thinking of him as her brother. She had used her influence with him to wrangle a meeting with Vishwamitra. The fact that Kaikesi's own family, especially her grandfather, had once been a close friend of Vishwamitra's father, King Gaadhi, was not mentioned. With good reason.

'Please don't tell anyone that I used my husband's name to arrange this meeting,' Kaikesi pleaded with Arishtanemi, as she led Kumbhakarna by the hand.

Arishtanemi nodded. He knew of the strained relationship between Vishrava and his first wife's children. Especially now that Vishrava had married again, bringing home a foreigner from Knossos as his wife. 'Don't worry. I won't.'

Kaikesi smiled. 'Thank you, brother.'

Arishtanemi led them into the guesthouse attached to the Koneshwaram temple, where Vishwamitra was staying. 'Wait here for a minute.'

Kaikesi was confused. 'But…'

'Just do as I tell you,' Arishtanemi said, before disappearing inside.

Standing outside the door, Kaikesi could hear snatches of the conversation.

'I don't have time to do all this, Arishtanemi. You should—'

Kaikesi walked in, pulling Kumbhakarna along.

A gigantic, barrel-chested man was sitting on the floor in the lotus position. Vishwamitra. He looked up as he heard Kaikesi walk in. He recognised her as Vishrava's wife. And the granddaughter of his father's closest advisor.

He made no attempt to hide his irritation. 'Listen Kaikesi, your grandfather caused enough trouble after my father's death and I am not—'

Vishwamitra stopped mid-sentence as he spotted the child standing next to Kaikesi, holding her hand. The six-year-old was big for his age and could easily pass off for a ten-year-old. He was also extraordinarily hairy. The rishi noticed the crude outgrowths from his shoulders and ears, which clearly established that he was a Naga. Only a doting mother would find a child as ugly as Kumbhakarna beautiful. But Vishwamitra had a big heart. Especially for those whom he perceived to be disadvantaged. His face creased in a smile. 'What a lovely child.'

Kaikesi looked at Kumbhakarna with pride in her eyes. 'He is.'

Vishwamitra beckoned to the boy. 'Come here, child.'

Kumbhakarna nervously slid behind his mother, clutching the end of her angvastram.

'His name is Kumbhakarna, noble Maharishi,' said Kaikesi respectfully.

Vishwamitra bent sideways to catch the child's eye. 'Come here, Kumbhakarna.'

Kumbhakarna took a quick peek at the rishi. Then retreated behind his mother.

Vishwamitra laughed softly. He turned to Arishtanemi and pointed at a plate. His previous visitors had left some homemade sweets for him. Arishtanemi brought the plate to the maharishi.

'I have some laddoos, Kumbhakarna,' said Vishwamitra with a smile, as he chose one and held it out.

At the mention of his favourite sweet, Kumbhakarna stepped forward hesitantly. He looked up at his mother. She smiled and nodded. He ran to the maharishi and grabbed the laddoo. Vishwamitra laughed and held Kumbhakarna affectionately, then made him sit by his side.

Kaikesi, not nervous any longer, went down on her knees before the seated Vishwamitra.

'Great Malayaputra,' said Kaikesi, 'I wanted to request... my son Kumbhakarna... He is...'

'Yes, I know. Sometimes the outgrowths bleed a lot. It's painful. And it can be fatal if not controlled,' Vishwamitra said, looking straight into Kaikesi's eyes. The great sages of yore had the power to read a person's thoughts merely by looking closely at their eyes. Vishwamitra, one of the greatest modern sages, also had this capability.

'You know everything, Guruji. Can you help him?'

'I can't cure it completely. That would be impossible. But I can reduce the bleeding. And I can certainly keep this adorable child alive.'

Tears of relief filled Kaikesi's eyes as she brought her head down to rest on Vishwamitra's feet. 'Thank you, thank you.'

Vishwamitra touched Kaikesi on the shoulder and bade her rise. 'But he has to take my medicines every day. He can never stop. Never. Or death will start closing in.'

'Yes, Guruji. I will never—'

'They are rare medicines. And difficult to obtain. Arishtanemi here will ensure that you get them regularly. Make sure you keep the medicines away from bright light and heat. And use them exactly as Arishtanemi tells you to.'

'Thank you. Thank you, Guruji. How can I ever repay you?'

'You can tell your grandfather to apologise to me for what he did all those years ago.'

Kaikesi didn't know what to say. Her grandfather was no more. She said nervously, 'Guruji, my grandfather... he...'

'He's dead?' asked Vishwamitra, surprised. 'Oh!'

'Guruji,' said Kaikesi, the tears flowing freely again.

'In the name of Lord Parshu Ram, stop crying and speak.'

'Noble Maharishiji ...'

Vishwamitra looked into Kaikesi's eyes. 'Someone else has the same condition?'

Kaikesi wiped her tears and said, 'Nothing can be hidden from you, Guruji. My other son, Raavan... He is also a Naga.'

Vishwamitra exhaled softly. He smelt an opportunity here. *Raavan was a Naga too?*

'He's a... he's a...'

Vishwamitra cut in. 'I know he is a smuggler.'

Kaikesi looked at Arishtanemi anxiously and then back at Vishwamitra. Tears poured down her cheeks. 'We went through some very difficult times, Guruji. He... he did what he had to. He's my son, Guruji... I can ask him to stop the...'

Vishwamitra sat quietly, his mind racing.

From what I've heard, Raavan is already gaining a reputation. He is young, but able to acquire and inspire followers. Efficient. Intelligent. Cruel, too. A potential warrior. He could serve my purpose. He could serve the purpose of Mother India.

Kaikesi was still crying. 'The growth on his navel has started bleeding, great Malayaputra. He will die like this. Please help him. He is not a bad person. Circumstances have forced him to become what he is.'

If his outgrowths bleed, he will always need my medicines to stay alive. He will be under my control. Always.

'Please, Guruji.' Kaikesi prostrated herself at Vishwamitra's feet again. 'Please help us. We are both from Kannauj, you and I. Please. Help me. Help my son.'

Vishwamitra smiled. 'It has been difficult. I know.'

Kaikesi sobbed silently, still crouched at the maharishi's feet.

Vishwamitra placed a benevolent hand on her head. 'I will have medicines sent every month for the both of them. I will keep them alive. As long as I can and must,' he said.

—ॐ—

As soon as Kaikesi and Kumbhakarna left, Arishtanemi turned to Vishwamitra. He looked puzzled.

'Guruji,' he said carefully. 'I don't understand why you want to help Raavan. Kumbhakarna is a child. He needs your help. But Raavan? I have heard stories of his ruthlessness. His cruelty. And he is not even an adult yet. He will only get worse.'

Vishwamitra smiled. 'Yes, he is cruel. And you are right, he will only get worse.'

Arishtanemi looked even more confused. 'Then why do you want to help him, Guruji?'

'Arishtanemi, the Vishnu will rise during my tenure as Chief of the Malayaputras.'

The Malayaputras, the tribe left behind by the previous Vishnu, Lord Parshu Ram, had two missions to fulfil. The first was to help the next Mahadev, the Destroyer of Evil, whenever he or she arose. And the second was to identify from their midst the next Vishnu, the Propagator of Good, when the time was right.

Arishtanemi looked shocked. 'Guruji, umm... I don't mean to question your judgement, but I'm not sure Raavan... you know... the role of the Vishnu is very...'

'Are you crazy, Arishtanemi? Do you think I would ever consider Raavan for the role of Vishnu?'

Arishtanemi gave a short nervous laugh, clearly relieved. 'I knew it couldn't be that... I was just...'

'Listen to me carefully. If you take away all the traditions and the hoopla, then who, or what, is the Vishnu to an ordinary Indian?'

Arishtanemi remained silent. He had a feeling that whatever he said would be the wrong answer.

Vishwamitra explained, 'A Vishnu is basically a hero. A hero that others willingly follow. And they follow the Vishnu simply because they trust their hero.'

'But what does that have to do with Raavan, Guruji?'

'What does every hero need, Arishtanemi?'

'A mission?'

'Yes, that too. But besides a mission?'

Arishtanemi smiled, as he finally understood. 'A villain.'

'Exactly. We need the right villain to act as the foil for our hero. Only then will people see the hero as their saviour, as the Vishnu. And only then will they follow the Vishnu along the path that we have determined. A path that will revive the greatness of this land. That will allow it to take its rightful place once again in the world. That will remove poverty and hunger. End injustice. End the oppression of the lower castes, the poor and the disabled. That will make the present-day Indians worthy of their great ancestors.'

'I understand now, Guruji,' said Arishtanemi, bowing his head. 'If all I've heard of Raavan is correct, he has the potential to be a good villain.'

'A perfect villain. For not only will he be a believable villain, he will also always be under our control,' Vishwamitra said.

'Yes. Without our medicines from Agastyakootam, he will die.'

Agastyakootam was the secret capital of the Malayaputras, hidden deep in the hills, in the sacred land of Kerala.

Vishwamitra nodded, as if confirming the plans to himself. 'We will help Raavan rise. And when the time is right, we will destroy him. For the good of Mother India.'

'For the good of Mother India,' Arishtanemi echoed.

Vishwamitra's expression changed as his mind harked back to the past. When he spoke again, it was with barely suppressed rage. 'That… that man will not stop me from fulfilling my destiny.'

Arishtanemi knew who Vishwamitra was talking about: his childhood friend turned mortal enemy, Vashishtha. But he knew better than to respond. He stood quietly, waiting for the wave to pass.

—रोI—

'Dada!' Kumbhakarna screamed excitedly, running down the stairs. His elder brother was walking into the house accompanied by Akampana and Mareech.

The massive profits Raavan had made over the last few years had turned the seventeen-year-old into one of the wealthiest traders in Lanka. But his success had only made him hungry for more. He spent most of his time out at sea, working hard. As a result, visits to his lavish new mansion, perched on one of the hills that surrounded Gokarna, were rare. And these rare visits were a source of delight for his eight-year-old brother, Kumbhakarna.

'Dada!' yelled Kumbhakarna again, rushing into the large courtyard that formed the centre of the mansion, straight towards Raavan. His belly jiggled as he sprinted.

Raavan dropped the gifts he was carrying and spread his arms, laughing, 'Slow down, Kumbha! You are too big for these games now!'

But Kumbhakarna was too excited to listen. He may have been only eight but he was already as big as a fifteen-year-old. The two extra arms on top of his shoulders shook wildly, as they always did when he was excited. With his unusually hirsute body, he resembled a small bear.

As Kumbhakarna jumped into his brother's arms, the impact caused Raavan to stagger. Kumbhakarna giggled happily.

Raavan swung his brother around, laughing. For a few moments, the ever-present pain in his navel was gone.

Kaikesi emerged from the kitchen in the far corner of the ground floor. From her bloodshot eyes, it was clear that she had been crying. 'Raavan.'

Raavan set Kumbhakarna down and looked at her, his expression changing to one of resignation. The pain in his navel was back. 'What is it, Maa?'

'Nothing.'

Raavan rolled his eyes. 'Maa, what is it?'

'If you need to ask, then you are not a good son.'

'Well, then, I am not a good son,' said Raavan, always on edge with his compulsively gloomy mother. 'I'm only going to ask you one more time. What is the problem?'

'You have come home after four months, Raavan. Don't you want to spend time with your family? Why do I have to keep demanding this? Is money all that matters to you?'

'I can spend all my time with you and we can live in a hovel, dying of hunger. Or I can work and keep all of you in comfort. I have made my choice.'

Mareech and Akampana shuffled their feet uncomfortably. These testy exchanges between Kaikesi and Raavan were becoming more frequent.

Kaikesi was on the verge of reminding her ungrateful son that it was because of her, and the medicines she had obtained by pleading with Vishwamitra, that he was still alive. But she thought better of it. Raavan now had an independent relationship with Vishwamitra. He didn't really need her.

Despite his young age, Kumbhakarna had already begun to assume the role of peacemaker between his beloved mother and brother. Now, gauging the tension in the air, he spoke up. 'Dada, you promised to show me your secret chamber!'

Raavan looked at his younger brother with a smile. 'But what about your gifts?'

'I am not interested in the gifts!' said Kumbhakarna. 'I want to see your chamber. You promised!'

The room that Kumbhakarna was so eager to see was on the topmost floor of Raavan's mansion. Off limits to everyone else, the room remained perpetually locked, with Raavan possessing the only set of keys. Even the windows were barricaded. During his short trips to Gokarna, Raavan spent hours by himself in the secret chamber. Nobody else was allowed in. Nobody.

But the last time he had come home, Kumbhakarna had managed to exact a promise from Raavan that he would be allowed into the chamber. There was almost nothing Raavan could refuse his not-so-little brother.

Raavan smiled broadly as he took Kumbhakarna's hand in his own. 'Come, Kumbha. Let's go.' As he was walking away, he pointed to where he had dropped the packages. 'Maa, your gift is somewhere in there. Take it.'

—ЃठI—

Raavan's secret chamber was much larger than Kumbhakarna had imagined. And darker. He coughed softly as the dust that had settled over the room in the past few months flew around, assaulting his nostrils.

'Wait here, Kumbha,' said Raavan, as he dropped the keys in a bowl placed on a side table. Torch in hand, he walked around, lighting all the other torches placed in the room. Large polished copper plates ran the length of the walls. They reflected the light of the torches, illuminating every corner of the room.

'Wow...' whispered Kumbhakarna, delighted that he was now privy to a part of his brother's life that nobody else was, not even their mother. He turned around and closed the door, pushing the latch in.

'Do you like it?' asked Raavan.

Kumbhakarna nodded, walking around in amazement, trying to soak it all in.

A majestic Rudra Veena was propped up against a wall. Kumbhakarna had heard the celestial sound of the instrument through closed doors, each time Raavan visited. Arranged in a row along the wall were other instruments—a tabla, dhol, damru, thavil, sitar, chikara, shehnai, flute, chenda and many others. Kumbhakarna had heard his brother play all of them.

'What's that, Dada?' asked Kumbhakarna, pointing at an instrument he had never seen before, or even read about.

The double-stringed musical instrument was kept on a gold-plated stand. Its bow was attached to a clip on the side.

'That is something I invented. I call it the Hatha.'

'Hatha?' asked Kumbhakarna. 'What does that mean?'

Raavan ruffled Kumbhakarna's hair and smiled before looking away. 'Hatha', in old Sanskrit, meant a man stricken with despair.

'I'll tell you some other time,' Raavan said, as the dull pain in his navel surged again.

'But if you have invented it, it should be named after you, Dada!' said Kumbhakarna.

Raavan looked thoughtful for a moment. His brother's suggestion was appropriate in more ways than one, considering the instrument's plaintive sound often reminded him of his own despair. 'Yes. You are right. I'll call it the Raavanhatha from now on.'

'Will you play it for me, Dada?'

'Some other time, Kumbha. I promise.'

Raavan had created the instrument in memory of the Kanyakumari. Playing it would only remind him of her.

Kumbhakarna squinted at the far wall. 'Are those paintings?'

Raavan reached for Kumbhakarna's hand. He wanted to lead him out of the chamber. He wasn't ready for this.

Not yet. But then, for some reason he couldn't understand, he restrained himself. He had held on to his pain for too long, all alone. He realised that, deep in his heart, he wanted Kumbhakarna to know. He wanted to share his pain with his brother. He wanted to share his hopes.

Tears welled up unbidden in Raavan's eyes.

Kumbhakarna ran towards the paintings.

Raavan walked slowly behind him, taking the opportunity to wipe his eyes. And take a deep breath. That always helped.

Kumbhakarna stared at the painting on the far left.

It was that of a girl. A girl no older than eleven or twelve. A round face. Fair-skinned. High cheekbones and a sharp, small nose. Long black hair, tied in a braid. Dark, piercing, wide-set eyes and almost creaseless eyelids. Her body was clad demurely in a long red dhoti, blouse and angvastram.

Divine. Distant. Awe-inspiring.

To Kumbhakarna, she looked like the Mother Goddess.

Kumbhakarna looked at his brother. 'Did you paint this, Dada?'

Raavan was too choked up to speak. He nodded.

'Who is she?'

Raavan took a deep breath. 'She is the Kan... Kan... Kanyakumari.'

Kumbhakarna observed the painting closely. Even to his young eyes, the display of devotion, of worship and love, was obvious in every brushstroke.

He glanced again at his brother's sad face, then turned back to the painting. That was when he noticed the other painting, to the right of the one he had been studying.

It was the same girl. Everything appeared to be the same. Except for the colour of her clothes. They were white.

He turned back to his brother. 'She looks older here.'

Raavan nodded. 'Yes. Exactly one year older.'

Slowly, Kumbhakarna walked along the wall, looking at the paintings. Each subsequent one depicted the same girl, only slightly older. Her breasts filled out. Her hips got curvier. She seemed to grow a little taller.

When he reached the tenth painting, Kumbhakarna stopped and stood quietly for a long time. It was the last in the series. The girl was now a woman. Perhaps twenty-one or twenty-two years old. Her clothes were a soft violet: the most expensive dye in the world and the colour favoured by royalty. She was tall. Striking. Long hair. Full, feminine body. Uncommonly attractive.

There was something otherworldly about her beauty. Her face. Her eyes. Her expression. She looked like a Goddess. The Mother Goddess.

'Does she pose for you every year?' asked Kumbhakarna, confused.

Raavan pointed to the first painting, of the adolescent girl. 'That was the last time I saw her.'

'So how did you paint these?'

'I see her growing older in my mind.'

'Why do you paint her, Dada?'

'Looking at her makes the pain go away, Kumbha…'

'What's her name?'

'I told you.' Raavan closed his eyes and took a deep breath to steady himself. 'Ka… Kanyakumari.'

'That's just a title, Dada. Even I know that. There are many Kanyakumaris. And she is probably not a Kanyakumari anymore if she is a grown woman. What's her real name?'

'I don't know.'

'Which tribe is she from?'

'I don't know.'

'Where is she now?'

'I don't know.'

Kumbhakarna's heart grew heavy. Tears welled up in his eyes. He walked up to Raavan and embraced him. 'We will find her, Dada.'

The tears were flowing down Raavan's cheeks now. There was no stopping them. He held his brother tight. The pain in his navel was excruciating.

'We will find her, Dada, we will! I promise.'

Chapter 7

'It's good to be home!' said Kumbhakarna, his extra arms shaking slightly, as they always did when he was excited. Though he was only ten, his voice had already begun to change.

Two years had passed since Raavan had allowed his younger brother into his secret chamber. They were now on their way back from a short trip to the Nicobar Islands, an important port en route to South-east Asia. It was Kumbhakarna's first trade voyage ever, and Raavan had wanted to ensure that it wasn't too long and uncomfortable.

Raavan sighed. 'I don't like coming home. I prefer the sea.'

'But home is home, Dada.'

'And maa is maa... I can't handle her constant crying. It's like she produces tears at will, just to irritate me. One of these days, I'll...'

Raavan stopped speaking as he saw Kumbhakarna's expression change. He knew that as much as his younger brother loved him, he did not appreciate these rants against their mother.

'All right, all right,' he said, patting Kumbhakarna's shoulder. 'You know I won't do anything drastic. But you handle her tears this time.'

The ship was slowing down gradually as it reached the mouth of the harbour. The brothers watched while the helmsman steered towards their allocated berth. As they passed other ships on their way in, heads turned to stare at the by now legendary ship as it prepared to dock. Its blinding speed on the high seas had given Raavan a huge competitive advantage in the cutthroat world of smuggling. With his fast growing profits, he had already built a fleet of five ships.

Raavan was conscious of being watched. He rather enjoyed the attention. But he continued to look straight ahead, pretending not to notice the admiring, and jealous, eyes gawking at him. He would not preen in front of others. That would be a sign of weakness. And nineteen-year-old Raavan did not believe in letting his weaknesses show.

The trader-prince, they called him. He liked that.

'Dada,' said Kumbhakarna, nudging Raavan to draw his attention.

Raavan turned. Akampana was standing at the port, waiting for them, clearly excited about something.

'Looks like the dandy has some news for us,' Raavan said, preparing to disembark.

— ?ठI —

'Raavan, I've found the secret! I've found the…'

'Quiet!' Raavan said severely, tapping him on the head.

Akampana stopped speaking, looking suitably chastened.

They were still in the port area, surrounded by people. Raavan knew that the success of any trading operation depended on reliable information about the commodities and goods that various ships were carrying, and the destinations they were headed for. It was critical to hold on to one's trade secrets.

He continued walking, as his bodyguards pushed people out of the way, clearing his path. Akampana fell into step behind him, smoothing his hair down. A few strands of hair had escaped their coiffure earlier, when Raavan had tapped him on the head. He turned to his assistant, who was walking alongside, for a towel. Some of the perfumed hair oil had come off on his hands.

—रोI—

'Now,' said Raavan. 'Start talking.'

They were in Raavan's private chamber in his well-appointed mansion. Raavan was leafing through the many messages that had arrived for him while he was away. Mareech and Akampana sat across from him, on the other side of a large desk. Kumbhakarna was sitting by the window, drinking lemon juice.

'I'm sorry, Raavan,' said Akampana nervously. 'I shouldn't have spoken up at the port and it—'

'Yeah, yeah,' Raavan interrupted, waving his hand dismissively without looking up. 'Get to the point. I don't have all day.'

Akampana leaned forward. The excitement in his voice was palpable. 'I've found it. I know what the secret is.'

Raavan put the papyrus scroll down and picked up a quill. He dipped it in the inkpot and started writing a note on the side of the message he was reading. 'You know I don't like riddles. Speak plainly. What have you found?'

'I've got the information we were looking for. From one of the descendants of King Trishanku Kaashyap.'

Raavan stopped writing. He replaced the quill in its hold, leaned back in his chair and said, 'Continue.'

'You do know that Trishanku Kaashyap's body was never found after—'

'I know Trishanku's entire story. Don't give me a history lesson. Get to the point,' Raavan snapped.

Trishanku Kaashyap was the first king of Lanka in the modern age. His kingdom had been established with the help of Vishwamitra. But over time, his subjects had wearied of Trishanku's violent and selfish ways, and he had been deposed. Even Vishwamitra, realising his mistake in supporting Trishanku, had helped the people's rebellion.

Mareech asked the question that was on everyone's mind. 'Have you found the secret?'

'Yes!' said Akampana triumphantly.

The secret in question related to Raavan's main ship, once owned by Akampana. Despite the remarkably inept way in which Akampana had handled it, the ship had never suffered any biofouling and had continued to travel at twice the speed of other ships. Akampana himself did not know what made his ship special. All he knew was that it had once belonged to a descendant of Trishanku Kaashyap.

'There is a special material that has to be ground and mixed with oil—an oil from Mesopotamia—and rubbed on the hull once every twenty years,' said Akampana. 'It keeps barnacles and other sea creatures away. It's as simple as that.'

Raavan leaned forward. 'And where does one find this special material, Akampana?'

'It's with your friends. The Malayaputras. They call it the cave material for some reason.'

'I guess that's because they found it in a cave,' said Raavan sarcastically.

'Perhaps you are right,' said Akampana, oblivious as usual.

Raavan rolled his eyes and turned to Mareech. 'Fix a meeting with them. Quickly.'

——ॐ——

'Why do you need the cave material, Raavan?' asked Vishwamitra.

By a strange coincidence, Vishwamitra and Arishtanemi had arrived in Gokarna that very week, en route to Sigiriya. Raavan had lost no time in going to meet them. But he had insisted on going alone. Without Akampana, or even Mareech.

'I have some plans for trading with it, Guruji,' answered Raavan, his head bowed. He was always polite and deferential with Vishwamitra.

'Are you planning to cut us out and sell directly to Kubaer? Are you planning to reduce our profits?'

Raavan knew that the Malayaputras sold the cave material directly to Kubaer. He had been told by Akampana that the material, whatever it was, was poisonous for humans. And that it was refined and used as a mixture in the fuel for the Pushpak Vimaan, the legendary flying vehicle owned by Kubaer. The other ingredients used for the fuel mixture were almost as costly. Which was one of the reasons the Pushpak Vimaan was used so rarely, and why similar vimaans had not been built. They were simply too expensive to run.

Raavan was prepared for the question. He looked up and folded his hands together in a namaste. 'No, Guruji. Would

I ever do that to the mighty Malayaputras? But having said that, Chief-Trader Kubaer isn't buying the material from you anymore because it's too expensive. As you know, he has even stopped using the Pushpak Vimaan.'

'So are you planning to buy the Pushpak Vimaan and use it yourself?'

Raavan had guessed that the Malayaputras were not aware that the cave material helped prevent biofouling on ships or they would have been using it on their own vessels. Listening to Vishwamitra now, he became certain of this. If all went well, he would be the only one with the competitive advantage of superfast ships.

'Leasing the Pushpak Vimaan is an option as well, Guruji. Chief-trader Kubaer never says no to an opportunity for making profits, does he?'

'And what are you going to do with the Pushpak Vimaan?'

'Oh, a little bit of this and a little bit of that.'

Although using the vimaan for trade would be a losing proposition because of the exorbitant running cost, Raavan did actually plan to use it. After all, he had to convince the ever-vigilant Malayaputras that he was buying the cave material only for the purpose of flying the vimaan. On prospecting trips maybe. Or even holidays!

Vishwamitra looked intently at Raavan, trying to read his mind. But he hit a blank wall. Raavan had by now learnt the technique of blocking even the most powerful rishi from reading his mind.

'All right,' said Vishwamitra. 'You will have to pay five hundred thousand gold coins per consignment. And you will have to take at least three consignments a year.'

It was a ridiculous price. Way beyond what Kubaer paid. And the insistence on a minimum purchase was unheard of.

But Raavan didn't flinch. He had done his calculations already. 'I agree to the price, Guruji. But I cannot agree to the minimum number of consignments. I don't know how often I will use the vimaan. I will try my best to buy three consignments every year. But there may be some years when I am unable to do so. I should not be penalised for that.'

Vishwamitra nodded. 'All right.'

Standing beside them, Arishtanemi could not believe his ears. Five hundred thousand gold coins per consignment! With that much money, the Malayaputras could begin the search for daivi astra material in earnest. The daivi astras were weapons of mass destruction, whose use had been severely restricted by the previous Mahadev, Lord Rudra. He had decreed that they could not be deployed without the permission of the Vayuputras, the tribe left behind by Lord Rudra. But Vishwamitra had plans of his own. He wanted the Vishnu to rise in his time. For that to happen, and to manage the course of events, he had to have independent control of the daivi astras. This deal with Raavan would give him the funds to seek out and quarry the material required for the manufacture of the divine weapons. Arishtanemi could not help but smile at the irony: it was the pirate Raavan who would free them from their dependency on the Vayuputras.

'Thank you so much, Guruji,' said Raavan, bending to touch the maharishi's feet.

'*Ayushman Bhava*,' said Vishwamitra, blessing Raavan with *a long life*.

—————

'I wonder what he is planning to do, Guruji,' said Arishtanemi.

'I'm confused too,' said Vishwamitra. 'The only use for the cave material, other than as fuel for the Pushpak Vimaan, is as a poison.'

'Yes. But for all practical purposes, it's a pretty useless poison.'

Arishtanemi was right. The cave material was a very slow-acting poison. One would have to administer it regularly to the victim, for many weeks, for it to have any effect. And when it was refined into a potent poison, it emanated a distinctively foul smell, which rather defeated the purpose. The intended victim would smell it from miles away!

'Maybe he wants to be the only one in the world with a flying machine, even if it bankrupts him. I had thought Raavan would serve our purpose. That he could grow into a worthy villain. But it looks like he's surrendered to mere vanity,' Vishwamitra said, looking disappointed.

'He can still serve our purpose, Guruji. With that much gold at our disposal, we can begin our search for the daivi astra materials in earnest.'

'True. But getting the cave material is difficult.'

'Please don't worry about that, Guruji,' said Arishtanemi. 'I'll ensure that we get all the material we need.'

—ॐ—

'Raavan, have you gone mad?' Mareech blurted. A steely look from his nephew forced him to control himself and check his tone. 'Listen to me, Raavan, we have worked hard… *you* have worked hard to build up all we have now. Five hundred thousand gold coins per consignment is too much. We can never—'

'My numbers are never wrong. I calculate that if we can build a fleet of two hundred ships as soon as possible, and run them continuously on the main trade routes—spice, cotton, ivory, metal and diamond—we will recover our investment in three years. After that, it's pure profit.'

'Two hundred ships? Raavan, I like your confidence, and I've always had faith in your vision. But this kind of scale is unimaginable. And unmanageable. The risks are too high.'

'On the contrary, scaling it up will reduce our risk.'

'But Raavan, no trader has ever owned a fleet of two hundred ships. It's unheard of!'

'That's because there has never been a trader called Raavan before this.'

Akampana tried to butt in. 'Are you sure we cannot negotiate further with the Malayaputras? Guru Vishwamitra and his followers live very frugal lives. I don't see what they need so much money for. Maybe there is still some room for negotiation...'

'I am not going back on a deal that I've signed already,' said Raavan firmly.

'Perhaps we can expand slowly, then? Start with say, twenty ships. One consignment of cave material is enough for that. We can see how it works and—'

Raavan cut in. 'No. We will begin with two hundred.'

'But, Raavan,' said Akampana, nervously fiddling with his many finger rings. 'Building two hundred ships means we will need ten consignments. That means we will need to pay five million gold coins.'

'That is correct.'

'Raavan, listen to me,' said Mareech. 'Five million gold coins is more than the annual revenue of most kingdoms in the Sapt Sindhu. We will have to mortgage everything we have to raise that kind of money.'

'Then we should do that.'

'Dada,' interrupted Kumbhakarna.

Raavan turned to his younger brother. 'Yes?'

'I have an idea.'

'What?'

'People talk freely in front of me because they think I am only a child and—'

'Please get to the point quickly, Kumbhakarna. You know Raavan does not like long-winded answers,' Akampana interjected. He looked at Raavan for confirmation, but withered on receiving an angry glare. Raavan had all the time in the world for Kumbhakarna.

'We may not need to borrow the money,' continued Kumbhakarna calmly. 'We can just steal it.'

Raavan shook his head. 'Not a good idea. We'll have to hit too many targets to raise five million. And each time we hit a place, the risk will increase.'

'Not really, Dada. All we need to do is hit one big target.'

'We can't target royal treasuries, Kumbha. The security is too tight.'

'I wasn't talking about a royal treasury.'

'There is someone in India, other than a king, who has five million gold coins?' Raavan raised an eyebrow, intrigued.

'Krakachabahu, the governor of Chilika.'

Mareech nearly choked on the cardamom-flavoured milk he was drinking. 'Krakachabahu? How can we steal from him? The entire Kalinga fleet will be after us. We will not have a safe harbour anywhere in the Indian Ocean.'

'But Uncle,' said Kumbhakarna politely, 'this is money that Krakachabahu has stolen from the king of Kalinga. He has been taking a cut from the Customs revenue for years. He keeps the money hidden in an underground vault in his palace. He will never be able to admit that he had it in the first place. That's the beauty of stealing from a thief; he cannot complain.'

'Hmm…' Raavan's eyes sparkled.

'I've also heard that a lot of his wealth is conveniently in the form of precious stones. Small, lightweight, and easy to steal. And they can be converted to gold at any port in the Indian Ocean.'

Raavan turned to Mareech and Akampana, a proud smile on his face. 'My brother!'

'But Raavan,' said Akampana, 'we can't just walk into Krakachabahu's palace. It's one of the best-guarded residences in India. And most of the guards are from his native land, Nahar.'

Mareech, who had begun to warm to the idea, countered Akampana. 'Yes, but the chief of the palace guards is Prahast.'

Raavan smiled as soon as he heard the name. 'He owes me one.'

'Exactly,' said Mareech. 'You saved his life once. And he has always wanted to work with you. The fact that he is greedy and ruthless makes him perfect for the job.'

'Let's start the preparations. We sail to Chilika in a month.'

Chapter 8

'The plan looks good, Dada,' said Kumbhakarna.

Two weeks had passed since Kumbhakarna had suggested looting Krakachabahu's treasure. The brothers were reviewing their strategy, late in the evening, in Raavan's wood-lined personal library, with its collection of thousands of manuscripts.

Knowledge was highly prized in India. Small manuscript collections were not uncommon in homes, though only universities and temples had large, well-stocked libraries. It was said, with reasonable confidence, that no individual had more manuscripts in his private collection than Raavan. What is more, he had actually read most of them.

'I came up with it,' said Raavan. 'Of course it's good!'

'Maybe, but I came up with our target!'

'Okay, okay,' Raavan said, laughing. 'You are the king of everything, Kumbha.'

Kumbhakarna bowed theatrically and laughed along. 'I want to read something interesting, Dada. Anything you'd recommend?'

Raavan looked around his huge library. He was extremely possessive about his manuscripts. He didn't allow anyone to borrow them. Except Kumbhakarna. There were very few things that he refused Kumbhakarna. 'How about I read you a poem instead?'

'A poem?'

'Yes.'

'Composed by whom?'

Raavan remained silent. He looked almost embarrassed.

Kumbhakarna raised his eyebrows. 'By you, Dada?'

'Yes.'

'By the great Goddess Saraswati, how did this miracle happen? I had no idea you composed poetry!'

'Will you keep quiet and listen?'

'Of course!'

Raavan picked up a scroll, looking nervous and excited at the same time. He cleared his throat, then said, 'It's called "The Ballad of the Sun and the Earth".'

'How eloquent! I like it already.'

'Shut up and listen, Kumbha.'

'Sorry, I'll try to be serious. Poetry is no joking matter after all.' Kumbhakarna smiled impishly.

'Well, it's a story as much as it's a poem. Now, listen:

'The Ballad of the Sun and the Earth

The Clouds rush to the Mountain...'

Kumbhakarna interrupted. 'What are the clouds and the mountain doing there? I thought this was about the sun and the earth.'

Raavan glared at Kumbhakarna, who immediately put his hands together contritely.

'No interruptions, I am warning you,' Raavan said. He took a deep breath and started again.

The Ballad of the Sun and the Earth

The Clouds rush to the Mountain,
they caress him gently,
they fight for his attention,
they rise to kiss his lips.
The Clouds believe the Mountain is smitten,
that he stands so high to not let them pass,
that he stands uncomfortably still, with rishi-like repose,
because he waits for their return every year.
There's no doubt in their mind:
The Mountain loves them.

It's sad that they'll never know
that the Mountain doesn't care for them,
he only wants the nourishing rain they carry,
he doesn't nudge them up to kiss them,
he does it to break them and get what he wants,
and by the time they understand,
it's too late.

It's sad that no Cloud survives to warn the others.

The River rushes to the Sea,
her instincts tell her this is her destiny.
She's grown up on stories of love,
on tales of blind and illogical passion,
and she's in too much of a hurry to
meet her lover, to stop and think.
But when she sees the Sea,
his immensity, depth, power,

she hesitates and meanders.
But her innate romanticism wins,
And she flows happily into his arms.

It's sad that she'll never know
that the Sea doesn't love her,
that the Sea is too lost in his own grandiosity
to even notice the River.
That her loving embrace doesn't change the Sea,
that the water she received as a gift from the Sea
was actually given to her by a philanthropic Sun.

It's sad that by the time the River realises the truth,
She's already lost her identity.

And then there's the Earth.
Unlike the others, she thinks more than feels,
Her mind is more powerful than her heart,
She sees the Sun,
Luminous and spirited, alone and magnificent,
Has so much and is so wasteful with it.
The Earth, being smart,
Uses the Sun's wasted energy,
Nourishes herself and grows,
in character, in mind, body and spirit.
She marvels at her own brilliance
and what she's done with her life.
She fears the Sun and his immense power,
and detests the way he lavishes his God-given gifts.

It's sad that she'll never know that the Sun could have
left,

Yet he stands there all alone, so that he can give to the Earth.
He burns himself, so she may benefit from it,
He wants to come closer, but he knows he can't,
He knows his passion is so strong that he'll hurt her,
So he stands apart and admires his Lady.

It's sad that no one's around to tell the Earth
Tell her just how much the Sun loves her.

Raavan put the scroll away and waited for his brother's response.

Kumbhakarna looked contemplative.

'Dada, that was powerful,' he said after a moment.

Raavan smiled. 'Do you really like it?'

'I love it! Trust me, Dada, there will come a time when even the Mahadevs and the Vishnus will quote this poem!'

Raavan laughed. 'You really do love me a lot, kid brother…'

'That I do! But seriously, Dada, you can play music, you sing, you write poetry, you are a warrior, you are wealthy, you are well-read, you are super-intelligent. There's no one like you in the whole wide world!'

Raavan puffed out his chest exaggeratedly. 'Quite right. There is nobody like me!'

They burst out laughing.

—१७१—

A month had passed since the decision to rob Krakachabahu had been made. Raavan and his crew were to sail out of the Gokarna port the following day. Considering the speed at which the ship could sail, they expected to be in Chilika within a few days. Akampana, Mareech and a hundred soldiers would accompany him. Kumbhakarna had insisted on tagging along too, and after a few unconvincing attempts at dissuading him, Raavan had relented.

Mareech and Akampana had already struck a deal with Prahast. He would first help Raavan steal Krakachabahu's treasure, and then leave Chilika with them. Most opportunely, Krakachabahu had recently sailed out to his homeland Nahar, situated in between the Tigris and Euphrates rivers. Half a world away from Chilika.

The night before the proposed heist, Raavan decided to visit his favourite courtesan, Dadimikali, the most expensive courtesan in the most elite pleasure house in Gokarna. Only the best would do for him!

He lay on the bed now, a sheet pulled up to his waist. Dadimikali was lying on her stomach, her head resting on Raavan's thighs. Nude as the day she was born. She was lithe of body and slim, with curves in all the right places.

'I don't think I'll be able to walk properly tomorrow,' she giggled. She turned towards Raavan and felt her way up. 'But it looks like you are ready for more.'

Raavan stretched his arms and cracked his knuckles. 'I don't think you can take it.'

Dadimikali gazed at his face lovingly. 'You know I can take anything from you.'

Raavan looked away. Bored. Dadimikali's affection was becoming increasingly cloying. His mind wandered to the dog he had killed a few months back. The one that had kept following him around.

Mangy, pathetic-looking creature. Disgusting. It needed to be put out of its misery.

'Raavan?'

Raavan didn't answer. He focused on his breathing. A long-dormant animal was slowly beginning to stir inside him.

'Raavan,' whispered Dadimikali. 'I think I love you.'

Raavan could feel the animal inside him awaken.

Dadimikali edged up and pressed her naked breasts against him. Love poured out of her eyes. 'You don't have to tell me you love me. I understand. I just want you to know that I love you.'

'What are you staring at?' growled Raavan.

He knew his swarthy skin was attractive to most women. But the pockmarks on his face always made him feel self-conscious. He was growing a beard and a moustache to hide as many of the marks as he could.

Dadimikali kept gazing at him. 'I'm looking at your beautiful face…'

She moved closer, pouting her lips in readiness for a kiss. Raavan grabbed her by the hair and yanked her head back.

'Which part of my face are you staring at?' he demanded.

Dadimikali knew that Raavan sometimes liked things rough. She lay back on the bed with her hands clasped behind her head. Surrendering completely. 'I am your slave. Do what you want with me.'

Raavan was gripped by desire. The desire to know what it would feel like to peel the beautiful skin off Dadimikali's face and see the pink flesh underneath. To slice through it. Hacking at the tissue and arteries. Reaching the bone. Sawing through the bone. He felt his breath quicken with excitement. The animal inside him was roaring now.

Oblivious to the reason for Raavan's excitement, Dadimikali edged closer once again. She kissed Raavan gently. Offering herself to him. Submissively.

He bit down on her lips. Hard. Drawing blood. She didn't cry out. She remained still. Waiting for Raavan to do more.

Raavan's breath quickened. His body urged him to finish what he had started. He felt intoxicated. Then, from the deep recesses of his mind, he heard a soft voice.

Dada...

Kumbhakarna's voice. Filled with innocence. And fear.

No. Not her. I can't keep it quiet here. Kumbhakarna will find out...

But the animal inside growled louder.

I have the money to keep it quiet.

He looked into Dadimikali's trusting eyes. Her puckered lips. Her heaving chest.

She wants it. She's asking for it. She's pathetic. Disgusting. She needs to be put out of her misery.

He wrapped his arms tightly around her. Crushing her. She whimpered slightly. But did not complain.

'I am yours. Do what you will with me...'

Suddenly, Raavan heard the familiar, calm voice in his head.

You can be better than this.

The voice of the Kanyakumari. The voice of a living Goddess.

His navel throbbed, the pain intensifying.

Raavan pushed Dadimikali away and leapt off the bed. She reached for him, trying to stop him from leaving. 'What happened? What did I say?'

'Get away from me!' he hissed.

Tears welled up in her eyes. 'Don't leave me... please...'

Raavan turned and slapped her across the face. Savagely. As she fell back on the bed, he picked up his clothes and stormed out of the room.

—ॐ—

Raavan and Kumbhakarna stood on the upper deck of the ship, admiring the view. They had just sailed into Chilika lake. Mareech and Akampana were on the lower deck, supervising the progress of the vessel towards the small island of Nalaban, in the centre of the lake.

The entire island had been reserved for Krakachabahu's use. His palace was on the top of a hill, right in the middle of the island. The hill was man-made, created from the earth that had been dredged up from Chilika lake to increase the depth of the water so large ships could enter. Much of the land around the house had been left undisturbed. Wild and lush. Nalaban was also a bio hotspot, welcoming large numbers of varied species of birds during their winter migration.

Krakachabahu was perceived to be a simple man, dedicated to his job. His apparent respect for Mother Nature and the simple gubernatorial palace helped him maintain appearances with the king of Kalinga, and hide his thieving. The truth was that he planned to take his illicit skimming of the Kalinga revenues and leave soon. He had stashed away enough money, and he intended to use it to raise an army to conquer Nahar. His long-term plan was to rule his home country.

But he didn't know that his plan was about to be upended by an upstart trader from Lanka.

'You remember my instructions, right?' Raavan asked his brother.

'I do, Dada, but can't I come with you?'

'No, you can't. We've discussed this already. Now repeat my instructions.'

'We'll sail to the secondary wharf on the island and present our manifest as a trading ship from Thailand. All of you will go in carrying empty chests, which you will fill with Krakachabahu's gold and precious stones. Then you will carry them back to the ship.'

Raavan laughed and ruffled Kumbhakarna's hair. 'Kumbha, that's what I need to do. Tell me what you are supposed to do.'

'Oh that, yeah... So, I'll be waiting at the wharf for you. In case I see any sign of trouble, I'll sound the ship's horn and sail out. I'll wait for you at the main wharf on the other side of the island. And you'll meet me there.'

The main wharf had been damaged a few months ago, when a craft lost control of its steering and rudder mechanism, and crashed into it. It was under repair now and all traffic had been directed to the secondary wharf.

'That's correct. Now, I am leaving some men here with you. But you will not attempt to be unnecessarily brave if there is trouble. You will sail out and meet me at the main wharf, the damaged one.'

'Yes, Dada.'

Raavan bent closer to Kumbhakarna. 'Promise me that you will sail away and not do anything foolish.'

'Have I ever disobeyed your instructions, Dada?' asked Kumbhakarna, looking hurt.

'Often,' said Raavan sardonically. 'Go on, promise me. Swear in the name of Lord Rudra.'

'Dada! I can't take Lord Rudra's name so casually.'

'Swear!'

'Fine! I swear in the name of Lord Rudra. I'll sail away at the first sign of trouble and meet you at the main wharf.'

'Good.'

—ꙄꙨꙊ—

'By the great Lord Indra!' exclaimed Raavan, turning the flawless pink diamond around in his hand. 'It's hard to believe this little rock is worth four hundred thousand gold coins.'

The colour of a diamond significantly determined its value. If a white diamond exhibited a yellow hue, its price went down. If it exhibited a pink hue, a much rarer phenomenon, its price shot up.

Mareech stepped closer to admire the precious stone. 'It's not little by any stretch of the imagination, Raavan. It's the biggest diamond I have ever seen.'

Akampana stood to one side, looking around nervously.

'Doesn't it look like it's bleeding from the inside?' asked Raavan, enchanted. 'I wonder how it got this pink hue.'

Nobody knew how or why a diamond acquired its colour. Some said it was because of the pressure exerted on the stone over many millennia. Others opined that the enormous forces unleashed by earthquakes caused a diamond's colour to change. A few even considered a pink diamond to be unlucky. A carrier of bad karma.

'Would you know?' asked Raavan, showing the diamond to Akampana.

'Raavan, it doesn't matter how it became pink. As long as it is pink. Let's leave. Please.'

Raavan laughed softly. 'Always so nervous, Akampana.'

He stepped back from the tiny, secret chamber that had been artfully built into the thick wall. He looked at Prahast, standing at the far end of the room. Prahast's loyal soldiers were positioned alongside him, their swords drawn. Dripping with blood. In front of them were three eunuchs on their knees. Part of Governor Krakachabahu's Naharin security team. They bore the wounds of the gruesome torture they had been subjected to, until they revealed the location of the secret chamber where the precious stones were kept.

Raavan nodded at Prahast. The men immediately swung their swords and decapitated the three eunuchs. Raavan's instructions had been clear. No eye-witnesses were to be left behind to identify the perpetrators of the robbery. Everyone in the palace—the security staff, the maids, the cooks, the helpers—had been killed. In cold blood.

Prahast had managed to corrupt half the security force, with loyalty earned over many years and large amounts of gold promised over the previous week. His men had launched a surprise attack on the other Naharins in the palace. Swift and clean.

Nobody outside had an inkling of the massacre that had taken place within the palace. In an attempt to mislead Krakachabahu, dead bodies had been brought into the palace earlier. Their faces had been smashed in to prevent identification. To convince the Naharin governor of Chilika that Prahast and the others in his security force had also been killed during the robbery.

It was a brutal plan. But also efficient and practical. Like Raavan himself.

On Prahast's advice, Raavan had decided against killing the workers whom they had seen repairing the damaged wharf, at some distance from the governor's residence. To kill them in the open was to risk exposure. In any case, the workers were never allowed near the palace or the secondary wharf. So the chances of them identifying Raavan and his gang were next to none.

Raavan's men had already carried the gold out of the palace in large chests. These were being loaded on the ship right now. He had stayed behind, with Mareech, Akampana and a few others to gather the precious stones. For just these stones were worth a little over two million gold coins.

Raavan stepped forward and stared at the decapitated bodies of the three Naharin eunuchs. As the blood continued to leak out of their gaping necks, he stood still, almost hypnotised. Drawn to the bloody spectacle before him.

He bent forward. Trying to distinguish the different arteries through which the thick red fluid was gushing out. The bodies were lifeless. But their hearts didn't seem to know that yet. They were still pumping. Weakly. But still despatching blood to heads that weren't there anymore.

Akampana touched Raavan's arm. 'Raavan...'

Raavan snapped out of his reverie and slipped the stone in his hand into the pouch tied to his cummerbund, where it clinked against the others. He took a deep breath and looked at the others. 'Let's go.'

Just then, the ship's horn sounded. Loud. Insistent.

'Run!' shouted Raavan.

Everyone reacted immediately. They knew what they had to do. The plan was clear. They had to rush to their horses and ride like the wind to the main wharf. Kumbhakarna would be waiting for them there, in Raavan's ship.

—१०१—

'Hyaah!'

Raavan and his men rode their horses hard. Ten of them. Mareech in the lead. Raavan bringing up the rear-guard. They were riding downhill, fast and furious.

'To the right!' shouted Mareech, pointing.

A fork in the road was coming up. The road to the right led downhill to the damaged wharf. The other one went straight to the secondary wharf, which was visible in the far distance. Where Raavan's ship should have been. But it was missing. From high up on the hill, they could see another large ship moored there. It had just cruised in, for the sails were still up. So was the flag. It was Krakachabahu's vessel. He had returned early.

'Faster!' shouted Raavan.

He could see riders racing out of the secondary wharf. Riding up the main road. Up the hill. Towards them. Perhaps Krakachabahu had sensed something was wrong.

'To the other wharf!' screeched Akampana. He was riding in the middle of the group. Nervous as a cat on a hot metal roof.

The horses swerved onto the road to the right. It was about a five-minute ride downhill to the wharf. Raavan could see a forward scout rider galloping up the straight road, towards them. Krakachabahu's man.

Raavan pulled his knife out of its scabbard, took the reins of his horse in his mouth, and focused for a moment. Holding his breath, he flung the blade at the rider. It rammed into the man's throat. As he fell from his horse, Raavan swerved to the right, riding hard behind his men.

'Hyaah!'

As they thundered down the road towards the damaged wharf, through the dense forest vegetation, Raavan could see the road more clearly. It was now a straight ride to the wharf, which meant they would be easy targets for Krakachabahu's mounted archers. And he was right at the back of the line. The first target.

Damn!

Thinking quickly, he yanked the string that crisscrossed his shoulder and pulled the shield tied on his back upwards. He could survive an arrow in his back. Not one that pierced his throat.

The wharf was just a little way ahead. The road was getting narrower. Much of it was taken up by the scaffolding built for port repairs. A few men were on the scaffolding, while others stood around on the road.

The horsemen thundered ahead.

'Move!' screamed Mareech, as he hurtled past.

The workers rushed to get out of the way, in a sudden state of panic. One of the more unfortunate ones came under Akampana's horse. The riders didn't slow down. The man was run over repeatedly by the many horses that followed Akampana's. By the time Raavan passed, he had been pummelled to a pulp.

Since there were no posts to tie the ship to, Kumbhakarna had had the sailors drop anchor. Keeping the ship as close as he could to the edge of the wharf, with the help of grappling hooks. The strongest amongst the sailors hung close to the anchor line, a large axe in his hands, ready to strike and cut the thick rope as soon as Raavan and the others were on board.

There was a wide gap between the wharf's edge and the ship. But the Lankan horses had been trained to jump high and far. Precisely for scenarios where a quick escape was necessary. Such as now.

Mareech did not slow down as he galloped through the damaged wharf.

'Hyaah!'

He whipped his horse to a frenzy, causing it to gallop harder. Faster and faster. Right at the edge of the wharf, he screamed, 'DASHA!'

Dasha was the old Sanskrit word for the number ten. Nobody knew why Raavan had insisted on this particular word when the horses were being trained, but his men had obeyed him unquestioningly, as usual.

Mareech's horse knew the command well, and leapt forward. High and far. He landed neatly onto the ship's deck. Mareech thundered on for a few feet more, clearing the way for the others behind him.

One after the other, the riders leapt onto the ship. One of Prahast's Naharin soldiers timed his jump wrong. His horse fell short and dropped into the water. The man banged his head hard against the shipboards, breaking his neck. He died instantly. Nobody stopped to look at him. They had no time.

'Come on!' screamed Mareech. He was standing by the balustrade of the ship now, having dismounted from his horse. Prahast came speeding forward, timing his jump perfectly, and landed safely on the ship. Raavan was next. The last of them.

Krakachabahu and his men were closing in. Just two hundred metres away.

'Come on, Dada!' screamed Kumbhakarna.

One of Krakachabahu's archers took his horse's reins into his mouth, positioned his riding bow in front of his chest, and released an arrow.

It was a lucky shot. At a fast-moving target.

The arrow slammed into the horse's digital flexor tendons on the lower part of his right hind leg. Severing it cleanly. It didn't seem like a big wound. There was hardly any blood. But it was debilitating for the galloping beast. The right leg, useless and incapable of bearing weight, collapsed. And the horse, because of the fearsome speed it was moving at, fell hard, its head hitting the ground, its neck twisting at an unnatural angle.

Raavan, alert as ever, had already untangled himself from the stirrups. Smoothly dismounting as the horse fell to the ground, he rolled away from it and was back on his feet almost instantly. He ran forward in the same smooth motion.

'Dada!' Kumbhakarna's voice was filled with anxiety and fear.

Everyone around him had the same thought.

Raavan is not going to make it.

Mareech looked at Kumbhakarna and then back at Raavan. 'Lord Rudra be merciful...'

There was no way a man could jump over the gap that most of the horses had strained to bridge.

But this was no ordinary man. This was Raavan.

He sprinted down the wharf. Dashing ahead, towards the edge. Towards the port crane meant for loading cargo on ships. It hadn't been used in months. It was about to be put to use in an unexpected way.

Krakachabahu's men were still raining arrows at him. Some flew past Raavan. Others missed him by a whisker. But none hit their target.

As he neared the edge of the wharf, Raavan leapt high and grabbed the hook block of the crane. One leg scissored out to kick the winch. His timing was perfect. The winch wound out quickly, allowing the hoist rope to spool out. Holding on to the hook, Raavan soared over the water, towards the ship, as arrows flew around him.

Kumbhakarna and the rest of the crew stood rooted to their spots. Transfixed by this adrenaline-charged display of athleticism.

As soon as he was at a suitable height, Raavan gathered momentum, swung his body forward, and let go of the hook. He soared high in the air, then dropped easily onto the ship's deck. He rolled smoothly to break his fall and was back on his feet immediately.

His men stood around him, awestruck. Silent.

'Let's go!' Raavan shouted.

Kumbhakarna turned to the man at the anchor rope. 'Cut it!'

The sailor swung the axe, and in one mighty blow, severed the thick rope. The grappling hooks were rapidly released.

'Row now! Quickly!' ordered Kumbhakarna.

On command, the pace setters in the galley deck below started beating their drums. The men began rowing in tandem. The ship lumbered ahead. Pulling out of the wharf.

Krakachabahu's men continued to shoot arrows at them.

'Get down!' shouted Raavan.

The men went down on their knees, taking cover behind the balustrades.

'Faster!' ordered Kumbhakarna. The pace setters pounded up the beat and the rowers picked up their pace.

'Unfurl sails!'

One of the sailors, who had been hiding behind the tabernacle, started turning the winch. This was an engineering innovation that Raavan had perfected. It allowed one of the sails to be unfurled rapidly, with the guidance of a winch rigged on the deck. The sail started spreading out quickly. It would catch the wind soon.

As the ship pulled away, Raavan could hear the angry shouts of Krakachabahu's men in the distance. Safe behind the balustrade, he looked at Kumbhakarna and grinned.

Mareech clapped Raavan on the shoulder. 'We've done it, Raavan! We've done it!'

Raavan smiled. He rose to his feet and made an obscene gesture at Krakachabahu's men in the distance. One of the Naharins shot an arrow that whizzed past his face.

Mareech pulled his nephew down. 'What are you doing? We are not out of danger yet. Stay down!'

Raavan's face was pale, his body strangely still.

'Dada?' Kumbhakarna said worriedly, feeling Raavan's body for any wounds.

Raavan pushed Kumbhakarna aside and rose to his feet. His gaze was directed at the workers who were cowering near the scaffolding. Another arrow whizzed by. But Raavan didn't duck.

Mareech pulled him down again. 'What is wrong with you? Stay down!'

Raavan fell back on the deck unsteadily. He looked like he had seen a ghost. His breathing was ragged. He pushed Mareech away and rose again.

This time an arrow hit him on the shoulder, slamming into him with brutal force. But Raavan didn't flinch. His eyes were glued to the scaffolding.

'Dada!' Kumbhakarna screamed in panic, pulling him down again.

He noticed the sudden tears in his elder brother's eyes.

'Ka...' Raavan was crying. 'Kanya...'

This time, Kumbhakarna rose. He narrowed his eyes and looked towards the fast receding shore. At the scaffolding. At the workers there. At one person in particular, standing in the centre.

It was her.

He recognised her from the paintings.

While everyone else was cowering, she stood there unmoving. Upright. Like the living Goddess that she was. The signs of hard physical labour marked her and yet her face was luminous. She watched the ship go, her expression stately and calm. She radiated a quiet dignity. Almost like she was willing them to stop the violence. With her moral force.

There could be no doubt. It was her.

Mareech reached out and pulled Kumbhakarna down as another arrow whizzed by. He shouted angrily at his nephews, 'What has gotten into you both?'

Kumbhakarna looked at Raavan. He said what Raavan couldn't find the strength to say. 'The Kanyakumari...'

As if energised by the divine word, Raavan broke the shaft of the arrow buried in his shoulder. He stood up again and turned around. Ready to jump into the lake. Ready to swim to her.

'Raavan!' screamed Mareech, grabbing his nephew. 'Stop this madness!'

'Let me go!' Raavan cried hoarsely, struggling to free himself. 'Let me go!'

Everyone on the ship stared at their leader. Wondering what was going on.

Kumbhakarna held Raavan tight. 'Dada, you can't go back now! You will be killed!'

'Let me go!' Raavan tried to push the others away and get to his feet.

'Dada! Listen to me, please. You will die before you reach her!'

'Let me go!'

'I will come back for her, Dada! I will find her!'

'Let me go!' Raavan repeated in desperation.

Mareech was too stunned to react. He had never seen Raavan like this.

'Dada!' Kumbhakarna wouldn't let go of his brother. 'Please, trust me. I'll come back for her. I'll find her. I give you my word. But right now, you need to stay with us.'

'Let me go.' Raavan's voice was ragged. Broken.

'Dada, I will find her. I promise.'

'Let me go…'

The mast unfurled completely and caught the wind. The ship sailed out and away from the shore. Away from Krakachabahu's arrows.

Away from her.

Away from the Kanyakumari.

'Let me go…'

Chapter 9

In a little less than a month, Kumbhakarna was back in Kalinga. After the daring robbery on Nalaban Island, they had sailed to Lanka in a sombre mood. They had reached Gokarna in a day and a half, and the precious merchandise had been quickly unloaded and stored in the basement of Raavan's mansion, in a specially built and well-guarded chamber, with multiple locks for additional security. Kumbhakarna had immediately set about preparing for his journey back to the island. He had purchased a new ship, one that could not be traced back to Raavan in any way. He had also hired a small crew of young men from southern Africa. All of this had been accomplished in three weeks.

Then Kumbhakarna set off again, sailing up north. Towards Chilika lake. Towards the Kanyakumari.

By now, news had got around that a band of Naharins who had planned to follow the governor of Chilika into rebellion had double-crossed him and taken him prisoner. They had sailed out to Nahar with the captive Krakachabahu, intending to hand him over to the king. When a rebellion fails, it is pragmatic for the rebels to betray their leader to the incumbent ruler and save at least their own hides. Without the money that Krakachabahu had amassed over the years, the Nahar rebellion was as good as dead.

Nevertheless, sailing directly into the lake would have been risky, Kumbhakarna knew. He may be young, but he was not rash. There could still be some loyalists of Krakachabahu in Chilika.

So, Kumbhakarna sailed up north, beyond Chilika, intending to enter Kalinga via the mouth of the Mahanadi. But on the way, he decided to stop at the famous Jagannath temple in Puri, which lay between the lake in the south and the river to the north.

The Jagannath temple was considered to be one of the holiest spots in India. It was close to the coast and clearly visible from the sea. Kumbhakarna anchored his ship and then set out on a rowboat to the shore, accompanied by ten African guards.

The temple complex, consisting of thirty temples, was built on an enormous stone platform spread over ten acres. The central temple, one of the tallest and largest in India, was the *Jagannath* temple; a shrine dedicated to the *Lord of the Universe*. The Vishnu. The Vishnu before all other Vishnus. The Vishnu who was the *Witness*. The *Saakshin*.

Unlike most idols in temples, which were made of stone or metal, the Jagannath idol was made of wood. The wood of a neem tree, to be precise. Every twelve years, it was replaced with a freshly carved one.

The dark idol had a massive head, emerging directly from the chest, without a discernible neck. The arms were in line with the upper lip. The eyes were large and round. The waist was where the form ended. No legs. No hands.

The Saakshin Vishnu was, strictly speaking, a witness. The rich *black colour, krishna* in old Sanskrit, was testimony to its provenance, that this God hailed from before the beginning of time. Before even light was created. For before light was created, all was dark. All was black.

The absence of hands signified that He would not enact any karma of His own. The absence of legs showed that He would not move, either towards you or away from you. He was neutral. He would take no sides in petty human rivalries. He was beyond personal likes and dislikes.

Some believed that it was inaccurate to even assign a gender to the God. He was beyond such petty divisions. He was unity. The source.

Most importantly, He had no eyelids. His eyes were forever open. He was always watching.

According to the ancients, this was the highest form of divinity that humans were capable of understanding. For the Saakshin Vishnu was the Primal Being. Floating through time. Witnessing it all, as people lived their lives and the universe breathed its karma.

The prayers that were offered to Him were also unusual.

Devotees did not go to the Jagannath temple to merely ask for His blessings. They went with a larger purpose, when they were ready to carry out their paramount karma. To ensure that it was recorded in the memory of the Primal Being. The account of their karma in the Saakshin Vishnu's memory would decide whether the devotee would get freedom from the cycle of birth and rebirth.

Kumbhakarna believed that he was about to embark on the greatest karma of his life. He went down on his knees in front of the great idol. His back bent. His head touching the floor.

Chanting. At long last, he rose and said what every devotee of the Saakshin Vishnu said when facing Him: 'Witness me, My Lord.'

Witness me as I carry out the greatest karma of my life.

—ॐ—

It had been three years since the Nalaban Island robbery. Twenty-two-year-old Raavan had become reclusive and rarely ventured out of Gokarna. While he was still involved in the business and made the decisions on all key strategic issues, he did not go out to sea or travel. He remained in Gokarna, watching the sea from the heights of his hilltop mansion. Waiting for Kumbhakarna.

All this time, Kumbhakarna had been sending regular updates from Kalinga. The dock-repair workers they had seen the Kanyakumari with had travelled westward, deeper into the heart of Kalinga. The next time Raavan heard from Kumbhakarna, it was with the news that they were encamped at Vaidyanath, close to the Mayurakshi River. It wasn't too far from Kalinga.

In the meantime, Mareech had started managing Raavan's vast business empire. He had used the money looted from Krakachabahu to commission the building of large new ships. The best ship-builders in Gokarna and across the land had their entire capacity blocked by Raavan's purchase orders. He was taking delivery of five or six ships every month; an unprecedented happening that shocked the trading community all across the Indian Ocean rim.

Gradually, Raavan built up a fleet of two hundred ships. An advance payment for the cave material had been made to the Malayaputras. Raavan's men took each new ship, as soon as it was delivered, to Unawatuna, a hidden alcove on the southern coast of Lanka. They careened the ships there. The cave material was then kneaded, mixed with other ingredients, and painstakingly rubbed on to each ship's hull. It was a long and laborious process. And done in secret by a small, loyal crew that was very well rewarded for its efforts.

As Raavan's fleet grew, so did its reputation for speedy travel. Manufacturers and artisans found it profitable to trade with him. They knew that their goods would be delivered and sold much faster if they went to Raavan, as compared to other traders. On Raavan's instructions, Mareech also began to use their vastly superior fleet to apprehend and loot other ships along the busy trade routes of the Indian Ocean. The pirate vessels would appear like the wind, plunder and kill the sailors on the target ships, and sink them to ensure that no trace was left of their crimes. Many of the ships they destroyed belonged to Kubaer. Because of the lack of witnesses, no one made the connection with Raavan. They believed the attacks to be the handiwork of pirates.

Of course, Raavan's plan did not end with merely raiding other ships for treasure. Exploiting the growing fear of pirate attacks at sea, he started building his own mini army under the leadership of Prahast. He claimed it was a protection force for his ships. Though it was unusual for a trader to have a standing corps of trained soldiers, many thought it was a logical way to protect profits. Some of the other traders started hiring the services of Raavan's protection force too. Not only did Raavan make profits from hiring out his force, his soldiers also became a source of information for him, about his rivals and their trading plans.

Profits flowed in at a tremendous pace. Raavan was already among the wealthiest traders in Gokarna. He would soon be one of the wealthiest traders in the world. Wealthy enough for even the richest man on the planet, Kubaer, to take notice.

Aware that they could not risk the Malayaputras finding out about the real use of the cave material, Mareech had gone about leasing the Pushpak Vimaan from Kubaer. He had negotiated very hard on the price so that it would seem like a credible deal. Kubaer, the ever-pragmatic trader, had readily agreed. The vimaan was so expensive to run that he had virtually stopped using it. And, like any machine not put to regular use, it was slowly rusting away. From his point of view, any deal was better than no deal.

When Mareech took over the Pushpak Vimaan, the first thing he did was to strip away all the luxuries that Kubaer had built into the flying craft. Out went the gold-plated bed with its soft mattress and the large, well-stocked kitchen for the preparation of exotic food. The vimaan was deprived of everything that smacked of ineffectual opulence without providing any practical value. Removing these luxuries vastly reduced the weight of the craft. The reduced payload meant that the quantities of cave material required to fly the aircraft came down drastically. This slashed the cost of running the craft.

Mareech also limited the use of the vimaan. It would now be used only for flights to distant lands. To seek information, and for trade in extremely valuable but light cargo, such as precious stones. Raavan sometimes accompanied him on these flights.

It was one such trip that Mareech had come to discuss with Raavan.

'Are you sure about this information?' asked Raavan gruffly, as he continued his workout.

Mareech and Raavan were on the first-floor balcony of his mansion. The house was situated on a tall hill that jutted into the sea. It afforded brilliant views of the Indian Ocean, which stretched as far as the eye could see. And beyond. Raavan came here every morning to perform the *Surya namaskar, salutations to the Sun God*; a perfect combination of exercise and spirituality.

'Yes, the sailor is from southern Africa,' said Mareech. 'It's first-hand news. He has seen the things he speaks of.'

The man in question was Lethabo, one of the African sailors who had travelled to Kalinga with Kumbhakarna. He had turned up a few months ago with a message for Raavan, but an injury had prevented him from returning to his post with Kumbhakarna, who was presently in Vaidyanath. Mareech had gone to visit the sailor at the Gokarna Ayuralay where he was being treated. And that's how he had learnt of the great mines full of precious stones, close to the southern tip of the African continent. Marked by a giant flat-topped mountain, which locals called the Table Mountain.

'Hmm…' Raavan remained non-committal as he finished his routine and did obeisance to the Sun God.

'Raavan, it may be worth taking the Pushpak Vimaan there. Even if we find just a few precious stones, it will cover the cost of the trip. And if we do find a mine… well, I leave it to your imagination.'

Raavan walked to the edge of the balcony and rested his hands on the railing. He looked towards the ocean, then away at the horizon.

'Raavan?'

Raavan remained silent.

'Raavan, what is your decision?'

There was no response.

Mareech sighed. He walked up to his nephew and touched him on the shoulder.

'Raavan…'

'Kumbha…'

'What?'

Raavan pointed to a ship at the edge of the horizon. Its sails raised high. A flag aflutter. The flag of Kumbhakarna.

'How can you make out the markings on the flag from this distance?' asked Mareech in disbelief.

'It's him. I know it is,' said Raavan, his face radiating delight.

He turned around and almost ran outside, hollering at his guards to follow. He would board a ship quickly and sail out to meet his younger brother. He was too impatient to wait.

He had to have news of her as soon as possible.

News of the Kanyakumari.

—रोI—

'Are you sure?'

Raavan had sailed out without delay, meeting his brother a few nautical miles from the Gokarna port. Kumbhakarna had been surprised by Raavan's sudden appearance, but he could understand his elder brother's anxiety. It had been three years.

After an emotional reunion, Raavan had taken Kumbhakarna aside, to one end of the upper deck. And fired his questions. Questions about the Kanyakumari.

'Yes, Dada, I am sure. I have seen her myself.'

Raavan's eyes lit up. 'You've seen her?'

Kumbhakarna smiled. 'Yes. Lucky me!'

Raavan smiled broadly. 'Indeed. But how far away is this place?'

'The village she stays in is quite far inland. In fact, it's close to the Vaidyanath temple.'

'Vaidyanath temple? Seriously? We stayed there for some time when you were a baby.'

'Yes, I know,' said Kumbhakarna. 'I've heard the entire tale from maa.'

'But the Vaidyanath temple is quite close to the local Kanyakumari temple, is it not? What is the name of the place? Trikut? Why would she go back to live as an ordinary woman in the land where she was once worshipped as a Goddess?'

'Apparently, it's quite common for former Kanyakumaris to settle down close to the temple where they once reigned as living Goddesses. It has been known to happen not just at the Trikut Kanyakumari temple, but at many other Kanyakumari temples across India. I guess with so many other former Kanyakumaris around, a support structure is available for them to rebuild their lives.'

'Hmm,' said Raavan, barely listening to what Kumbhakarna was saying.

I should have gone to Vaidyanath much earlier. It was the logical thing to do, to search for her there. How foolish I have been! I've wasted so many years.

'Dada...'

'What?' asked Raavan, bringing his mind back to the present.

'I just want to say that there is a slight problem.'

'What problem?'

'Umm...'

'Come on, out with it. There is nothing that your dada can't handle.'

'Dada, the Kanyakumari… She's… she's married.'

Raavan waved his hand in dismissal. 'Oh, that's no problem. We'll handle it.'

'Handle it? How?' Kumbhakarna looked anxious.

'Don't be stupid, Kumbha,' Raavan scoffed. 'We will not kill her husband. How can we? He's the Kanyakumari's husband. We'll buy him off.'

'But…'

'You leave that to me. How quickly can we leave for Vaidyanath?'

'We can leave in a few days.'

'Good!'

Kumbhakarna laughed and mock-saluted Raavan. 'At your command, Iraiva!'

Iraiva was a title that Akampana used for Raavan. It meant 'True Lord' in the dialect that was spoken in Akampana's homeland, far away in the Pashtun regions of north-western India. The title had caught on. Many of Raavan's sailors now called him Iraiva.

Raavan embraced his brother and ruffled his hair. Kumbhakarna, despite being nine years younger than Raavan, was nearly as tall as he was.

'But you haven't asked me the most obvious question, Dada,' said Kumbhakarna. 'I guess I've been away too long. And you're getting slower as time passes.'

Raavan pulled back from Kumbhakarna and frowned. 'What question is that?'

'Something you've wanted to know since forever. Ask me. I have the answer.'

Raavan's face brightened as he caught on. 'You know it? You know her name?'

Kumbhakarna nodded, laughing softly.

Raavan grabbed his brother by the shoulders. 'Tell me, you fool! What is her name?'

'Vedavati.'

Raavan held his breath. Letting the ethereal name echo in his ears. Through his body. Through his spirit.

Vedavati.

The embodiment of the Vedas.

Raavan looked away from his brother, towards the sea. He felt as if his heart would burst at the sound of that divine name. He dared not speak it out loud. His soul wouldn't be able to handle it. He let the name echo softly in the confines of his mind.

Vedavati...

Chapter 10

The brothers were to leave the next morning. The fastest ship in their fleet had been prepared for the journey ahead.

Surya, the Sun God, had called it a night. Fortunately, Som, the Moon God, had taken up the baton. It was a beautiful full-moon night. Some parts of the sea and the exquisite coastline of Gokarna were illuminated in the glimmer of the diffused moonlight. There were almost no clouds in the sky, and the star-studded night resembled a jewelled canopy. A cool, moist sea breeze soothed the senses. The discordant noises of the city had died down. Raavan looked up towards the sky.

Love was in the air. And the pirate-trader breathed it in.

'I can't wait till tomorrow!' he said, drinking some more wine.

Kumbhakarna smiled. He had begged off sharing the wine with his elder brother. Their mother was home.

Raavan savoured the elegant flavour of his drink, holding the glass up in appreciation. He glanced at the bottle. Then at Kumbhakarna's empty hands.

'Seriously?' asked Raavan. 'She actually told you not to pick up my bad habits? Sometimes I think I should just—'

Kumbhakarna interrupted his elder brother. 'Dada, does it really matter? She is our mother...'

Raavan sighed. He drank some more wine.

Though Kumbhakarna respected his mother's wishes, at least in her presence, Kaikesi's well-meaning warnings to her younger son went unheeded. Kumbhakarna idolised Raavan. His elder brother had always been his hero. Bad habits? He wanted to emulate *every* habit of Raavan's. The only thing he wished his brother wouldn't do was insult their mother.

'So, tell me more about her,' said Raavan. 'The Kanyakumari...'

Kumbhakarna had noticed that despite knowing her name, Raavan could not bring himself to say it. He wondered what else he could tell Raavan about Vedavati. He had already described her physical form. It was remarkable how closely she resembled the woman in Raavan's paintings.

'She truly is extraordinary, Dada,' said Kumbhakarna. 'You know how hard life is for most people, right? Taxes have gone up and jobs have been difficult to come by.'

The anti-trader policies of most of the Sapt Sindhu kingdoms had resulted in a dramatic decline in business activities. An equally dramatic decline in tax revenues had followed. At the same time, royal expenditure had gone up due to the imperial preoccupation with war. So tax rates had been increased. This had further diminished the prospects for business and impacted job opportunities. In this atmosphere of desperation, crime too had increased. And as usual, the common folk suffered the brunt of it all. Mini rebellions were breaking out all over the country, especially against the petty nobles and landlords who served the kingdoms' rulers. But Raavan was not interested in the condition of the people at this moment.

'Tell me about the Kanyakumari.'

'It's linked to that, Dada. The Kanyakumari's husband…'

Kumbhakarna stopped as he saw Raavan's jaw clench.

Raavan looked away for a moment and then back at his brother. 'Yes, what about him?'

Kumbhakarna continued, 'His name is Prithvi. He is, or was, a businessman from Balochistan, in the far western corner of India. He settled in Vaidyanath many years ago and tried his hand at some business. But he ended up making heavy losses.'

'Loser.'

Kumbhakarna decided to let Raavan's jealous remark pass without comment. He had been told that Prithvi was an honest, straightforward, decent man. Even if he wasn't the sharpest businessman going.

'These losses in business,' continued Kumbhakarna, 'left him heavily indebted to the local landlord. To repay his debt, he is now working for the man.'

'So the Kanyakumari is stuck doing some menial job because of her idiot husband?'

'It appears she is there by choice, Dada. She too works for the landlord. Everyone in the area knows that she was the Kanyakumari and they respect her. Therefore, she is able to broker peace between the common people and the landlord, whenever it becomes necessary. The landlord ensures that there is enough food for his people. He also gets them jobs wherever he can, on his farm, or at construction sites in and around Chilika. They are reasonably content because of this and have no reason to rebel. Theirs is one of the more peaceful villages you will find in the Sapt Sindhu. Which is an achievement in these times of penury and anger. And it is all underwritten by the moral authority of Vedavatiji.'

Raavan's takeaway from all this was just one thing. 'So, all we have to do is repay the debt to a petty village landlord and the Kanyakumari is free?'

'Umm… Dada, I don't know if it will be that simple.'

'It *is* that simple. There is so much you have to learn about life, Kumbha. You are still very young.'

—ॐ—

Raavan's ship was sailing up the eastern coast of India, towards Branga. Towards the mouth of the holy Ganga. They intended to sail up the river, to the point where it came closest to Vaidyanath. The crew would then march overland to the sacred temple town. The river Mayurakshi began its journey close to Vaidyanath, and flowed east to empty itself into the westernmost distributary of the Ganga. An amateur sailor might make the mistake of thinking that sailing up the Mayurakshi would be the fastest way to reach Vaidyanath. But Raavan was not an amateur. He knew that the Mayurakshi was a flood-prone river with treacherous and fast-moving currents. Sailing on it would be hard work, and slow. Better to sail further up the Ganga, and then walk or ride the rest of the way.

'Are you sure you are fit enough to ride all the way to Vaidyanath?' asked Raavan, playfully patting Kumbhakarna's immense belly.

The brothers were on the upper deck of the ship, walking down the corridor, towards the captain's cabin. Raavan had just finished an hour of dance practice on the open deck, accompanied by his favourite musician, Surya. He had hired Surya at considerable expense some time ago, and persuaded him and his wife Annapoorna to accompany them on the voyage so he could continue to practice the dance form he was currently attempting to perfect.

'Don't worry about me, Dada. I am not the one who goes breathless at the mere mention of that "divine name",' said Kumbhakarna, a mock-devout expression on his face.

Raavan burst out laughing and Kumbhakarna thumped him on the back, laughing even more loudly. They entered the cabin and Kumbhakarna shut the door behind them. Raavan walked up to an ornate cabinet and fetched a glass decanter and goblet. He poured himself some wine.

'Maa is not here, Kumbha,' said Raavan, holding the glass high. 'You should try some.'

'I have tried some already, Dada!' Kumbhakarna grinned. 'But I don't like drinking at sea. It makes me feel like vomiting.'

'Yuck,' grimaced Raavan, 'I did not need to know that.' He flopped down on a chair placed near a porthole, across from his brother. 'Anyway, now that I know you have tried wine already, I have to get you to try women. There are some very good courtesan-houses on the way. We'll stop at one of them. Let you experience… shall we say, a woman's touch.'

Kumbhakarna giggled. Embarrassed and excited at the same time. He had heard stories. But he had no idea what he was supposed to do with a woman.

'The only problem with women is their mouth,' continued Raavan. 'They talk. And what is more, they talk utter nonsense. You do know that in some parts of the world, they believe that heaven is above and hell is below, right? Well, it's the exact opposite with women. With women, there is heaven below and hell above!'

Raavan laughed aloud at his own joke. Kumbhakarna joined in somewhat uncertainly.

'That is not true of all women, Dada,' he offered. 'When Vedavatiji speaks, one can sense the wisdom—'

Before he could complete the sentence, Raavan cut in. 'The Kanyakumari is not just a woman. She is a living Goddess.'

'Of course, Dada.'

Raavan looked out of the porthole, sipping his wine. Thinking of what he would tell her when he saw her. How he would woo her.

Why will she refuse me? Especially when she finds out how I feel about her. When she gets to know how rich and powerful I am... and worthy of her love.

'Dada, I just want to be honest about something. You should consider it seriously too.' Kumbhakarna's voice interrupted Raavan's thoughts.

Observing his younger brother's grave expression, Raavan became serious too. 'What is it?'

'It's just that...' Kumbhakarna hesitated.

'What happened, Kumbha? Out with it.'

'Dada... don't take this the wrong way... but honestly, I just don't think the Kanyakumari will be impressed by your dancing. So don't dance for her, please. I can guarantee that she will run away from you if you do.'

Raavan picked up a small cushion that lay nearby and threw it at Kumbhakarna, who collapsed in peals of laughter.

Raavan was laughing too. 'You are certainly not the good little boy who maa fears I will corrupt.'

Kumbhakarna grinned. 'Trying to follow your example, Dada!'

Raavan picked up another cushion that was at hand and threw it at Kumbhakarna. His younger brother caught it effortlessly, and put it behind his back. 'I think I'm comfortable enough now, thank you. I won't be needing any more!'

Laughter filled the cabin. As he wiped away the tears of mirth, Raavan looked at his younger brother with love. And pride. For these few light-hearted moments, even the ever-present pain in his navel seemed to have disappeared. Joy and hope filled his heart.

—रेॊI—

Kumbhakarna couldn't stop smiling as he walked unsteadily back to the ship.

Raavan put his arm around his little brother's shoulders, leaned in close and whispered, 'How was it?'

They were in Mahua Island and Kumbhakarna had just visited a courtesan-house for the very first time. The island was at the mouth of the western-most distributary of the Ganga, at the point where the great river, burdened with water and silt, sluggishly met the Eastern Sea. There was a courtesan-house here, owned by a woman called Vasantpala, which was renowned across the region. Raavan had decided it was the perfect place for his brother's initiation into the world of carnal pleasures.

He had taken Vasantpala's advice and chosen a famous courtesan called Zabibi for his younger brother. Zabibi was from Arabia, and had come to India only recently, to make her fortune. She was no less than an *apsara*, a *celestial nymph*. Long-limbed and supple, she was blessed with lustrous black hair. Though new to the land, she was already famed for her beauty and her impeccable taste in clothes and jewellery. And most importantly, she was experienced in the art of love.

Only the best would do for Kumbhakarna.

'I think I am in love,' whispered Kumbhakarna, looking stricken and intoxicated at the same time.

Raavan burst out laughing. He continued walking, then stopped when he realised his brother was not next to him.

Kumbhakarna was standing still. Looking dreamily at the early morning sky. The two extra arms on his shoulders drooped, as if they too were inebriated. 'I am not joking, Dada. I think I am in love.'

Raavan raised his eyebrows.

'I don't want to leave her here. Can't I have her forever? Can't I marry her?'

Raavan walked back to where Kumbhakarna stood, put his arm around his shoulders, and started walking his reluctant brother along.

'Dada, I am serious…'

'Kumbha, women like Zabibi are meant to be used, not loved.'

The flash of anger on Kumbhakarna's face gave Raavan pause.

'Dada! Don't speak of Zabibi that way!'

'It was a transaction, Kumbha. She gave you pleasure, you gave her money. She is not interested in you. She is interested in the money.'

'No, no! You don't know what she told me. She couldn't believe that I was just a boy. She said she had never been with a man like me.'

'I paid her, Kumbha. She is a professional. Of course she said things that you wanted to hear.'

'But she didn't lie to me and say things to make me feel good. She meant what she said. She didn't say that I was good looking. I know I am not. But she did say that I was intelligent. Which I am. And that I am strong. And…' Kumbhakarna smiled shyly, 'and good in bed.'

Raavan couldn't help laughing again. 'My naïve little Kumbha! This world is full of selfish people. They will tell you what you want to hear in order to get what they want from you. To protect yourself, you must know how to use them to get what you want. That's the way the world works.'

'But Dada, Zabibi is different. She is—'

'She is no different. She is just clearer about what she wants. She wants money. And she'll give you sex in return. It's simple. Some men want honour. Why? I don't know. But they do. So, give it to them. Give them an honourable way to die. And profit from it. Some women believe that flaunting their beauty is empowering. So, compliment them, have sex with them, and cast them away. Use people before they can use you. Most people in the world are contemptible. Many hide behind pretentions. The ones who succeed are the ones who are honest with themselves. Zabibi is honest. She doesn't care about you. She cares about herself. She's here for a few years to earn enough money, and then she'll go back to her husband in Arabia.'

Kumbhakarna was shocked. 'She's married? She lied to me!'

'Yes, she lied to you. But she didn't lie to the most important person in her life—herself! You should not be shocked. Instead, you should learn from her. Be clear about what you want. But hide it well. It will help you get what you want.'

Kumbhakarna was silent for some time, thinking over what his brother had said. Finally he said, 'That's why we are attacking Kubaer's ships, right? But we do it in such a way that everyone thinks it's the work of pirates.'

'Exactly. Now you are learning. Kubaer's strength is his wealth, and the more of it we take away, the more insecure he will get. In his desperation, he will turn to the only person in Lanka with a league of well-trained and armed men—me. He will seek my help to secure his wealth. I will obviously help the hapless man. And become the chief of the army of Lanka. From there, it will be a short distance to becoming the king.'

Kumbhakarna's chest puffed out with pride. 'My brother, the king of Lanka!'

Raavan smiled. 'Always remember why we are strong, why we are successful. Because we don't fool ourselves that we are honourable or good. We know who we are. We accept it. We embrace it. That's why we beat everyone. That's why we will continue to beat everyone.'

'Yes, Dada.'

Raavan walked on, with Kumbhakarna ambling along beside him.

Chapter 11

'We have to go back, Dada!'

'Kumbha, you are being silly. Go to your cabin.'

Their ship was to leave Mahua Island in a few hours. Kumbhakarna had just come rushing into Raavan's cabin with some news. Earlier, when he had been with Zabibi, enjoying the courtesan's attentions, he had barely noticed the very young girl, not more than eight years of age, who had served him alcohol and food. Before she left the room, he had seen her linger beside the chair on which he had casually flung his angvastram. He hadn't thought much of it then.

Back in his cabin, he had noticed a small knot tied to the end of the fabric. He had opened it to find a tiny piece of papyrus. With two words written on it, in a childish handwriting. He handed the note to Raavan.

Raavan read it aloud. 'Help me.'

'We have to.'

'Help whom?'

'The little girl in the courtesan-house.'

'How do you know it was her?'

'I just know, Dada. She looked troubled. Now that I think about it, there was fear in her eyes. She needs our help.'

'Kumbha, I gave you a long lecture only half an hour ago! We succeed because of our ability to exploit people. Not because we are do-gooders.'

'Dada, you were the one who once told me that if you find someone vulnerable and in serious trouble, help them—and then make them your slave for life. If she is being abused, and we help her, she will be loyal to us forever. She could be useful.'

'Nonsense, Kumbha. You just want to help her and you are trying to find a justification for it.'

'Maybe I am. It will cost us very little. How much does it take to buy the services of a young girl after all? She will be worth it. I saw fire in her eyes.'

'A moment ago, you said you saw fear in her eyes. Which was it? Fear or fire?'

'Dada, I am telling you. This girl could be useful.'

Raavan shook his head in dismay. Then he pointed a finger at Kumbhakarna. 'This is the last time I am helping some random person because of you.'

'It's not help, Dada. It's business. It will be profitable. Trust me.'

—ॐ—

'Vasantpala, it is a good price and you know it,' said Raavan impatiently. 'Ten gold coins. Take it and be done with it. Don't waste my time.'

Raavan and Kumbhakarna had returned to Vasantpala's establishment, accompanied by twenty guards. Raavan had thought this would be a quick negotiation. But he was in for a surprise.

The little girl Kumbhakarna wanted to rescue was standing by the wall. Head bowed. Hands clasped together. She was shaking. Perhaps in fear. Perhaps in anticipation of freedom.

'It's not that simple, my lord,' said Vasantpala. 'Ten gold coins may not be enough for her.'

Raavan was irritated. 'You have made more than enough money from me over the years, Vasantpala. Don't be a fool. You can easily get another serving girl or boy. Who has jobs these days?'

'She is not just a serving girl.'

Raavan looked at the girl again. He noticed the ligature marks on her hands and feet; marks that indicated that she was often tied up. He knew that some men liked to have sex with very young girls and boys, even tie them up during the act. He had never understood it. It was disgusting. Abominable.

'How much, then?' he asked.

'Two hundred gold coins. She is profitable.'

Raavan held his right hand out. One of his aides stepped up and gave him a papyrus sheet and pen. Raavan wrote on it, marked it with his seal and threw it at Vasantpala. 'One hundred gold coins is my final offer. You can cash this *hundi* anywhere.'

Vasantpala picked up the sheet and read it carefully. She smiled. 'Thank you, my lord, but this will not be enough.'

'I am not haggling with you, Vasantpala. This is my final offer. Or we can tear up that hundi and—'

Vasantpala interrupted him. 'I wasn't asking for more money for myself, my lord. This is good enough for me. But you will need to pay somebody else too.'

Raavan frowned. 'Who?'

'Her father,' answered Vasantpala.

Raavan turned towards the little girl, shocked. But only for a moment. *All fathers are assholes. Just like mine.*

The little girl raised her head and looked at Vasantpala. Her eyes were burning with rage. And hatred. But almost immediately, her expression changed. She seemed stoic once more. Head bowed. Docile.

Woah! This girl may actually be worth it.

Raavan turned towards Vasantpala. 'Her father?'

'Who do you think sold her to us?'

—ॐ—

The little girl's father lived a short twenty-minute walk away from the courtesan-house. One of Vasantpala's aides led Raavan and his entourage there. On the way, he informed Raavan that the girl never spoke. They didn't know if she had been born dumb. Raavan had a feeling that the girl's loss of speech had more to do with the torture she had suffered at such a young age.

They reached the place to find a modest house in a relatively deserted locality. But it was in better shape than Raavan had expected, considering the state of the little girl. The area around the house was clean. The walls had been reinforced recently with fresh bricks. The roof looked new. There was a small garden outside, with a flower bed. All very tastefully done.

Vasantpala's aide knocked on the door and stepped aside. A middle-aged man answered the door. He was shorter than Raavan and thin, except for a small potbelly. He wore an expensive silk dhoti. A thick gold chain gleamed around his neck. His long hair was neatly oiled and tied.

'Is this your daughter?' asked Raavan, pointing at the little girl.

The man looked at her and then back at Raavan. He noticed the daunting musculature of the pirate-trader. His eyes took in the expensive clothes and jewellery. Obviously, a rich customer. 'Yes, she is.'

'I have something to ask. I want to know—'

The man cut in. 'One gold coin per hour. You can use a room in my house. If you want to do something different, like with her mouth or backside, the rates go up. However, if you want to tie her up, or beat her, we will have to negotiate. Because if you break any bones, she will not be able to earn anything for a few months at least.'

Raavan stepped closer to the man.

'So, what will it be?' asked the father, a little uncertainly.

In answer, Raavan swung his fist viciously at the man's face. Hitting him squarely on the nose. The sickening crunch confirmed that he had broken a bone. As the man fell to the ground, blood spurting from his nose, Raavan turned to look at the little girl. She was staring at her father. At her father's blood.

She didn't blink. She didn't look away.

Raavan turned to his men. 'Tie him to that tree. On his knees.'

The man was howling in pain.

Raavan's men dragged him to a tall coconut palm close by and tied him to it. On his knees. Hands behind the trunk. Both legs secured. Face towards Raavan. Utterly helpless. Still screaming at the top of his lungs.

'In the name of Lord Indra, cover this idiot's mouth,' said Raavan, his face screwed up in revulsion.

One of the guards immediately produced a piece of cloth and stuffed it into the man's mouth. They gagged him with another, longer piece of cloth which was then secured around the trunk of the tree. Not only could he not create a racket now, he could barely move his head. Only soft, muffled sounds escaped his mouth.

Raavan turned to look at Kumbhakarna. Communicating with his eyes. *Watch and learn.*

'You,' said Raavan to the little girl. 'What's your name?'

The girl didn't say anything. Kumbhakarna was about to remind Raavan that she couldn't speak, but his elder brother signalled for him to be quiet.

'Come here,' Raavan said to her.

She stepped closer. The tall and extravagantly muscled Raavan towered over her. She barely came up to his waist. Suddenly Raavan pulled out a knife. The girl stepped back in alarm.

'Don't be afraid. This knife is for you.' Saying this, Raavan flipped the knife around and handed it, hilt first, to the girl.

She studied it closely. It was long, with a firm, metal hilt and cross-guard. The blade was sharp on the outer side and serrated on the inner. The sharper side helped the blade slide smoothly into flesh. The serrated side caused maximum damage and pain while pulling the knife out. Manufactured by the talented metalsmiths of Gokarna, it had been designed by Raavan himself.

The little girl held the knife tightly. Her hands were trembling. Then she looked at her father. The man's eyes widened with fear. His muffled cries became more high-pitched.

I am your father…

Forgive me...

I am your father...

'Come with me,' said Raavan. He walked up to the pathetic figure tied to the tree. The little girl followed.

The man was now shaking, and in a state of utter panic. He struggled against the ropes that confined him. But he had been trussed up well. His muffled cries were the only sounds to be heard. Everyone else was silent.

Raavan slapped the man hard. 'Oh, shut up!'

Raavan turned to the girl and pointed to the place on her father's neck, at the base, where the jugular vein and carotid artery carried blood between the head and the heart. Almost as if imparting a lesson, he said to the little girl, making a slashing action with his hand, 'Make a large, deep cut here, and your father will die in a few minutes.' Then he pointed to the heart and pressed a hand on the man's chest. 'Stab here, and he will die much faster. But you have to make sure you get it right. You don't want the knife to get deflected by the ribs. That is hard bone. Sometimes, the knife can ricochet back from the ribs and you may end up hurting yourself. So, I wouldn't recommend trying it right now. You can train for it later.'

The little girl nodded. Like an eager student. A ferociously eager student.

'Or,' continued Raavan, pointing to the man's lower abdomen, 'you could stab him here. In the guts. No bones to deflect the knife. But the problem is that it will take time for him to bleed out. We may have to hear him scream for twenty, maybe even thirty minutes, as he bleeds to death. And if the wound is not deep enough, the blood flow will be very slow. It could take hours. And I don't have that much time to waste on your father. So, if you are going to stab him here, make sure it's a deep wound.'

The desperate man was struggling to free himself.

'It's up to you now,' said Raavan.

The little girl looked at her father. All her reserves of self-control seemed to have run out as she shook in fury. She gripped the knife hard in both hands. Her father's eyes were pleading for mercy. Tears mixed with sweat and blood.

Raavan stood aside, waiting for the girl to decide.

But even he was surprised by how quickly it happened.

The girl acted fast. No second thoughts. No hesitation. She stepped up and stabbed her father in the guts. Thrusting her shoulder forward as she did so. Choosing the slow, painful death for him. The man emitted a sound of sheer agony. His eyes were wide in panic and pain. His reactions only seemed to egg the girl on. She pushed the knife in harder, using both her hands. When she finally yanked it out, a fountain of blood spurted out. Dyeing her hands red. Her clothes. Her body. Everything.

She didn't flinch. She didn't step back. She stood there drenched in her father's warm blood.

Raavan smiled. 'Good girl.'

But the girl was not done. She stepped forward and stabbed her father again. And again. And again. And again. Always in the abdomen. Always in the guts.

She was silent through it all.

No sounds of anger. No screaming. No shouting.

Just pure, silent rage.

She kept stabbing her father until his abdomen was ruptured, and the intestines started spilling out.

Kumbhakarna said to Raavan, 'Dada, make her stop.'

Raavan shook his head. *No.*

His eyes were fixed on the girl.

She raised the knife and stabbed her father again.

When she finally stepped back, she had inflicted nearly twenty-five wounds on his flailing body. Her face, her hands, her body, her clothes, were slick with blood. It was almost like she had bathed in her father's blood.

She turned around and looked at Raavan. He was momentarily staggered.

She was smiling.

She walked up to Raavan, went down on her knees, and placed the bloodied knife at his feet.

Raavan placed his hands on her shoulders and pulled her to her feet.

'What is your name?' he asked.

The girl said nothing.

Raavan said, 'I am your master now. You will work for me. You will be loyal to me. And I will protect you.'

The girl remained silent.

Raavan repeated his question. 'What is your name?'

The little girl had heard what Raavan's followers called him. Iraiva. The True Lord.

She finally spoke. In a childish voice that was disconcertingly calm. 'Great Iraiva, my name is Samichi.'

Chapter 12

Raavan and his entourage had reached the bungalow in Vaidyanath that Kumbhakarna had rented for their stay. It was a nondescript building at a safe distance from the temple complex, and had none of the luxuries Raavan was now used to. But the brothers had decided to keep a low profile. With so many major temples in the region, many members of the royalty and nobility from across the Sapt Sindhu frequented the area. That meant high security. And a well-known smuggler would be a prize catch for the tax inspectors and the police in the Sapt Sindhu. The brothers had even chosen fake names for themselves: Jai and Vijay, rather than Raavan and Kumbhakarna.

Within an hour of reaching their place of stay, Raavan and Kumbhakarna set out to find Vedavati. She was an hour's ride away, in a village called Todee.

Historically, temples in India were not just centres of worship, but also hubs of social activity around which community life revolved. Most temple complexes had ponds for the use of the local population. Food was provided for the poor, in the form of prasad. Free primary education was made available for children who lived in the villages nearby. Temples in larger towns offered higher education as well. Villagers could access basic medical help at temples in their neighbourhood. In addition, most temples acted as storehouses where essential grains were kept, to provide for people when the rains failed. If they were exceptionally wealthy, they even paid for local building projects, such as houses for the poor and check dams on streams. All of this was made possible because of the donations that the temples received from people, rich and poor.

But like most things now, the system was fraying. As trade declined, so did the donations. Even at the major temples, funds were beginning to dry up. To make matters worse, the royal families were using some pretext or the other to take over temples—ostensibly, to 'run them better'. Soon, a significant portion of the temple donations was being siphoned off into royal treasuries.

Naturally, the charitable work that most community temples funded also began to suffer. Local infrastructure too was badly hit.

But this was not the case in Todee. Here, the local landlord, Shochikesh, was working with the villagers to create a check dam on a stream that flowed close by. It would help conserve water for the dry season. The landlord had supplied the material and the villagers provided the labour. Everyone would benefit.

This seemingly impossible collaboration had only been made possible because of Vedavati. For, while the villagers did not find it easy to trust the landlord, everyone trusted the Kanyakumari. Everyone.

And there she was, supervising the operation. Standing on a slightly raised platform, uncaring of the sweat gathering on her forehead and the dust flying all around.

Work on the check dam was progressing quickly. All the able-bodied men of the village were on the job, with hardly any breaks. The landlord stood on the same platform as Vedavati, observing the work. They were racing against time and he felt the pressure. He had even managed to convince his wayward son, Sukarman, to come and help out. The check dam had to be completed very soon. Not because the rainy season was upon them—there were still many months to go for that. The reason was Vedavati.

She was pregnant. Very obviously pregnant. Work on the dam had to be finished before she went away to the hospital attached to the nearby Vaidyanath temple, to give birth to her child. Neither the villagers nor the landlord's men were sure they could work together without her calm presence. She was the only one who was capable and trustworthy enough to resolve all their disputes satisfactorily.

Raavan and Kumbhakarna tethered their horses a few hundred metres away from the worksite, and cautiously made their way towards it on foot. Raavan had decided they would spend the first day observing the Kanyakumari, without showing themselves.

'Dada,' began Kumbhakarna.

'Softer!' shushed Raavan. 'Someone may hear us.'

Kumbhakarna looked around. There was no one to be seen. But he dutifully lowered his voice to a whisper. 'Dada, why are we hiding? Nobody knows us here. We can tell people that you are a trader visiting the Vaidyanath temple and that you stopped here on your way back to your rest house. You can then go and speak with the Kanyakumari. Only she will recognise you.'

Raavan shook his head.

Kumbhakarna wondered if he was the reason for Raavan's cautiousness. 'I have been here before, Dada. The people around here do not have any biases against Nagas. I'm safe here.'

Raavan looked at Kumbhakarna. 'I'll rip out any eyes that glare at you,' he said quietly. He was walking carefully. Avoiding dry leaves or twigs that might snap under his feet.

Kumbhakarna smiled to himself. His big brother was nervous.

'Do you know that we lived close to Todee for a few days when you were a baby?' asked Raavan, keeping his voice low.

'You've told me, Dada.' Kumbhakarna raised his hand and held up three fingers. 'Only three times in the last five minutes.'

'Oh, have I? I guess I must have…'

Kumbhakarna smiled broadly this time. He had never seen his brother so anxious.

— ऱॐI —

The brothers had found the perfect hiding spot, behind some dense vegetation. It had a clear view of the worksite at the stream. None of the workers had noticed their approach. Nobody had noticed them hiding. They were pirate-traders after all. Concealing themselves when required was a necessary professional attribute.

There were over fifty people at the worksite. But Raavan had eyes for only one of them.

He was transfixed. Practically paralysed. His gaze focused on Vedavati, as she walked among the villagers.

He couldn't help thinking that the muse had truly blessed him, for she looked uncannily like his own paintings of her. She was tall for a woman. Fair, round face, high cheekbones, and sharp, small nose. Black, wide-set eyes with creaseless eyelids. Her long, black hair flowed down her back in a tight braid. Her image was burned into his mind. He had painted her as a curvaceous woman, with a full feminine body. She looked even more voluptuous now. Her frayed, yet clean clothes did not detract from her magnetism.

Kumbhakarna whispered, 'I'm sorry, Dada. I didn't know that the Kanyakumari was pregnant. It didn't show earlier...'

But Raavan wasn't listening. He just kept looking at her, unable to believe that he was finally in her presence.

It took Kumbhakarna a while to realise why, despite the resemblance, Vedavati looked just that bit different from Raavan's paintings of her. It was not her baby bump. It was something else. On Raavan's walls, she appeared divine and awe-inspiring, but also quite aloof and distant. She was different in real life. She still looked divine, yes. Awe-inspiring, yes. But there was nothing distant about her. Warmth and kindness shone in her eyes as she moved among the villagers. Like a Mother Goddess.

'Dada,' whispered Kumbhakarna.

Raavan placed his hand on Kumbhakarna's shoulder. He didn't say anything, but the gesture was enough.

Stay quiet, little brother. Let me look... Let me finally live my life...

Kumbhakarna said softly, 'Dada, don't you think it's time we...'

He stopped speaking, as Raavan raised his hand to signal for silence.

A whole week had passed since their arrival in Vaidyanath. They had been coming to the worksite every day, changing their hiding place each time. Getting a different perspective of the worksite. Getting a different view of the people there. Getting a different darshan of the Kanyakumari.

What didn't change was the fact that they hadn't spoken to her yet. Not even made their presence known.

Kumbhakarna was at a loss. His mighty, indomitable brother simply couldn't muster up the courage to speak to Vedavati. His confidence and easy charm with women seemed to have abandoned him. Bereft of his usual bravado, he just stood in hiding and stared at the object of his devotion.

His Kanyakumari. His Goddess.

But Kumbhakarna could not keep staring at the Kanyakumari forever. So he observed the others at their work, and at rest. Over the past week, he had seen enough of the villagers, and their interactions, to start forming opinions of them. Shochikesh, the landlord, seemed like a genuinely good man. He wasn't attired as grandly as most landlords in Lanka, but he seemed to care for the villagers. The villagers appeared to respect him, even if they did not trust him. Shochikesh's son Sukarman, on the other hand, was a spoilt brat. Lazy. Selfish. Slacking off, and once, even stealing money when nobody was looking. But always on his best behaviour whenever the Kanyakumari or his father were close by.

Why am I wasting my time looking at these idiots?

Kumbhakarna turned to his brother. 'Dada...'

Raavan raised his hand again for silence.

Kumbhakarna refused to be silenced this time. He was at his wits' end, waiting for Raavan to make a move. He imagined spending the rest of his life hiding behind foliage and keeping an eye on the Kanyakumari. No, he had to do something. 'Dada, why don't we just kidnap her?'

Raavan glared at Kumbhakarna, horrified. 'What the hell is wrong with you? She's a Goddess! How can—'

Kumbhakarna interrupted his brother, laughing softly, 'Dada, I still remember your speech in Mahua Island. The Power-of-using-and-exploiting-people speech. I thought we were good at that! What are we doing hiding behind bushes and looking at villagers going about their business?'

Raavan looked outraged for a moment. Then he smiled and shook his head. '*Vaamah kaamo manushyaaNaam yasmin kila nibadhyate; jane tasmiMstvanukroshah snehashcha kila jaayate.*'

He was quoting the words of a brilliant philosopher, one of the great Valmikis, the tribe left behind by the Lady Vishnu, Mohini. The line in old Sanskrit, a statement of helplessness by a man in love, translated as: *It is ominous for a man to feel desire; for a man who is bound up in desire feels compassion and fondness.*

The unspoken truth: such a man would be weak.

Kumbhakarna's eyes twinkled with mischief as he smiled at his elder brother.

Raavan turned to look at Vedavati in the distance and whispered, 'Tomorrow... We'll go speak to her tomorrow.'

—१७२—

'Yes,' said Kumbhakarna, politely folding his hands together in a namaste. 'We are traders who came to visit the great

Mahadev temple in Vaidyanath. We were on our way to the rest house when we heard that there was a check-dam project going on here. So, we thought we would come and see it.'

As decided, Kumbhakarna and Raavan had finally emerged from their self-imposed hideout. Both the brothers had, wisely, come dressed in relatively simple clothes. In these impoverished times, amidst a community that was making the best of its constrained circumstances, it would have been impolite, even dangerous, to show off their wealth. Kumbhakarna was only thirteen years old, but he understood one of the most basic of human emotions: jealousy.

Of course, to the landlord and the villagers, Kumbhakarna looked like a grown man of at least twenty. And to his credit, Shochikesh did not even glance at the outgrowths that marked Kumbhakarna as a Naga.

'You are most welcome to share our lunch, noble travellers,' said Shochikesh. 'We may not be well-off, but we know our dharma. *Athithi devo bhava.*'

Kumbhakarna folded his hands and bowed his head in respect, acknowledging Shochikesh's recitation of an old Sanskrit line from the Taittiriya Upanishad. *Any guest is like God.* He nudged his elder brother, who followed suit. But Raavan's attention was focused elsewhere. On the woman who was walking towards them.

The Kanyakumari.

The Virgin Goddess.

Vedavati.

'What did you say your names are?' asked Shochikesh.

'My name is Vijay,' said Kumbhakarna. 'And my elder brother's name is Jai.'

Shochikesh smiled. 'Both your names mean victory. Your parents must have had high hopes!'

Kumbhakarna laughed genially. 'And we dashed those hopes!'

Shochikesh smiled. He pointed at his red hair. 'Well, my parents named me *Shochikesh*. One with *hair like fiery flames*, apparently! But there is nothing else about me that is fiery!'

'Maybe it is the duty of all children to disappoint their parents?' Kumbhakarna kept the banter going, hoping his brother would snap out of his reverie soon.

Shochikesh chuckled. On some unspoken instinct, he turned to look at his son, Sukarman, who was sitting not far away, watching the others at their work. And the smile was wiped off his face. *Sukarman* meant *One who did good deeds*. Harsh truths, even when garbed in humour, continue to inflict pain. 'In any case, you are most welcome to have lunch with us.'

Kumbhakarna did not get a chance to respond to Shochikesh. For Vedavati had made her way up to them. Her left hand was on her distended belly, supporting her unborn child. Kumbhakarna looked at her and smiled. Raavan, on the other hand, stood staring at the ground.

'Our noble landlord Shochikesh is right,' said Vedavati. 'You are most welcome to have lunch with us.'

Raavan lifted his head slightly and smiled. This was the voice he had ached to hear all these years. It was like a salve for his soul. He let it echo inside him, in his entire being. The words themselves were of little consequence.

He tried to say something. To respond. But his vocal chords seemed constricted. No sound escaped his mouth.

Kumbhakarna looked at his tongue-tied brother, and then at Vedavati. The painful truth was obvious to him. Vedavati had no idea who Raavan was. She didn't recognise him at all.

Kumbhakarna bowed and said politely, 'Great Kanyakumari, it is—'

'I am not the Kanyakumari anymore,' interjected Vedavati, smiling warmly.

Kumbhakarna nodded. 'Of course, noble Vedavatiji. But I don't know if we can stay for lunch. Because we have to—'

'We'll stay!'

If Kumbhakarna had not felt the firm hand of his elder brother squeezing his shoulder, he would probably not have recognised the voice. It was an alarmingly childish squeak. Not the usual baritone of the powerful Raavan.

'Wonderful!' Vedavati smiled at Raavan. Then she turned and walked away.

Kumbhakarna stared at his brother, who was now smiling absurdly at Vedavati's retreating form. He had a bizarre look on his face. Of ecstasy. He couldn't have been happier.

Kumbhakarna swallowed a lump in his throat. He had read somewhere that there was nothing worse than unrequited love. But they were wrong. There was something worse: Unrequited love that was not even aware of it being one-sided. He couldn't watch his brother, the man he admired above all, succumbing to such heart-break.

He looked away, his mind racing to find solutions to this strange new predicament.

Chapter 13

'It was quite shocking,' said Vedavati. 'We were going about our work as usual, when suddenly these people emerged out of nowhere and killed one of our colleagues. This is what the powerless are subjected to in our society.'

Raavan and Kumbhakarna were in Todee again. They had been coming back regularly for the last few days, under the pretext of wanting to learn the techniques of check dam construction.

On this particular day, they were having lunch with Shochikesh and Vedavati. Far enough from the work camp to be away from the dust.

Kumbhakarna had been curious to know more about safety measures at the work site. And they had got talking about past incidents and accidents that they had themselves encountered, or heard about. It was Shochikesh who had brought up the episode of a workman who had lost his life while working on a wharf three years ago. At Chilika Lake. Near Governor Krakachabahu's residence.

Kumbhakarna had stiffened at the mention of the incident, though he had controlled himself in time. Raavan, however, had remained unruffled as they listened to Shochikesh, and then Vedavati, talk about that day, about the cruel men whose horses had trampled over the hapless young worker.

Shochikesh had gone on to expound some sketchy details of the robbery at the governor's residence. Kumbhakarna had tried his best to pretend he was hearing it all for the first time. With appropriate expressions of shock and outrage.

'From what we found out later,' said Shochikesh, 'the attack may have been the work of Governor Krakachabahu's enemies from his native land, Nahar. When two elephants fight, the grass gets trampled. We were the grass.'

'But this is adharma,' said Vedavati. 'Whatever quarrels the Kshatriyas have with each other, they have to ensure that no innocents are harmed.'

Raavan nodded in agreement, his expression giving nothing away.

'That's true,' said Shochikesh. 'But who cares about dharma these days? We have forgotten our traditions and culture. We are an embarrassment to our ancestors.'

Kumbhakarna once again thanked his stars that he had been on the ship during the raid at Chilika, too far away for these people to recognise him. He assumed Raavan had ridden by so fast that nobody had got a good look at him, especially not Vedavati. Also, Raavan's beard was fuller than it had been three years ago. And his face looked very different with the handlebar moustache he now sported.

Maybe it's a blessing that she doesn't recognise him at all. Either from father's ashram or from Chilika.

—ॐ—

Vedavati was in the last stages of her pregnancy by now, and judging by the kicks that often took her by surprise, she was carrying a strong baby. And a strong baby needed robust nutrition. Rice cooked in milk, with a dash of cardamom and ginger, was considered excellent for the mother and her unborn child. But the small village of Todee did not grow or have access to cardamom. Black cardamom was usually grown in the foothills of eastern Nepal, Sikkim and Bhutan. It was expensive and difficult to obtain.

But what was difficult for others was easy for Raavan. He had sent out his men and procured five sacks of the fragrant spice. It was a huge amount, considering how little was required for one meal. He presented the cardamom to Vedavati, telling her that it was for the use of the entire village. He had also got some tools which he knew would make the construction work easier.

It was a deeply grateful Vedavati who sat with Raavan over lunch the next day. Shochikesh was away in Vaidyanath. And Kumbhakarna had suddenly, and conveniently, remembered that he had some unfinished work in the village.

As the two sat eating quietly, Raavan retained his calm demeanour, despite the storm in his heart.

'Jai,' said Vedavati, using what she had been told was Raavan's name. 'Are you from the Indraprastha region? From your accent, it appears that you are.'

Raavan did not want to reveal his antecedents to Vedavati. Not yet. 'I have spent some time there. But not much.'

Vedavati looked uncertainly at him. 'Jai, we are grateful for your generosity, of course, but I do hope you haven't stretched yourself too much for us. If you don't mind my asking, what is it that you do? How can you afford to do so much charity?'

'Oh, I work in… trade. Importing things people here may need, and exporting items from here that people in other lands may fancy.'

'I see. And it's profitable?'

If I had misplaced that money spent on the cardamom and the tools, I wouldn't even have noticed it.

Raavan kept his thoughts to himself, and said, 'Yes. It's a little difficult with the new licenses and restrictions. But I can make ends meet.'

'That's good to know,' said Vedavati. People who are innately decent and straightforward tend to accept others at face value. 'Thank you, Jai. Your help means a lot to my village.'

Raavan shrugged. *It's nothing.*

'Not everyone who can help, does,' continued Vedavati. 'Not in these times.'

'Not everyone is… Jai,' Raavan said, laughing, and stopping himself just in time from giving away his real name.

Vedavati smiled, ignoring his conceit. 'These villagers have suffered greatly. They are the real victims of all that's going on these days. And most people don't care about helping those less fortunate than themselves. The tradition of charity is slowly being forgotten in India. We are forgetting our dharma.'

Raavan blanched but held his tongue.

'I don't mean someone like you,' said Vedavati, misinterpreting Raavan's expression. 'But across the land today, dharma has been reduced to just rituals and talk. The philosophy that underpins the rituals, and the reason why we follow them, is being forgotten.'

'Oh, I agree with you,' Raavan said. 'There is a great deal of uncalled out hypocrisy everywhere. But…'

'But what?' asked Vedavati.

'Well, I don't think these villagers should be thought of as victims.'

Vedavati stopped eating, surprised. 'You think they aren't?'

'Oh, they *are* victims.'

Vedavati smiled, shook her head and resumed eating. 'I don't understand what you are saying.'

'Of course they are victims,' Raavan said. 'Just like every other person in the world. All of us are victims in some way or the other. But that doesn't mean we should *think* of ourselves as victims.'

Vedavati looked up at Raavan, intrigued.

He continued, 'All of us have been through times when life seemed unfair. In such situations, we can choose to see ourselves as victims and blame the rest of the world. We can drown ourselves in the false comfort of knowing we are not responsible for our difficulties and expect others to change our lives. Or, we can pick ourselves up. Be strong. And fight the world.'

'It's true that all of us face adversity in life, Jai, but surely not everyone's troubles are the same. Some people are at a greater disadvantage than others. And they need our assistance. Of course, nobody should expect others to solve their problems entirely but the strong must help...'

'...help the "cult of victimhood"?' interrupted Raavan.

'What?'

'The lot who just want to whine and complain.' Raavan put his hands up and mimed in a high-pitched voice, 'Oh, poor me. Look at me. Look at how much I'm suffering. Somebody come and take care of me. I'm a victim of society.'

Vedavati bit her lip as though to stop a smile from forming, then frowned. 'Jai, we shouldn't indulge the weaknesses of others, but we shouldn't mock them either.'

'I'm... I'm not... Noble Kanyakumari, perhaps it was wrong of me to make fun of them. I'm sorry. But this is the way I see it: There is a lion and a deer within each of us. Only if we nurture the lion will we make something of ourselves. If we indulge the deer, we'll be running and hiding all our lives.'

'So... the hunter and the hunted.'

'Yes.'

'And we should always aim to be the hunter, I suppose? Because the hunted cannot possibly have any virtues to recommend them?'

'If we cannot fight for ourselves, how will we protect and provide for those who depend on us?'

'So that's how you see it? Every hunter is a magnificent warrior, and the hunted deserve no respect?'

'You don't agree, great Ve... Veda... Kanyakumari?'

Vedavati looked at him sympathetically. She thought Raavan had a stutter that became acute whenever he had to speak a name, especially one that began with a 'v'. So she had yielded to being called Kanyakumari by him.

'Jai, have you heard of the Panchatantra?'

Raavan nodded readily. 'Of course!'

Panchatantra, literally the five treatises, was a part of the primary learning of every child in India. It contained stories of talking animals, with a moral lesson embedded in each tale.

'Sometimes,' said Vedavati, 'we don't have to depend on animal fables to learn lessons in dharma. Sometimes, we can learn from real animals too.'

Raavan leaned forward, his curiosity aroused.

'This happened a long time ago,' said Vedavati. 'I was still a Kanyakumari. I had travelled a great deal, including to the wonderful lands of the brave Andhras. Close to the river port of Amaravati.'

'I've been there. It's stunningly beautiful. Truly a city worthy of its name.'

'Yes, there are people who believe that the modern city of Amaravati is located in exactly the same place where, sometime in the faraway past, Lord Indra, the king of the Devas, lived.'

'Yes, I have heard that too. For all you know, it could be true.'

'Anyway, while we were there, the local ruler wished to take us on a tour of the jungle that lies between the holy Krishna and Godavari rivers. Much of it was open grassland, and we travelled on elephant back. Sometime during the day, we saw an old lion, with his cubs.' Vedavati paused before asking, 'Do you know what happens to many lions in their old age?'

'Yes.' Raavan nodded. 'There is no sight more painful than that of a powerful hunter past its prime. I've seen it often enough: an old lion challenged by another, usually younger, lion. If he is defeated but lucky enough to survive, he has to flee the territory. The young challenger takes over the pride, and the lionesses switch their allegiance to him. This younger lion might even kill the cubs of the older lion. The mothers watch from the side lines, helpless. They probably see it as a command from their new master—new rules in the new pride.'

'The ways of the jungle can be cruel.'

'Now, if this older lion you saw had his cubs with him, he must have managed to save them somehow. Maybe he and his cubs together escaped the wrath of the young challenger.'

'Very possible,' Vedavati said. 'So, as you know, hunting is difficult for an old lion. And if you happen to be one with a few cubs to feed, life can become a huge struggle. This lion's cubs were starving. He was starving. They were weak. And desperate.'

'What happened next, noble Kanyakumari?'

'When we saw this lion, he was at the other end of the grassland, with his three cubs behind him. He had just spotted a few deer that had probably got separated from the main herd. A mother, with her babies. There were four fawns. One of them was clearly weaker than the others. The runt of the family.'

'Food for his cubs...'

Vedavati noticed that Raavan's first thought was for the lion and his hungry cubs. He seemed to identify with the hunter, even when the hunter was old and weak. 'Of course. But remember, the lion was old. A hunter past his best days. What do you think he did?'

'Why, he would have gone for the weakest fawn, of course. It would provide less meat, but at least he could be certain of catching it and feeding his cubs. A little food is better than no food. His cubs and he would survive another day. Become a little stronger.'

Vedavati smiled. 'You understand the hunter's mind-set well, Jai.'

Raavan returned her smile, though he wasn't entirely certain she meant it as a compliment.

'So, as you correctly guessed, the lion charged at the runt among the deer,' continued Vedavati. 'The doe, sensing danger, lifted her head up, her eyes searching for any movement. On spotting the lion, she moved instantly, alerting the fawns, and they fled towards the tree line, running and leaping over each other. They were swift. All except one. The lion increased his pace. He was weak, but he was still a lion. He began closing the distance to the tiny fawn. It was just a matter of time, a few seconds perhaps, before he would catch up with his prey. It seemed that the lion and his cubs would finally get their meal.'

'And then?'

'Then, much to our surprise, the doe slowed down. The bigger fawns had reached the edge of the clearing, and would vanish into the foliage any moment. Away from the lion. But the runt was still at risk. The mother stopped running, then came to a stop.'

Raavan found that he was holding his breath. 'Then?'

'The lion turned towards the doe. A full-grown deer would last him and his cubs much longer than the little one. He changed course. Since the mother deer was practically stationary, he was upon her in no time at all.'

'Didn't the doe bolt away at the last minute? Now that she had deflected attention from her baby?'

Vedavati shook her head. 'No. She just stood there, watching the little one get to safety.'

'What did the lion do?'

'The lion also came to a halt. Just a few metres from the doe. He seemed confused. The runt, meanwhile, had caught up with his siblings. They turned to look at their mother, bleating frantically, as if pleading with her to flee. But the doe remained where she was. She made a sound, just once. Like she was ordering her children to run away. Perhaps she did not want them to see what was to follow.'

Raavan remained silent. *What a mother…*

Vedavati said, 'The story doesn't end there.'

'So what happened next?'

'The lion looked at the fawns, way out of his reach now. Crying and bleating for their mother. Then he looked at the mother deer, standing just one short leap away. And he seemed paralysed. Like he couldn't bring himself to kill the splendid deer in front of him. And then, he turned to look at his own cubs in the distance. Hungry and waiting to be fed.'

Raavan watched the changing expressions on Vedavati's face as she relived those moments in the jungle.

'What should the lion do? What does dharma say? Should he be a good father and kill to feed his starving children? Or should he exercise his goodness and gift life to a magnificent mother?'

'I… I don't know,' answered Raavan.

'We assume that animals cannot think in terms of dharma. Perhaps they are not able to *express* dharma, since they cannot speak. But why should we assume that dharma does not touch them too? Dharma is universal. It touches everyone.'

Raavan remained silent, listening with his head and his heart.

Vedavati continued to speak. 'Dharma is complicated. It is often not about the *what*, but the *why*. If the lion had been hunting for pleasure—which most animals are not capable of—we might call it an exercise in adharma. Since he was hunting to feed his starving children, it's fair to say he was following his dharma. If the deer had allowed circumstances to overwhelm her and not attempted to save her children, it would have been adharma. But her sacrifice to save her children can only be thought of as dharma. In the field of dharma, intentions matter as much, if not more, than the act itself. But one thing is clear. *Only* if you put your duty above yourself do you even have a chance of attaining a life of dharma. Selfishness is the one thing that's guaranteed to take you away from it.'

'Life was unfair to both the lion and the deer,' Raavan remarked thoughtfully. 'Both were victims.'

'Life is unfair to everyone. As Sikhi Buddha said, the fundamental reality of life is *dukha*. There is no escaping the *grief* that permeates every corner of this illusory world. Accepting this basic truth is the first step towards trying to overcome it.'

'Everyone is struggling... I suppose we must try to understand and learn, rather than judge.'

'Precisely. If you don't judge, you can open the space in your heart to help others. And that will take you towards dharma.'

'But how did it all end, noble Kanyakumari? Did the lion kill the doe?'

'That's not the point of this story, Jai.'

Raavan smiled. And stopped asking questions.

—१७१—

'This is taking too long, Dada,' said Kumbhakarna. They had been in the Vaidyanath area for nearly a month already. 'Mareech uncle had wanted us to return as soon as possible. There's that business in Africa—'

Raavan stopped him with a gesture. 'It's nothing that Mareech cannot handle on his own.'

'But Dada, what about our crew? And Samichi. They're all sitting around doing nothing, probably wondering why they are cooped up in this guesthouse with no—'

Raavan interrupted his brother. 'Just give them something to do, Kumbha. Send them on some short trade mission or something.'

Kumbhakarna fell silent. Raavan looked dreamily out of the window. It was late at night. All they could hear was the chirping of crickets. Occasionally, an owl hooted in the distance. Raavan had returned to the guesthouse in the evening after a long conversation with Vedavati. He stared at the moon and sighed.

'Isn't it beautiful today?'

Kumbhakarna turned and stared at the moon. It looked pretty ordinary to him. He exhaled softly and looked back at Raavan. 'Dada...'

'Shhh!' Raavan picked up the Raavanhatha lying next to him. 'Listen. I've composed something new.'

He strummed the instrument, as though testing its sound. And began.

From the first time he had heard it, Kumbhakarna had thought of the Raavanhatha as an instrument of grief. It tugged at your heart and brought tears to your eyes.

But tonight, Raavan's deep, attractive voice, the lilt of the melody he had composed, and the whisper of the wind, combined with the ethereal sound of the Raavanhatha to create an island of ecstasy and bliss. He managed to coax the musical instrument of grief to create a melodious tune of joy.

The possibility to turn negative into positive always exists. But it takes a Goddess to inspire the change.

Chapter 14

What do you do when a woman you love deeply, a woman you have dreamt of and worshipped, is lost to you forever? You steel your heart and reconcile yourself to life without her.

Then, by a twist of fate, you meet her again. And you find out that she is committed to someone else. You try to ignore this truth. Ignore the existence of another in her life. Suppress the instinctive hatred you feel.

But you cannot keep away from her. You get to know her better. Fall even more deeply in love with her—if that's possible. And then, you meet the other man. The… husband. And he is everything you did not expect. He is handsome. Honest. Kind. Generous. He is noble, in a way that you know you can never be.

And he loves her. Perhaps as much as you love her. He respects her. Perhaps more than you respect her.

And somewhere deep in your heart, a soft, monstrous, unwelcome voice is heard. You are forced to listen to the truth that you don't even want to acknowledge: that maybe, just maybe, he is better for her than you are.

What do you do then? What do you do?

The only logical thing to do is to hate and despise that man, even more than you did earlier.

It *was* logical. Raavan told himself that.

Prithvi, Vedavati's husband, had returned to the village. When he heard this, Raavan decided to stay away for a few days, pleading some personal work. Until, one day, he took the bit between his teeth and made his way to the worksite with Kumbhakarna.

It was late in the afternoon and a welcome breeze cooled the hot day. Shochikesh was away, ostensibly to make arrangements for some materials that were required for work to continue on the check dam. But Raavan knew better. Shochikesh's son, Sukarman, had been caught stealing from the temple donation-box again; he claimed he had gambling debts to pay off. Shochikesh was trying to get the money back quietly, before word got around. Raavan kept the news to himself. He didn't want to cause any distress to the pregnant Vedavati.

'Thank you once again, Jai,' said Prithvi, addressing Raavan. Like many people from the Baloch region in the far west of India, Prithvi was tall, with clean-cut features and a clear, fair complexion. Even Raavan had to admit that he was a handsome man. 'The tools you donated have really helped pick up the pace of work here. It's heartening to meet a businessman who believes in dharma and charity.'

Raavan smiled and waved his hand awkwardly, not sure how to react to compliments from a man he loathed.

'So how was your trip, Prithviji?' asked Kumbhakarna.

Prithvi glanced at Vedavati before replying. 'It went very well. I made a good profit this time. Around six hundred and fifty gold coins.'

Raavan found it hard not to snigger. *That's a good profit? I earn as much in an hour.*

'Finally, I have enough to take care of my wife and child,' said Prithvi, taking Vedavati's hand in his.

Vedavati rested her head on Prithvi's shoulder. Raavan looked away, focusing on some birds on the treetops close by.

'And you have returned just in time,' said Kumbhakarna.

'Yes!' said Prithvi proudly. 'Just a few more weeks now before our child enters the world.'

Kumbhakarna nodded in agreement. 'By the way, I was thinking that some more tools might help advance the work on the check dam. If you have some time, I could show you what I mean.'

Prithvi looked at Vedavati.

'I'd much rather rest, Prithvi,' said Vedavati. 'My back is killing me.'

Prithvi smiled and caressed Vedavati's face gently. 'I'll be back soon.'

After Prithvi had left with Kumbhakarna, Raavan relaxed a little. 'How bad is it? Should I send for some medicines from Vaidyanath?'

Vedavati shook her head. 'No, I don't think that's necessary. We'll be leaving for Vaidyanath in a week in any case.'

Raavan nodded, trying not to let his feelings show.

'He is a good man, you know,' said Vedavati.

Raavan looked at her, startled. 'Of course he is. I would never think otherwise.'

'And I love him. He is my husband.'

'I… of course… I mean…'

Vedavati held Raavan's gaze steadily. She was making sure her message carried without hurting his feelings.

'So where did we first meet?' she asked suddenly.

Raavan was taken aback. He wasn't sure what she meant.

'I asked Vijay one day, why it is that you both look at me like you know me from before. From my days as a Kanyakumari, perhaps. For some reason I can't be sure of, you seem familiar to me as well. Not Vijay, to be honest. I would certainly have remembered him.' Vedavati was too polite to state the obvious—Kumbhakarna's Naga features made it difficult for anyone to forget him. 'So, I am certain you and I have met before. But where did we meet?'

The lie came smoothly to Raavan's tongue. 'It could be when I came to Vaidyanath many years ago. I visited the Kanyakumari temple and you blessed me. It was so long ago, though. We were both children. It's amazing that you find anything even remotely familiar about me.'

Vedavati stared into Raavan's eyes. For a moment, he thought she was going to tell him that she knew he was lying. But she merely nodded.

'So you are a devotee of Lord Rudra?' Vedavati asked.

Raavan smiled and touched his ekmukhi rudraaksh pendant. 'Yes, I am. Jai Shri Rudra!'

'Jai Shri Rudra,' repeated Vedavati, smiling and clasping her own rudraaksh pendant. 'So, let me ask you: Are you a devotee of His actions or what He represents as the Mahadev?'

Raavan frowned. 'Is there a difference?'

'Of course there is.'

'How so? A person is defined by what he or she does. By his vocation or career. Karma defines the individual. A person without karma may as well be dead.'

Vedavati smiled. 'I didn't say that karma is not important. But it's not the *only* thing that's important. There are other things too.'

'And what are those other things?'

'*Swatatva*, in old Sanskrit. Literally, the *essence of your Self.* Or more simply, your Being.'

'Being?'

'Being is a complex word, and not easy to understand. Like dharma.'

'I understand dharma.'

'Do you?' Vedavati smiled.

'All right. I admit dharma is a complex concept. We could debate its nuances for many lifetimes. But surely, Being is not so complex.'

'It is. But to understand Being, you first need to understand karma. Your actions are your karma. It is what you do. Tell me, why do you perform any action that concerns others? Because you expect a reaction—hopefully, a reaction that will make you happy.'

'So, are you saying that karma is transactional and hence, selfish?'

Does she know that I donated things to this pathetic village only to be close to her?

Vedavati shook her head. 'Don't get into what is good or bad. It is what it is. That's all. Karma is most certainly transactional.'

'And Being isn't?'

'No, it isn't. That's what makes it so important. And powerful.'

'I don't understand.'

'I'm sure you've been told that the only way for the mind to find peace is by learning to be calm and centred.'

'Yes,' said Raavan, rolling his eyes.

'Why did you roll your eyes?'

'I didn't mean to. I'm sorry.'

Vedavati laughed. 'I didn't say it was wrong. I just asked why you did it.'

Raavan laughed softly. 'Because it's very easy to counsel people that they should be calm and centred. But no one tells you how to do it!'

'Exactly. That is the problem. People keep thinking that they have to do something to achieve that state. Be successful in their profession, perhaps, or go on a holiday, or make the right friends, or find a different spouse…. But even after they make that change, they find they are not calm. So then they think they have to do something more. Something different. It's a never-ending cycle. Basically, calmness and centeredness are always elusive because people assume they have to do something, gain good karma, to get there.'

'So, the problem is with our focus on karma?'

'Yes. It's very difficult to be calm and centred if your entire focus is on that. For karma is action in the hope of something in return. Like, if you give charity to someone, you expect at least respect in return. It's a transaction. And if the result of your actions is not what you expected, you feel let down and become unhappy. Even worse, if the karma you get in return for your actions *is*, in fact, what you expected, you discover that the happiness you derive from it is fleeting. If dissatisfaction is guaranteed, how can you find peace of mind?'

'How?'

'Simply by Being what you are meant to Be. By staying true to your *Swatatva*.'

Raavan leaned back. The beauty of the logic filled his mind.

Vedavati continued, 'I am not saying we shouldn't focus on action. Without our karma, we may as well be dead. But karma should not be the centre of our lives. If we truly discover our Being, our Swatatva, and live in consonance with what we are meant to be, then everything becomes easy. We don't have to try hard to carry out our karma. Because we will not do anything in the vain hope of something else. We will do it simply because it is in consonance with our Being. With what we were born to Be.'

Raavan had never felt as centred or calm as in these last few weeks with Vedavati. She had answers for him. Answers to questions that he didn't even know he had. 'And what do you think I am born to Be, great Kanyakumari? What is my Swatatva supposed to be?'

'A hero.'

Raavan burst out laughing. Vedavati remained silent, confident in the truth of her assertion.

Raavan controlled his mirth and said, 'I apologise, Kanyakumari. I am not a hero. You certainly are. But not me. I am as close as anyone can be to a...' Raavan stopped before the word 'villain' could escape his mouth.

Vedavati leaned forward. 'Your Swatatva is demanding it of you. You want to be a hero. You want to be an *arya*. You want to be *noble*. That's why, whatever your reasons for leaving the Sapt Sindhu, you came back here. I have been told that you live in Lanka. That's where all the rich people in the Sapt Sindhu are escaping to. But you keep coming back here. Why? Because you want the acceptance and respect of the aryas here. You will never have peace of mind till you accept who you are.'

Raavan remained silent. His eyes glazed over. He was a small child again. Desperately seeking the approval of Vedavati. Of the Kanyakumari. His heart picked up pace. He could smell her fragrance again. The scent from all those years ago. He could hear her commands, her young voice, in his mind.

You are better than this. At least try.

No, I am not.

Yes, you are. This is who you want to be.

I just want to hurt my father. I hate him.

Do you want to defeat him?

Yes.

Defeat your father, by all means. But don't do it by hurting him. Do it by being better than him.

'Jai?'

Vedavati's voice pulled Raavan out of his internal, tumultuous world. 'Sorry… what?'

'I am not suggesting that you desire the respect of the nobility in the Sapt Sindhu. There is nothing "arya" about them, no real nobility. But I can see you want the respect of the true aryas. Those who still remember our old ways. Those who are genuinely noble. Who may not be powerful today, but are dharmic. You want their acceptance. Jai, all you have to do is to accept who you are. And you will find peace.'

She looked at him intently. 'At least try.'

—ॐ—

'That didn't go as planned,' said Kumbhakarna.

He had just come back from Todee. Raavan had sent him to offer a job to Prithvi and had been waiting for him eagerly at the guesthouse. But the news was disappointing.

'Did you tell them everything?' asked Raavan. 'Including the bit about the money?'

'Yes I did, Dada. I know how important this is for you.'

'All that idiot will have to do is to be my personal secretary,' said Raavan. 'Write letters. I am sure even he can manage that. I am willing to pay him two thousand gold coins every year for it! Why did he say no?'

'Perhaps the offer was too kind for Vedavatiji.'

'The Kanyakumari? Why did she get involved in this?'

'Well, Prithviji was very enthusiastic about the offer. He said they could leave for Lanka a few months after the birth of their baby. Then he went to ask Vedavatiji about it. And she said no.'

'But why? I thought she wants me to…'

'Wants you to what?'

'Nothing. Why did she refuse?'

'She wouldn't say.'

'But did you ask her?'

'I did, Dada.'

Raavan looked away. Staring out of the window.

'And then she said the strangest thing.'

'What?'

'She told me to tell you that it took her some time, but she finally remembered.'

'Remembered what?'

'About the hare and the ants.'

Raavan turned to look at Kumbhakarna, stunned. He had been recognised. How much did she know? Did she know about the robbery too? She would hate him if she did. 'Did she say anything about Chilika? About Krakachabahu?'

'No. Why would she? I don't think she connects that with us.'

Raavan remained silent.

'But, Dada, what did she mean by the hare and the ants?'

Raavan did not respond.

Chapter 15

'I thought you wanted to encourage me to do good,' said Raavan.

Raavan had come to Todee by himself to meet Vedavati. He knew he could not prolong his stay much longer and would have to leave for Lanka soon. He had been away too long. But how could he leave without her? Raavan was desperate—he had to convince her, somehow.

'I can't travel,' said Vedavati.

'After your baby is born? Perhaps you can come then.'

Vedavati remained silent.

'Please… I am begging you.'

'You know you don't need me.'

'I do! Please… Nothing needs to change. You can remain married to him. To… Prithvi. I will not make any demands on you. I just need you to be in Lanka. Just be there… just let me look at you every day. That's all I ask for. Please… please… Veda… Ve… Please, great Kanyakumari.'

'You don't need me,' Vedavati repeated calmly.

There were tears in Raavan's eyes. 'I do… I know what I need.'

'No. You don't know what you need. For then you would know that you already have it.'

'But I don't!' Raavan couldn't conceal his agitation. 'I need you! I need you!'

'You don't need me. You need yourself.'

'What does that mean? I don't…'

'Think about it. What have I been to you so far? Only an image in your mind. It's you who wanted to be a better version of yourself. All you needed was an excuse. An excuse to motivate you, help you improve what you had become as a reaction to what your father did to you. You hung on to me as that excuse. What I am trying to tell you is that you don't need the excuse anymore. In fact, you should never need someone else to better yourself. That is dangerous. I could die tomorrow. Then what will you…'

Raavan clenched his fists. 'I will destroy anyone who hurts you. I will rip their—'

'Why do you assume someone will hurt me? I could die of an illness. There will be nobody to blame then, right?'

Raavan fell silent.

'When you start on the most important journey of your life, you cannot be dependent on anyone else. For you would be binding your *purpose*, your *swadharma*, to the fate of another person. That is dangerous. Especially for someone as important as you are.'

'I am not…' Raavan stopped himself from cursing. 'I am not important. I am not even a good person. You don't know the kinds of things I've done.'

'Don't be so hard on yourself. You've been taking care of your mother and your younger brother since you were a child. You have built a trading empire almost single-handedly. You have strength, you have courage, and you are a capable man.'

'I… I have done some terrible things to build my empire. I am…' Raavan was struggling to be completely honest for the first time in his life. 'I am a monster. I know I am a monster. I enjoy being a monster. I need you to save me. You are my chance. My only chance, if I am to make something… something noble of myself.'

'That's where you are wrong. I am not your chance. You are your own chance. You think you are a monster? Which great man does not have a monster inside him?'

Raavan stared at Vedavati. Silent.

'What you term a monster is the fire every successful man has within him,' continued Vedavati. 'A fire that will not let him rest. A fire that drives him to work hard. To be smart. To be relentless. Focused. Disciplined. For those are the ingredients of success. That fire is like a monster that will not allow you to lead an ordinary life. But there is one thing that differentiates a successful man from a great man. One key thing: Does the monster control you or do you control the monster? Without the monster, you would have been ordinary. With the monster, you have a chance to attain greatness. Not a guarantee, but a chance. To seize that chance, you need to control the monster and use your unique and enormous abilities, in the cause of dharma.'

'I can't do it without you.'

'Me? I'm nobody.'

'You are the Kanyakumari! You are a living Goddess! You are noble in a way I could never be. You are kind and generous. You are the purest person I have ever met. I am an impure, selfish bastard.'

Vedavati looked at him steadily without saying anything.

Raavan immediately turned contrite. 'I didn't mean to curse. I'm sorry.'

'There is no need to use an expletive to emphasise a point.'

'I'm sorry.'

Vedavati smiled. 'So, you think I'm pure? Have you noticed that there are no fish to be found in water that is too pure?'

Raavan was quiet. It took him a few moments to realise that Vedavati was right.

'I may be pure, but have I made any real difference in the lives of people? I may be noble in my actions, but I am not capable of commanding the attention of those outside my village. Only those who can reach millions of people can improve the lives of millions of people. Nobility without capability is limiting, it only results in good theory.'

'But…'

'Listen to me, Raavan. Truly great people, who have left a positive stamp on history and in the hearts of millions of followers, combined a cold, ruthless mind with a warm, dharmic heart.'

'I don't have it. I don't have a heart. I don't…'

Vedavati leaned forward and took Raavan's hand in hers. It was the first time she had touched him. His heartbeat seized for a moment.

'You *do* have a warm heart, Raavan. Don't use it just to pump blood through your body. Let it also propel dharma through your soul. Rise to do good. Do good for this land of ours, which is suffering in poverty, chaos and disease. Help the poor. Help the needy. Do good.'

Tears pooled in Raavan's eyes.

'Lead India back to greatness, make it truly *Aryavarta* once again. Make it a *noble land* once more. And then I will come and live in Lanka. Not as your Goddess. But as your devotee. My husband and I will worship you.'

Raavan didn't know what to say. He was surprised to see himself through Vedavati's eyes. Was he really as capable as all that?

'I have faith in you. You can do it. This long-suffering motherland of ours has enough villains already. It desperately needs a hero. Rise to become one.'

Raavan sat quietly, listening.

'You are a devout worshipper of Lord Rudra, aren't you?' asked Vedavati, her voice kind and gentle.

Raavan looked up and nodded. *Yes.*

'I am sure you know what the Lord's name means. Rudra is the "One who roars". The One who roars to protect good people. And what do you think Raavan means? What have you been told it means?'

Raavan didn't say anything.

'What did your father tell you? What does it mean?'

'He told me it means "One who scares people". Raavan is one who puts fear into people.'

'Your father was only half right. The root of the word "Raavan" is "Ru". So Raavan would be "the One who roars to frighten people".'

'Are you saying that the root of my name and that of Lord Rudra's is the same?'

'It is. But the question is, what will you roar for, Raavan? Will you roar to frighten people? Or will you, like Lord Rudra, roar to shield those who need protection?'

Vedavati's words sent a flood of positive energy and inspiration coursing through Raavan. More than ever, he felt connected to the Mahadev, the God of Gods.

'Roar, noble Raavan,' said Vedavati. 'But roar in favour of dharma. Roar to protect the innocent, the poor, the needy.

Be a true follower of the Mahadev. Be aggressive, but for the good of others. Be tough, but only to nurture the weak. Be fearsome, but only to fight for the virtuous. That is what Lord Rudra stood for. Follow the Lord's example.'

Raavan didn't say a word.

'Jai Shri Rudra,' said Vedavati.

'Jai Shri Rudra!'

Vedavati smiled and gently let go of Raavan's hand.

The first step on the path for all true followers of the Mahadev is a ritual sacrifice of the ego. Raavan knew what he had to do. He kneeled in front of the seated Vedavati. Taking a deep breath, he bent his hitherto unyielding back and brought his head down to the Kanyakumari's feet. For the first time in his life, he sought the blessings of another living person.

Vedavati put both her hands on Raavan's head and blessed him. 'May you always live in dharma. May dharma always live in you.'

Raavan drew himself up to his full six feet and three inches, and pulled out a sheet of papyrus from the pouch tied to his cummerbund. 'Please accept this, noble Vedavati. Don't say no.'

For the first time, Raavan's heart was in control as he spoke aloud that divine name. He didn't stutter.

'No to what?' she asked.

'My first act of genuine goodness.'

'Why do you run yourself down like that? You have done good before. You have done good for your brother. For this village. For...'

'Those were selfish acts. I protected those who were my own. Even the stuff I handed out here was meant to impress you. When I wrote and sealed this hundi, I had a selfish reason for it, but I don't anymore. I am giving it to you because I know you will do good with it.'

'Raavan, I cannot take money from you.'

'It's not for you, noble Vedavati. This is a hundi for fifty thousand gold coins, and it's for this entire region. I know you will use it well.'

'But…'

'Please don't refuse. Don't stop me in my first act of genuine kindness. I will consider it a blessing.'

Vedavati took the hundi from Raavan's hand, touched it to her forehead and said, 'It is my privilege, noble Raavan. I will use it for the good of the common people.'

'That means a lot to me. I intend to come back here as an arya and ask for what is due to me then.'

'And it will not be denied. Prithvi and I will be honoured.'

Raavan folded his hands together in a namaste. 'I will take your leave now, gentle Vedavati. My blessings for your unborn child. He or she is truly lucky to have a mother like you and a father like Prithvi.'

'Thank you, great Raavan.'

Every time Vedavati said his name out loud, a pleasurable current ran through Raavan's being. 'Till we meet again, Vedavati. Jai Shri Rudra.'

'Jai Shri Rudra.'

As Raavan walked away from her, he felt a lightness in his being that he had never felt before. Positive energy coursed through him. Even the pain in his navel had ceased to bother him. He walked with a spring in his step, the name of the Mahadev on his lips and the Kanyakumari in his heart.

A man with a purpose.

A man walking with dharma.

Neither he nor Vedavati noticed Sukarman, Shochikesh's son, hiding behind the bushes. He had been there the entire time and had heard everything. But only four words from the conversation reverberated in his mind. *Fifty thousand gold coins!*

—₹6I—

'This is generous,' said Kumbhakarna, his eyebrows raised in surprise.

'This is only the beginning,' Raavan responded, a serene smile on his face.

Kumbhakarna had never seen his brother smile as much as he had over this past week. In the seven days since Raavan had last met Vedavati, he had transformed into a new person—full of hope and enthusiasm. He had been planning how to use his immense wealth to help India. He was contemplating the conquest of a small kingdom in the Sapt Sindhu, to be set up as a model dominion for the common people

He also wanted to build a large hospital attached to the Vaidyanath temple, which would treat poor people from across the Sapt Sindhu, free of cost. The amount he was thinking of donating was sizeable and had led to Kumbhakarna's comment on his generosity.

'Are you sure, Dada?' asked Kumbhakarna. 'This is a huge amount of money.'

'It's only a drop in my ocean of wealth, Kumbha. You know that. Now, take the hundi to the local moneylender and get the gold. We will donate it and then leave for Lanka. There is a lot to do and not enough time.'

Kumbhakarna smiled and nodded. 'Your word is my command, great devotee of the Ka... Ka... Kanyakumari.'

Raavan punched Kumbhakarna on his arm. 'Stop teasing me, will you!'

Kumbhakarna was still laughing as he left the room.

—ऱुॐI—

'Wow,' said the moneylender. 'Two hundis from the great Raavan on the same day.'

Kumbhakarna took the receipt from the moneylender and put his seal on it. The moneylender would use this signed receipt and Raavan's original hundi to get the amount reimbursed through Raavan's closest trading office, in Magadh. And of course, earn a generous commission on the transaction.

'Eighty thousand gold coins,' continued the chatty moneylender, 'is a lot of money for our small Vaidyanath. And all in the same day!'

'And a good commission for you as well,' said Kumbhakarna, good-humouredly.

'Yes!' beamed the moneylender. 'I can finally buy the piece of land my wife and I have been eyeing for some time now.'

Kumbhakarna smiled as he handed the receipt over and took the outsized bags of coins. Two soldiers from his posse of armed men picked up the bags and moved towards their bullock cart. Kumbhakarna thanked the moneylender and turned to leave.

Then suddenly, he stopped. His sixth sense prickled.

'The woman who came earlier to redeem Raavan's other hundi,' said Kumbhakarna. 'Did she—'

'Not a woman,' interrupted the moneylender. 'It was a man. He was here just an hour ago.'

It was Prithviji then.

'A very young man he was too,' continued the moneylender.

Kumbhakarna felt a sense of foreboding enter his heart. 'Show me the receipt.'

The moneylender shook his head. 'I can't show you the receipt. It would…'

He stopped talking as Kumbhakarna dropped fifty gold coins on the counter and extended a hand commandingly. Without any further hesitation, the moneylender reached into the small cabinet below the counter and fished out the receipt. Kumbhakarna took one look at it, turned, and ran for his horse.

He was soon galloping through the streets to the main stables of Vaidyanath. That was where a man would go, to hire a horse or find a place on a departing cart, if he wished to travel beyond the city limits.

He knew he had to rush. There was little time.

For the name on the receipt had been clearly inked: Sukarman.

Chapter 16

Raavan slapped Sukarman viciously across the face. 'Did you actually think you would get away with this?'

Kumbhakarna had reached the horse stand just in time. Sukarman and his five associates were about to leave with their ill-gained wealth. Kumbhakarna and his guards had easily overpowered the six youths and confiscated the coins they were carrying. The thieves had then been presented before Raavan.

'You are lucky I am a changed man,' growled Raavan. 'Otherwise your tortured body would be lying here, half-dead by now.'

Sukarman strained against his captors, looking terrified.

Kumbhakarna gestured to the other five, who stood clustered around Sukarman. 'Who are these men, Sukarman? I don't recognise them. They are not from your village,' he said.

Sukarman was shivering now, too petrified to answer.

'Let's take him back to Todee, Dada,' said Kumbhakarna. 'We can let Vedavatiji decide what is to be done with him.'

Raavan continued to stare at Sukarman. Despite the show of anger, he was quite in control of his emotions. At the mention of Vedavati, he felt even calmer. 'We could, but I suspect she will forgive him. And this bastard does not deserve forgiveness.'

Sukarman suddenly lost control of his bladder and wet himself. Raavan's first reaction was to laugh, but then he stopped.

A thought too painful to consider mauled its way into his consciousness. For a few seconds, he was paralysed, afraid even to acknowledge it.

Oh Lord Rudra… No…

Stricken with horror, Raavan turned to look at his younger brother. His heart sank when he saw that Kumbhakarna's expression mirrored his own. He turned his gaze to Sukarman, as if in a trance. The colour had vanished from the man's face. He stood there, trembling, a wretched figure. Raavan felt his heart turn to ice. This wasn't just a robbery… This was…

Lord Rudra, have mercy!

It was Kumbhakarna who gathered his wits first. He moved swiftly, shouting as he ran, 'Guards! Everyone! We are riding out to Todee! Now!'

—ॐ—

Less than an hour later, Raavan's entourage of over one hundred soldiers thundered into Todee. Only Samichi had been left behind on Kumbhakarna's orders. Sukarman had been tied to the back of a horse, whose reins were in the hand of one of Raavan's mounted warriors. His five companions were being hauled back to Todee in a similar manner.

As the horses galloped into the village, it became immediately obvious that something was amiss.

There was a deathly silence all around.

Raavan whipped his horse and continued to race ahead, leading the way to Vedavati's house at the centre of the village. There was a massive crowd in the open square right outside it. Almost the entire village seemed to have congregated there.

Raavan vaulted off his horse and ran towards the house, pushing people aside. His heart was pounding. His mouth felt dry with foreboding.

Kumbhakarna was close behind him.

As Raavan shoved a scrawny villager out of his way, he nearly tripped over something lying on the ground.

Without so much as a glance, he straightened up and stumbled on, towards the modest hut that belonged to Vedavati and Prithvi.

It was Kumbhakarna who realised what it was that Raavan had tripped over.

Prithvi's bloodied and mutilated body.

Oh Lord Rudra…

There had clearly been a struggle. Prithvi had been stabbed multiple times, and had probably bled to death. It was clear that he had died slowly. A trail of blood on the ground suggested that he had tried to drag himself towards his house, till his body gave way.

Kumbhakarna looked up. Towards Prithvi's house. Where the pregnant Vedavati would have been.

And then he heard a cry.

It was the sound of raw, unfathomable anguish. The broken voice of a soul struck down with unimaginable grief.

He ran towards Vedavati's hut, roughly pushing aside everyone in his path. He emerged through the crowd to see Raavan on his knees outside the open door. Sobbing uncontrollably.

Steeling his heart, Kumbhakarna looked through the open door into the one-room hut. The sight made his blood curdle. Vedavati lay on the floor, her right arm twisted at a strange angle. Her left hand was on her belly, as if she was protecting her unborn child. Or had died trying to protect it. For most of the stab wounds were on her belly. She had been knifed at least fifteen to twenty times. The blood had flowed and congealed around her, a macabre red shroud cradling her dead body. Her face, always so still and serene, had not been spared either. The attacker had jabbed the knife straight into her left eye. By the look of it, it was a deep wound. Perhaps the wound that had finally killed her. The blow that had snuffed out the light of the Living Goddess.

Kumbhakarna bent over, unable to believe what he was seeing. Blinded by tears, he stumbled towards his brother and reached out to touch his shoulder.

Raavan shrank back at the touch, as though seared by fire. He looked at his younger brother. Tears streaming down his face.

Kumbhakarna collapsed on his knees. 'Dada…'

Raavan looked up at the skies. To the cloud palaces where the Gods were supposed to live. 'YOU SONS OF BITCHES!! WHY?! WHY HER?! WHY?!!'

Kumbhakarna embraced Raavan, not knowing what else to do, or say.

They say tears can wash away grief. They lie.

There are some kinds of grief that even a million tears cannot wash away. Which haunt you for life. For all time.

They say time heals all wounds. They lie.

Sometimes, the grief one is cursed with is so immense that even time surrenders to it.

The brothers held each other. Crying inconsolably.

—रावण—

Raavan's men had slowly gathered around Raavan and Kumbhakarna. None of them truly understood what was going on. But they could see that their trader-prince was devastated.

The villagers, too stunned to do anything, stood around weeping.

Shochikesh slowly staggered up to Raavan. His eyes were swollen with tears and his body stooped with grief. 'I am so sorry, Jai... I...'

He still had no idea who Raavan was.

'Where the hell were all of you when this happened?' Raavan snarled. The rage of the entire universe seemed to sweep through him.

'Jai... There's nothing we could have done... We rushed here when we heard noises... but they were armed...'

Raavan felt the fury rise again within him. He looked around. There were at least two hundred villagers assembled near the hut. He looked at Sukarman and his five accomplices, each one securely tied to the trunk of a tree beside the hut.

Two hundred against six.

Raavan's voice dropped to a menacing whisper as he addressed Shochikesh. 'She was your Goddess. She held up this entire pathetic village. Cared for it like a mother. And all of you together could not protect her from six thugs?'

'I am so sorry… we… Many got scared and ran away…'

Raavan rose to his full height, towering over Shochikesh. 'Ran away? You sons of bitches ran away?'

Shochikesh looked at the Lankan trader's bloodshot eyes, his own panic rising. He tried to reason with Raavan. 'But… But what could we…'

The words remained frozen on Shochikesh's lips. His eyes widened as he looked down to see a knife buried deep in his body. He stood in shock for a moment, before he let out an agonised scream. Raavan had drawn his long knife in one smooth, rapid arc and thrust it into the other man's abdomen. The scream infuriated Raavan even more. He rammed the knife in further, twisting it viciously. The blade ripped through to the other side, the point bursting out of Shochikesh's back. Raavan yanked his weapon out and pushed Shochikesh back. The flame-haired man fell to the ground, bleeding copiously. It would be a slow, painful death.

The villagers stood rooted to their spots, paralysed with fear.

Raavan looked down at Shochikesh's body for a moment. Then the trader from Lanka hawked and spat on the Todee landlord.

Continuing to look down, Raavan ordered in a low growl, 'Kill them all.' Then he pointed to where Sukarman and his gang were tied up. 'Except them.'

The villagers scattered and ran screaming in all directions as Raavan's soldiers rushed to obey their lord's command. The residents of Todee did not stand a chance. Every one of them was killed.

Corpses littered the ground. Men. Women. Children. Cut down where they stood. It was all over in just a few minutes.

Raavan stood next to one of Sukarman's associates, while Kumbhakarna stood on his other side. The Lankan soldiers, holding their bloodied swords, were at the back. Sukarman's hands had been nailed to a door that faced the trees where his associates had been tied up. He could see exactly what was being done to them.

Raavan held a burning log to the man's arm, letting the fire incinerate the skin and roast the flesh. The sickening smell of burning flesh pervaded the atmosphere. The blood-curdling screams of the man being slowly burnt alive rent the air.

But Raavan wasn't even looking at the victim of his torture. His eyes were focused on Sukarman's face. 'Did you do this only for money? Or were you ordered by someone to kill her?'

The petrified Sukarman began to blabber. 'I... so sorry... forgive me... please... forgive me... take all the money...'

Pure, unadulterated rage flashed in Raavan's eyes. He raised the flaming log and held it closer to his agonised victim's face. Then he turned his attention back to Sukarman. 'You think this is about money?'

Kumbhakarna spoke up. 'Where is the Kanyakumari's baby?'

When Vedavati's body was examined, her womb had been found to be empty. Which meant that she had given birth to her child before she was killed.

However, there was no trace of the baby.

'Sukarman, I asked you a question. Where is the baby?' growled Kumbhakarna.

Sukarman remained silent, looking down at the ground. Fear had made him lose control of his bladder again.

'Sukarman.' Kumbhakarna's fists were clenched tight. 'You'd better talk.'

Suddenly, one of Sukarman's associates spoke up. 'He ordered me to do it. Sukarman did. I didn't want to.'

'What did you do?' snarled Kumbhakarna, glaring at the man.

'He ordered me to. It's his fault…'

'WHAT DID YOU DO?'

The man fell silent.

Kumbhakarna strode up and looked him fiercely in the eye. 'What did you do? Tell me. And you will have mercy.'

The man looked at Sukarman and then back at Kumbhakarna. 'He ordered me to… throw the baby into the wild. And let the animals… eat… I mean…' His words stumbled to a stop. Even his pathetic barbarian soul was ashamed of the terrible crime he had committed.

Indians believed that to kill a baby was a horrific sin, and it would pollute one's soul for many births. Sukarman's gang had thought they would get around this commandment by letting wild animals do the deed for them.

Kumbhakarna looked at Raavan, too shocked for words. He had not expected such an answer. Even for savages like these, this seemed abominably cruel.

A baby left in the wild for wild animals to feast on… Lord Rudra have mercy.

'Mercy,' pleaded the man. 'I told you the truth… Mercy…'

Kumbhakarna glanced at Raavan again. Raavan nodded. Kumbhakarna drew his sword and beheaded the man in one clean strike.

The decapitated head of the criminal flew in the air and hit the head of his associate tied up next to him. He screamed in panic, as a bloody fountain erupted through the gaping neck, on to him.

A loud flapping of wings made Raavan and Kumbhakarna look up. A kettle of vultures was descending on the village. They watched as one of the birds tentatively pecked at one of the dead bodies that lay scattered about on the ground. On discovering meat that was still warm, the bird squawked in delight and began feasting on it.

Raavan turned his attention back to the man burning beside him. Uncontrollable tears of rage flowed from his eyes as he looked at the now insensate, almost unrecognisable creature slumped against his bonds. He felt no pity, no remorse. Only fury.

—ॐ—

Raavan and Kumbhakarna sat on the ground, their backs against the wall. The five dead men were still tied to the trees. Sukarman, barely alive, had been yanked away from the door to which he had been nailed, and tied to a tree. Some of his bloodied flesh still clung to the nails. He had fallen unconscious under the slow burning and torture. But Raavan was careful to ensure that Sukarman didn't die. He had to suffer as much pain as was humanly possible. Pain, the very memory of which would terrify his soul for several lifetimes.

Meanwhile, Raavan's soldiers had carried the lifeless bodies of Vedavati and Prithvi to the village landlord's house. They had to be washed and clothed before the cremation ceremonies.

By now, the vultures had been joined by other creatures of the wild. Crows. Wild dogs. Hyenas. There was enough meat for everyone. The animals ate quietly. They didn't fight with each other. They didn't make too much noise. They knew there was enough food to last them for several days.

It was an eerily macabre sight. Wild animals everywhere, feasting silently on dead human bodies. An unconscious man tied to a tree. Soldiers with bloodied swords standing to attention. And two brothers, braving their broken souls, sitting outside the house of the woman they admired. The person they loved. The Goddess they worshipped.

Raavan's eyes were bloodshot and swollen, his face drained of all expression. Kumbhakarna took his brother's bloodied hands in his own. The blood of the criminals who had killed Vedavati had soaked their limbs but it had done nothing to cleanse their grief. What words could alleviate anguish such as this?

At last, Raavan spoke. 'I hate this...' He stopped as tears began flowing down his cheeks again.

Kumbhakarna looked at his brother. Silent.

Raavan's voice emerged, raw with grief and anger.

'I hate this cursed land.'

Chapter 17

Each time Sukarman slipped into unconsciousness, a bucket of water drenched his face. He had to be kept conscious, to experience every moment of the torture. Though his body hung limp, the taut ropes kept him upright against the tree. He had been stripped bare except for his loincloth. Blood oozed from his numerous lesions and almost every inch of him was either scorched or slashed. Except his face.

When Sukarman finally managed to open his eyes, he saw the Lankan pirate-trader standing in front of him.

Raavan.

Among the richest men in the world. Certainly, the angriest man alive. A man with an intense craving for vengeance. 'Why didn't you just take the money?' Raavan's voice was a mixture of rage and desperate sadness. 'Why? Why did you have to kill her?'

Hope flickered in some corner of Sukarman's mind. He thought he might still have a chance to explain himself. And the thought fired some energy into him. 'I did try... I tried so hard... But she wouldn't... listen.'

Raavan looked at Kumbhakarna and then back at Sukarman.

'I told her that she'd never cared about money before... so why now? But she wouldn't agree... she was being... stubborn... Even that husband of hers suddenly grew a spine and snubbed me. She asked me to take everything else they owned... but she wouldn't give me... your hundi... But everything else they owned was worth nothing... and I needed to settle my gambling debts... My debtors would have killed me... I told her that... but she was being so... unreasonable,' he wheezed.

Raavan stared at Sukarman in disbelief.

Sukarman's voice was barely audible as he continued, 'I told her... that you would give her more... that you... are fabulously rich... wouldn't care... but she refused to listen... She said she would not part with the hundi... said the hundi was holy... it had been given by someone who had discovered dharma... that she would not surrender Raavan's chance to discover the God within him...'

A low moan escaped Kumbhakarna, as he clutched his hair in despair. But Raavan just kept staring at Sukarman, unable to respond.

Sukarman was not done. Misreading Raavan's silence, he mumbled, 'I was trying to reason with her, but one of the others lost his patience... I can't blame him... She was being... stubborn.'

Raavan had had enough. He lunged at Sukarman and unleashed a vicious upper cut that caught him on the chin. Sukarman's head snapped back and hit the trunk of the tree. Kumbhakarna stepped up and grabbed him by the hair, holding his head steady as he punched him squarely in the jaw, breaking it with an unmistakable crack. Then he pushed the broken jaw down, forcing Sukarman's mouth open.

Raavan picked up a small piece of half-burnt coal and pushed it into the slack mouth.

Sukarman's body convulsed as the red-hot coal singed the skin of his mouth before being pushed down his throat. Kumbhakarna held his mouth open, while some of the Lankan soldiers rushed forward with more pieces of burning coal. Raavan took them one by one and stuffed them down Sukarman's throat. He was using his bare hands, unheeding of the pain. As more and more pieces of burning coal found their way down Sukarman's oesophagus, his body flailed in agony.

He was being burnt alive, from the inside out.

But Raavan and Kumbhakarna would not stop. They kept forcing more coal pieces into Sukarman's digestive tract.

After some time, he stopped moving.

A pungent smell of burnt flesh permeated the air. Smoke was coming out of Sukarman's mouth. His stomach seemed aglow. As though his insides had caught fire. The wretched man was being cooked alive.

Still, the brothers did not stop.

Rage had taken over their souls completely.

They had lost everything.

Their Goddess. Their world. Their sanity.

They had lost it all.

—— ऽ७I ——

Preparations for the ceremony were complete. Two large pyres had been prepared. The bodies of Vedavati and Prithvi had been cleaned, bathed and dressed in fresh white clothes. Sacred Vedic chants had been whispered into their ears. It was believed that the power of the mantras would give the souls of the departed the strength to continue on their journey.

Once all this had been done, holy water was poured into their mouths and tulsi leaves placed on their lips. Some more tulsi leaves were bunched together and placed in their nostrils and ears. Vedavati's hands were arranged on her chest, with her thumbs tied together. The big toes of her feet had also been tied together. The same was done for Prithvi. It was believed that this helped conjoin the right and left energy channels, thus ensuring the movement of energy in a circle within the body. Earthen lamps were lit at the precise spots where Vedavati and Prithvi had been found dead, with the flame facing south, in honour of Lord Yama, the God of Death and Dharma.

Through all of this, Raavan and Kumbhakarna remained outwardly calm. There was no space here for undignified crying and indecorous mourning. Dignity. Respect. Honour. That was what the Goddess deserved. The great Kanyakumari would leave this earth in the same manner in which she had lived. With dignity, respect and honour.

The two brothers stood beside Vedavati's unlit pyre. She would be cremated first, and then Prithvi.

Holy ghee was brought in an earthen pot. Kumbhakarna held the vessel as Raavan scooped out dollops of ghee and poured it over Vedavati's body. As he did so, both the brothers chanted from the *Garuda Purana*. When Raavan wiped his hands clean, some of his men came up and placed more wooden logs on Vedavati's body. Soon, only her face was visible.

As Raavan stepped back, a wooden log was brought to him, lit with holy fire.

Kumbhakarna gathered the courage to look at Vedavati's face one final time. The punctures had been covered. A patch had been put over the hole where her left eye had been.

Her face—even now, after all that she had suffered—was calm and gentle. Like that of a Goddess. Kumbhakarna struggled to hold back his tears. He would not be undignified. Not in front of her. Not in front of his Goddess.

He had heard it said enough times, that the tears of loved ones made it difficult for the departed soul to leave the world. The living had to control and suppress their grief, for the good of the dead.

He looked at Vedavati's still body waiting to be engulfed in flames, and unexpectedly, all of a sudden, the rage left him.

He looked around in a daze, as though waking up from a long sleep. In the village beyond, he could see that wild animals were still feasting on the dead bodies of the villagers. Men and women who could be called cowards, but not criminals. He looked back at Vedavati's face and was ashamed. Of himself, and of what he had done.

He knew that she would be disappointed in him and his brother. He turned to look at him now.

Raavan was holding the log with the holy flame and walking up to the pyre.

Kumbhakarna stepped back.

Raavan pushed the log into the pyre, setting it ablaze. Letting *Lord Agni*, the all-purifying *God of Fire*, consume the body of the Goddess.

Someone handed Raavan an earthen pot filled with holy water. He punctured it and, following the sacred tradition, started walking anti-clockwise around the blazing pyre. Water trickled out of the small hole in the pot as he walked. He performed the circumambulation three times. In doing so, he was, in effect, stating to the world that he would assume the responsibility for repaying Vedavati's debts. Not monetary debts, for money was meaningless to the soul—he was promising to repay her unfinished karmic debt and ensuring that she would be free of all attachments and responsibilities in this world. Her soul could then, hopefully, travel towards *moksha*, and be *liberated from the cycle of births.*

Kumbhakarna looked at his brother as he circled the pyre, and then at the village they had destroyed.

There was much to do. Much to atone for.

He hoped they wouldn't let her down.

—१६१—

It was late in the morning the next day, when Raavan and Kumbhakarna woke up. They had spent the night on the banks of a lake not far from the village. Despite the exhaustion of the day, they had managed barely a few hours of sleep.

Both the pyres were still smouldering, though the flames had died out. The physical bodies of the noble Kanyakumari and her gentle husband had been reduced, mostly, to ash. Twenty of Raavan's soldiers had been stationed at the cremation ground through the night, to keep away any wild animals that might choose to venture there. Their fears were unfounded, though. There was enough food to keep the animals in the village.

After their ritual bath, Raavan and Kumbhakarna went back to the cremation site. A few ceremonies still remained to be done. They began with Vedavati's pyre.

A bucket of holy water had been arranged. Tulsi leaves floated on its surface. Raavan took a coconut and smashed it on the ground. It broke vertically, from one narrow end to the other. This was rare and considered auspicious; the soul would certainly find moksha. The coconut water was added to the water in the bucket. The solution was stirred by hand as Sanskrit hymns were chanted. When this was done, Raavan ritually drizzled the holy water onto the smouldering pyre, extinguishing the last of the flames.

Four Lankan soldiers came up and removed the ashes from the platform. Kumbhakarna and Raavan bent over the pile and painstakingly sifted through it for the *asti*, the small pieces of bone that hadn't been reduced to ash in the pyre. Almost everything else that formed part of the body—flesh, organs, muscles—had been consumed. The ashes were to be returned to Mother Earth in an easily usable form. What remained of the bones would be immersed in the holy waters of the Ganga.

Raavan knew that *asti* was the root for the Sanskrit word *astitva,* which meant *existence*. These bones, which had tenaciously refused to be consumed by the holy fire, symbolised the remnants of existence. They had to go back to the source of it all, to the Mother Goddess, in the form of the flowing, nurturing river. They would merge with the water, in the bosom of the Mother Goddess, so that even the residual bits of existence could find peace.

Raavan and Kumbhakarna carefully washed each of the small bones, then placed them in an earthen pot. It was almost impossible to distinguish which part of the body they had been a part of. Then, to his utter surprise, Raavan came upon the bones of two fingers which seemed almost intact. The flesh, the muscles, the tendons, had all been burnt away. What survived were three bone phalanges from each of the two fingers. Six phalanges in all. Clearly distinguishable.

When most of the skull had not survived, what were the chances of these phalanges surviving?

As he held the fragile bones in his open palm, it struck Raavan—these were probably the vestiges of the hand with which Vedavati had held his hand. For the first time. Just a few days ago. She had never touched him again.

He would never see her again. But he could still hold her hand.

Raavan couldn't control himself anymore.

He wept as he touched the bones to his forehead, like they were hallowed relics of the most divine Goddess. And then he kissed them lightly.

She had left these for him.

He knew, then, that he would survive. That he would find a way to live the rest of his life. For he knew that he could hold her hand any time he wished to.

She had left these for him as a crutch. So that he could walk through the agony that he knew the rest of his life would be. With her hand as support.

With her hand to hold.

—ॐ—

Raavan turned the urn over and let Vedavati's remains slip into the holy river. Further down, Kumbhakarna did the same for Prithvi.

It had been three days since the cremation. The brothers had ridden out towards the river with all their soldiers, picking up young Samichi on the way. Despite Kumbhakarna's repeated pleas, Raavan had refused to conduct funeral ceremonies for the villagers of Todee and had left their dead bodies where they were. As rotting food for wild animals. He had no qualms about condemning their souls to suffering for all eternity.

Raavan watched closely as the earthly remains of Vedavati disappeared into the holy river. The asti were a part of the Mother now.

But he hadn't surrendered all of it. He had kept the finger phalanges, the remnants of Vedavati's hand. They hung around his neck now, bunched together to form an unlikely pendant.

He started up the steps of the river ghats, with the urn still in his hand.

'Dada,' said Kumbhakarna, stepping out of the water. 'You have to drop the urn into the river too.'

Raavan looked down at the urn—empty and bereft. As though it, too, was in mourning.

'Dada…'

Raavan did not respond. He looked around him. At the holy Ganga, the verdant banks, the dense forest cover… at the land of India. The land blessed by the Gods.

He closed his eyes. A feeling of disgust overcame him.

A country that cannot honour its heroes doesn't deserve to survive.

'Dada… the urn…' Kumbhakarna reminded him.

To Kumbhakarna's surprise, Raavan turned and started walking back towards the shore.

'Dada?'

Raavan reached the river bank, bent down, and picked up some soil—the earth of the Sapt Sindhu—and put it in the urn. Then he started walking back into the river, at a furious pace, like a man possessed.

'Dada, what are you doing?'

Raavan bent and dipped the urn in the water, so that the soil was washed away. Like he was immersing the asti of the land itself.

'Dada?' Kumbhakarna's voice conveyed his mounting anxiety.

Raavan filled the urn with water and poured it over his head. Like the ritual bath at the end of a funeral ceremony.

'No, Dada!' Kumbhakarna rushed forward, frantic to stop Raavan. But he was too late.

, Raavan broke the urn on his arms and let the pieces fall into the river. Then he turned towards Kumbhakarna, eyes blazing and fists clenched tight. Rage poured out of every cell of his body. He gritted his teeth and said, 'This country is dead to me.'

'Dada, listen to me...'

'Control the monster, did she say?'

'Dada, what are you saying? Listen to me...'

'I will unleash the monster! I will destroy this land!'

Chapter 18

'Magnificent piece, Dada,' said Kumbhakarna.

Two long years had passed since Vedavati's death.

Twenty-four-year-old Raavan had been playing a raga dedicated to the *Devi*, the *Goddess*. Most of the ragas created in honour of the Goddess celebrated her motherly embodiment. There were others dedicated to her manifestation as a lover, a daughter, an artist and so on, but very few were dedicated to the warrior Goddess. The raga Raavan had composed captured the essence of this form—fierce, angry, and wild. Like nature in all its tempestuous and uncontrollable glory.

He called the Raga *Vaashi Santaapani*. The *roar of the furious Goddess*.

'I have yet to hear another piece that's as powerful,' said Kumbhakarna. 'In fact, I think it's the most beautiful raga I have heard in my life.'

Raavan nodded absentmindedly. He didn't seem to care too much for the compliment.

'Even the word Vaashi is so appropriate, Dada. The sound of a blazing flame—isn't that its original meaning? I doubt you can get more evocative than that.'

'Hmm.'

Kumbhakarna touched his brother on the shoulder almost tentatively. 'You know, they say grief and tragedy often bring out the best in an artist.'

Raavan looked at his brother in irritation. 'And who are these "they"? Whoever they may be, they are morons! Nobody goes looking for tragedy. Nobody wants to experience grief just to be able to create art.'

Kumbhakarna realised his brother was not in the mood for this conversation. He tried to change the subject. 'I am happy that work is consuming more and more of your time, Dada. Drowning oneself in work is the best way to push negative thoughts away.'

Raavan truly had been busy. Over the previous year and a half, he had leveraged his vast wealth and control over the only credible armed force in Lanka, to inveigle himself closer to the Lankan throne. Kubaer, the ruler of Lanka, had come to depend on him to provide security for his trading ships. Many other traders had taken to paying for the services of Raavan's security forces. And since, unknown to most, Raavan controlled both the pirates and the militia, whenever someone hired his men for protection, the pirate attacks on their ships stopped. Raavan's wealth and resources had grown exponentially, as had his clout and reputation. He was now on the verge of being formally appointed as the head of the Trading Security Force of Lanka. His plan was simple: to get his private militia appointed as the official Lankan Security Force. Not only would the cost of maintaining and arming his soldiers fall to the Lankan treasury, the soldiers would remain loyal to Raavan, even after their transfer. Over time, he would expand the force to make it as large and well-equipped as a regular army. An army trained to take on the Sapt Sindhu empire.

'Yes,' said Raavan. 'Work is a good distraction.'

Kumbhakarna smiled, glad to get a few words out of his brother. But he wasn't prepared for what came next.

'This silly female notion maa has, that talking about problems can help one come to terms with grief, is utter nonsense. The masculine way is better. Drown yourself in work. Suppress the grief. Don't think about it and don't let it come out. Let it remain trapped in some deep, dark dungeon of your heart, even if it festers there. And when you are old and tired, have a nice fatal heart-attack, and it's all over,' Raavan finished.

Kumbhakarna thought it wise to not say anything. It was obvious. Let alone suppress his grief, Raavan remained crushed by it. He had thrown himself into work with the single-minded ambition of bringing the Sapt Sindhu down, but nothing seemed to give him pleasure anymore. Kumbhakarna had thought he would tactfully broach the suggestion his mother had made, of an early marriage. But perhaps this was not the right time to speak of it.

—ॐ—

Kubaer looked extremely nervous. 'Raavan, I am not sure it's advisable to take on the most powerful empire in the world.'

Four years had passed since Vedavati's death.

Kubaer and Raavan were in the Lankan ruler's private office. Raavan and Kumbhakarna had moved to Sigiriya some time back, leaving their mother in Gokarna. As soon as he had been appointed head of Lanka's Trading Security Force, Raavan had started making preparations to move closer to the

Lankan throne. He had bought a huge mansion not far from Kubaer's palace.

Since moving to the Lankan capital, Raavan had also started working on his plan to trigger a war against the Sapt Sindhu. He needed a plausible reason to provoke the empire into attacking the small island kingdom, and he knew what it could be. As a first step, he proposed reducing the share of the profits that the Sapt Sindhuans appropriated from cross-border trade. After months of persuasion, he had finally managed to engage Kubaer in a discussion on the matter. Kubaer, a prudent sixty-nine-year-old compared to Raavan's impetuous twenty-six, was not a warrior; he was a businessman who valued pragmatism. He privileged profit over pride and thought caution was a necessary quality. His skill lay in charming and negotiating a beneficial deal, not inviting trouble.

'I've said it before and I'll say it again: Why should we give up nine-tenths of our profits to the Sapt Sindhu?' asked Raavan. 'Why should we do all the hard work and let them take most of our money?'

'We are not actually giving them ninety per cent, Raavan,' said Kubaer with a sly smile. 'Our accounts are creative. We overstate our costs. In actual fact, they don't get more than seventy per cent.'

Raavan had already anticipated Kubaer's comeback, but he decided to play along. He would not make the mistake of underestimating the chief-trader of Lanka, like the Sapt Sindhuans did, solely because of his physical appearance. Kubaer's round, cherubic face and smooth complexion belied his advanced age. But he was so obese that he waddled ponderously, like a duck. He usually wore brightly coloured clothes; today, it was a shocking blue dhoti and a yellow angvastram, and his body was bedecked with ornate jewellery. His effeminate mannerisms and life of excess had made him an object of ridicule for the warrior class. But Raavan knew the effete exterior hid a sharp, ruthless mind, devoted to one cause alone: profit.

'But even seventy per cent is too high!' he countered.

'Thirty per cent is good enough for me. I save a considerable part of it, while the Sapt Sindhu squanders away most of its share. So my wealth is greater than theirs. And do you know why they don't save anything?' Kubaer asked.

'Forget about their savings, Great One. Why should we care about how much money Ayodhya or its subordinate kingdoms have? We should care about our own wealth. If we reduce their commissions, we will have more profit for ourselves.'

'You didn't answer my question. I'll tell you why we have higher savings than they do, even though we earn less. It's because the Sapt Sindhu wastes a lot of money on unnecessary wars. We don't. War is bad for business, it's bad for profits and wealth. If we reduce the commissions, they will certainly attack us. We will then be forced to mobilise our army and spend money, no, *waste* money, on a silly war. And that's—'

Raavan interrupted Kubaer. 'What if I agree to fund our war effort?'

Kubaer frowned with suspicion. 'The entire war?'

'Everything. You won't have to spend a single coin. I'll pay for it all.'

Kubaer had the natural mistrust of an astute trader for a deal that sounded too good to be true. Raavan, he knew, was too shrewd to do something only for glory. 'And why, pray, would you help me at all?' he asked.

'Because you will then share half the increased commissions with me.'

Kubaer smiled. Any kind of selfish interest, he understood and respected. Experience had taught him that the best business deals were struck when both parties were honest about their own interests. 'So, let me make sure I understand this. You can't declare war without my approval. And you think this war will be profitable.'

'Yes to both.'

'But what guarantee is there of victory?'

'None. But is there any guarantee that our ships will not sink in the sea when we send them out to trade? We estimate the probabilities and take the best bet. A calculated bet. We are traders. That's what we do.'

'All that is very well, but what if we lose?'

'Then you should do the pragmatic thing.'

'If we lose the battle,' said Kubaer, choosing his words carefully, 'the pragmatic thing would be to tell the Sapt Sindhuans that this was all your idea.'

'You are right. That would indeed be the pragmatic thing to do. If we fail, let me take the blame. It's my idea, after all. Keep yourself, and the other traders of Lanka, safe. But if we win, I get half the increased commissions.'

Kubaer smiled. 'All right, Raavan. You will have your war. Just make sure I don't make a loss. Nothing spoils my day like an unanticipated loss.'

'Honourable One, have I ever let you down?' Raavan asked with a smile.

—ᜠᜦᜱ—

Kumbhakarna was worried. 'Dada, we may be over-reaching with this…. Are we biting off more than we can chew?'

The brothers were at home in Sigiriya, the capital of Lanka.

'We are not, Kumbha,' said Raavan. 'We'll bite it all. We'll chew it all. We'll digest it all.'

'Dada, the Sapt Sindhu rulers do nothing except fight wars. We are traders. Our soldiers are essentially pirates. They fight for money, and money alone. If there is no profit in sight, they will abandon the battle. But the Sapt Sindhu soldiers actually celebrate "martyrdom" in battle. They die for bizarre causes like honour and glory. How are we supposed to defeat such morons?'

'Through good tactics.'

'I think you…'

'No, I am not being overconfident.'

'But even if we can defeat them, how are we going to turn a profit from it? The cost of the campaign will be too high.'

'Don't worry. Once we win, we will start taking ninety per cent of the profits, if not more.'

Kumbhakarna nearly choked on the wine he was drinking. 'Ninety per cent! For us?'

Raavan frowned. 'Yes, of course.'

'Dada, I don't think we can enforce a treaty like that. It will be too much for the Sapt Sindhu kings to swallow. They will have no choice but to keep on fighting. The ensuing rebellions will destroy them, but they will wear us out too. And we simply don't have enough soldiers to control all the Sapt Sindhu kingdoms and their people in peacetime.'

'We'll break their spirit in one major battle. Destroy their entire army. I am not interested in imposing our rules on their citizens, so where is the need to control them? We'll only impose our trade conditions on them. And slowly suck them dry.'

'But, Dada,' said Kumbhakarna, 'a commission this big will destroy the Sapt Sindhu economy over time. We would end up killing the golden goose that feeds us.'

Raavan's expression gave little away as his eyes met Kumbhakarna's.

'Precisely,' he said.

—१७—

Burly soldiers rowed the large boat in quick strokes towards the shore. Raavan sat in front, his right hand on the gunwale. Kumbhakarna sat behind him, observing his flexed arms, the massive triceps that were visibly tense.

Dada is upset.

Raavan looked straight ahead, towards the *Sapt Sindhu*— the *Land of the Seven Rivers*.

Kumbhakarna looked to his left, at Kubaer's boat being rowed rhythmically towards the shore by ten sailors.

It had only been a year since Raavan had convinced Kubaer to wage war against the Sapt Sindhu. Events had proceeded rapidly after that.

Within a matter of months, Raavan had mobilised and trained his army. He had also brought in mercenaries from around the world, promising them a rich share of the spoils.

Once the Lankan army was ready, Kubaer had sent an official communication to the emperor of the Sapt Sindhu, Dashrath. When his message reached Ayodhya, the capital city from where Dashrath ruled all the northern parts of the Indian subcontinent, it immediately set teeth on edge.

The old-elite royal families of the Sapt Sindhu, with their disdain for the trader-class Vaishyas, considered the effete Kubaer an upstart. They just about tolerated his existence. To receive a 'royal communication' from the trader-ruler of Lanka was seen as an affront. Traders were not supposed to send royal communications to emperors of ancient imperial dynasties. They were supposed to send humble, grovelling petitions. And as if that wasn't outrageous enough, the demand to reduce the empire's commissions on profits was seen as an intolerable insult to Kshatriya pride. Such a dishonour could not be stomached.

Dashrath had immediately rallied all of his subordinate kings across the land and mobilised an army. The plan was for his troops to march to Karachapa, one of Kubaer's biggest trading hubs, on the west coast of the Sapt Sindhu. Dashrath planned to destroy the Karachapa fort and trading warehouses. He had assumed that this would be enough to bring Kubaer to his senses. If not, some of the other ports held by Kubaer would also be destroyed, and ultimately, Lanka itself would come under siege.

Raavan had anticipated that the Sapt Sindhuans would take exception to Kubaer's message and march out to war immediately. His own troops were in a state of readiness. His specially designed ships, buffed with the enigmatic cave material, were prepared for battle. As soon as he received intelligence of the Sapt Sindhu army mobilising, and the direction of their march, the ships set sail, moving quickly up the western coast of peninsular India, to arrive at Karachapa.

There were too many ships in Raavan's navy for even the massive Karachapa port to accommodate. Besides, Raavan knew the Sapt Sindhuans had spies within Karachapa and the last thing he wanted was to generate curiosity about the radically different designs of his ships. They were a part of his battle plan, his secret weapon. So most of the ships were anchored offshore.

Later in the day, Raavan and Kumbhakarna boarded a rowboat and headed up to the beach of Karachapa. The rowboat hit the sand with a lurch and four soldiers jumped off, into the shallow waters, and pulled the boat onto the beach. Raavan remained immobile. Looking straight ahead.

Kumbhakarna could feel his breath quickening. They were returning to the Sapt Sindhu after five years. The last time they were here, they had immersed Vedavati's ashes in the holy Ganga.

It is said, and rightly, that whatever the memories associated with the past, every person's heart beats faster when they return to the land of their roots. The pain of separation, and the joy of homecoming, are universal. And nothing can compare to the sheer relief of returning to the lap of your mother, the most comfortable place in the world.

Kumbhakarna jumped off as soon as the boat was out of the water. He bent down and picked up some wet sand, the soil of his motherland, and with great veneration, brought it to his forehead. He touched it to both his eyes and kissed it. As he placed the sand back on the ground with utmost respect, he whispered, 'Jai Maa.'

Glory to the Mother.

He saw Raavan, who had gone slightly ahead of him, bend down to pick up some sand too. Kumbhakarna smiled.

Perhaps returning to the motherland has finally thawed his heart.

Kumbhakarna watched as Raavan brought his hand closer to his face and stared at the sand in it for what seemed like an eternity. He hesitated to go closer. Perhaps he should let his brother have this moment to himself.

He felt a vast sense of relief that the past was finally behind them. His elder brother had been through so much, raged against the world for so long, but it seemed he was finally ready to welcome some peace within. This war would be fought, of course. It had to be done. For profit. But, at least, returning to the motherland had alleviated some of Raavan's deep-seated sorrow. Or so Kumbhakarna thought.

Raavan opened the palm that cradled the sand, bringing it closer to his mouth. Then, slowly, deliberately, he hawked and spat into it. His entire body seemed to convulse in rage as he flung the sand to the ground and crushed it under his foot.

'Fuck this land.'

Chapter 19

'Shouldn't we be going over to their camp?' asked Kubaer nervously.

Dashrath, the overlord of the Sapt Sindhu, had marched right across his sprawling empire, from Ayodhya, its capital, to Karachapa. Within just a few hours of his arrival, he had sent a terse message to Kubaer, summoning him for a discussion on the terms of ceasefire.

In the early years of his reign, Dashrath had built on the powerful legacy he had inherited from his father, Aja. Rulers in various parts of India had either been deposed or made to pay tribute and accept his suzerainty, thus making Dashrath the Chakravarti Samrat, or the Universal Emperor.

'We are not going to his camp, noble Chief-Trader,' replied Raavan, trying hard to keep his irritation in check. 'The Ayodhyan will see it as our weakness. If we have to meet, it has to be on neutral ground—neither their camp, nor ours.'

'But...'

'No buts. We have come to fight, not to surrender.'

Raavan's approach had been clear from the start. Over the last week, he had ordered his troops to destroy all the villages in a fifty-kilometre radius around Karachapa. Standing crops had been burnt down. Harvested grain and livestock had been confiscated and commandeered as food for the Lankan soldiers. Wells had been poisoned with the carcasses of dead animals.

A scorched earth policy.

The Lankan army would be well fed and rested within the Karachapa walls. However, the Sapt Sindhu army, camped outside the city, would find it difficult to feed their five hundred thousand soldiers, given the ravaged countryside. Their numerical advantage would turn into a liability.

'But what if Emperor Dashrath doesn't retreat despite the food shortage?' asked Kubaer, anxiously. 'What if he attacks immediately?'

Raavan smiled. 'I am counting on you, great Chief-Trader, to provoke Dashrath to do precisely that. I will take care of the rest.'

'*Emperor* Dashrath,' corrected Kubaer.

Raavan preferred to speak only the man's name. No unnecessary respect towards an enemy. 'Just Dashrath,' he said quietly.

—ऱ७I—

Dashrath was in no mood for extended parleys.

'I order you to restore our commission to the very fair nine-tenths of your profits and, in return, I assure you I will let you live,' he said firmly.

After exchanging some terse messages, the adversaries had finally decided to meet on neutral ground. The chosen site was a beach, midway between Dashrath's military camp and the Karachapa fort. The emperor was accompanied by his father-in-law King Ashwapati, his general Mrigasya and a bodyguard platoon of twenty soldiers. Kubaer had arrived with Raavan and twenty bodyguards.

The Sapt Sindhu warriors could scarcely conceal their contempt as the obese Kubaer waddled laboriously into the tent. The chief trader had disregarded Raavan's advice to wear sober clothes and had dressed, instead, in a bright green dhoti and a pink angvastram. The jewellery he wore was flashier than usual. He had reasoned that a display of his fine taste would earn him the appreciation of the Sapt Sindhu leaders. What it did was to convince his opponents that they were dealing with an effete Vaishya; a peacock who knew little of warfare.

'Your Highness…' said Kubaer timidly, 'I think it might be a little difficult to keep the commissions fixed at that level. Our costs have gone up and the trading margins are not what they—'

'Don't try your disgusting negotiating tactics with me!' shouted Dashrath as he banged his hand on the table for effect. 'I am not a trader! I am an emperor! Civilised people understand the difference.'

Raavan clenched his fists under the table. Kubaer was not following any part of his advice, either in demeanour or in speech.

Dashrath leaned forward and said with controlled vehemence, 'I can be merciful. I can forgive mistakes. But you need to stop this nonsense and do as I say.'

Kubaer shifted uneasily on his chair and glanced at the impassive Raavan, who sat to his right. Even seated, Raavan's height and rippling musculature were surprising to the Sapt Sindhuans. They had not expected to find a warrior like this amidst what they derisively called a trader's protection force.

Raavan's battle-worn, swarthy skin was pockmarked as a result of a childhood encounter with disease. His thick beard, accompanied by a handlebar moustache, only added to his menacing appearance. His attire was unremarkable and sober, consisting of a white dhoti and a cream angvastram. His headgear was designed to add to his intimidating presence, with two threatening six-inch-long horns reaching out from the top on either side. The message was clear: Raavan was no mere soldier; he was a bull among men.

The Sapt Sindhuans kept glancing at the well-built Lankan general sitting amongst them, expecting him to say something. But Raavan sat still, offering neither opinions nor objections.

Kubaer turned back to Dashrath. 'But, Your Highness, we are facing many problems, and our invested capital is—'

'You are trying my patience now, Kubaer!' Dashrath snapped. 'You are irritating the emperor of the Sapt Sindhu!'

'But, my lord…'

'Look, if you do not continue to pay our rightful commissions, believe me, you will all be dead by this time tomorrow. I will first defeat your miserable army, then travel all the way to that cursed island of yours and burn your city to the ground.'

'But there are problems with our ships, and labour costs have—'

'I don't care about your problems!' Dashrath was shouting now.

'You will, after tomorrow,' said Raavan softly.

The emperor had lost his temper. The time was right.

Dashrath swung around to look sharply at Raavan. 'How dare you speak out of—'

'How dare you, Dashrath?' asked Raavan, his voice clear and ringing.

Dashrath, Ashwapati and Mrigasya sat in stunned silence, shocked that this mere sidekick of a trader should have the temerity to address the emperor of the Sapt Sindhu by his name.

Raavan suppressed a smile. They were behaving exactly as he had expected. *These people are so easy to play. Their egos will be their undoing.*

The time had come to twist the knife.

'How dare you imagine that you can even come close to defeating an army that I lead?' asked Raavan with a half-sneer on his lips.

Dashrath stood up angrily, and his chair went flying back with a clatter. He thrust a finger in Raavan's direction. 'I'll be looking for you on the battlefield tomorrow, you upstart!'

Slowly and menacingly, Raavan rose from his chair, with his fist closed tight around the pendant that hung from a gold chain around his neck. Holding her hand gave him strength. It was also a constant reminder of why he was doing all this.

As Raavan's fist unclenched, Dashrath stared at the pendant. It was obvious that the emperor was horrified by what he saw. He probably thought the Lankan to be a monster who vandalised the bodies of his enemies.

Let Dashrath believe I am a cannibalistic beast. It will be a competitive advantage in battle.

'I assure you, I'll be waiting,' said Raavan, with a hint of amusement lacing his voice, as he watched Dashrath gape at him. 'I look forward to drinking your blood.'

That's enough. Let him stew in his anger.

Raavan turned around and strode out of the tent. Kubaer wobbled out hurriedly behind him, followed by the Lankan bodyguards.

—ॐ—

'You weren't able to sleep either?' asked Kumbhakarna.

Raavan turned towards his brother and smiled, letting go of the pendant in his hand.

It was the fifth hour of the fourth prahar—just an hour before midnight. Raavan had been standing on the ramparts of the Karachapa fort, looking towards the Sapt Sindhu camp and the many fires lit there. The night was quiet, and the sounds of conversation and laughter carried all the way to the fort.

'Looks like the enemy isn't sleeping either,' said Raavan.

Kumbhakarna laughed. 'These Sapt Sindhu Kshatriyas think war is a party.'

Raavan took a deep breath. 'By this time tomorrow, we will own the Sapt Sindhu.'

'Technically, won't it be Kubaer who owns it?'

'And who the hell do you think owns that fat slob?'

Kumbhakarna burst out laughing, and a moment later, Raavan joined in. Kumbhakarna put an arm around his brother.

'You should laugh more, Dada,' he said. 'She would have liked that.'

Raavan's right hand instinctively sought the pendant again. 'The best way to honour her is to destroy the army that defends the filthy society that killed her.'

Kumbhakarna remained silent. He knew there was no point in saying anything to Raavan about this.

Raavan stared at the inky black sea. He couldn't see them, but he knew his ships were there, anchored more than two kilometres from shore. Those ships, with their unusually broad bow sections, were crucial to his battle plans.

'The ships are to remain where they are,' said Raavan. 'I don't even want the rowboats to be lowered.'

'Obviously,' said Kumbhakarna.

Raavan liked how his brother always seemed to read his mind. With the Lankan ships far away, and the rowboats still aboard, the Ayodhyans would assume that the vessels would have no role to play in the battle. Even if there was a reserve force on board those ships, it would not be possible to bring them into combat quickly enough.

And that's how the trap would be set.

'Do you think they will fall for it?' asked Kumbhakarna.

'They have taken every bait so far, haven't they? I have faith in their arrogance. Their assumption that we are stupid traders and incapable of battle is what will cause them to make mistakes tomorrow. Also, remember they have five hundred thousand soldiers. We have a little over fifty thousand in the city. The odds must look very good to them. And people do reckless things when they think the odds are in their favour.'

'But unless the emperor commits them to an attack formation on the beach, our ships will be useless.'

'Precisely,' said Raavan, turning to look at Kumbhakarna. 'That's what I wanted to talk to you about.'

'I'll do it, Dada. I'll lead some of the battalions outside the city walls and offer them—us—up as bait. And when the Ayodhyans charge at us, you can do the rest with the ships.'

'You know almost exactly how my mind works,' said Raavan, smiling.

Kumbhakarna grinned. 'Almost? I always know what you are thinking.'

'Not entirely. We'll follow the battle plan that you just laid out. Except, I'll be the bait. And you'll be leading the ships.'

Kumbhakarna was aghast. 'No, Dada!'

'Kumbha…'

'No!'

'You've said to me often enough, that you'll do anything for me.'

'Yes, I will. I'll put my life at risk. And you'll win the battle.'

'Kumbha, I'm asking you to do something far more difficult. I want you to allow me to put my own life at risk.'

'That's not possible, Dada.'

'Kumbha, listen to me…'

'No!'

'Kumbha, that arrogant fool Dashrath hates me. I am the one who can drive him to act rashly. I have to be here.'

'Then I'll stay with you. Let Uncle Mareech lead the ships.'

'My life will be at risk, Kumbha. You are the only one I can trust to have my back.'

'Dada…'

'You are the only one who will ensure that I don't die.'

Kumbhakarna raised his hand to cover Raavan's mouth. 'Shhh! Maa has told you not to speak of your own death. Just because the Almighty has given you a mouth doesn't mean you have to use it to say stupid things!'

'Then make sure that I don't have to speak of it again. Lead the ships.'

'Dada!' Kumbhakarna was exasperated.

'It's an order, Kumbha. I can trust only you. You have to do this for me. You have to ensure that the ships sail in on time.'

Kumbhakarna clasped Raavan's hands tightly, not saying anything.

'We will win tomorrow,' said Raavan. 'And then our era will begin. History will never forget the names of Raavan and Kumbhakarna.'

—ۏۏI—

The next day, by the fourth hour of the second prahar, Raavan was battle-ready. Mounted on his warhorse, and waiting at the frontline.

Much to the shock of his enemies, and even some of his own followers, he had surrendered the immense defensive benefits of staying behind the well-designed fort walls. Instead, he had arranged about fifty thousand soldiers—most of his army—in standard chaturanga formation outside the fort walls, on the beach.

The Lankans now had their enemy to the front and the fort walls behind them. Presenting a seemingly soft target to Dashrath and his army.

A Lankan bait for the warriors of the Sapt Sindhu.

And the bait had been taken.

The emperor of Ayodhya had arranged his army along the beach, in a *suchi vyuha*, the *needle formation*. Dashrath knew that charging the fort from the landward side was not an option. Raavan's hordes had planted dense thorny bushes all around the fort, except along the wall that ran beside the beach. Dashrath's army could have cleared the bushes and created a path to reach the fort, but that would have taken weeks. With the Lankan army having scorched the land around Karachapa, and the resultant absence of food and water outside the fort, the option was simply not viable. The army had to attack before they ran out of rations.

Dashrath should have stopped to consider why Raavan had blocked all possible options of engagement except for the one along the beach. The king of Ayodhya had never lost a battle in his illustrious military career. His strategic instincts should have alerted him. But Raavan's insulting words the previous day still played on his mind, and he had let his pride get the better of his judgement.

The beach was wide by most standards, but it wasn't enough for a large army—hence Dashrath's tactical decision to form a suchi vyuha. The best of his troops would take position alongside him, at the front of the formation, while the rest of the army would fall into a long column behind them. They intended a rolling charge, whereby the first lines would strike the Lankan ranks, and after twenty minutes or so of battle, slip back, allowing the next line of warriors to charge in. It would be an unrelenting surge of battle-hardened soldiers aiming to scatter and decimate the enemy troops of Lanka.

Ashwapati, the king of Kekaya and Dashrath's father-in-law, had misgivings about this strategy. He had pointed out that only a few tens of thousands of their soldiers would be engaged in battle at any point of time, while most of the others waited at the back. By forcing the battle along the narrow beach rather than a large battleground, Raavan had negated the huge numerical advantage of the Sapt Sindhu army. But Ashwapati's concerns had been brushed aside by a confident Dashrath.

To Dashrath's mind, the Lankans were traders who were incapable of sophisticated battle tactics. The apparently stupid move of positioning the army outside the fort walls had only convinced him that Raavan and his troops had no understanding of what they were doing.

Far away, at the other end of the beach, Raavan looked to his right, to where his ships lay at anchor more than two kilometres out at sea. The rowboats were not visible. Kumbhakarna was following his instructions perfectly.

Raavan turned his gaze back to the Sapt Sindhuans.

His arrogant and overconfident enemies had not even sent spy boats out to investigate the broad bow sections of his ships. They really should have done that.

A smile played on his lips. *Bloody fools.*

Raavan flexed his shoulders and arms. The most irritating part of battle was the waiting. Waiting for the other side to charge. You couldn't allow yourself to be distracted and you couldn't waste energy either. He had warned his troops not to tire themselves out by screaming obscenities at the enemy or chanting war cries. They had been ordered to wait silently.

Clearly, Dashrath had given no such instructions to his soldiers. They were roaring their war cries, their voices rising and falling in a frenzy. Charging themselves on adrenaline. And tiring themselves out in the bargain.

Raavan had worn his trademark battle helmet with its six-inch horns sticking out threateningly from the sides. It was a challenge to his enemies; to Dashrath.

I am here. Come and get me.

Dashrath, meanwhile, was on his well-trained and imposing-looking war horse, surveying his amassed troops. He ran his eyes over them confidently. They were a rowdy, raucous bunch, with their swords already drawn, eager for battle. The horses, too, seemed to have succumbed to the excitement of the moment, making the soldiers pull hard at their reins, to hold them in check. Dashrath could almost smell the blood that would soon be shed; the massacre that would lead to victory!

He squinted as he observed the Lankans and their commander up ahead in the distance. He felt a jab of anger as he remembered Raavan's words from their last meeting. The upstart trader would soon feel his wrath. He drew his sword and held it aloft, and then bellowed the unmistakable war cry of his kingdom, Kosala, and its capital city, Ayodhya. '*Ayodhyatah Vijetaarah!*'

The conquerors from the unconquerable city!

Not everyone in his army was a citizen of Ayodhya, and yet they were proud to fight under the great Kosala banner. They echoed their emperor's war cry. 'Ayodhyatah Vijetaarah!'

Dashrath roared as he brought his sword down and spurred his horse. 'Kill them all! No mercy!'

'No mercy!' echoed the riders of the first charge, taking off behind their fearless lord.

Riding hard, riding fearlessly, riding to their own destruction.

As Dashrath and his finest warriors charged down the beach towards the Lankans, Raavan's troops remained immobile. When the enemy cavalry was just a few hundred metres away, Raavan unexpectedly turned his horse around and retreated from the frontlines, even as his soldiers held firm.

Raavan's strategy was clear—what was important was victory, not a display of manhood and courage. For Dashrath, however, brought up in the ways of the Kshatriyas, personal bravery was the most important trait of a general. Raavan's apparent cowardice infuriated him. He kicked his horse to a gallop, intending to mow down the Lankan frontline and quickly reach Raavan. And the Ayodhyans followed their lord, racing hard.

This was exactly what Raavan had hoped for. The Lankan frontline swung into action. The soldiers suddenly dropped their swords and picked up unnaturally long spears, almost twenty feet in length, which had been lying at their feet. Made of wood and metal, they were so heavy that it took two men to pick one up. The soldiers pointed these spears, tipped with sharp copper heads, directly at Dashrath's oncoming cavalry.

The mounted soldiers could not rein in their horses in time, and rode headlong into the spears, which tore into the unprepared beasts. Their riders were thrown forward while the horses collapsed under them. Even as the charge of Dashrath's cavalry was halted in its tracks, Lankan archers emerged, high on the walls of the Karachapa fort. They started shooting a continuous stream of arrows in a long arc from the heights of the fort ramparts, into the dense formation of Dashrath's troops at the back, shredding the Sapt Sindhu lines.

Many of Dashrath's warriors, who had been flung off their impaled horses, stumbled up to engage in fierce hand-to-hand battle with the enemy. Their king led the way as he swung his sword ferociously, killing all who dared to come in his path. But all around him, he could see the devastation being wrought upon his soldiers, who rapidly fell under the barrage of Lankan arrows and superbly trained swordsmen. Minutes later, Dashrath gestured to his flag bearer, who raised his flag high in response. It was the signal for the soldiers at the back to join the charge, in support of the first line.

This was the moment Raavan had been waiting for.

On Kumbhakarna's orders, the Lankan ships abruptly weighed anchor. Big ships always stay offshore, unless there is a proper harbour available. Naval warriors are transported to the beaches in small rowboats. But Kumbhakarna did not lower the rowboats. He ordered the ships themselves to speed to the beach! The sailors, who had been on full alert, extended oars and began to row rapidly to the shore. The ships' sails were up at full mast to help them catch the wind. Within minutes, arrows were being fired from the decks into the densely packed forces under Dashrath's command. The Lankan archers on the ships ripped through the massed ranks of the Sapt Sindhuans.

No one in Dashrath's army had factored in the possibility of the enemy ships beaching with speed; ordinarily, it would have cracked their hulls. What they didn't know was that these were amphibious crafts with specially constructed hulls that could absorb the shock of grounding. Even as the landing crafts stormed onto the beach with tremendous velocity, the broad bows of the hulls rolled out from the top. These were no ordinary bows of a standard hull. They were attached to the bottom of the hull by huge hinges, and they simply rolled out onto the sand like a landing ramp. This opened a gangway from the belly of the ships straight onto the beach. Cavalrymen mounted on disproportionately large horses imported from the West thundered out of the ships and straight onto the beach, mercilessly slicing through the men who blocked their path.

The Sapt Sindhuans were now battling at both ends—at the frontlines against Raavan's soldiers at the Karachapa fort walls, and at the rear, with the unexpected attackers from the ships, led by Kumbhakarna.

The trained instinct of a skilled warrior seemed to warn Dashrath that something terrible was ensuing at the rear guard.

As he strained to look beyond the sea of battling humanity, he detected a sudden movement to his left and raised his shield just in time to block a vicious blow from a Lankan soldier. With a ferocious roar, the king of Ayodhya swung brutally at his attacker, his sword slicing through a chink in the armour. The Lankan fell back, as his abdomen was ripped open and blood spurted out, accompanied by slick pink intestines that tumbled out in a rush. Dashrath turned away and looked behind him, to his troops in the rear formations.

'No!' he yelled.

A scenario he had never foreseen was playing out in front of his eyes. Caught in the vicious pincer attack of the archers and the foot soldiers at the fort walls in front, and the fierce Lankan cavalry from the beached ships at the back, the spirit of his all-conquering army was collapsing rapidly. Dashrath stared in disbelief as some of his men broke ranks and began to retreat.

'No!' he thundered. 'Fight! Fight! We are Ayodhya! The Unconquerables!'

Meanwhile, with everything going exactly as he had expected, Raavan kicked his horse into a canter and led some of his men down the beach on the left, skirting the sea. It was the only flank that was open to counter-attack by the Ayodhyans. Accompanied by his well-trained cavalry, Raavan hacked his way through the outer infantry lines before they could regroup. He had to hold his position at the fort walls while Kumbhakarna massacred the rear lines.

Raavan wasn't interested in killing Dashrath. That didn't matter at this point. His focus was on victory. And to achieve that, he had to break this last remaining holdout of the Ayodhyans.

Slowly but surely, hemmed in by the soldiers at the fort walls, the attackers led by Kumbhakarna at the rear, and the crushing attack by Raavan's men along the flanks, Dashrath's army fell into disarray. Panic set in among the ranks. And before long, a full disorderly retreat began.

This was not a battle anymore. It was a massacre.

But Raavan did not stop. He did not order a ceasefire. He did not allow his troops to show mercy.

His orders were clear and he shouted them aloud: 'Kill them all! No mercy! Kill them all!'

And his soldiers obeyed.

Chapter 20

Raavan tapped his empty wine goblet reflectively. An attendant at the other end of the chamber began making his way forward, but slowed as he noticed Kumbhakarna rising from his seat to attend to his brother.

Kumbhakarna refilled the goblet before pouring some wine for himself. Then he looked up and signalled to the attendant to leave. The man saluted and withdrew from the room.

It had been five months since the rout of the Sapt Sindhu army in the Battle of Karachapa. Dashrath had barely survived, saved by the bravery of his second wife, Kaikeyi, the daughter of the king of Kekaya, Ashwapati.

'Do you think we should have killed the emperor?' asked Kumbhakarna, taking a sip of wine and settling back in his comfortable chair.

'I did consider it,' said Raavan, shaking his head. 'But I think it's better this way. A quick death on the battlefield would have been a blessing for him. The humiliation of the defeat will extinguish his spirit little by little. The military failure, and the treaty we have imposed, will destroy his mental peace. With an unstable and insecure leader, the morale of the

Sapt Sindhu is unlikely to recover. They are not going to give us any trouble as we slowly squeeze the empire dry. If we had killed Dashrath, we would have turned him into a martyr. And martyrs can be dangerous. They can trigger rebellions.'

'So you think the bravery of Queen Kaikeyi has actually helped us.'

'She wasn't trying to help us, she was only trying to save her husband. But she is a brave woman. And I have no doubt she will be treated poorly by her ungrateful subjects. They don't know how to honour their heroes.'

'Apparently, Emperor Dashrath and his first queen Kaushalya were blessed with a son the day we defeated him in Karachapa. They call him Ram.'

'After the Vishnu?' asked Raavan, laughing softly in derision. Ram was the birth name of the sixth Vishnu, more commonly known as Parshu Ram. 'They must have high expectations of that baby!'

'The funny thing is, they blame the poor child for their defeat in Karachapa. Apparently, he brought them bad luck.'

'So our victory had nothing to do with my brilliant war strategies? It was all because some queen went into labour at the same time?!' Raavan laughed.

Kumbhakarna grinned back at him.

'You should laugh more often, Dada,' he said. 'Vedavatiji would have liked you to.'

'Stop telling me that again and again.'

'But it's the truth.'

'How do you know it's the truth? Did her soul come and inform you?'

Kumbhakarna shook his head. 'Dada, you will not be healed till you are able to think of her with a smile on your face. If you feel sadness and anger each time you remember her, you'll turn a beautiful memory into poison. It's been so many years. You have to learn to move on.'

'Are you saying I should forget how she died? That I should live in a state of foolish oblivion?' Raavan snapped.

Kumbhakarna remained calm. 'I did not say that. How is it possible for us to forget how she died? But that's not the only memory of her we have, right? It's one of the many memories she left behind. Spend time with those other memories too. The happy times you had with her. Then you will not drown in sadness whenever you think of her.'

'Maybe I like the sadness. It comforts me.'

'If you spend enough time with anything, you start liking it, even sadness.'

Raavan shook his head. Clearly, there was to be no more conversation on the subject.

Kumbhakarna fell silent.

'Anyway, when is the first instalment of the war reparations reaching Sigiriya?' asked Raavan.

'In a few weeks, Dada. In a few weeks, Lanka will go from merely rich to fantastically wealthy. Perhaps the wealthiest kingdom in the world.'

Before the Battle of Karachapa, Lanka was entitled to retain only ten per cent of the profits from its trade with the Sapt Sindhu. Ninety per cent belonged to Ayodhya, the representative of the empire. Ayodhya would, in turn, share this commission with its subordinate kingdoms. After the battle, Raavan had unilaterally slashed Ayodhya's commission to just nine per cent, keeping the rest for Lanka. In addition, he had drastically reduced the prices of all manufactured goods purchased from the Sapt Sindhu. If that wasn't enough, he had also ordered Ayodhya to return, with retrospective effect, the surplus amount that the kingdoms had been paid over the previous three years, going by the new calculation—as war reparations. Raavan knew that this sweeping reduction in commissions would pauperise the empire over time, while making Lanka extremely prosperous. Of course, since he was going to keep half the increased Lankan profits, he would soon be stupendously rich as well. And powerful.

'What next, Dada?' asked Kumbhakarna.

Raavan walked over to a large window in the chamber and looked out at the verdant gardens beyond. His mansion in Sigiriya was a short distance from the giant monolithic rock that housed the palace of Kubaer—chief-trader of Lanka and the richest man in the world.

Kubaer may not have known too much about warfare, but he did understand the need to protect his immense wealth. Over the last few decades, he had vastly improved the defensive systems of the city. Sigiriya was surrounded by rolling boulder-strewn hills. Each of the tall boulders had structures built on their flat tops, to house soldiers who could fight off any trespassers from an unassailable height. This was in addition to the sturdy walls and moats that surrounded the city.

But Kubaer did not concern himself only with security. Despite his garish taste in clothes and jewellery, he had a surprisingly fine eye for architecture. And he had turned what was already an achingly beautiful city into a truly exquisite symbol of grace and elegance.

The city, built on a large plateau, was adorned with stunning gardens and public walkways. Beautifully landscaped lawns, irrigated by waterways and underground channels, dotted the outskirts, while tall, evergreen trees spread their branches on either side of the main roads. Even the many boulders within the city had been incorporated into what the Sigiriyans called boulder gardens, with intricate fountains adding to their grace and beauty. There were tastefully designed halls for public functions, libraries, amphitheatres, lakes for boating, and everything else that was required for civilised living. Lanka was a part of the larger Vedic world and many temples to different Vedic Gods graced various parts of the city. The largest of the temples, of course, was dedicated to Lord Parshu Ram, the sixth Vishnu and the founder of the Malayaputra tribe. This temple had been built and consecrated by the great Rishi Vishwamitra himself.

Raavan, however, was not swayed by all of Sigiriya's fineries. His attention was focused on the monolith called Lion's Rock, which rose a sheer two hundred metres from the surrounding countryside. The city was named after this rock; Sigiriya harked back to the Sanskrit *Sinhagiri* or *Lion's Hill*. At the top of the monolith was the massive palace of Kubaer. It represented the triumph of human imagination over nature's bounty. Colossal, and yet delicately refined.

At the base of the monolith were roughly concentric terraced gardens that showcased the skilful use of water-proofed brick walls. Each of these gardens rose a little higher than the one next to it, and a winding road led up to the rock, through lush parks speckled with fountains. The pathway from the northern side led up to one of the most stunning architectural achievements of Sigiriya: The Lion Gate.

The Lion Gate was called so because there actually was a gargantuan lion's head carved high above the entrance. The gate stood between the lion's two front paws, each the height of an average man, while the massive head reared up, visible to all the citizens of Sigiriya from far and wide. The monolith itself was shaped like the body of a colossal lion, seated in regal splendour, its head surveying its territory from high above.

It was a magnificent sight.

On top of the monolith, across an area spread over two square kilometres, stood the massive palace complex of Kubaer, complete with pools, gardens, private chambers, courts, offices, and unimaginable luxuries designed to please the richest man in the world.

'What is next is that we take control of that,' said Raavan, pointing towards Lion's Rock.

'What!' Kumbhakarna couldn't conceal his shock. 'Isn't it too early to get rid of Kubaer, Dada? We are still not strong enough and...'

Raavan frowned. 'Not that,' he clarified. 'That.'

Kumbhakarna followed the pointing finger more closely this time. Raavan was pointing towards Lion's Rock, but not at Kubaer's palace. The steps going up from the Lion Gate led to a mid-level terrace, about one hundred metres lower than the top of the monolith. The pathway carved into the rock and leading to the terrace had a wall alongside it that was made of evenly cut bricks covered with polished white plaster. So highly polished that anyone walking by could see their reflection in it. It was called, rather unimaginatively, the Mirror Wall. Beyond the Mirror Wall, the rock was designed to look like a cloth saddle for the massive lion that the monolith represented. The saddle was covered with gorgeous frescoes depicting beautiful women. Nobody knew who these figures represented. They had been painted during Trishanku Kaashyap's time, and had been lovingly maintained. Beyond the frescoes, the pathway led to the lower-level palaces, behind lavish gardens, ponds, moats and ramparts which protected the upper-citadel, where Kubaer's personal palace stood.

It was these lower-level palaces that Raavan was pointing at.

'Meghdoot?' asked Kumbhakarna.

The lower-level palaces housed some of the concubines and younger wives of Kubaer. But one of these palaces was the home of Meghdoot, the prime minister, who was in charge of revenues, taxes, Customs and general administration. Raavan, being the general in command of the Lankan army and the police was, effectively, the head of all the muscle power. Meghdoot was head of all the money. Together, they ran the kingdom for Kubaer. If Raavan were to add Meghdoot's portfolio to his own, he would effectively have more power than the chief-trader. After that, replacing him would only be a matter of time. A soft coup.

Kumbhakarna was careful with his words, even though they were alone. 'You do realise that we would have to—'

'Yes, I do,' interrupted Raavan. 'But it must look like an accident. Otherwise it will be difficult for me to take over.'

'Hmm...'

'It's a difficult task. We can't have a thug do it. We need an artist.'

'I'll find someone,' Kumbhakarna said thoughtfully.

—१६१—

It had been a month since Raavan had ordered the assassination of Meghdoot, the prime minister of Lanka, but Kumbhakarna had been unable to find a way forward. He had finally turned to their uncle for help. And today, Mareech had informed him that the man for the job had been found.

Eager to update his brother with this news, Kumbhakarna went looking for him, but he was nowhere to be found. Finally, he went down to the secret chamber hidden away in the deep interiors of the palace. No one apart from the two brothers was permitted entry here, just like in Raavan's private chamber in Gokarna.

As soon as he walked in, Kumbhakarna turned and locked the door behind him. A single torch had been lit. His brother was inside.

The first thing he saw in the semi-darkness was a gold-plated Raavanhatha. It lay on the ground, broken, its strings ripped apart. In the deathly quiet of the chamber, he thought he heard the sound of someone crying.

As his eyes adjusted to the darkness, Kumbhakarna saw Raavan slumped on a tall wooden stool, his back to the door. His head was in his hands and his entire body shook as he cried. Deep, anguished sobs wrenched from the depths of sorrow and despair.

In front of Raavan stood an easel. On it, a vaguely familiar image had been scratched out with rough, angry strokes that nearly concealed its outlines. It took a moment for Kumbhakarna to decode the drawing, but then he saw that it was an unfinished profile of Vedavati. Pregnant, her form full and voluptuous. The outlines sketched and ready for the colours to be filled in. The eyes were half drawn—and that's where Raavan seemed to have given up.

Kumbhakarna knew that Raavan had stopped painting Vedavati since that day of the gruesome killings. Until then, she had grown older in his imagination, gradually, year after year. And he had been able to see her in his mind's eye, in fine detail, almost as though she stood beside him while he painted. But after her death, the will to paint had died too, and now, when he sought to capture her on canvas again, it seemed that the blessing, the power of creative vision, had vanished.

Kumbhakarna was aware that even he couldn't fully comprehend the rage and resentment his brother felt. Only an artist can understand the despair of being abandoned by his muse, his lifelong inspiration. Only someone who has loved can know the immeasurable agony of losing the object of one's passion. Only a devout believer who has touched the Divine can know the soul-emptying misery of his Goddess being taken from him.

Kumbhakarna walked over to Raavan quietly.

He knelt beside his elder brother and put an arm around him. Raavan turned and buried his face in his brother's shoulder, weeping as though nothing could comfort him again, ever.

They held each other for a long while, not saying anything. Their shared grief drowned everything else out—all thoughts, all words.

It was Raavan who broke the silence. 'I need control… of Lanka… quickly.'

'Yes, Dada.'

'I need to destroy… I need to… those bastards… Sapt Sindhu… destroy completely…'

Kumbhakarna remained silent.

Raavan controlled himself with some effort, then said, 'Get me that assassin.'

'Yes, Dada.'

'Quickly.'

'Yes, I will.'

When you fill a clogged drain with more water than it can hold, it's bound to overflow and contaminate everything around it. When grief overwhelms someone, when they are enraged at what fate has done to them, their fury often overflows and is inflicted upon the world.

That's the only way in which they can cope with their own life—a life that holds no meaning anymore.

—रॐI—

'Are you sure?' asked Raavan, his expression quizzical.

Raavan and Kumbhakarna had travelled to Gokarna for this meeting. They didn't want to risk anyone in Sigiriya getting even a whiff of their plan.

Mareech and Akampana had just entered the house through a side entrance, hidden from view. They were accompanied by a young, wiry man.

Mareech said to Raavan, his voice soft but confident, 'Trust me. I have seen some of his work myself. He is exceptional. Right up there with the Vishkanyas.'

The *Vishkanyas*, or *poison-bearing women*, were renowned assassins. They were raised from a very young age to be killers, with small doses of poison being administered to them daily. Eventually they became immune to the poison. But even a kiss from them was known to be fatal. And if their poison didn't get you, their weapons would. They were the deadliest killers the world had ever known.

'Right up there with the Vishkanyas?' Kumbhakarna did not try to hide his scepticism, as he looked at the man who stood next to Akampana. 'Really, Uncle, there has to be some limit to exaggeration.'

Mareech looked at the potential assassin. He could see why they did not think much of him. Of small build, with long curly hair and dimples on both cheeks, he exuded a genial charm. There was not a scar in sight. More than a cold-blooded assassin, he looked like a no-good philanderer who knew only how to seduce women.

'Who's next on the list?' asked Raavan, irritated that he had come all the way to Gokarna to meet someone who was evidently unfit for the job.

Mareech didn't answer. He turned to the assassin and nodded.

The lithe body moved with lightning speed, reaching behind Akampana in a flash. Before the dandy trader could even react, a finger had jabbed him hard and precisely on a pressure point at the back of his neck. Instantly, Akampana was paralysed from the neck down. The attacker grabbed him by the shoulders and gently let him slide down to the ground.

Akampana was able to move his head, just about. His eyes swivelled left and right in panic. 'I can't feel anything! I can't feel anything! Help me! Oh Lord Indra!' He called out to Raavan. 'Iraiva! Iraiva! Please help!'

But his 'true lord' was laughing. Positively surprised by what he had seen. He turned to his brother. 'This chap isn't bad, Kumbha!'

Kumbhakarna wasn't amused, however. He said to Mareech, who was laughing along with Raavan, 'Uncle, tell him to let Akampanaji go at once. This is not right. He is one of us.'

Akampana was still jabbering in terror. 'Lord Raavan! Iraiva! Don't kill me! Please! I haven't done anything!'

Raavan controlled his mirth and asked Mareech, 'Uncle, this is reversible, right?'

'Yes, my lord.' The cause of all the anxiety answered Raavan directly. 'I can release the hold. But, if I have to, I can also kill him peacefully while he is still paralysed.'

Hearing this, Akampana moaned again in panic, 'Iraiva! Help!'

'Oh, shut up, Akampana!' said Raavan, before turning to the assassin with keen interest. 'So does the victim feel anything?'

'Not when I work this particular pressure point. There are others that will leave him paralysed but feeling the pain.'

Raavan didn't conceal the fact that he was impressed. 'What is this man's name, Uncle?'

'His very name means death,' said Mareech. 'Mara.'

Raavan turned back to the young man. 'All right, Mara. You are hired.'

'Iraiva!' screamed Akampana. 'Release me!'

Raavan looked at Akampana and then at Mara. 'Can you release his body but paralyse his tongue?'

Everyone burst out laughing. Even Akampana smiled weakly.

Kumbhakarna was still not amused. The two extra arms on top of his shoulders were stiff. He turned to his elder brother, disapproval writ large on his face. 'Dada...'

'All right, all right,' Raavan said.

He gestured to Mara. 'Release him.'

Chapter 21

'Not bad,' said Vishwamitra, clearly impressed. 'Not bad at all.'

Vishwamitra and Arishtanemi were in Agastyakootam, the hidden capital of the Malayaputras. It had been a year since the Battle of Karachapa.

'Yes, Raavan truly is turning out to be the perfect villain,' said Arishtanemi. 'There is no person more hated in the Sapt Sindhu than him. Not only did he defeat the empire comprehensively, he has imposed such an extortionate treaty on them that they will soon go from being the wealthiest land in the world to among the poorest.'

'When I heard of the conditions he had proposed, I assumed Raavan was asking for an outrageous cut so that when he finally settled for less, his magnanimity would be lauded. Clearly, that is not what he had in mind. He is actually ramming the terms of the treaty down their throats. Ayodhya has never been so weak. Which means that finally, that... that... spineless abomination of a man has been shown his place.' Vishwamitra couldn't bring himself to speak the name he despised above all.

Arishtanemi knew his guru was referring to Vashishtha, the *raj guru*, the *royal sage* of the Ayodhya court and chief adviser of the royal family. As always, the mere thought of Vashishtha was enough to agitate Vishwamitra.

Arishtanemi smoothly changed the subject. 'Yes, Ayodhya is weaker now than it has ever been. And the way Raavan forced Kubaer's hand was masterly, for the chief-trader himself would never have pushed the treaty and the war reparations to this extent. He may be greedy, but he is also a coward. And let's not forget, the assassination of Meghdoot was a deft touch, impeccably timed.'

'Are you sure about that?' asked Vishwamitra, forgetting about Vashishtha for the moment. 'Because I have heard conflicting reports. There are enough people who believe that his death was caused by drowning—accidental drowning.'

'I am sure, Guruji. He didn't drown. He *was* drowned.'

'But—'

'It was beautifully planned. Everyone knew that Meghdoot was rehearsing for his role as the doomed poet Kalidas, in his favourite play, *Jalsandesh*. And we all know how that famous lake scene played out.'

'But I heard a wine glass and a decanter were found next to the pool where he drowned.'

'Also a part of the setup. Meghdoot was a colourful character who liked his wine and women, so it made sense to place a glass of wine there. A red herring, if there ever was one. Besides, there was no sign of injury on Meghdoot. No signs of any struggle. The post-mortem showed there was water in his lungs. He died by drowning. Everything fits too well to be true, Guruji. There is no reason for anyone to suspect anything.'

'So, you think it was too perfect?'

'Exactly. Real life is messy. Nothing is ever perfect, but this death was. That's what got me suspicious, and I decided to investigate.'

'So, who is the person behind this?'

'Someone called Mara. That's obviously not his real name. Which mother would name her child "death"? I don't know anything about his background yet, but wherever he came from, he is a genius. I suspect he is young and still honing his craft. There are things he needs to work on.'

'Such as?'

'Well, for one, he is not secretive enough. He has shown his face to too many people. He is good, but he can be trained to improve.'

'Is that what you intend to do?'

'I do believe Mara could be a useful asset for us, Guruji.'

'I'll leave that to you. Do what you have to. I am more interested in what Raavan is going to do next. When do you think he will take Kubaer out?'

'I don't think he will, for now. With Meghdoot gone, he controls both the revenue department and the military directly—the first Lankan minister to do so. He has, in fact, already started excluding Kubaer from *sabhas*, saying that the voice of the chief-trader is too pure to be heard in these petty *administration meetings*. He is, for all practical purposes, already the king of Lanka. There is no need for him to upset the balance by overthrowing Kubaer.'

'Hmm… clever move. But I am a bit sceptical about the wisdom of enforcing such ridiculous terms on the Sapt Sindhu. He will end up killing the golden goose that feeds him.'

'Is that relevant, Guruji? We have him exactly where we need him. He is setting himself up to be the perfect villain. All of the Sapt Sindhu will grow to dread him. We should start searching for a Vishnu now.'

'Of course. But we can't lose sight of Raavan's motives either. We need to know what's going on in his mind so that we can control him better. It is important to understand exactly what is pushing him to take this position on Ayodhya. I don't think it's just his lust for money and power. He seems to be driven by a sort of unbridled, almost unhinged rage. Because his actions defy all logic—of business and politics.'

'I'll find out, Guruji.'

'Also, let's start charging him more for the cave material and the medicines.'

Arishtanemi chuckled. 'Yes, Guruji. I was thinking that too. We'll certainly put the money to better use than he will.'

—ॐ—

Raavan flung open the door to the ship's cabin and walked briskly in, his face sweaty and flushed.

Kumbhakarna, looking similarly exhausted, followed his brother. There were two Lankan soldiers with him. As he entered the cabin, he stopped the soldiers outside. 'Keep your swords drawn and stay vigilant. Don't allow anyone else in.'

Raavan had already poured two goblets of wine for them. He handed one to his younger brother.

'Thanks, Dada,' said Kumbhakarna, regarding the bloodstained goblet for a moment before draining the wine in one gulp. There was nothing like good wine after the exertions of a battle.

Raavan downed his glass just as efficiently. He was still trying to catch his breath.

It had been two years since the Battle of Karachapa. With the Sapt Sindhu having capitulated completely, money was pouring into Lanka at a furious pace. Raavan was now the prime minister of the island kingdom and the general of the Lankan army, making him the most powerful man in the land. Kubaer had been reduced to a ruler in name only.

Mareech and Akampana ran the twenty-nine-year-old Raavan's business empire under Kumbhakarna's able supervision. Mareech had been tasked with expanding the business as far and wide as possible and dominating global trade. He had already appointed 'approved key traders' in every kingdom of the Sapt Sindhu. All trade with the empire was done only through these appointees. This was a strategic move—it gave the Lankans greater control over their trade with the Sapt Sindhu, and also allowed them to build loyal allies in each kingdom.

Akampana's task was to ensure that the accounting and financing of this vast enterprise—the biggest business corporation in history—was clean, with no scope for either employees or associates to drain money out through corruption.

All their plans had been executed smoothly so far. Raavan was now wealthier than Kubaer and had begun to focus more on enjoying his immense wealth. The richest man in the world wanted his lifestyle to reflect his newfound status—the finest wine and food, the most beautiful women, music and dance—only the best of everything would do for Raavan. He indulged in all that satiated his *desire*, his *kaama*.

The palaces situated on the lower levels of Lion's Rock had been taken over soon after the previous prime minister's unfortunate death. Raavan had evicted Meghdoot's family and Kubaer's junior wives and concubines, merging their palaces into a sweeping, opulent estate over which he presided with all the pomp of a ruler.

He had also begun to travel for pleasure—something he had rarely done before—accompanied by Kumbhakarna and a few of his chosen concubines. It was as they were sailing peacefully over calm seas towards the Arabian Peninsula that one of the ship's officers had burst into Raavan's cabin, with the news that a pirate vessel had been spotted speeding towards them. The brothers had just returned to the cabin after taking care of the unwanted diversion.

'Fools!' said Raavan. 'Attacking us! What were they thinking?'

Kumbhakarna rose from his chair, wine glass in hand, took Raavan's from him and walked over to the table. He put them down before cleaning his bloodied hands with a towel. Then he wiped the goblets clean. When he was done, he poured out some more wine and walked back to his brother, bearing the two goblets and the piece of cloth. 'Here, Dada. Use this to wipe your hands. Lord Indra alone knows whose blood that is.'

Raavan looked down at his bloodied hands. His clothes were stained red too. But not one speck of blood on his expensive clothes or his body was his own. There was not a cut on him. He sniffed the blood on his hand before sticking out his tongue and licking it.

'Yuck!' Kumbhakarna made a face.

'Hmmm,' said Raavan, thoughtfully. 'It's an interesting taste.'

Kumbhakarna, still looking nauseated, held the goblet away from Raavan. 'You need to clean your mouth first.'

'I'll just wash it down,' Raavan said, as he took the goblet from Kumbhakarna and gulped down the wine. He wiped his mouth with the back of his hand, smearing some more blood on his face. 'So, what were we talking about? Before those bonehead pirates attacked?'

Kumbhakarna shook his head, trying not to think about what he had just witnessed. 'We were talking about meeting Vibhishan and Shurpanakha. You promised maa you would, remember?'

After Vishrava and his second wife, Crataeis, had passed away, Kaikesi had decided to adopt their children, Vibhishan and Shurpanakha. The two children, accompanied by some others from the ashram of the great sage Vishrava, had found their way to their wealthy half-brother Raavan's abode in Lanka, seeking refuge. They had not anticipated the reception they would get there. Raavan, still angry with his father, had thrown his half-siblings out of his home and refused to shelter them. But Kaikesi had stood up to her son and insisted on bringing them back, saying she had responsibilities towards them.

Raavan did not approve of his mother's act of apparent altruism. 'Kumbha, you know what maa is really like. Her compassion is all fake. She's only taken them in to show the world how virtuous she is.'

'Dada, what's wrong with you? How can you say that about maa?'

'I haven't said anything untrue. Tell me, what has she done to deserve any of this? What sacrifices has she made for our happiness? I am the one who is working hard and paying for her comfortable life in that magnificent mansion. I am the one who pays for all the charity that she does—and publicises.

And I am the one who is paying for those useless half-siblings of ours whom she has decided to adopt and shower with attention. She just struts around exclaiming, "Oh, look! Look, how great I am."' Raavan opened his eyes wide and mimicked his mother's slightly high-pitched voice. 'She's a fraud. Let her try to build her own life by herself. Then she can prance around the world teaching lessons in morality, for all I care. I am tired of her virtue signalling.'

'Dada, I wish you wouldn't be so harsh on her. Besides, what do Vibhishan and Shurpanakha have to do with any of this? They are little children.'

The outgrowths on Kumbhakarna's shoulders were stiff and straight, a clear sign that he was upset.

Raavan sighed. 'You are too genuinely kind for your own good, Kumbha.'

Kumbhakarna remained silent.

Raavan threw his arms up in surrender. 'All right, all right! I'll meet them when I get back to Sigiriya.'

Kumbhakarna smiled. 'That's my boy.'

'Excuse me!' said Raavan, straightening up. 'What do you mean "boy"? Don't forget I am your elder brother.'

'Yeah, yeah,' said Kumbhakarna, laughing.

Raavan smiled at him. 'I let you get away with too much.'

'That's because you can't manage without me.'

'Well, my life manager, tell me, what have you done about Kubaer?'

'We've discussed this already, Dada. There's no need to try and remove him. He's practically your prisoner in any case. He can't step out of his upper citadel without passing through our lower terraces. His bodyguards are our men. We control his life.'

'But what is the point of having him around at all?'

'Listen to me, Dada. Kubaer's idea of doing away with taxes within Lanka was brilliant. We don't need tax revenues in any case, with the flood of money coming in from the Sapt Sindhu. And by proclaiming that all citizens are exempt from paying any taxes at all, he has bought the loyalty of his subjects for life.'

Raavan shook his hand. 'No. It's been too long. I want to be known as the king of Lanka.'

'Sounds to me like you already have a plan.'

'Obviously. That's why I am talking to you.'

'What do you want me to do?'

'I'll tell you… but only after we're finished with these guys.' Raavan drained his glass and threw it away, then he got up and strode briskly to the door.

Kumbhakarna followed in his brother's footsteps.

They were on the main deck of the ship in no time. It was a pleasure boat, so the deck was massive and grand. At the moment though, it resembled a battleground. The bodies of the pirates lay all over. Not one Lankan had been killed, though a few had suffered minor injuries. Next to the large ship, bobbing in the sea, was the much smaller pirate craft, attached to Raavan's vessel with grappling hooks. The pirates had assumed their target carried some rich, chicken-hearted businessman whose crew could be easily overpowered. They had chased down Raavan's ship and boarded it, screaming fierce battle cries. Regrettably for the pirates, that had been the extent of their fierceness. They had come face to face with soldiers who were amongst the finest warriors in the Indian Ocean. Most of the pirates were dead within the first few minutes of battle. The rest, many of them grievously injured, had been lined up at the far end of the deck, shackled and on their knees.

The brothers walked up to the prisoners, their loyal Lankan soldiers close behind them. They stopped in front of a stocky young man who was on his knees, blood flowing from a deep cut on his forehead.

'So, Dada, what do you want to do with these morons? Should we find out who they work for? Maybe we can sell them as slaves somewhere in the Mediterranean?'

By way of answer, Raavan simply flexed his shoulders, then drew his sword and in one swift, mighty blow, beheaded the man kneeling in front of him.

Kumbhakarna shrugged. 'Or we could do that.'

The Lankans followed the example of their lord and commander. They drew their swords and put every one of the pirates out of their misery.

Chapter 22

Three years had passed since the Battle of Karachapa. Raavan was now the sole ruler of Lanka, having got rid of Kubaer. It had been surprisingly easy.

The main contact for trade in Ayodhya for the Lankans was a woman called Manthara. Over the years, Kubaer had come to trust her implicitly. However, a message from Raavan asking her to choose between higher commissions for compliance on the one hand, and severe punishment in case of disobedience on the other, had made the pragmatic Manthara switch sides in a hurry. On Raavan's instructions, she had put the idea in Kubaer's head that Raavan had hired an assassin to get rid of him. This was not the truth, but Kubaer believed it. To nudge him further towards the edge, Manthara let him know that his former prime minister, Meghdoot, had not died by accidental drowning but had, in fact, been assassinated on Raavan's orders. This, of course, was the truth.

The terrified Kubaer had quickly abdicated the throne, publicly announcing that he had nothing more to achieve. He now wished to retire to Devabhoomi in the Himalayas, he said, and perhaps even go further, to Kailash. He was seen off in Lanka with the respect and honour due to someone who was on his way to taking *sanyas*. But *ascetism* was far from Kubaer's mind, especially since Raavan had allowed him to leave with most of his personal wealth, as well as his wives and favourite concubines. He had even allowed Kubaer the use of the Pushpak Vimaan to travel north—the flying vehicle was now officially Raavan's property. And Kubaer had been appropriately obsequious while publicly appreciating Raavan's generosity.

To ensure that there were no counterclaims or even grumbling about Raavan's right to the Lankan throne, Kumbhakarna had suggested that Kubaer himself crown the new king before he left. The ever-reasonable trader was only too willing to place the crown on Raavan's head. Once a ruler had publicly abdicated his throne in favour of another, there could be no earthly reason for the latter to assassinate him. It was only logical.

As soon as he became the undisputed king of Lanka, Raavan abandoned the rather tame title Kubaer had preferred, of chief-trader. Instead, he assumed far more grandiose ones, such as the King of Kings, Emperor of Emperors, Ruler of the Three Worlds, Beloved of the Gods, and a few others. When Kumbhakarna joked about the pompous new titles, he was told by his brother to shut up.

With everything going just the way he wanted it to, Raavan should have been happy and satisfied. However, right at this moment, he didn't look particularly pleased.

'I don't know why I let you talk me into this,' he said.

Raavan and Kumbhakarna were on their way to the lower-citadel palace that was now Kaikesi's abode. The brothers had moved into Kubaer's magnificent palace on top of Lion's Rock. To reach the lower citadel, they had to pass through the large, flat piece of ground that had been converted into a landing pad for the Pushpak Vimaan. They were followed by a phalanx of one hundred bodyguards, who maintained a discreet distance from the king and his brother.

'Dada, I know you are unhappy about this, but they moved into their palace a week ago. They have been delaying the *grahpravesh puja* just for you. You know delaying such a ceremony is inauspicious. We can't keep them waiting anymore,' Kumbhakarna replied.

'She has deliberately brought some priests from the Sapt Sindhu for the ceremony. She knows that will irritate me. When will you understand how devious our mother is?' Raavan snapped.

Kumbhakarna thought it best to ignore his elder brother's dark mood and continued walking.

As they neared the palace, they could see Kaikesi standing at the entrance, with the young Vibhishan and Shurpanakha hiding behind her. Both children were under ten years of age, and were terrified of Raavan. The priests Kaikesi had invited were standing next to her, issuing instructions in a low voice. At least a hundred maids stood behind them, responding to every demand. Kaikesi was enjoying the luxuries that came with her son's good fortune.

As soon as Raavan was within hearing distance, Kaikesi glanced at the sun and declared, 'You are late.'

'I can leave,' said Raavan.

His mother pursed her lips and muttered something under her breath. Then she took the puja thali from the priest standing next to her and looped it in small circles around Raavan's face. Three times. As Raavan stepped aside, she repeated the action for Kumbhakarna.

'Come in,' she said gruffly, waiting for Raavan and Kumbhakarna to enter before her. As Raavan was about to cross the threshold into the palace, she said loudly, 'Right foot first.'

Raavan stopped, glanced at his mother, then at the priests standing next to her, and put his left foot forward.

'Dada!' Kumbhakarna exhaled noisily in frustration, then conscientiously and carefully placed his right foot over the threshold. 'The palace looks beautiful, Maa,' he said. 'You have done a wonderful job, and in such little time.'

Kaikesi looked at her son and sighed, tears welling up in her eyes. 'Forgive me for being so emotional, my son. It's just that it's rare for me to receive compliments these days. I do so much for others, yet no one appreciates me.'

Raavan turned around abruptly and barked, 'I need to leave quickly, Maa. I have lots of work to do. Where is this stupid puja supposed to happen? Let's get it over with.'

Kaikesi raised her voice immediately. 'Mind your words, Raavan. It's not a stupid puja! It's the way in which we honour our ancestors and our culture. Don't be disrespectful!'

Raavan stepped closer to his mother. 'You're right. It's not a stupid puja. It's a *very* stupid puja.'

Kumbhakarna had had enough of this childishness. 'Stop it, both of you!' He looked around to see all the maids studiously examining the floor, while the priests seemed absorbed in setting out the materials for the puja. Only young Vibhishan and Shurpanakha looked visibly petrified. Kumbhakarna turned back to his mother and elder brother. 'Let's do the ceremonies quickly. Then you will not have to cause each other any more grief.'

'He doesn't need me to cause him any grief,' said Kaikesi bitingly. 'He's quite capable of doing it to himself.'

Raavan turned to her, fists clenched tight. 'What do you mean, Maa?'

'You know exactly what I mean.'

'I dare you to say it openly. What do you mean?'

Kumbhakarna tried to calm tempers once again. 'Listen, let's do this puja later. We'll come back. Let's...'

Kumbhakarna fell silent as Raavan raised his hand. He stepped closer to his mother, towering over her. The air between them bristled with hostility. 'Say it, Maa. What did you mean?'

Kaikesi didn't step back. The source of all her wealth and power was her eldest son, yet she had grown to despise him. She also knew that however angry he was, Raavan would never harm her. She could get away with saying almost anything. 'Don't forget that I am your mother. I know every little detail of what happens in your life. And you know who I am talking about.'

'Who are you talking about? Say it. Say it!'

Kumbhakarna pleaded with them again. 'Maa, please don't say anything.' He turned to Raavan. 'Dada, let's go. Come on.'

Raavan continued to glare at his mother, molten rage in his eyes. 'Say it!'

'It was all your fault! If you had honoured your mother and listened to her as a good son should, none of this would have happened! Understand that the Gods punished you. They punished someone innocent because of you. It was because of your lack of dharma that the Kanyakumari, the noble Vedavati, was killed!'

'MAA!' Raavan screamed as he reached for his knife.

'Stop!' Kumbhakarna rushed to stand between them, pushing Raavan back and away from their mother. 'Dada, no!'

Raavan was out of control now. He stabbed the knife in the air as he raged at his mother. 'You bitch! You can't survive a day without my protection! And you dare to take her name! You dare to insult the Kanyakumari! You dare to insult Ved...'

Raavan's voice continued to resonate through the corridors as Kumbhakarna almost dragged his brother out of the palace.

—रोI—

'Love?' asked Vishwamitra, genuinely surprised.

Following the great maharishi's orders, Arishtanemi had investigated the likely cause of Raavan's attitude towards the Sapt Sindhu. And he had, by chance, stumbled on the truth.

'Yes. Apparently, he was in love with a Kanyakumari.'

'Which Kanyakumari?'

'Vedavati.'

Vishwamitra narrowed his eyes and looked at his lieutenant. 'Arishtanemi, how am I supposed to know which Kanyakumari that is? You think I know all their birth-names? Which temple? And for what period?'

'Sorry, Guruji. She was the Kanyakumari of Vaidyanath. And this was a long time ago. Probably two decades at least.'

'So he met her when he was a child?'

'Yes, I believe so.'

'But we never saw her with him, did we? Not since we began tracking him.'

'Apparently they met in his father's ashram and didn't see each other for many years after. Then they met again, perhaps eight or nine years ago. I'm not entirely sure of the time.'

'So you are saying he was in love with her all this time, through his childhood? Even though he didn't meet her for several years?'

'Apparently so.'

'What sense does that make?'

'It makes no sense, but that's what happened. In any case, when he found her again, with his brother's help, she was married to someone else.'

Vishwamitra leaned back as the realisation hit him. 'Lord Parshu Ram be merciful! Is this the former Kanyakumari who was killed in her own village? What was the name of that place... Todee?'

'Yes, Guruji.'

'Her husband was also killed, wasn't he?'

'Yes.'

'And the entire village was exterminated? Brutally?'

'Yes. Nobody really knows what happened, since there were no survivors. Some people from a neighbouring village discovered the bodies a few days later. They chased the wild animals away and performed the funeral ceremonies for all the dead villagers of Todee.'

'But I remember hearing that the corpses of the Kanyakumari and her husband had been cremated with full Vedic honours.'

'Yes. That's what I heard as well.'

'There's only one interpretation possible then,' Vishwamitra said.

Arishtanemi nodded. 'I was thinking the same thing, Guruji. Raavan was attracted to Vedavati, but by the time he found her, she was married to someone else. She must have refused to leave her husband for him, and enraged at her rejection, Raavan killed her and her husband. Perhaps he tried to rape her... we will never know the complete truth. To wipe out any evidence of his crime, he must have massacred the entire village.'

Vishwamitra was too appalled to speak. He'd had a long life—there were some who thought he was at least a hundred and fifty years old—and had seen some terrible things in his time. The world had never been a kind place, but savagery of this magnitude was beyond his imagination. Not since the reign of Trishanku Kaashyap could he remember hearing of anything like it.

'Well, Guruji,' said Arishtanemi, 'we wanted a villain, and we've got one. A monstrous one at that.'

'Kumbhakarna could not have been involved in this, surely,' Vishwamitra said. He had always had a soft spot for the little Naga boy who had come to see him with his mother many years ago.

'I cannot be sure, Guruji. But he is completely under Raavan's thumb.'

Vishwamitra clasped his hands under his chin, deep in thought. Then he took a deep breath and shook his head. 'I met that Kanyakumari once, the Kanyakumari from Vaidyanath... I remember her. She was still a child then. Joyous, and kind to everyone, even animals. How a person treats those weaker than them is a good indicator of their character. Yes, I remember her... She could mimic the sound of a hill myna almost accurately. And she mimicked me as well.' Vishwamitra smiled as he said this. 'A wonderful girl, pure of mind and heart... a truly noble soul. She did not deserve to die the way she did.'

'We have to create an India where such purity and nobility are respected once again, Guruji.'

There was a brief silence, then Vishwamitra said decisively, 'We have to find the Vishnu now. Yes, we have to… We have to revive our great land. We have to make it worthy of our ancestors once again.'

'We have the villain we were looking for,' said Arishtanemi. 'Now, we need to quickly identify the noble Vishnu who will take our plan to fruition.'

Master and disciple looked at each other, their eyes alive with a sense of mission.

—ॐ—

'Dada!' Kumbhakarna's voice was low and uneven. He seemed to be struggling with his emotions.

It had been five years since the Battle of Karachapa. Raavan had been the ruler of Lanka for more than two years now. The royal family's problems had spilled out into the open, with Kaikesi telling almost anyone who would listen to her that Raavan was not her son anymore, and she did not wish to be associated with him. Instead, she said, Vibhishan and Shurpanakha were to be treated like her own children.

It was obvious to everyone that Kaikesi's status in Lanka— all the luxuries she enjoyed, the charities she funded, the honour she was accorded, and the power she wielded—was founded on her identity as Raavan's mother. But no one had the courage to say this to her face. In fact, many fed her insecurities to get favours for themselves in return.

But of one thing there was no doubt: there was only one true power centre in Lanka, indeed in the entire Indian subcontinent, if not the world, and that was Raavan. And no one dared to confront Raavan. On the contrary, they rushed to obey his every command and followed every instruction unquestioningly. Some went a step further in the hope of winning his approval. It was one such excess that was tormenting Kumbhakarna greatly.

'What is it, Kumbha?' sighed Raavan. 'Just manage whatever needs to be managed.'

'There is nothing left to be managed, Dada.' Kumbhakarna's tone was unfailingly polite, as it always was when he spoke to his brother in public, but he was visibly distraught.

Raavan stared at Kumbhakarna for a moment, and then nodded to the dainty woman sitting on his lap. She got up, picked up her blouse in a single, languid movement, and left. The other dancers in the chamber followed suit.

'So what do you want me to do?'

'You must remove Prahast from the army.'

Raavan's forces were divided into two contingents. One of them, led by officers who had been given the title of MahiRaavan, were responsible for the territories on land. The other group, commanded by officers called AhiRaavan, managed the seas and the ports. Among the AhiRaavans was Prahast, who, since betraying the governor of Chilika, had become an officer in Raavan's army and was greatly feared for his brutality.

'Kumbha, if we need to control the seas, we need ruthless officers like Prahast. Are you forgetting that it's thanks to him that we captured Krakachabahu's wealth many years ago?'

'Dada, there is a difference between ruthlessness and adharma.'

'Don't be immature, Kumbha! There is nothing called dharma or adharma. There is only success and failure. And I refuse to be a failure, ever. I am Raavan.'

'And I am Kumbhakarna, Dada. Nobody in this world loves you as I do. And my job is to stop you from committing a great sin.'

'The only real sin is to be poor and powerless, as we once were. Do you remember how helpless we were in our childhood? We will never go back to those days.'

'Dada, how much more wealth and power do we need? You are the wealthiest man in the world. You are the most powerful man in the world. You don't need more.'

'Yes, I do. You say I am the wealthiest man in the world. Well, I cannot rest till I am the richest man in history. And once I achieve that, who knows, I may want to become wealthier and more powerful than the Gods! Maybe that's not a bad idea, actually. The citizens of Lanka should learn to worship me as a God.'

'Dada, if you want to be a God, then consider how a God would behave. Would he allow the kind of crimes that Prahast has committed?'

'Let me be the judge of how I should behave.'

'Dada, what Prahast has done in Mumbadevi is beyond evil!' said Kumbhakarna.

'Once again, let me be the judge of that. What did he do?'

The Mumbadevi port was situated on the western coast of India, at a strategic point on the sea route between the Indus–Saraswati coast and Lanka. Raavan wanted absolute control over trade in the Indian Ocean—the hub of global trade. Whoever dominated this ocean would dominate the world.

He had managed to gain control over most of the major ports across the Indian subcontinent and the coasts of Arabia, Africa and South-east Asia. In all of these places, he had managed to enforce his usurious Customs duties. He had also, through his ally, King Vali in Kishkindha, put restrictions on the land trade routes south of the Narmada River. He now had the most prosperous region in the world, the Sapt Sindhu, in a vice-like grip. And he squeezed it for riches for himself and for Lanka.

Mumbadevi alone stubbornly refused to charge high Customs duties or turn away any sailor who sought refuge there. The Devendrars, the ruling community of Mumbadevi, believed that commerce had to go hand-in-hand with service, and they would not veer from doing their duty, their dharma. Raavan had decided he had to stop this for the good of his business. There could be no challenge to his vice-like grip: not only would it mean a loss of revenue, it would also weaken his image as the all-powerful king of Lanka.

'He has taken control of the Mumbadevi port,' Kumbhakarna began.

'So? *I* ordered him to take control of the port. Are you questioning my orders?'

'No, Dada! I am not questioning your orders. I am questioning your subordinate's methods.'

'I don't care about the methods. He was supposed to deliver results. If he has, then that's good enough for me.'

'Dada, all of Mumbadevi is destroyed.'

'So what? We can use the Salsette Island close by as a port.'

Kumbhakarna was shocked. 'Dada, did you hear what I just said? Forget about Salsette. All of Mumbadevi is destroyed. Every single Devendrar is dead. Their palace has been burned to the ground, their houses lie demolished. No one has survived—men, women, children. Their bodies were piled high on a mass pyre. The half-charred body of the kindly King Indran was also found. It looks like they were all burned alive.'

Raavan did not react. It appeared that he was momentarily staggered by the news.

'They were all non-combatants,' continued Kumbhakarna. 'They were not warriors. Killing them like this is an act of adharma. I have heard that some of our soldiers were so disgusted by Prahast's actions that they have deserted the army. He has lost nearly a third of his five-thousand-strong brigade. Prahast has come back to Lanka with all the wealth of the Devendrars, hoping that mere gold will stop us from punishing him.'

Raavan looked down, deep in thought. His right hand instinctively reached for the pendant around his neck.

Kumbhakarna moved to kneel beside his brother. 'Dada, you have to punish Prahast. We cannot allow adharma like this. An example has to be set.'

Raavan remained silent for some time before looking up at Kumbhakarna.

'Dada?'

'Yes, an example has to be set,' Raavan said. 'So, here's what we will do. Prahast will be transferred. The wealth he looted from Mumbadevi will be confiscated and added to the Lankan treasury. And we will send out raiding parties after the deserters. A few of them will have to be publicly executed.'

Kumbhakarna looked at his brother in shock.

'Kumbhakarna, I agree with you. Prahast overdid it. But we cannot remove him from the army. We are hated by most of the world. We need his ruthlessness on our side. Also, we simply cannot allow desertions. It would destroy our army. We don't have to go after them all, that would take too much effort. We just need to find a reasonable number, maybe one or two hundred of the deserters. And execute them. That should serve as a warning for the rest.'

'Dada... but...'

'Do it, Kumbha,' said Raavan, the tone of his voice brooking no further disagreement.

The king of Lanka turned towards the door and clapped his hands. The dancers came rushing back in, some of them removing their blouses as they ran. Kumbhakarna knew that the meeting was over.

Chapter 23

Eleven years after the Battle of Karachapa, Lanka's domination of global trade was complete. Not only had Raavan's personal wealth grown beyond measure, but he had transformed the small island kingdom into a world power. The heavy taxes levied on the Sapt Sindhu were bleeding the Land of the Seven Rivers dry, but even in its vastly reduced state, it remained wealthy. There was plenty for Lanka to continue to extract from.

Lanka by now had absolute control over the trade routes and every major port in the Indian Ocean. Consequently, it dominated the flow of trade across the world. The kingdom glittered with riches and had come to be known as Golden Lanka—with zero taxes, heavily subsidised living, free healthcare and education, twenty-four-hour water supply to homes through lead pipes, sprawling public gardens, sports stadiums, concert halls, and so on. There were no poor people in Raavan's Lanka.

Raavan himself, now thirty-eight, had acquired a God-like status in the kingdom. People had begun to worship his likeness in a few temples that had come up over the past year. Only his mother Kaikesi dared to oppose this deification: she had publicly declared that Raavan was dishonouring the ancient Vedic ways by encouraging such worship while he was still alive.

On the personal front, too, things had changed for Raavan. He had finally given in to Kumbhakarna's persuasions and taken a bride. Mandodari was the pious and beautiful daughter of a minor noble called Maya, who was the landlord of two small but prosperous villages in central India. Unfortunately, it soon became clear to her and to others around them, that Raavan had only married her to spite the land he professed to hate. As though he wanted the great empire of the Sapt Sindhu to acknowledge that he had the power not only to defeat their armies and seize their wealth, but to take away their women too. The only positive consequence of the ill-fated union was the birth of a son, Indrajit, whom Raavan truly loved.

The twenty-nine-year-old Kumbhakarna, meanwhile, had become increasingly melancholic. He cherished his brother but was unhappy about some of the things that he was forced to do because of his unwavering loyalty to him. Torn between his love for his brother and a desire to follow his dharma, he had begun to look for excuses to escape Lanka as often as he could. He travelled far and wide, sometimes on trade missions and negotiations, and other times on military expeditions, to put down the menace of piracy on the high seas. He grasped at any legitimate reason to stay away from Sigiriya.

It was on one such trip that Kumbhakarna found himself in the Ethiopian kingdom of Damat, a long-standing ally of Lanka. For as long as anyone could remember, trade between the West and India had flourished via the Western Sea, access to which was through the narrow Mandab strait in the Red Sea or the strait of Hormuz in the Persian Gulf, also called Jam Zrayangh by the locals. Any Egyptian or Mesopotamian trading ship had to enter the Western Sea at either of these points before sailing on to India. In a master stroke, Raavan had conquered the ports of Djibouti and Dubai, which controlled the two straits. Now, ships from Damat and other kingdoms that lay further west had to pay heavy Customs duties at either of these two ports to enter the Western Sea and the main Indian Ocean trade routes.

Kumbhakarna was in the kingdom to meet its ruler and fix the trade quotas and Customs duties for the next year. After the meetings were done, he had decided to stroll around the markets of the city of Yaha-Aksum, the capital of Damat. With just a day to spare before he left for Lanka, there wasn't enough time to explore all the sights and sounds of this beautiful city he was visiting for the first time.

Suddenly, a familiar sound caught his attention—a drumbeat that he did not expect to hear so far from home.

Dhoom-Dhoom-danaa-Dhoom-Dhoom-danaa.

Dhoom-Dhoom-danaa-Dhoom-Dhoom-danaa.

He started walking in the direction of the sound, as if pulled by an invisible thread.

Dhoom-Dhoom-danaa-Dhoom-Dhoom-danaa.

A few minutes later, he found himself in front of a graceful stone structure that looked unexpectedly like an Indian temple—a large platform made of red sandstone at ground level and a spire shooting high up into the sky, like a namaste to the Gods. The outer walls were decorated with beautifully sculpted figures of celestial nymphs, rishis, rishikas, kings and queens, all of whom were dressed Indian-style. The only difference was that their faces were distinctly African.

Kumbhakarna had met a few people from the African continent who had settled in India. He also knew of some rishis and rishikas who were originally from Africa. However, nothing had prepared him for a temple dedicated to Lord Rudra in the heart of Yaha-Aksum.

As he entered the temple, the drumbeats grew louder.

Dhoom-Dhoom-danaa-Dhoom-Dhoom-danaa.

Large stands were placed at different points in the main temple hall, before the sanctum sanctorum. On each of these stands were placed three massive drums, in a row. Tall muscular men, holding long drumsticks, stood on the sides, beating the drums rhythmically. The temple compound was filled with people dancing. A dance of sheer, ecstatic abandon.

The mood was electric, and it instantly infected Kumbhakarna. His body began to move of its own volition, and soon he was dancing as well. The booming ecstasy of Lord Rudra's music filled his mind and soul.

As the beat picked up pace, the dancing grew frenzied. The temple compound was alive with the raw energy of Lord Rudra's devotees. Gradually, the tempo built up till it reached a crescendo and ended with a loud triumphant cry of 'Jai Shri Rudra!'

Kumbhakarna raised his voice in ecstasy to join the call to the Lord.

Glory to Lord Rudra!

'Jai Devi Ishtar!'

Glory to Goddess Ishtar!

Kumbhakarna looked around at the happy faces around him, sweaty from the exuberant dancing. Some had tears of happiness flowing down their cheeks. Some were still in a trance. Strangers hugged, wishing each other well. Kumbhakarna too was embraced. No one seemed to notice that he had deformities, that he was a Naga.

'What brings you here, Kumbhakarna?'

Kumbhakarna turned to see a tall, distinguished-looking man with unblemished chocolate-coloured skin. While his features made it plain that he was a local from Damat, he was dressed in a saffron dhoti and angvastram, the colour of detachment and monkhood. A knotted tuft of hair at the top of his shaven head announced that he was a Brahmin. A flowing salt-and-pepper beard softened his face, and despite his imposing physical presence, he conveyed an impression of tranquillity, with his calm, gentle eyes. He was clearly a man at peace with himself.

Kumbhakarna frowned. 'I've seen you before.'

The Brahmin smiled and nodded.

'Yesterday, at the court?'

'Right,' said the man. 'I was standing at the back. You are observant.'

'I tend to notice important people,' said Kumbhakarna, smiling politely and folding his hands in a respectful namaste. 'But I didn't know you are a fellow devotee of Lord Rudra. What is your name, my friend?'

The man smiled and responded with a namaste. 'You can call me M'Bakur, my friend.'

'M'Bakur?' Kumbhakarna was surprised. 'Do you know, there's an old Sanskrit word called Bakur—it means a war trumpet.'

'I do. And, in our language, when we add the sound *M* to it, it means a *great* war trumpet.'

Kumbhakarna smiled broadly. 'Great name. But you seem to be a man of peace.'

'I've had enough of war. And I have the scars to prove it.'

'So the mighty sword has been put down in favour of temple drums?'

M'Bakur laughed softly. 'Dancing is much more fun than fighting, wouldn't you agree?'

Kumbhakarna laughed too, and nodded.

'I had my reasons for becoming a temple priest,' said M'Bakur. 'What is your reason for being a trade negotiator when your heart is clearly not in it?'

'Excuse me? Are you telling me I am not good at it?' Kumbhakarna was not sure whether to take offense.

'I didn't say that. I just said your heart isn't in it. I watched the negotiations yesterday. I was surprised. You could have asked for better terms. You left too much on the table for us.'

Kumbhakarna remained silent.

'It seemed to me that you were compensating for something. Overcompensating, perhaps. Like helping us would take some load off your mind.'

Kumbhakarna looked around. The temple had largely cleared out. Most of the devotees had left. He looked back at M'Bakur. 'Who are you?'

'Sit with me, my friend,' said M'Bakur in a gentle voice.

They sat in the main temple hall, resting their backs against the pillars. Kumbhakarna looked towards the sanctum sanctorum in the distance. It housed a life-size idol of Lord Rudra: a tall, muscular figure with long, open hair and a flowing beard.

Lord Rudra, as he had been in real life—magnificent and fearsome.

Kumbhakarna folded his hands together and bowed in deep reverence, as did M'Bakur.

The idol of a Goddess placed to the right side of Lord Rudra was nearly as tall as the Lord himself. The serene face had African features, though the body was dressed in an Indian-style dhoti, blouse and angvastram. An egg in the left hand and a long sword in the right identified her as the Goddess of Love and War. Kumbhakarna and M'Bakur bowed to the idol of Lady Ishtar as well.

The Lankan asked once again, 'Who are you?'

'Someone who can help you,' answered M'Bakur.

'Who says I need help?'

'Not everything needs to be said. When you see someone attempting to harm themselves, it is evident that they need help. But I guess you're wondering if you can trust me…'

Kumbhakarna remained silent.

M'Bakur bowed forward and whispered, 'I am a friend of Hanuman.'

Kumbhakarna looked at him, startled. Hanuman was a member of the legendary Vayuputra tribe. A gentle giant with a heart of gold, he was always on hand to help anyone in need. He had saved Kumbhakarna's life once, a long time ago. But he had extracted a promise from him never to speak of it, and Kumbhakarna had honoured that promise. However, he had remained forever grateful to Hanuman, and had always looked for an opportunity to repay that debt.

Any friend of Hanuman's was a friend of his.

'Are you a Vayuputra?' asked Kumbhakarna.

M'Bakur nodded. *Yes.*

'And you don't hate me?'

M'Bakur laughed softly. 'Why should I hate you?'

'I mean…' Kumbhakarna sighed. 'I am…'

'Go on.'

'Look, you are from the divine Vayuputra tribe. The tribe left behind by Lord Rudra. You are tasked with protecting the holy land of India. And I am the brother of the man who is destroying India.'

'Destroying India! Really?' asked M'Bakur, his eyes widening in mirth. 'Do you think your brother is all that powerful?'

Kumbhakarna was nonplussed. He was used to people speaking of his brother in exalted tones. He had never heard someone question his power or the extent of his influence. 'What? I don't understand.'

M'Bakur smiled. 'Tell me, how do you feel about someone destroying India?'

'It's... it's my land. I love my motherland.'

'And is your motherland so weak that one man can destroy it? Or, let me put it another way. If a land is so fragile that a single man can destroy it, does it even deserve to survive?'

'What are you saying?'

'Have you heard of *Matsya Nyay*?'

'Who hasn't? The bigger fish will always eat the smaller fish. I suppose you could call it *the law of the fish*.'

'You do know the law does not just apply to fish, right?'

Kumbhakarna laughed. 'Yes, I do.'

'It's about the law of Mother Nature. The survival of the fittest.'

'Yes, and it's a cruel law. That's why we've moved away from it. We don't kill those who are weaker than us. We protect them.'

'That is the human code of conduct, but nature doesn't work that way. Cruelty and kindness are human concepts.

Nature prioritises balance. And balance sometimes calls for tough love.'

'Tough love?'

'There's love that weakens you, and then there's love that prepares you for what lies ahead. Sometimes that love may appear tough, but it's necessary. If you are a parent who is only concerned with the here and now, you will give your child whatever she wants, because you want to see a smile on her face. But if you are a parent thinking of your child's future, you will realise that spoiling your child is the worst thing you can do.'

'Yes, but if you are too tough, the child will break.'

M'Bakur smiled. 'And that is the difference between nature and us. Mother Nature doesn't keep track all the time, she lets the laws of survival take over. And yes, sometimes the weak break and go extinct. But human beings are different. We can think and… well, we can keep track. We can modulate the tough love to the right level; tough enough to strengthen, but not so tough as to break.'

'What does this have to do with my brother, or me?'

'Have you ever stopped to consider whether, like the play of Mother Nature, there are some larger forces controlling our lives too? That possibly, your brother is a puppet in the hands of such a force?'

Kumbhakarna was too surprised to answer.

M'Bakur changed tack suddenly. 'Have you ever seen forest fires?'

'I have.'

'Are they good or bad?'

'It depends.'

'Depends on what?'

'Depends on whether the fire is controlled or uncontrolled.'

'Exactly. A controlled forest fire removes all the deadwood; deadwood, beyond a point, can turn toxic and destroy the forest. If small, controlled forest fires are not used to clear the ground, the chances of a massive, uncontrolled fire breaking out would increase. And an uncontrolled forest fire could destroy everything. That's not good, right?'

'That's not good at all.'

'Exactly. So a small forest fire is like using a small poison to kill a bigger poison.'

Kumbhakarna stiffened. 'My brother is not a poison.'

M'Bakur smiled. He didn't answer. He didn't apologise either.

Kumbhakarna got up, ready to leave.

'We haven't finished,' said M'Bakur.

'What makes you think you are so much better than my brother?' Kumbhakarna asked, sitting down again. 'To me, your casual acceptance of people suffering for some apparent "long-term good" seems as wrong as what my brother does.'

'You know, from Mother Nature's perspective, the opposite of right is not wrong, it's left.'

'That's just sophistry. What the hell do you mean?'

'I mean that there is no one right way, no ideal solution. The world usually suffers most at the hands of those who believe in perfection, those who don't realise that there is no one ideal. The truly wise, however, realise that you can only look for an optimal solution, not an ideal solution. A solution that could help *most* people is worth pursuing. Because there can't be a solution that will help *all* people. India is suffering because the Kshatriyas have become all-powerful, and in their arrogance, they have been oppressing the Shudras and the Vaishyas. We need to break their stranglehold before society can be set right again. And that is the role that Raavan is playing. He can break the Kshatriyas.'

'Why are you telling me all this? I could go and tell my brother how you are using him.'

'And you expect him to listen to you?' asked M'Bakur. 'Do you think he will suddenly turn dharmic?'

'Do you expect me to believe that you people are dharmic?'

M'Bakur smiled. 'If only questions on dharma could be answered so simply.'

'Try me.'

'Dharma is complex. We could spend whole lifetimes discussing what it is and what adharma is. But what truly matters is whether our intentions are dharmic—the outcome is beyond our control and cannot therefore be a measure of dharma.'

'Intentions?'

'Someone may try to do good for others, like the Vayuputras, for instance, are trying to do. Will we actually succeed? Only time will tell. But we know that our intentions cannot be doubted. We are thinking of the good of others, and not just our own objectives. That is the first step towards dharma. When you ignore your own selfish interests for the sake of others.'

Kumbhakarna leaned forward. 'Once again, why are you telling me all this?'

'Because Raavan's demonic nature may well be used for the greater good. But we want his soul to be saved as well.'

Kumbhakarna frowned. 'And you think I am naïve enough to believe that the Vayuputras care about him?'

'Why not? We care about everyone. We may not be able to help everyone, but we care about everyone.'

'But what do you want from me?'

'We hope that you will help your brother.'

'And what do you think I have been doing?'

'Negotiating bad deals does not help your brother.'

'We have more money than we can ever use. I may as well spread it around a bit. At least some good will come of it. Every bit spent in charity is good for dharma.'

M'Bakur smiled. 'Have you heard of Lord Vidur?'

'Of course I have,' answered Kumbhakarna. 'Who has not heard of the great philosopher, one of the most brilliant men in history?'

'Lord Vidur said that there are two ways to waste money. One, by giving charity to the unworthy. Second, by not giving charity to the worthy.'

'I have been…'

'Your trade concessions help the rulers and traders in my kingdom. They don't need charity. It's the poor who need help. Not only in Damat, but everywhere. Find them and help them. Help them in the name of your brother. Earn some good karma for him. Don't give in to melancholy. Find purpose. I know your brother saved your life at birth. Now it is your duty to help his soul.'

Kumbhakarna looked thoughtful as he listened intently to M'Bakur's words.

'And don't give up on him,' continued M'Bakur. 'We live in a period of constant change. I am sure an opportunity to save Raavan's soul will come again. He may be too ignorant to see it, but he will need you to help him when the time comes.'

Kumbhakarna spoke softly, his eyes moist. 'I have lost my brother. I love him, but I have lost him. I have lost him to his anger. To his pain. I have lost him to his grief over…'

'Over the death of Vedavati,' said M'Bakur. 'I know.'

Kumbhakarna stared at M'Bakur. Shocked that he knew something about Raavan that was so personal. And a secret from most.

'Don't forget that he loves you too. You and his son Indrajit are probably the only people alive whom he truly loves.'

'Indrajit loves him in return. Perhaps even more than I do.'

M'Bakur smiled. 'I know. But he is a little child. He cannot help his father, at least not yet. So it becomes your responsibility to save Raavan. That is your swadharma in this life. Do it well.'

—ᴚᴏI—

'Dada, this money makes no difference to us.' Kumbhakarna was upset and angry. The two extra arms on top of his shoulders stood stiff and straight.

It had been seventeen years since the Battle of Karachapa. Kumbhakarna was in Raavan's private chamber. As usual, there were some half-naked women dancing in the centre of the massive room. Raavan was on his reclining chair, his fingers idly playing with the hair of the woman on his lap. He had a marijuana-infused chillum in his free hand.

Kumbhakarna could have performed the act of charity by himself, with his own money. But he wanted this specific donation to go from Raavan's personal income. It had to be that way.

Raavan took a deep drag of the chillum and stared at Kumbhakarna, a lazy, inebriated smile on his lips. He spoke through the smoke rings. 'I will burn all my money, but I will not let any of it go to the Sapt Sindhu. Even if it is for a hospital in Vaidyanath.'

Kumbhakarna looked around the chamber. The women, the smoke, the alcohol, the marijuana, the excesses. 'You are burning your money already, Dada.'

'Well, I've earned it… I can do what I want with it.'

Kumbhakarna turned to the dancers and said sharply, 'Leave us.'

The women stopped dancing, but didn't leave the hall. They stood where they were, half defiant, half afraid, waiting for Raavan's order.

Kumbhakarna gestured to the woman on Raavan's lap. 'Get out.'

The woman tried to get up, but Raavan pulled her roughly back against his chest. 'Don't cross your limits, Kumbhakarna,' he snapped.

Kumbhakarna stepped forward and pointed at the pendant that hung around Raavan's neck. 'This hospital was a promise you made in the name of the Kanyakumari, Dada. We took on her karmic debts at her cremation ceremony. You may have forgotten it, but I have not. I am going to get that hospital built. It will treat patients free of cost and it will save lives. And you will stamp this hundi with your seal.'

Raavan was silent. There was no expression on his face, neither anger nor remorse, not even grief. He had sought refuge from his pain in drugs, alcohol and silly women. The price for that asylum was the surrender of his mind.

Kumbhakarna stepped forward, took hold of Raavan's hand and pressed the ring on his forefinger, with the royal seal, on the document. The charity was now authorised to spend Raavan's money.

Kumbhakarna glanced at the woman perched uncomfortably on his brother's lap and said, 'You have a wife, Dada. She should not be insulted like this.'

Raavan didn't answer.

Kumbhakarna turned and walked out of the chamber.

The woman on Raavan's lap edged closer to him and caressed his cheek. With an air of affected concern, she whispered, 'I don't like the way your brother speaks to you.'

Raavan's reaction was swift. His fist shot out and hit the woman hard on her face. Breaking her nose. As she tumbled to the ground, screaming in pain, he shouted at the dancers in the distance, 'Get out of here! All of you!' He pointed at the sobbing woman lying at his feet, her face red, her nose streaming blood. 'And take this bitch with you!'

As the women ran from his chamber, Raavan fell back in his chair and held Vedavati's fingers tightly. Tears forced their way through his closed eyes and ran down his cheeks.

You can be better than this. At least try.

Chapter 24

'I don't know if I am doing the right thing. I seem to be causing him a lot of stress,' said Kumbhakarna. 'He is very weak these days.'

It had been a few months since Kumbhakarna had forced Raavan's hand over building a charitable hospital in Vaidyanath. He was now in the temple-town, checking on all preparations before construction began. Money had been allocated. Doctors had been identified and hired. The building was to be ready in a few months. M'Bakur, who had remained in touch with Kumbhakarna over the years, was also in Vaidyanath to help wrap up work.

'Your brother may be many things,' said M'Bakur, 'but he is certainly not weak.'

'The truth is, it's depressing to see him these days. He has almost surrendered to drugs and alcohol. He's nearly forty-five years old, he can't keep abusing his body like this. And I am making it worse with all the stress I am causing him.'

'You're wrong. Stress is good.'

'Oh, come on, M'Bakurji. How can stress be good?'

M'Bakur gestured to a small stove on a platform behind them, on which was placed a vessel filled with water.

Cooking in this boiling water was a simple lunch of eggs and potatoes.

'You see this boiling water?' M'Bakur said.

'What does that have to do with stress?' asked Kumbhakarna.

'It will help you understand.'

Kumbhakarna sighed. 'Why can't you people not speak in riddles?'

'Because speaking in riddles is fun. And you will understand a thought better if you decode it through a riddle. As someone said: *Parokshpriyaa Vai Devaaha.*'

The saying in old Sanskrit roughly translated to, *the Gods like indirect speech.*

'So, philosophy can never be conveyed directly?' questioned Kumbhakarna.

'It can, of course. But it's much more interesting to have it conveyed in the form of a complex riddle. Deciphering the message keeps the fun of philosophy alive. Also, the understanding thus derived feels like an achievement. If there is no sense of achievement or wonder, even the most important message fails to find its target.'

'So, I am expected to understand the bigger point you're trying to make with this boiling water?' asked Kumbhakarna.

'Not only will you understand it, you will arrive at it yourself.'

Kumbhakarna threw up his hands in exasperation. 'All right, then. In answer to your question, yes, I see the boiling water.'

'Both, the eggs and the potatoes, are in the same water, right?'

'Yes, obviously. I can see that.'

'So, they are both being cooked in water boiled to the same temperature, in the same atmosphere, and in the same vessel that is on top of the same fire?'

'Yes.'

'What will happen to the egg in this boiling water?'

'It will become a boiled egg.'

M'Bakur laughed. 'That much is obvious. What I want to know is, how is the boiled egg different from the original egg?'

'It's harder.'

'Absolutely! Now, consider the potatoes. How will they fare in the water?'

Kumbhakarna smiled. 'They will become softer.'

'You see? The same boiling water, the same vessel, the same temperature, yet the eggs harden and the potatoes soften.'

'So the boiling water is like stress. Different people react to it differently. It hardens some and softens others. Is that your point?'

'That's the obvious point, but think about it a bit more. What is the egg like before the stress of the boiling water hits it?'

'It has a tough shell, but the inside is liquid.'

'So the egg is hard on the outside but soft inside. And the boiling water, the stress, makes it hard inside as well, does it not?'

'Yes.'

'Now consider the potato. How would you describe it?'

'It has a flimsy peel—so, soft on the outside and hard on the inside.'

'People respond to stress in much the same way. Those who are soft on the inside become harder with the right amount of stress, and those who are hard on the inside become softer. If you think about it this way, then the right amount of stress becomes necessary to balance your character. Too much stress is not good—it may break you. But no stress is not good either. You need the right amount of stress to balance your character and make you grow.'

'So, are you saying that the stress I'm causing my brother will toughen him up again?'

M'Bakur shook his head. 'I am not talking about your brother. I am talking about you.'

Kumbhakarna frowned, taken aback.

'There are people across the world with biases against your kind, the Nagas. You have a hard, scary exterior. But inside, you are gentle and sensitive. You are one of the finest men I have had the pleasure of knowing.'

Kumbhakarna didn't say anything, though he flushed with pleasure at the unexpected compliment.

M'Bakur continued, 'The truth is that you are the one who is feeling the stress of what's happening to your elder brother. The stress is toughening you up. It's preparing you to face what will come.'

'What will come?'

'The Vishnu.'

'The Vishnu?'

'The seventh Vishnu will come. It will be a tough time for those on the path of adharma. The responsibility of guiding and bringing your brother's soul on to the right path will be yours, Kumbhakarna. You will also have to save the innocents of Lanka. You will need to be tougher.'

'I have heard nothing about a Vishnu coming...'

M'Bakur smiled. 'Only fools react to a fire when it is upon them. The wise see it coming many years before it's even been lit.'

'But why will the Vishnu go after my brother?'

M'Bakur looked at Kumbhakarna, his eyebrows raised at the obviously stupid question.

Kumbhakarna retreated quickly, a little shamefaced. 'Who is this Vishnu? What is his or her name?'

M'Bakur hesitated for a split second before he replied, 'The answer is not clear.'

M'Bakur knew he could not tell Kumbhakarna the truth, but he wasn't lying either. At least, not technically.

—ॐ—

'You called for me, Dada?' asked Kumbhakarna loudly, standing at the door of the chamber.

Twenty years had passed since the Battle of Karachapa. The previous year had witnessed a change in Raavan's attitude. The forty-seven-year-old had worked consciously to subdue his addictions. He had started taking control of his business once again. He would even occasionally inquire about the hospital in Vaidyanath, though he had never visited it.

Kumbhakarna assumed his brother had been shaken out of his apathy and self-indulgence by the tragedy that had suddenly befallen Sigiriya a few years back. A mysterious plague had taken the city in a vice-like grip and all attempts to end it had failed. Strangely, its effects were most evident amongst children. Babies were being born prematurely, and many had died during childbirth. Those who survived were growing up with learning disabilities, loss of appetite, almost constant abdominal pain, sluggishness and fatigue. Some experienced hearing loss and had frequent convulsions or seizures. Adults weren't free of pain either. Many of them suffered debilitating joint and muscle pains and crushing headaches. Large numbers of pregnant women suffered miscarriages and stillbirths and many had died during labour.

While the physical symptoms caused widespread distress, even more harmful was the lowering of morale across the land. The finest doctors in Lanka were unable to understand the cause of the plague, let alone find a cure for it. With almost the entire population suffering in some way or the other, rumours had started up about some kind of a curse that had fallen on Sigiriya.

What worried Raavan the most about the plague was the weakening of his army. He could have strengthened the Lankan forces by recalling a few battalions from the various trading outposts across the Indian Ocean, but that would have left those ports defenceless. Also, it would have alerted Lanka's enemies to the fact that all was not well in the island kingdom, and that, in turn, would have stoked rebellions.

While Raavan applied himself to the task of supplementing the city's defences without word getting out to the Sapt Sindhu, Kumbhakarna's approach to the problem was to invest more money in research and the training of doctors and nurses. He was thinking about this now as he waited for his brother to respond.

Then he heard Raavan's voice. 'Yes, Kumbha. Come on in.'

Kumbhakarna entered Raavan's secret chamber, where many of his elder brother's favourite musical instruments and some of his most treasured manuscripts, numbering in the thousands, were stored. Most importantly, his precious paintings of the Kanyakumari were kept there.

'Why is the lighting so low?' He asked.

Raavan pointed to the torches on the wall. 'You can fire them up now. I needed soft diffused light to complete this last part.'

Kumbhakarna lit the torches and reached his brother's side to see what he had been working on. He gaped at the sight of the canvas.

Raavan asked, 'What do you think?'

Kumbhakarna stopped himself from saying the words that came to his mind. *Scary and magnificent at the same time.*

It was a painting of Vedavati, but not the Vedavati he had known. In the painting, she was the same age she had been when she died, but that was where the resemblance ended. This woman was strong and powerful, her body muscular and sinewy. She was much taller than she had been in real life. Though Raavan had not meddled with her proportions, her curves looked less pronounced because of the more athletic frame. The cumulative impact of all of Raavan's changes meant she looked less nurturing and more fierce, like a warrior princess. She was riding a magnificent horse, her open hair flying in all directions. One hand held a bloodied sword that was raised high, ready to strike again. In front of her, on the muddy ground, on their knees, were many of the kings of the Sapt Sindhu. They looked desperate and fearful. Some had their mouths open in a scream. A few had been beheaded already, while the others were clearly pleading for mercy. In the background, far in the distance, were the common people— the Indians—poor and worn out, but exuberantly cheering their Goddess as she massacred their oppressors.

Scary and magnificent at the same time.

'What do you think?' asked Raavan again.

'It's… it's spectacular, Dada! I don't know what to say,' Kumbhakarna stuttered.

'I am glad you think so,' said Raavan. 'This is how the world should remember her. This is how the world will remember her.'

But this is not how she was.

Kumbhakarna kept his thoughts to himself.

'Look at her face. I have painted her exactly as she was when we last met.'

'Yes, Dada. It's amazing that you still remember her so clearly, even after twenty years and more.'

'How can a soul forget the reason for its existence?'

Before Kumbhakarna could respond, Raavan turned and picked up a letter, his eyes sparkling with excitement. 'Look at this.'

Kumbhakarna took the letter and read it quickly. 'What does this mean?'

'What does it mean?' asked Raavan. 'Are you blind? Read it again. It's clear as crystal.'

'Yes, but…'

'But what?'

'It's an invitation from the kingdom of Mithila to attend Princess Sita's swayamvar.'

Mithila was a kingdom in the Sapt Sindhu whose best days were well behind it. It had been a wealthy river-port town once, settled near the Gandaki River. But the change in the course of the river many years ago, due to an earthquake, had vastly reduced the town's prosperity, and power. However, even in its diminished state, Mithila commanded respect across the Sapt Sindhu. It was a city loved by the rishis and rishikas, and at least in spiritual and intellectual terms, it remained one of the most venerated kingdoms in India.

'Exactly.'

'But why would…'

'Why would I go?'

'This is a trap, Dada. You know the Sapt Sindhu royals hate you. Why would they invite you? Please don't go.'

Raavan looked surprised. 'I thought you wanted me to try and make peace with the Sapt Sindhu.'

Kumbhakarna looked at the painting of Vedavati briefly before turning back to Raavan.

'I began that painting many months ago. I am willing to make a fresh start,' Raavan said. 'This invitation has made me think that maybe we can actually get along with the Sapt Sindhuans. Maybe our wealth can be used for some good too. The question is, are you with me?'

Kumbhakarna remembered M'Bakur's words from more than eight years ago. *I am sure an opportunity to save Raavan's soul will come again… he will need you to help him when the time comes.*

He stepped up to embrace Raavan. 'Of course I am with you, Dada!'

If we can walk away from adharma, the Vishnu will have no reason to attack us.

———र७ऽ१———

Akampana was confused. 'But Iraiva, I don't understand. Mithila? They're… they're nobodies. They're only respected as intellectuals and philosophers. They have no real power.'

Akampana's true lord, Raavan, would normally have told him to shut up and do as he was told. But men of consequence, men who do big deeds, usually have a weakness: they like to speak of their big deeds. They like to hear how great they are, if not in words, then with a look of admiration in the eyes of their acolytes. Raavan was no different. He normally spoke of his plans only to Kumbhakarna. Indrajit was still too young, and Raavan had little respect for anyone else. But lately, communication between the brothers had been strained. Kumbhakarna's constant talk of dharma had begun to weary Raavan.

'You will swear to never speak of this to anyone,' said Raavan.

Akampana immediately made a pathetic attempt at the standard Lankan salute. 'Of course, Iraiva.'

'Not even to Kumbhakarna.'

Akampana's chest swelled with pride. At last, his true lord had realised his value. He was placing greater trust in him than in his own blood. 'Wouldn't dream of it, Iraiva. I swear. I swear on the great Lord Jagannath.'

'So here is what I am going to do. As soon as I win the swayamvar, I will take over Mithila and have King Janak follow my commands. I will force him, and his rishi council, to acknowledge me as a living God. Mithila may be powerless in temporal matters, but when it comes to spiritual matters, it is among the most respected, perhaps even rivalling Kashi. Only the land along the Saraswati River commands greater reverence. If Mithila starts worshipping me as a God, then many other Sapt Sindhu kingdoms will follow its example. They will build temples to me while I am still alive. Then, and only then, can I be assured of immortality.'

There was another aspect to the swayamvar that excited Raavan. His marriage to Princess Sita would be the ultimate humiliation for the Sapt Sindhuans; it would show them that he was capable of taking not only their ports and wealth, but also their women. He had married Mandodari for similar reasons. But Mandodari was the daughter of a mere landlord. Sita was the daughter of a king—a true princess. The thought of snubbing the royals by marrying one of them gave Raavan immense satisfaction. But he couldn't say this to Akampana. Loyal servant though he was, Raavan couldn't possibly discuss his personal life with him.

The loyal servant, meanwhile, was still reeling with shock. 'But Iraiva, do you think that they will…'

'They will.'

'Who am I to disagree with you, great Iraiva? But, I mean… the Sapt Sindhu people are stubborn. They are not as open-minded as we Lankans are. Even the Vishnus and the Mahadevs did not have temples built to them while they were alive.'

Raavan leaned forward, his face close to Akampana's. 'Are you saying that I am less than a Vishnu or a Mahadev?'

'I wouldn't dare suggest it, noble Iraiva! You are greater than them, of course. But I don't know if the Sapt Sindhuans will see this obvious truth. Sometimes people refuse to acknowledge that the Sun God has risen even though it is midday!' Akampana said with an unctuous smile.

'You don't need to worry about that. They will see the truth for what it is. Trust me.'

'I am sure you are right, Iraiva. Why else would they think of inviting you?'

'They didn't think of it. I got them to do it.'

'Really?' Akampana was impressed.

'Yes. Kushadhwaj, the king of Sankashya, is the brother of King Janak of Mithila. He is deep in debt to Lanka. His business affairs have been a mess since his prime minister, Sulochan, died suddenly of a heart attack some years ago. We forgave much of his debt and he arranged the invitation.'

'That was very well handled, great Iraiva.'

Raavan looked pleased with Akampana's compliment. 'Yes, I did handle it well.'

'By the way, we have someone in Mithila too, my lord.'

Raavan had official trade representatives in every kingdom of the Sapt Sindhu. But that was not all. He had also established a secret spy network throughout the kingdoms. These spies and loyalists worked for him undercover, quietly ensuring that his agendas were effectively pursued.

'I didn't think Mithila was important enough for us to have someone stationed there,' said Raavan. 'But I suppose it will serve us well. Who is it?'

'Well, we haven't been actively managing her for years. As you say, my lord, Mithila is not a very important kingdom, and we don't do much trade with it. But our spy is quite high up in the kingdom's administration—the chief of police and protocol in Mithila.'

'Who is he?'

'She, my lord. Her name is Samichi.'

Raavan froze at the mention of the girl. He had not wanted to associate with anyone, except Kumbhakarna, who had been with him when Vedavati was killed. Their presence only reminded him of that terrible day. All the Lankan soldiers who had accompanied him to Todee had been sent to nondescript posts where he would never have to see them again. Hearing

Samichi's name brought back memories and reminded him yet again of his failure to protect Vedavati.

'You speak to her and make sure everything is arranged in my favour,' he said.

'Of course, Iraiva.'

'Nothing must go wrong.'

'Absolutely, Iraiva.'

'And I don't want to see or meet Samichi when I am there. Is that clear?'

Akampana was confused, but he readily agreed. 'Whatever you say, Iraiva.'

—ᚱᚯᛁ—

The Pushpak Vimaan hovered in the air for some time, as its rotors decelerated slowly. Then, very gently, it descended to the ground. Raavan had excellent pilots working for him.

As the doors slid open, Raavan emerged from the innards of his legendary flying craft, followed by Kumbhakarna. Vali, the king of Kishkindha and scion of the legendary Vaanar dynasty, stood at a safe distance, his entire court in tow.

Raavan's corps of ten thousand soldiers had already left for Mithila, sailing up the east coast of India and then up the Ganga. They would march onward to Janak's kingdom after disembarking from their ships, and wait for Raavan to arrive. Since there were enough days in between, Raavan had decided to stop at Kishkindha on his way to Mithila.

Strewn with massive boulders and rocky hills, the terrain of Kishkindha resembled a moonscape. The mighty Tungabhadra, flowing north-east, meandered through this surreal land before merging with the Krishna River up north.

In consonance with the nature- and idol-worshipping ways of most of the Vedic people, great temples had been built in many parts of the city, venerating the sacred Tungabhadra, the land around it, and the ancient Gods. Each district of Kishkindha was built around a temple, which was surrounded by markets, amphitheatres, libraries, parks and houses. Vali was a wise and strong ruler. His land was prosperous and his people happy. And his reputation for bravery, honour and dignified conduct had spread far and wide.

'Something is wrong,' whispered Kumbhakarna, as they walked towards their waiting hosts.

There was no sign of the traditional Vedic welcome they had expected. No bedecked elephants, no ornamented cows, and no holy men holding ceremonial prayer plates. Not only that, the welcoming party was shrouded in an uncomfortable silence—there was no music or sounds of chanting.

Vali stood quietly at the head, his hands folded in a polite namaste. The king of Kishkindha was a fair, unusually hirsute and extraordinarily muscular man of medium height. He was dressed in full ceremonial attire, but he seemed distracted.

'I don't see Sugreev,' whispered Raavan to Kumbhakarna.

Sugreev was Vali's younger half-brother, and in Raavan's opinion, an effete moron. Most people agreed with Raavan's low opinion of the man, seeing in Sugreev the spoilt, indolent sibling of a great king, one who could not match the accomplishments of his over-achieving elder brother and managed his insecurities by drinking and gambling. Sugreev had committed enough indiscretions to deserve being kicked out of the kingdom, but the protection of their mother, Aruni, had ensured that Vali had not expelled his younger brother.

'Neither do I,' said Kumbhakarna softly.

Raavan smiled, sensing an opportunity.

—रोI—

Kishkindha had a matrilineal society. The ascendency to the throne did not pass from father to son, but from mother to daughter. The husband of the daughter succeeded the husband of the mother as king. But Lady Aruni, headstrong and powerful, had broken with tradition and made her capable elder son the king. She hadn't been blessed with a daughter, and rather than letting the royal line pass to her younger sister's female descendants as tradition dictated, she had decided to keep the throne within her immediate family.

Raavan was familiar with this history, but that was not what interested him right now, as he sat beside Vali in the guest wing of the Kishkindha royal palace. No one else, except Kumbhakarna, was around, not even Vali's bodyguards.

Raavan's expression was carefully calibrated to show concern. 'You look distracted, King Vali. I hope the share of Customs duties being given to you is not too low? My men can be a little greedy at times,' he said.

Vali smiled wanly. 'Your people know that I cannot be pushed around. I am Vali.'

Raavan laughed heartily. 'You're the man, my friend.'

Vali looked at Raavan, a sad expression on his face. Though he remained silent, his bereft eyes seemed to convey a message. *Man? Me?*

Raavan was now confident that the information he had received this morning from his spies was correct. But he had to be certain before he made his move.

'My friend,' he said. 'Where is Angad? I don't see him anywhere. I hope he is well?'

Angad was Vali's five-year-old son and the apple of his eye. The tough, stern and distant Vali, more respected than loved, was a different man when he was with his only son. He played and laughed with him, and indulged him any chance he got. Even occasionally becoming a horse for Angad to ride around on. Since Angad's birth, Kishkindha's citizens, and even the royal family, had come to see a casual, fun-loving side to Vali.

'Yes… Angad… he's…' Vali stopped speaking, his face a picture of agony, his voice choked.

Raavan was now certain his information was correct. He controlled his breathing. He couldn't allow his excitement to show.

Later. I'll take over Kishkindha later. After I've taken Mithila.

Kumbhakarna, on the other hand, was shocked at the distraught look on Vali's face. He had never seen the mighty Kishkindha king like this. 'Great king,' said Kumbhakarna, 'is everything all right?'

Vali suddenly got up and stood in front of them, his hands clasped together. 'Forgive me, my friends. I… I must go. I will come back in a while.'

Raavan and Kumbhakarna also rose immediately.

'Of course, Vali,' said Raavan, his face a picture of concern. 'Please let us know if there is anything we can do.'

'Thank you. We'll speak later.' Saying this, Vali rushed out of the chamber.

Kumbhakarna stared at Vali's retreating form and then turned to his elder brother in bewilderment. 'I didn't realise King Vali was so close to his mother.'

Vali's mother Aruni had passed away just a month ago, after a brief illness.

'It's not about his mother,' said Raavan.

Kumbhakarna looked surprised. 'Then what is it? He looks almost frail. I've never known him to bow down to any misfortune. Something is worrying him.'

Raavan cast a quick glance at the doorway, making sure that they were, indeed, alone. 'What we are speaking of will remain between us. Strictly between us.'

'Of course,' said Kumbhakarna immediately. 'What is this about?'

'It's about Angad.'

'Angad? Has something happened to that lovely child?'

'Nothing has happened to him yet. What matters is what happened before he was born.'

'Before he was born?'

'Yes. Are you familiar with the tradition of niyoga?'

Kumbhakarna was taken aback. Niyoga was an ancient tradition by which a woman, whose husband was incapable of producing a child, could request and appoint another man to impregnate her. For various reasons, this man was usually a rishi.

For one thing, most rishis were revered for their high intellectual prowess, a quality they would hopefully pass on to their offspring. More importantly, since most rishis were wandering mendicants, it was almost certain that they would not lay claim to the child. According to the law, any child produced as a result of a union sanctioned by niyoga would be considered the legitimate child of the woman and her husband; the biological father could not claim fatherhood and would have to remain anonymous.

'From what my spies tell me,' continued Raavan, 'Vali was once very seriously injured while trying to save Sugreev. This happened many years back, during a hunt. The side effect of the medicines that saved his life was that he couldn't have children. This was, for obvious reasons, kept secret.'

'That useless brother of his,' said Kumbhakarna in disgust. 'So, you mean King Vali's wife Tara decided to…'

'Not Tara,' Raavan interrupted him. 'It was apparently his mother. The Queen Mother decided that Vali's child should rule Kishkindha after him. And turned to niyoga for a solution.'

'So what?' asked Kumbhakarna. 'What difference does it make if Angad is not his biological son? The rules are clear. Since King Vali is Queen Tara's husband, he will be considered the father of her son, even if the child was sired by someone else. And Angad is a wonderful boy. He will make a great ruler one day. I can see, even at this young age, that he has his noble father's spirit, drive and intelligence.'

'Well, it's a little more complicated than that.'

'How so?'

'You know what Aruni was like.'

'I have heard stories, yes, of the Queen Mother's headstrong ways…'

'Yes, in any case, I think when people are close to death, they start thinking about their souls. They want to repent for their sins and "speak the truth".'

'What truth did she tell King Vali?'

'Apparently, when Aruni decided that a niyoga was necessary for the sake of an unbroken lineage, she didn't want to take Vali's wife to a rishi.'

'So what did she do?'

'She wanted to ensure that it was *her* bloodline that continued to rule. So she…'

'Oh my God!' Kumbhakarna exclaimed, as the truth hit home.

Sugreev.

Kumbhakarna held his head, feeling Vali's pain. 'I can't even imagine how distraught he must be. Angad is his pride and joy. And now… to know the truth… that it's Sugreev's cowardly blood that runs in Angad's veins…'

'Exactly,' said Raavan.

'Does Angad know?'

'As far as I know, he does not.'

'So the Queen Mother told King Vali this?'

'Yes. On her deathbed, apparently.'

'Why didn't she just remain quiet about it?'

'Guilt? She must have known that she did not do right by Vali and wanted to confess to him before her death.'

'How incredibly selfish! To cleanse her own soul of bad karma, she confessed to her son and gifted him a lifetime of trauma.'

'You know how selfish mothers can be…'

Kumbhakarna ignored the barb. 'Did King Vali confront that coward, Sugreev?'

'Yes, and he confessed to it, said he had no choice in the matter. That he had only complied with their mother's order.'

'Bullshit!' said Kumbhakarna. 'I am sure Sugreev was delighted at the prospect of his child ascending the throne someday.'

'Vali threw Sugreev out of the kingdom when he found out the truth,' said Raavan. 'I would have killed him!'

'Lord Rudra have mercy!' said Kumbhakarna. 'What a mess.'

Raavan sympathised with Vali, but he couldn't help feeling pleased about the good fortune that had fallen into his lap. He could now use the fight between Sugreev and Vali to wipe out the Vaanar dynasty and bring wealthy Kishkindha under the Lankan yoke. Vali's army would become his to command and could then be used for the defence of Lanka, if he so wished.

He breathed a sigh of relief. He might finally have found a solution to the problem he had been struggling with for so long: the depleting strength of his forces in Lanka.

But he didn't think Kumbhakarna would approve of his plan. He would have to handle this alone.

Chapter 25

The Pushpak Vimaan flew smoothly, thousands of feet above the holy land of India, travelling from Kishkindha to Mithila. Raavan and Kumbhakarna were seated in comfortable chairs, strapped in for safety. They would land in Mithila soon, in time for Raavan to attend Princess Sita's swayamvar.

At the moment, though, their minds were not on Mithila, or Sita.

'Celibacy, Kumbha?' sneered Raavan. 'Seriously? Women were created for one purpose alone. And you would deny them that purpose by turning celibate?'

'Seriously, Dada, why are you so disrespectful towards women?' asked Kumbhakarna. He knew he had annoyed his elder brother by announcing that he would undertake the forty-one-day oath that would allow him to travel to Shabarimala, the sacred Lord Ayyappa temple in the deep south of India. Raavan saw this as yet another sign that his brother was moving away from him and towards a strictly dharmic way of life.

'Would you rather I respect them, dear brother?' asked Raavan, laughing. 'Trust me, women are not looking for respect or honour. They want someone to pay their bills and to give them protection. In return, they are prepared to give love, or something resembling it!'

'Dada, you are about to get married for the second time. I really think you need to update your views on women.'

'Listen, Kumbha, I have more women in a fortnight than you have had in your entire life. I know how they think. They may say they like nice, sensitive men. But remember, women never say what they mean. In reality, they dismiss the gentle, domesticated sort of men as weak and unreliable. They want real men—tough, strong men.'

'Our dharma says that a real man is one who respects women.'

'So a real man is one who surrenders himself and becomes a doormat for women?'

'I never said that. A real man is one who respects himself and treats others with respect too.'

'Bullshit. I can tell you from personal experience, four women don't add up to the worth of one man. In fact, even four hundred women do not add up to the worth of one man.'

'What nonsense! Do you even hear yourself, Dada?'

'All the time. And I don't hear anything wrong!'

Kumbhakarna took a deep breath to control his irritation. 'Forget it. Your views cannot shake my beliefs or the vows that I will undertake for Lord Ayyappa.'

'How does your being celibate please a God?' sniggered Raavan, clearly trying to annoy Kumbhakarna.

'It's not only about celibacy, Dada,' Kumbhakarna explained patiently. 'By taking the *vow*, I am pledging my loyalty to Lord Ayyappa, the son of the previous Mahadev, Lord Rudra, and the Vishnu, Lady Mohini. Though Lord Ayyappa is worshipped across the land in thousands of temples, the *vratham* applies only to the temple of Shabarimala. A small forest-dwelling community in that region, led by Shabari, the Lady of the Forest, maintains the temple. And for all devotees, the rules are clearly laid out.'

Kumbhakarna ticked off the rules on his fingers: 'We will not eat meat or consume alcohol during the period of the forty-one-day vratham. We will sleep on the floor. We will not hurt anyone, either physically or with our words. We will stay away from all social functions. The point is to live simply and focus on high thinking.'

'All that sounds very noble. But tell me something, you keep talking about how much you respect women. You do know that women are not allowed into the Shabarimala temple? Isn't that disrespectful to them?'

'Women are allowed! Of course they are. Only women who are in the reproductive stage of their life are not allowed in this particular temple. Basically, women who are capable of menstruating are forbidden entry.'

'Aha! So you think reproduction is impure? And menstruating women will contaminate the temple? Do you know that in the Kamakhya temple in north-east India, menstrual blood is considered sacred and worshipped?'

'You are misunderstanding me on purpose, Dada. The ban on menstruating women has nothing to do with menstrual blood being impure. How can any Indian think that? It's about the path of *sanyas*, of *renunciation*.'

Kumbhakarna continued, 'As you know, practically all the temples in India follow the *gruhasta* route, the path of the *householder*. The rituals in these temples are built around the worldly life, celebrating relationships like that between a husband and wife, or a parent and child, or a lord and his subjects. The *renunciates* or *sanyasis* have temples too, many of them being rock-cut caves in remote mountainous regions; non-sanyasis are not allowed entry into these. The only way of entering a sanyasi temple is by giving up all worldly attachments, renouncing one's family and material belongings, and permanently joining a sanyasi order.'

Raavan pretended to be alarmed. 'Are you becoming a sanyasi? Are you going to leave me? What the hell!'

Kumbhakarna laughed. 'Dada, listen to me. The Shabarimala temple is not for those who have taken permanent sanyas. We just have to be sanyasis for the forty-one days of the vratham. It essentially gives us a short experience of the life of a sanyasi. If you understand this, then all the vows I mentioned earlier make sense. For these forty-one days, we have to stay away from all the pleasures and comforts of life, as well as extreme emotions. That's why the rule against consumption of intoxicants or meat, and sex. The temple is dedicated to the male sanyasi route, women in their reproductive phase are not allowed in, but young girls and older women are welcome. Similarly, there are temples dedicated to the female sanyasi path, where adult men are not allowed, like the Kumari Amman temple. There are temples for the sanyas of transgender people too. Misunderstandings arise because you worldly people don't know enough about our sanyasi ways.'

'Okay, okay, I give up,' said Raavan, holding his hands up in mock surrender. 'Go for your pilgrimage. When is it? In a few months?'

'Yes.' Kumbhakarna smiled and murmured, *'Swamiye Sharanam Ayyappa.'*

We find refuge at the feet of Lord Ayyappa.

While he may have been mocking his younger brother, Raavan was not about to disrespect Lord Ayyappa. The forest Lord was, after all, the son of Lord Rudra and Lady Mohini. He was considered to be one of the greatest warriors that ever lived.

He repeated after Kumbhakarna, 'Swamiye Sharanam Ayyappa.'

Before Raavan could say anything more, a loud announcement was heard. 'We are about to land. Please check your straps.'

Raavan and Kumbhakarna double-checked the straps with which they were secured to their chairs. The hundred soldiers within the Pushpak Vimaan did the same.

Raavan looked down at *Mithila*, the *city for the sons of the soil*, through the portholes. From up in the air, Mithila looked very different from the other large Indian cities, which were mostly located on the banks of rivers. Mithila had originally been a river-port town, but after the Gandaki River had changed course to flow westward a few decades ago, the fate of Mithila had altered dramatically. From being counted among the great cities of the Sapt Sindhu, it had witnessed a speedy decline. It was now far poorer than the other cities of the empire, which were themselves being rapidly impoverished by Raavan. So much so that Raavan had dismissed his appointed sub-traders in Mithila. There simply wasn't enough work for them.

'It's rare to see such a dense forest coming almost all the way up to the city,' said Raavan.

Being a fertile, marshy plain that received plentiful monsoonal rain, the land around Mithila was extremely productive. Since the farmers of Mithila had not cleared too much land, the forest had used the bounty of nature to create a dense border all around the city.

'Look at the moat,' said Kumbhakarna, surprised.

From the air, they could see a body of water around the fort that must have served as a defensive moat once, with crocodiles in it for preventive security. Now, it was a lake to draw water from.

The lake circumscribed the entire city within itself so effectively that Mithila was like an island. Giant wheels drew water from the lake, which was carried into the city through pipes. Steps had been built on the banks for easy access to the water.

'They don't have a proper defensive moat anymore!' said Raavan, astonished.

'I think it's a smart move. They don't need one. Why would anyone attack Mithila? There is no money to be looted here. And they freely distribute their only treasure: their knowledge.'

'Hmm… you're right.'

As the brothers looked at the moat around the fort, they observed an inner wall, about a kilometer inside the main fort wall. The area between the outer and the inner fort walls was neatly partitioned into plots of agricultural land. The food crops appeared ready for harvest.

Raavan was impressed. 'Good idea. At least someone in Mithila has military sense.'

Growing crops within the fort walls would secure the food supply during any siege. Also, since there was no human habitation there, this area would be a killing field for anyone who managed to breach the outer wall. An attacking force would lose too many men in the effort to reach the inner wall, without any hope of a quick retreat.

Kumbhakarna agreed with his elder brother. 'Yes, it's a brilliant military design; two fort walls with uninhabited land in between. We should try it too.'

As the Pushpak Vimaan hovered over the ground for a little while, they could see one of the main gates of Mithila. There were no coat of arms emblazoned across the gate, unlike in most forts in India.

Instead, an image of *Lady Saraswati*, the *Goddess of Knowledge*, had been carved into the top half of the gate.

There was a couplet inscribed below the image, but it was not readable from this distance.

'I wonder what the couplet says,' said Raavan.

'I remember Akampanaji telling me about it,' said Kumbhakarna.

> '*Swagruhe Pujyate Murkhaha;*
> *Swagraame Pujyate Prabhuhu;*
> *Swadeshe Pujyate Raja;*
> *Vidvaansarvatra Pujyate.*'
>
> *A fool is worshipped in his home.*
> *A chief is worshipped in his village.*
> *A king is worshipped in his kingdom.*
> *A knowledgeable person is worshipped everywhere.*

Raavan smiled. Truly, a city dedicated to knowledge. Truly, a city beloved of the rishis. Truly, a city that would serve his purpose well.

Small, circular metal screens descended over the portholes, blocking the view.

'We're landing,' said Kumbhakarna.

As the thunderous sound of its rotors dipped, the Pushpak Vimaan slowly descended to the ground. It touched down in the space earmarked for it, far outside the outer fort wall, in the clearing ahead of the forest line. Raavan's bodyguard corps of over ten thousand soldiers had already gathered there, in orderly formation.

Raavan took a deep breath. 'Time for action.'

—ॐ—

'Something is not right, Dada,' said Kumbhakarna. 'Let's leave.'

Raavan had set up camp outside Mithila. Safer to be there, surrounded by his soldiers, than within the city walls of a Sapt Sindhu kingdom. A kingdom that he had, through his trade policies, impoverished.

'But King Kushadhwaj invited me himself!' said Raavan, outraged. He had been waiting for Kumbhakarna and his aides to return from their visit to the royal court in Mithila, where they had gone to announce his arrival.

'I know, but he was quiet throughout. So was King Janak.'

'Then who the hell was speaking?'

'Guru Vishwamitra.'

'What in Lord Indra's name is Guruji doing here? There is no debate during a swayamvar ceremony!'

'I don't know what he is doing here, but I can tell you that he seemed to be making all the decisions. And I was not even allowed to meet Princess Sita.'

'What does this mean?' Raavan was getting more and more agitated. 'I am Lanka. Ruler of the most powerful kingdom in the world. The richest land on earth. I have done Mithila a favour by agreeing to come here to win the hand of Sita. How can they treat me this way?'

'Dada, let's just leave. The Sapt Sindhuans will never accept us. You tried. You did it with a clean heart. You wanted to make a fresh start. But these people won't let that happen. To hell with this "Aryavarta". Let us be happy in Lanka, in our own corner of India. Let's leave.'

'And let the entire world know I was humiliated? So that any insignificant bastard can rebel against me tomorrow? Never. I will not leave!'

'Dada, listen to me. Guru Vishwamitra was trying to tell me, without actually saying so, that you would not be welcome at the swayamvar. Each time I looked at King Kushadhwaj, he was busy examining the floor. He didn't say a word. None of this bodes well.'

'Why didn't you tell them that we were invited by that fool Kushadhwaj?'

'What's the point, Dada? He did not want to acknowledge us. We are not welcome here. Let's just leave.'

'No, we will not!'

'Dada…'

'Raavan will not be insulted this way! Lanka will not be insulted this way! I don't care what they think. I will go to the swayamvar and I will win. I will leave with Sita, even if I just throw her into the dungeons of Sigiriya afterwards. I will win this swayamvar. I will redeem my honour!'

'Dada, I don't think that—'

'Kumbhakarna! My decision is final!'

—१७—

On the day of the swayamvar, Raavan and Kumbhakarna left their camp, accompanied by thirty soldiers. Fifteen marched ahead of them and fifteen behind. The soldiers were dressed in their ceremonial best, as the representatives of the richest kingdom in the world ought to be. They carried the standard of Lanka: black flags, with the head of a roaring lion emerging from a background of fiery flames.

Given that they were not welcome at the swayamvar, Kumbhakarna had arranged for a battalion of a thousand soldiers, armed to the teeth, to follow Raavan and his bodyguards. They were to wait outside the venue of the swayamvar. Kumbhakarna wanted to play it safe, but without provoking the Malayaputras.

The Lankans crossed the pontoon bridge over the lake and marched through the open gates of the outer wall, and then past the inner wall. The soldiers behind Raavan and Kumbhakarna blew on their conch shells, attracting as much attention as they could.

Most of the citizens of Mithila were headed to the swayamvar, or had already got there. The few who remained in the city came out of their houses to stare at the procession. The procession of the richest and most powerful man in the world. Faced with the pomp and grandeur of the Lankan party, the peaceful inhabitants of Mithila withdrew. They did not want to offend or aggravate the Lankans in any way.

Raavan kept his eyes on the path ahead, his posture that of a king returning victorious from battle. He refused to even glance at the meek citizens of Mithila.

The swayamvar had been organised in the Hall of Dharma, inside the palace complex, instead of at the royal court. The building had been donated by King Janak to the Mithila University and the hall regularly hosted debates and discussions on various esoteric topics—the illusion of this physical world, the nature of the soul, the source of Creation, the value and beauty of idol-worship, the philosophical clarity of atheism… King Janak was a philosopher-king who focused all his kingdom's resources on matters of spiritual and intellectual interest.

The circular hall was crowned with a large, elegant dome. Its walls were decorated with portraits of the greatest rishis and rishikas from times past. In some ways, the circular design embodied King Janak's approach to governance: a respectful regard for all points of view. During debates, everyone sat at the same level, as equals, without a regulating 'head', deliberating issues openly and without fear.

For the purpose of the swayamvar, temporary three-tiered spectator stands had been erected near the entrance to the hall. At the other end, on a wooden platform, was placed the king's throne. A statue of the great King Mithi, the founder of Mithila, stood on a raised pedestal behind the throne. Two thrones, only marginally less grand, were placed to the left and right of the king's throne. A circle of comfortable seats lined the middle section of the great hall, where kings and princes – the potential suitors – were seated.

Accompanied by the loud cacophony of Lankan conch shells, Raavan and Kumbhakarna made their grand entry along with their entourage of thirty bodyguard. The battalion of one thousand soldiers waited outside the hall. Out of sight, but close at hand. Ready to charge to the aid of their king if summoned.

Raavan and Kumbhakarna walked ahead, looking around at the arrangements.

The upper levels of the three-tiered spectator stands were packed with ordinary citizens, while the nobility and the rich merchants occupied the first platform. The contestants sat in a circle, on comfortable chairs, in the middle section of the hall. Every seat was occupied. Princess Sita would be able to see all that was going on without being visible herself, as she had decided to make it a *gupt swayamvar.*

In the centre of the hall, placed ceremoniously on a table top, was an unstrung bow. The legendary Pinaka, the bow of Lord Rudra Himself. A number of arrows were placed beside it. Next to the table, at ground level, was a large copper-plated basin. Competitors were required to first pick up the bow and string it, which itself was no mean task. They would then have to move to the basin, which was filled with water, with more trickling in steadily from the top. This created gentle ripples within the bowl, spreading out from the centre towards the edge. To make things more difficult, and unpredictable, the drops of water were released at irregular intervals.

A hilsa fish was nailed to a wheel, which was fixed to an axle that was suspended from the top of the dome, a hundred metres above the ground. The wheel revolved at a constant speed. The contestants were required to look at the reflection of the fish in the unstill water below, and use the bow to fire an arrow into the eye of the fish. The first to succeed would win the hand of the bride.

Raavan did not pause to look at the task set for the potential suitors. Neither did he appear to notice that his entry into the hall had interrupted the speech of the great Malayaputra, Guru Vishwamitra. This was an unprecedented insult to the maharishi. But Raavan did not seem to care. For something else had caught his attention. Every seat in the competitors' circle was occupied.

They haven't reserved a place for me! The bloody bastards!

Raavan's entourage moved to the centre of the hall and halted next to Lord Rudra's bow. The lead bodyguard made a loud announcement. 'The King of Kings, the Emperor of Emperors, the Ruler of the Three Worlds, the Beloved of the Gods, Lord Raavan!'

Raavan turned towards a minor king who was sitting closest to the Pinaka, grunted softly, and gestured with his head. The terrified man rose without question and scurried away to stand behind another competitor. Raavan walked towards the chair, but did not sit. He planted his right foot on the seat and rested his hand on his knee. Kumbhakarna and his men fell in line behind him. Then, almost lazily, Raavan turned his gaze to the other end of the hall, where the thrones were placed.

Maharishi Vishwamitra was seated on the royal throne of Mithila, the one customarily reserved for the king. The present king of Mithila, Janak, sat on the smaller throne to the right of the great maharishi, while the king's younger brother, Kushadhwaj, sat to the left of Vishwamitra.

Raavan spoke loudly to Vishwamitra in the distance. 'Continue, great Malayaputra.'

Raavan did not even deem it fit to apologise for the great insult of interrupting the chief of the Malayaputras in the middle of his speech.

Vishwamitra was furious. He had never been treated so disrespectfully. 'Raavan...' he growled.

Raavan stared back at him with complete insouciance.

Vishwamitra managed to rein in his temper; he had an important task at hand. He would deal with Raavan later. 'Princess Sita has decreed the sequence in which the great kings and princes will compete.'

Raavan took his foot off the chair and began to walk towards the Pinaka while Vishwamitra was still speaking. The chief of the Malayaputras completed his announcement just as Raavan was about to reach for the bow. 'The first man to compete is not you, Raavan. It is Ram, the prince of Ayodhya.'

Raavan's hand stopped a few inches from the bow. He looked at Vishwamitra and then turned around to see who had responded to the sage. He saw a young man, around twenty years of age, dressed in the simple white clothes of a hermit. Behind him stood another young, though gigantic man, next to whom was Arishtanemi. Raavan glared first at Arishtanemi, and then at Ram. If looks could kill, Raavan would have certainly felled a few today.

This is that little kid born in Ayodhya on the day I defeated his father! And Vishwamitra has the gall to put this child up against me? Against the king of Lanka? Against the ruler of the world?

Raavan turned to face Vishwamitra, his fingers wrapped around Vedavati's finger-bone pendant that hung around his neck. He needed her. He needed her voice. But he couldn't hear anything. Even she had abandoned him during this great humiliation.

Raavan growled in a loud and booming voice, 'I have been insulted!'

Kumbhakarna, who stood behind Raavan's chair, was shaking his head imperceptibly. Clearly unhappy.

'Why was I invited at all if you planned to make unskilled boys compete ahead of me?!' Raavan's body was shaking with fury.

Janak looked at Kushadhwaj with irritation before turning to Raavan and interjecting weakly, 'These are the rules of the swayamvar, Great King of Lanka…'

A voice that sounded more like the rumble of thunder was finally heard. It was Kumbhakarna. 'Enough of this nonsense!' He turned towards Raavan. 'Dada, let's go.'

Raavan suddenly bent and picked up the Pinaka. Before anyone could react, he had strung it and nocked an arrow on the string. Most people could not even lift the mighty Pinaka easily. Yet Raavan, in a supreme display of strength and skill, had smoothly picked it up, strung the bow and nocked an arrow before anyone could react. The speed and dexterity with which he moved was mind-numbing. Even more remarkable was the target of his arrow.

Everyone sat paralysed as Raavan pointed the arrow directly at Vishwamitra, the great maharishi and the chief of the legendary Malayaputras.

The Malayaputras were the tribe left behind by the previous Vishnu. So their chief was, in a way, a representative of the Vishnu. For someone to even say a rude word against the chief Malayaputra was unprecedented. But for someone, even a man as powerful as Raavan, to point an arrow at Vishwamitra? It was unthinkable.

The crowd gasped collectively in horror as Vishwamitra stood up, threw his angvastram aside, and banged his chest with his closed fist. 'Shoot, Raavan!'

Everyone was stunned by the warrior-like behaviour of the great maharishi. Such raw courage in a man of knowledge was rare. But then, Vishwamitra had been a warrior once.

The sage's voice resounded in the great hall. 'Come on! Shoot, if you have the guts!'

I should shoot him. The pompous nutcase... But the medicines... For Kumbhakarna... For me...

Raavan shifted his aim ever so slightly and released the arrow. It slammed into the statue of King Mithi behind Vishwamitra, breaking off the nose of the ancient king.

The king of Lanka looked around. He had insulted the founder of the city. The ancient king was respected and idolised by all. His memory remained sacred even today. Raavan expected at least some Mithilans to respond with righteous rage.

Come on! Fight for King Mithi's honour. Give me an excuse to order all my soldiers in and massacre all of you!

But no Mithilan stood up. Shamefully, swallowing their pride, they remained seated even at the public insult to the memory of the founder of their kingdom.

Cowards!

Raavan dismissed Janak with a wave of his hand as he glared at Kushadhwaj. He threw the bow on the table and began to walk towards the door, followed by his guards.

In all this commotion, Kumbhakarna stepped up to the table, quickly unstrung the Pinaka, and reverentially brought the bow to his head with both hands.

My apologies, great Lord Rudra. My brother did not mean any insult to your sacred bow. He has surrendered to his emotions. Please don't hold this against him.

With utmost respect and dignity, Kumbhakarna placed Lord Rudra's bow, the Pinaka, back on the table. Then he turned around and briskly walked out of the hall, following a seething Raavan.

Chapter 26

'How dare they!' Raavan was pacing up and down inside the stationary Pushpak Vimaan. 'How dare they? I am Lanka! I am their lord! How dare they?'

Kumbhakarna tried to calm him. 'Let it be, Dada. I told you what to expect. Let's just leave.'

'Leave? Leave? Are you crazy, Kumbhakarna?'

Kumbhakarna knew that if his elder brother was calling him by his proper name instead of 'Kumbha', he was in no mood to listen to any brotherly advice about staying calm.

'These pathetic losers have insulted me,' Raavan hissed, his fists clenching and unclenching. 'They have humiliated me in public. They will pay the price!'

'Dada,' Kumbhakarna said, his tone even. 'What do you intend to do?'

Raavan pointed towards Mithila. 'I'll burn the city to the ground! I'll kill everyone in it! I'll grind this city of the sons of the soil into the soil!'

'Dada, why punish innocent civilians for the crimes of their leaders?'

'If civilians don't rebel against the crimes of their leaders, then they are criminals too!'

'But Dada—'

'No buts! I said they are criminals too!'

Kumbhakarna changed tack, trying to appeal to reason rather than compassion. 'Dada, the crown-prince of Ayodhya is in there. Apparently, he won the swayamvar for Princess Sita's hand. He will not abandon his wife and escape Mithila. My intel also tells me that, over the last few years, Prince Ram has become Emperor Dashrath's favourite son. If we end up killing him, the emperor will almost certainly declare war on us. And if the emperor calls for war, treaty obligations will force other kingdoms to join too. You know we cannot afford to fight a war right now. It's only our reputation that keeps us safe.'

Raavan cursed. Kumbhakarna was right. The plague had weakened the Lankan army. An all-out war was out of the question.

But Raavan's anger would not be pacified easily. 'Whatever it is, we are not leaving,' he said.

'Dada, I was told by Akampana, who had it from Samichi, that there are nearly four thousand policemen and policewomen in Mithila. They will be able to put up a fight.'

'But we have ten thousand Lankan warriors.'

'Even a five-to-two advantage will be negated by their defensive double walls. You know that.'

Raavan was not ready to give up. 'I've heard that there's a secret tunnel on the eastern side of that inner wall. We can send a small force to enter the city through the tunnel. Once our soldiers overpower the guards at the gateway and fling the main city gates open, the army can take over. We will massacre them!'

Kumbhakarna had also heard about the secret tunnel from Akampana, who had sourced the information from Samichi.

Akampana had told Kumbhakarna that while agreeing to lead them through the secret tunnel, Samichi had exacted a promise from the Lankan that Princess Sita would not be harmed during the attack. This was a bizarre demand from someone who had sworn loyalty to Raavan and Lanka. Maybe all the talk of a secret tunnel was a trap. Kumbhakarna doubted Samichi's loyalty. Clearly, Raavan did not.

'Prepare for an attack,' he said.

'Dada, I still think—'

'I said, prepare for an attack!'

Kumbhakarna took a deep breath, bowed his head and whispered unhappily, 'Yes, Dada.'

—र्ठI—

It was late at night, the fourth hour of the fourth prahar. Torches lined the Lankan camp. Raavan's bodyguards had been working feverishly through the evening, chopping down trees in the forest and building rowboats to carry them across the moat. Simply marching across was out of the question since the Mithilans had destroyed the pontoon bridge.

Raavan was standing beside the lake, looking across the water to the fort walls. He wore armour that covered his torso. Two swords and three knives hung from his waist. Two smaller knives were hidden in his shoes. An arrow-filled quiver was tied to his shoulders, across his back. He held a bow in his left hand. Raavan was ready for battle.

Standing next to the king of Lanka was Kumbhakarna. He had even more weapons on his person than Raavan, since the extra arms on top of his shoulders were also capable of flinging knives.

Their soldiers were armed and ready too. Ten thousand Lankans stood at a distance, close to the boats—on full alert, and with a reputation to protect.

Raavan lowered the scope he was looking through. 'They have nobody on the outer walls.'

Kumbhakarna pulled up his own scope and looked through it, examining the walls thoroughly. 'Hmm. That makes sense. They want us to scale the outer wall. Most of their soldiers are on the ramparts of the inner walls. While we are rushing towards the inner walls, they will fire arrows on us and hope to kill as many of our soldiers as possible in that zone of death.'

Raavan sniggered. 'Somebody in that namby-pamby city of intellectuals has battle sense, but not enough to match ours. We won't be climbing over the inner walls. We'll be racing through the open gates.'

Kumbhakarna nodded.

'When are we likely to get news?' asked Raavan.

Kumbhakarna continued to stare at the fort as he replied, 'The fact that we haven't got news till now does not bode well.'

'I don't care. We are not retreating.'

Kumbhakarna turned to his elder brother. 'I know, Dada.'

Just then, Akampana came rushing towards them. 'Iraiva! Iraiva! It was a trap!'

'Softly, you fool!' hissed Raavan.

'What happened?' asked Kumbhakarna.

'The secret tunnel had already collapsed onto itself, great Iraiva. Even worse, that traitor Jatayu and his Malayaputras were on top of the wall, firing arrows at us. We lost half the platoon. Ten of the men escaped somehow to give me the news. Perhaps Samichi has been discovered and forced to reveal our battle strategy to them.'

'Or Samichi lied to us,' said Kumbhakarna.

'It doesn't matter,' said Raavan. 'We are still attacking.'

'Dada…'

'I have a backup plan.'

Kumbhakarna looked towards the boats. Large wooden contraptions were being loaded on to them. 'What's that?'

'My backup plan,' said Raavan. 'Let's go.'

The soldiers began to push their boats into the moat. It would take half an hour for all the ten thousand soldiers to cross the lake and assemble on the other side of the water, outside the fort.

The Battle of Mithila had begun.

—ᚱᚦI—

The Lankans organised themselves outside the outer walls with great efficiency.

Since there was no resistance—no Mithilan soldiers on the ramparts shooting arrows at them or pouring down boiling oil—they could move about freely.

Kumbhakarna, meanwhile, was staring in wonder at Raavan's innovation—his backup plan.

'This is brilliant, Dada. It just might work,' said Kumbhakarna.

'It *will* work!' said Raavan.

'You're the man! You still have it.'

'I never lost it!' said Raavan.

The object of Kumbhakarna's admiration, a device Raavan had invented, was simple in design and devastating in its potential to destroy. It consisted of a large stand with an enormous bow, almost the size of a man, fixed at the far end, horizontal to the ground. The bow was fastened to an axle at the centre, with an extremely thick bowstring attached to it. A rough seat had been built at the other end of the stand, where the archer would sit. The job of the archer was to load an enormous arrow, almost the size of a small spear, onto the bow, then pull the bowstring back with both hands and let it fly. A system of gears and pulleys allowed the stand to be adjusted so that the direction and angle of the arrow could be controlled.

There were a thousand of these stands, with one thousand bows mounted on them.

Essentially, Raavan had adopted the standard tactic of an attacking army firing arrows at soldiers on a fort wall and turbo-charged it.

They already knew, thanks to Samichi's information, that the 'soldiers' on the Mithila side were mere police personnel, not warriors. They would not have metallic shields, only wooden ones. Shields that were good enough to stop a hail of arrows but were certainly not sturdy enough to stop missiles the size of spears.

'They won't know what hit them,' Kumbhakarna said. 'They'll keep wondering how we are managing to reach them with spears thrown from outside the outer walls. They'll wonder if we have monsters and giants in our army!'

Raavan grinned, the bloodlust rising in him. Nothing got his heartbeat going like the heat of battle. 'They won't have time to wonder. They'll be too busy dying.'

'Should I order the attack?'

Raavan looked around. Long ladders had been set up against the outer walls of the fort. Spotters had been stationed on top of the ladders, each with a scope, to focus on the inner walls of Mithila and report the destruction that would follow shortly. Raavan expected the Mithilan soldiers to flee as soon as the attack of the spears began. But a good general trusts hard data more than his expectations. Unlikely though it was, there was still the chance that a few courageous Mithilans would put up a fight. Once he received confirmation that there were no Mithilan defenders in sight anywhere near the inner fort wall, the Lankan soldiers would scale the outer walls and charge.

Raavan looked at Kumbhakarna. 'Let's begin the massacre.'

Since this was a charge at night, orders could not be conveyed through flags. Kumbhakarna turned to his herald and nodded. The herald immediately raised a conch shell and blew into it. The signal rolled out, the length and the breaks in the sound conveying Raavan's message to the soldiers. The other heralds across the Lankan lines repeated the signal.

The archers began putting arrows to the massive bows. After a brief pause, the conch shells signalled again and a fusillade of Lankan spears was released. A thousand missiles flew together on their deadly journey towards a city built for knowledge and not war. The Mithilans cowered behind their wooden shields. Shields that were utterly inadequate for blocking the spears coming their way.

Raavan and Kumbhakarna waited for a sign from the lookouts. A moment later, each of them could be seen raising a closed fist, almost in unison.

A loud cheer went up from the Lankans on the ground below. '*Bharatadhipa Lanka!*'

Lanka, the Lord of India! Or more accurately, *Lanka, the ruler of India!*

'Direct hit!' roared Raavan. The spears had torn into the Mithilan ranks amassed at the inner fort wall. 'No time to waste! Fire one more volley.'

The archers bent to their task immediately. It would take a few minutes for all the bows to be ready.

'We cannot fire once our men scale the outer wall,' said Kumbhakarna. 'We may hit our own soldiers while they are running towards the inner wall.'

'That is why I want another round of spears fired,' said Raavan. 'I want the Mithilans in retreat before we charge.'

Kumbhakarna looked up at the lookouts. Almost all of them had both hands above their heads in a swinging motion.

'Look, Dada! We may not have to fire another round,' said Kumbhakarna. 'They are in retreat already.'

Raavan grunted in disgust. 'Bloody cowards. Can't even withstand one volley!'

'Should we charge?'

'No. Fire another round for safety's sake.'

The lookouts were now holding their arms over their heads, crossed together. The Mithilans were in full retreat.

Kumbhakarna looked at Raavan as another booming, ominous whoosh was heard. A thousand more spears sprang out of the bows and flew towards the inner ramparts, ripping into the stragglers among the fleeing Mithilans.

At least one thousand of the four thousand Mithilan warriors were downed in those devastating few minutes. Without a single Lankan life being lost.

The lookouts were now clapping their open palms together above their heads. The signal was clear. There were no Mithilans on top of the inner wall anymore. They were either dead or had run away.

'Charge!' roared Raavan.

The heralds announced the orders down the line, and the Lankans began scaling the outer wall, roaring their battle cries.

Weapons drawn. Ready to kill. Ready to destroy the hapless residents of Mithila.

They were in for a surprise.

Mithila was a poor city, and the little wealth it had was distributed unfairly. The rich were too rich. And the poor, too poor.

As a consequence of this, the rich lived in luxurious mansions in the heart of the city, while the poor lived in decrepit slums and hovels close to the walls of the fort. Sita, the princess of Mithila and its prime minister, had not been able to countenance such injustice. So she had raised money, through taxes and support from outsiders, to redevelop the slums. Since there wasn't enough land to construct large houses for all the slum-dwellers, she had come up with an ingenious solution—a four-storied honeycomb structure, which extended right up to the inner fort walls.

Because of its shape, this massive building that had replaced the slum was called the Bees Quarter. Many of the former slum-dwellers had punched windows through the walls of the fort, which were also now the walls of their homes. Sita had not stopped them. Considering the minor status of Mithila within the Sapt Sindhu power structure, security had never been as paramount for her as the upliftment of the poorer citizens.

The windows in the walls had been temporarily sealed for the swayamvar, with wood-panel barricades. But now, the Mithilans had quickly broken and removed these barricades, giving them a clear view of the empty grounds between the two fort walls—and an easy outlet for shooting arrows at the Lankans who came rushing from the outer fort wall towards them. Since the Mithilans were inside the Bees Quarter, the roof protected them from any further missile attacks.

Basically, a makeshift improvisation in urban engineering had turned into an immense strategic advantage during battle!

The Lankans, unaware of the danger that awaited them, were charging forward in a frenzy. They ran towards the inner wall, carrying ladders. Ready to scale the second wall, weapons in hand, and ravage the hapless citizens of Mithila. They expected no resistance.

'Kill them all!' thundered Raavan, running shoulder-to-shoulder with his soldiers, bloodlust in his eyes. 'No mercy! No mercy!'

In the tremendous din that the Lankans were making, Raavan didn't hear a loud command in the distance. From within the Bees Quarter. An order bellowed by Sita and her husband, Ram. 'Fire!'

To the shock of the charging Lankans, arrows suddenly came raining down on them. Raavan looked up at the inner ramparts before realising that the arrows were being shot from the windows lower down, within the wall. Windows they did not even know existed.

The Lankans were caught off-guard as the arrows cut through their lines. The losses were heavy, with almost every missile finding a mark, since the soldiers had been hurtling forward in dense formations. In the confusion, part of the charge stalled, with some of Raavan's men running helter-skelter to avoid the projectiles aimed at them, while others cowered behind their shields. The Mithilans shot their arrows without respite, killing as many of the enemy as they could.

The soldiers around Raavan and Kumbhakarna pulled their shields forward, protecting the brothers.

'Retreat, Dada!' shouted Kumbhakarna. 'We are in a death zone.'

'Never!' roared Raavan. 'All we need to do is scale the inner wall. Our army will finish them off! A few more minutes!'

'Dada! In a few more minutes, you will not have an army left!'

Kumbhakarna could see that Raavan was seething. He also knew he could not give the order to retreat without Raavan's permission. 'Dada, they are shooting us down like fish in a barrel! Give the order!'

Behind the protective barrier of shields, Raavan looked around. At his loyal soldiers falling all around him, cut down ruthlessly.

The king of Lanka nodded, the movement barely visible in the darkness.

Kumbhakarna turned to his herald. 'Retreat!'

The conch shells were sounded, and their tune was picked up by heralds across the Lankan line. But this time, they played a different strain. At the signal, the Lankans turned and ran, retreating as rapidly as they had arrived.

A loud cheer went up from the Mithilans in the Bees Quarter.

The first Lankan attack had been repelled.

Chapter 27

It was the fifth hour of the first prahar the following day.

The sense of shock in the Lankan camp was greater than the actual devastation. They had expected an easy victory against the apparently peace-loving Mithilans. What they had not expected was a strong counter-attack.

Raavan had initially been incensed at the previous night's outcome, but on reflection, he realised the odds were still in their favour. The Lankans had lost a thousand men the previous night. But so had the Mithilans, according to the intelligence from Samichi. The loss of a thousand soldiers weighed a lot more on the smaller Mithilan force. While Princess Sita's army was now made up of three thousand irregular soldiers drawn from the police force, the Lankans still had nine thousand battle-hardened veterans. Furthermore, they had received word from Samichi that the ordinary citizens of Mithila were horrified at the devastation wrought by the Lankans the previous night. Morale was at an all-time low and Princess Sita was trying hard to rally her citizens to fight, but it seemed unlikely that she would succeed.

The more he thought about it, the more Raavan was convinced that his forces still had the strength to conquer and destroy the city of King Mithi. And now, more than ever, it was a matter of prestige.

The Lankans had been hard at work all night. The injured were being treated inside makeshift hospital tents, while parts of the forest were being cleared at a rapid pace. By the morning, they had enough wood for their needs. Some of the soldiers worked in groups to saw and shape the hardwood into planks. Others linked these planks into giant rectangular shields with sturdy handles on the sides as well as at the base. Each shield was capable of protecting twenty men.

Raavan, accompanied by Kumbhakarna, walked up and down the lines, supervising the work.

'The tortoise shields are coming along well,' said Kumbhakarna. Though he had not been enthused at the prospect of battle at first, Kumbhakarna knew that leaving was out of the question. If they retreated after their unsuccessful first attempt, news would spread throughout the Sapt Sindhu that a tiny, powerless kingdom had managed to beat back the mighty Lankans in battle. This would electrify Raavan's enemies. If they had avoided battle in the first place, the effect would not have been as devastating. But it was too late now. They would have to fight and defeat Mithila to forestall other rebellions.

'Yes,' said Raavan. 'Tonight, we will charge again. We will break the outer walls, there's no need to scale them. In any case, no Mithilan will be out there. Once we are past the outer walls, protected by our tortoise shields, we'll breach the inner walls. These fools are not prepared for a siege. We underestimated them earlier. We will not make the same mistake again.'

Kumbhakarna nodded. But it continued to bother him that Guru Vishwamitra and some of his Malayaputras were still inside the fort. One never took the mighty Malayaputras lightly. Never.

Raavan's mind was still on the battle to come. 'Once we breach their walls, we will destroy them all. Nobody should be left alive, not even the animals.'

Kumbhakarna did not say anything.

'You continue checking the shields,' said Raavan. 'I want to read the spy reports.'

'Yes, Dada.'

Kumbhakarna walked away, deep in thought. He knew they had to fight this battle, but he couldn't shake off the sense of foreboding that gripped him.

He was moving among the men, checking the tortoise shields, when he heard the unmistakable sound of an arrow whizzing through the air. He ducked instinctively, only to see the arrow slam into a plank of wood at his feet. He looked up in surprise.

Who in Mithila can fire an arrow that travels this distance with such unerring accuracy?

He stared at the walls. All he could make out were two unusually tall men standing on the inner wall ramparts, and a third, who was a trifle shorter. The third man held a bow; he seemed to be looking directly at him.

Kumbhakarna stepped forward to examine the arrow that had buried itself in the wood. There was a piece of parchment tied to its shaft. He tugged it off, untied the note, and read it quickly.

Lord Rudra have mercy!

—ॐ—

'You actually believe they will do this, Kumbhakarna?' asked Raavan, snorting with disgust as he threw the note away.

Kumbhakarna had come running to Raavan and taken him aside to show him the note. It was from Ram, the crown-prince of Ayodhya and now the husband of Sita, the princess-prime minister of Mithila. The short note warned, very clearly, that the Malayaputras had set up an Asuraastra missile on the inner fort walls of Mithila, out of reach of the Lankan soldiers. And that if the Lankans did not demobilise their army and retreat, Ram would fire the Asuraastra. Raavan had one hour to decide.

'Dada,' said Kumbhakarna, 'if they fire an Asuraastra, it could be—'

'They don't have an Asuraastra,' interrupted Raavan. 'They're bluffing.'

The Asuraastra was considered by many to be a daivi astra, used as a weapon of mass destruction. Lord Rudra, the previous Mahadev, had banned the unauthorised use of daivi astras many centuries ago, and practically everyone obeyed his diktat. Anyone who broke the law, he had decreed, would be punished with exile for fourteen years. Breaking the law for the second time would be punishable by death. The tribe left behind by Lord Rudra, the Vayuputras, would enforce this punishment strictly.

However, there were those who insisted that the Asuraastra was not, strictly speaking, a weapon of mass destruction, only of mass incapacitation. And since it could not be termed a daivi astra, it could possibly escape Lord Rudra's ban. Raavan did not concern himself with whether the Asuraastra qualified as a daiva astra or not. He simply refused to believe that the Malayaputras had an Asuraastra at all. He knew it was extremely difficult to access the core material for building one—there was none to be got in India for sure. He did not see the point in worrying about a weapon that his enemy was unlikely to possess.

'But Dada, the Malayaputras do have—'

'Vishwamitra is bluffing, Kumbhakarna!'

Shocked to hear Raavan refer to Guru Vishwamitra by his name alone, Kumbhakarna fell silent.

—ॐ—

Nearly three hours had passed since the Lankans had received the warning. By now, even Kumbhakarna had begun to wonder if the note had been a bluff, though the vague sense of impending doom refused to leave him.

'Are you convinced now, Kumbha?' asked Raavan. 'You know I am never wrong.'

Kumbhakarna wished he could share his brother's conviction, but his own instincts said otherwise.

'You are aware of the punishment for firing a daivi astra, right?' asked Raavan. 'Do you expect the Malayaputras to break Lord Rudra's law? Guruji knows very well that even if we kill everyone else in Mithila, we would not dare touch them. They are safe.'

What Raavan didn't know was that the Malayaputras were out of options. Even though they were mindful of Lord Rudra's laws, they had to protect Sita at any cost.

Kumbhakarna's instincts were right.

'Can I please have your permission to step out now?' asked Raavan sarcastically.

On Kumbhakarna's insistence, Raavan had grudgingly remained within the parked Pushpak Vimaan. One of the metals used to build the fuselage of the vehicle was lead, and it was well-known that lead was an inhibitor of the effects of various daivi astras, including the Asuraastra. That's why it was sometimes called a magic metal. Kumbhakarna had been keeping an eye on the section of the Mithila fort from where the warning arrow had been fired. At the first sign of trouble, he intended to close the vimaan door, so that his brother would be safe.

Kumbhakarna shook his head. 'No, Dada. Please. It's my job to protect you.'

'And it's my job to protect you from your own stupidity! Step aside now. I need to go check if the boats are ready for the weight of the tortoise shields.'

'Dada, please listen to me.'

'In the name of Lord Rudra, have you gone insane, Kumbhakarna?' Raavan asked, exasperated.

'Please, Dada. Your safety is most important.'

'I am not a child who needs your protection!'

'Please stay here, Dada,' said Kumbhakarna. 'I will go and check the boats.'

'Dammit!'

'Dada, just think you are doing it to humour me. I have a bad feeling—'

'We can't make battle plans based on your "feelings"!'

'I beg of you. Stay in the vimaan. I'll go and check on the boats.'

Raavan sat back angrily. 'Fine!'

—१६१—

Kumbhakarna was at the lake, instructing the Lankan soldiers to load the tortoise shields on the boats. He still had one wary eye on the fort, checking for any sign of the Asuraastra being fired.

He turned to look at the vimaan parked some distance behind him and was relieved to see a scowling Raavan standing just inside the flying craft.

Kumbhakarna gestured for Raavan to remain where he was, then turned back to watch the work on the boats.

All of a sudden, that sense of foreboding inside him seemed to strengthen. Painfully. Like someone had grabbed his guts and was squeezing them dry.

He looked towards the fort. Towards the section of the inner wall that had the Bees Quarter abutting it. His eyes widened in alarm.

What Kumbhakarna did not know was that the Malayaputras had finally found someone to trigger the Asuraastra. Someone to take the blame, and the punishment, for possibly breaking Lord Rudra's commandment. Someone whose desire to save the woman he loved was strong enough to make him break the law, something he would not normally consider—Sita's husband, Ram.

A flaming arrow shot by Ram was tearing through the air at a fearsome speed.

Lord Rudra have mercy.

Kumbhakarna turned around instantly, screaming, 'Dada!'

He charged towards the Pushpak Vimaan, running as hard as his legs would allow.

Meanwhile, at the top of the Bees Quarter, the flaming arrow slammed into a small red square on the Asuraastra missile tower, pushing it backwards. The fire from the arrow was captured in a receptacle behind the red square, and from there it spread rapidly to the fuel chamber that powered the missile. There was a flash of intense light, and a series of soft explosions. A few seconds later, heavy flames gathered near the base of the tower.

Kumbhakarna reached the vimaan and leapt for the entrance, throwing his weight on his elder brother, who went flying backwards into the vimaan. Kumbhakarna's momentum carried him inside as well.

But the door of the craft was still open.

The Asuraastra missile took off and flew in a high arc over the walls of Mithila, covering the distance in a few short seconds. The Lankan soldiers on the outer side of the moat-lake looked up in surprise and panic. The missile could mean only one thing.

A daivi astra.

They were doomed. They knew that.

There was no time to react. No time to run. And where would they run and hide?

They were out in the open. Easy prey for the Asuraastra.

Even while devastation sped towards them, none of the Lankans could tear their eyes away from the spectacle. As the missile flew high above the moat-lake, there was a small, almost inaudible explosion, like that of a firecracker meant for a child.

The terror in the soldiers' hearts was quickly replaced by hope.

Maybe the daivi astra had failed.

But the Malayaputras and the princes of Ayodhya, who stood at the top of the Bees Quarter, knew better. They had covered their ears, as instructed by Guru Vishwamitra.

The assault of the Asuraastra had not yet begun.

Kumbhakarna, meanwhile, had sprung to his feet, even as Raavan lay sprawled on the floor of the vimaan. He rushed to the door and hit the metallic button on the sidewall with the full weight of his body. The door of the vimaan began to slide shut slowly. Too slowly.

The door will not close in time.

Without a second thought, Kumbhakarna took up position. Just inside the vimaan. Just behind the doorway. As the sliding door moved into place, closing slowly, agonisingly slowly.

Kumbhakarna. Blocking the still open part of the doorway with his gigantic form.

So that the effects of the explosion would not travel beyond him.

Kumbhakarna. Ready to sacrifice himself. For the man he loved.

For his brother.

For his dada.

The Asuraastra hovered above the Lankan soldiers for a moment, and then exploded with an ear-shattering sound that shook even the walls of Mithila in the distance. The Lankans felt their eardrums burst painfully, the air sucked out from their lungs.

But this was only a prelude to the devastation that would follow.

An eerie silence followed the explosion. Then spectators on the Mithila rooftops saw a bright green flash of light emerge from where the missile had splintered. It burst with furious intensity and hit the Lankans below like a flash of lightning. They stayed rooted, stunned into a temporary paralysis. Fragments of the exploded missile showered down on them.

Kumbhakarna saw the flash of green light just as the door of the Pushpak Vimaan slid shut. Even as the door sealed and locked automatically, saving those inside the flying vehicle from any further injury, Kumbhakarna collapsed, unconscious.

'Kumbhaaaaaaa!' Raavan rushed to his younger brother, screaming.

Outside the vimaan, the Asuraastra was still not done. The real damage was yet to come.

A dreadful hissing sound radiated out, like the battle-cry of a gigantic snake. Simultaneously, the fragments of the missile that had fallen to the ground emitted demonic clouds of green gas, which spread like a shroud over the stupefied Lankans.

The gas was the actual heart of the Asuraastra. The real weapon. The explosions and the paralysing green light primed the victim. The thick green gas was the slayer.

In a few minutes, the deathly gas enveloped the Lankans, who lay paralysed in the clearing outside the Pushpak Vimaan. It would put them in a coma that would last for days, if not weeks. It would kill some of them. But at the moment, all was deceptively calm. There were no screams and no cries for mercy. No one made an attempt to escape. They simply lay on the ground, motionless, waiting for the fiendish astra to push them into oblivion. The only sound in the otherwise grim silence was the hiss of the gas spewing from the missile fragments.

Inside the vimaan, a devastated Raavan was on his knees, holding his younger brother in his arms. Tears streamed down his face as he shook the body of his paralysed brother repeatedly, trying to wake him up. 'Kumbha! Kumbha!'

—३६१—

Some thirty minutes had passed. The Asuraastra had completed its devastation of the Lankan troops.

A small, skeletal crew present inside the craft had escaped. One of them was a doctor. As standard operating procedure, the vimaan was always manned and ready for flight.

The doctor had managed, with the help of his emergency kit of medicines, to release Kumbhakarna from the paralytic effects of the missile. His body was still immobile and his breathing was ragged, but he could move his head a little. He lay on the floor of the vimaan. Blood seeped very slowly from his Naga outgrowths. His head was on his elder brother's lap.

He tried to say something, but his tongue was swollen and his speech was slurred and unintelligible.

'Be quiet,' whispered Raavan, his cheeks wet with tears. 'Rest. You will be fine. I won't let anything happen to you.'

'Thatha… thuuu… thokay?'

Raavan's tears flowed more strongly as he understood what his younger brother was saying. Even in this state, Kumbhakarna was more concerned about Raavan's wellbeing. The king of Lanka kissed his younger brother's forehead gently. 'I am okay. You rest, little brother, you rest.'

Kumbhakarna's partially paralysed face shaped itself into a crooked smile. 'Thuuu… thowe… thmee.'

Raavan smiled through his tears. 'Yes. Yes, I owe you, my brother. I owe you.'

Kumbhakarna shook his head slightly, the crooked smile still on his face. 'Thust… thoking…'

'Rest, Kumbha. Rest…'

Kumbhakarna closed his eyes.

Raavan held his brother's head close to his chest, crying. 'I am so sorry, Kumbha. I am so sorry. I should have listened to you.'

'My lord,' whispered one of the Lankan soldiers, looking through a porthole.

Raavan looked up.

'The gas is still visible,' the man said. 'It has wrapped itself around our men. What do we do?'

Raavan knew what that meant. All his soldiers who lay on the ground outside the Pushpak Vimaan would be paralysed for days, if not weeks. They would be in a coma, from which some of them would never awake. He couldn't step out either. For the effects of the gas could still be strong.

The Battle of Mithila had been lost. His bodyguard corps was destroyed. He had no soldiers left, besides the few within the vimaan. There was nothing he could do.

But that didn't seem to matter so much now.

He looked down at his brother. And pulled him closer.

All that mattered was his brother. He had to get Kumbhakarna back on his feet.

Raavan looked at the pilots of the Pushpak Vimaan. 'Fly us out of this cursed place.'

Chapter 28

Raavan breathed deeply. 'Finally, a chance to get back at the Malayaputras,' he said.

A little more than thirteen years had passed since the Battle of Mithila. Raavan and Kumbhakarna were in Sigiriya, in the king's private office in the royal palace. The memory of the battle had faded with time, but the wound was still raw for Raavan.

The humiliating defeat and the devastating destruction of Raavan's ten-thousand-strong bodyguard corps had not had as much of an impact across the Sapt Sindhu as he had feared. For a short period after the Battle of Mithila, others within the Sapt Sindhu had started dreaming of challenging Lankan authority. They had even begun to see Ram, the prince of Ayodhya, as the leader of the resistance. But before the movement could gather force, Ram had been banished for fourteen years from the Sapt Sindhu by King Dashrath, for the unauthorised use of the daivi astra, in accordance with the laws of the previous Mahadev. All dreams of a rebellion had died with his departure. The fact that Ram's wife Sita, the princess of Mithila, and his younger brother Lakshman had left with him had hit morale further.

Raavan had endured a loss of prestige too. His people had expected him to return to Mithila and destroy it to avenge the defeat he had suffered, but Raavan knew that the Lankan army was in no condition for an all-out war. Besides, the Malayaputras had left Mithila with the Lankan soldiers, who had been revived and then imprisoned. The price for returning them was Raavan's solemn oath, in Lord Rudra's name, that he would not attack Mithila or any other kingdom in the Sapt Sindhu.

To ensure that Raavan kept his word, Guru Vishwamitra had warned him that if he so much as thought of mobilising his army to attack the Sapt Sindhu, he would stop receiving the medicines that kept him and Kumbhakarna alive. To drive the point home, he had further raised the price of the medicines and the cave material. Though burning with humiliation, Raavan had had no choice but to accept these terms. But he had been waiting for a chance to get back at the Malayaputras, and it seemed now that an opportunity had finally presented itself.

'It's not about vengeance, Dada,' said Kumbhakarna. 'It's about getting what we want. We have to be careful. Very careful.'

'That may be true for you. For me, getting back at the Malayaputras is just as important. But I would never do anything silly, or in anger. I am not stupid.'

Kumbhakarna threw up his hands in acceptance. 'All right.'

'The important thing is, they have a Vishnu now. And an interesting choice of a Vishnu too,' Raavan said thoughtfully.

'Yes,' said Kumbhakarna. 'Suddenly a lot of things are making sense. For instance, I could never understand why the Malayaputras were so desperate to save Mithila. They used the Asuraastra, defying the ban by Lord Rudra and possibly damaging their relations with the Vayuputras permanently. An insignificant kingdom like Mithila was surely not worth such a risk. But it's apparent now that they were not trying to save their precious city of sages, but their Vishnu! They knew that you were so angry, you would have killed everyone there that day.'

Raavan nodded. 'True. They don't care for their own lives. They care only about their mission. And for their mission to succeed, they need the Vishnu.'

'Princess Sita.'

'Who would have thought they would select someone from tiny, powerless Mithila for a Vishnu,' said Raavan, flexing his right shoulder. He was close to sixty years old now, and aches and pains had become a constant part of his life. Also, the medicines that kept him alive were taking a toll on his strength. The mysterious plague ravaging Sigiriya was only causing further damage.

'She wasn't the only candidate,' said Kumbhakarna.

Raavan looked at his younger brother, surprised.

'The Vayuputras and Guru Vashishtha believe that Ram should be the next Vishnu,' said Kumbhakarna.

Vashishtha was the raj guru and chief adviser to the Ayodhya royal family. But his position within the Sapt Sindhu royalty wasn't the main reason he was held in such high esteem across the land. He was also a *maharishi*, a *great man of knowledge*, whose intellect was unmatched. His only equal, perhaps, was the chief of the Malayaputras, Maharishi Vishwamitra. It was also well known that Maharishi Vashishtha was very close to the Vayuputras, the tribe left behind by the previous Mahadev, Lord Rudra.

'Ram? Really?'

'Yes.'

'That's awkward,' said Raavan. 'What are the Vayuputras and Guru Vashishtha trying to do? Create marital discord between Ram and Sita?'

Kumbhakarna laughed. 'In any case, what the Vayuputras or Guru Vashishtha think about the Vishnu has no bearing on the final choice. The Vishnu is selected by the Malayaputras alone. And Guru Vishwamitra has made his choice. Sita will be the next Vishnu.'

Raavan leaned back in his chair and took a deep breath. 'What is the cause of this fight between Guru Vashishtha and Guru Vishwamitra? Weren't they friends once?'

'I don't know, Dada. That's something for another story, another book. It has nothing to do with us.'

'But you do know a lot about most things,' said Raavan. 'How did you find out so much about this Vishnu business?'

'It's best if you don't know.'

'Why?'

'Just trust me, Dada.'

Raavan stared at Kumbhakarna. 'Why do I get the feeling sometimes that we are pawns in a much bigger game?'

'Every human being is a pawn, Dada. But in chess, the pawn that breaches the other side suddenly becomes very powerful.'

Raavan raised his eyebrows and smiled. 'There is a difference between chess and real life, little brother.'

'Of course. But chess is a representation of real life. How you play chess says a lot about how you live as well.'

'Wise words,' said Raavan. 'In any case, I trust you completely, Kumbha. Any time I have not trusted you, I have suffered.'

Kumbhakarna laughed and stifled a yawn.

'Feeling sleepy again?' asked Raavan, a guilty look on his face.

The Asuraastra had had a debilitating effect on Kumbhakarna. Born a Naga, he had suffered aches and discomfort since his childhood. His outgrowths were painful at the joints, and would bleed profusely during his childhood. The Malayaputra medicines had helped keep the pain and bleeding in check. However, exposure to the noxious Asuraastra's green light had caused a massive deterioration in his condition. Furthermore, at fifty-one, he was not as strong as he had once been. The renewed bleeding and pain were almost unbearable now.

The Malayaputra physicians had visited Sigiriya and formulated some new medicines that helped manage the pain and the bleeding to some extent, but they also made Kumbhakarna extremely lethargic. He slept for most part of the day, every day. The only way he could get his focus back was by avoiding having the medicines for a few days. But the pain would return almost immediately, and the bleeding would restart if he skipped the medicines for more than five days. Anything beyond that, and his life itself would be at risk.

And all this because he had put himself in danger to save his brother's life during the Battle of Mithila.

Raavan had not been able to forgive himself. He had curtailed all his other plans over the last thirteen years— from the expansion of the Lankan empire to the takeover of Kishkindha. He focused instead on ensuring that his younger brother remained alive and as healthy as possible.

Kumbhakarna smiled at Raavan. 'I'm all right, Dada.'

Raavan smiled and patted his brother's shoulder.

'In any case,' Kumbhakarna continued, 'we have nothing to do with the Vayuputras or Guru Vashishtha. We only need the Malayaputras under our control. And that will happen when we take the Vishnu away. They will want to free her at any cost, and that's when we can really squeeze them dry. We'll demand the medicine supply we need for the next twenty years in one shot—without paying their ridiculous prices. Nothing stops us from demanding more from the Malayaputras as long as the Vishnu remains imprisoned in Lanka.'

Raavan nodded.

'Do we go ahead then?' asked Kumbhakarna.

'Yes, we have to kidnap Sita.'

'Remember, Dada, it's not about vengeance. We will only ask for what we want. We just need some leverage over the Malayaputras. We will not kill the Vishnu.'

Raavan nodded.

'She will be our prisoner.'

'Yes.'

'A political prisoner. She will be kept in one of the palaces in Lanka, not in the dungeons.'

'I get it, Kumbha! You don't have to go on about it!'

Kumbhakarna smiled and put his palms together in apology.

—ऱ्ऻI—

'Dada, I don't think this is a good idea,' whispered Kumbhakarna.

Raavan was in his private chamber in the royal palace of Sigiriya, with Kumbhakarna. Raavan's son, the twenty-seven-year-old Indrajit, was also present. Indrajit had the same intimidating physical presence as his father. He was tall and astonishingly muscular, with a voice that was deep and commanding. He had also inherited his mother's high cheekbones and thick brown hair, which he wore in a leonine mane, with two side partings and a long knot at the crown of his head. An oiled handlebar moustache sat well on his smooth-complexioned face. His clothes were sober—a fawn-coloured dhoti and a creamy white angvastram. He wore no jewellery, except for the ear studs that most warriors in India favoured. The plague that was ravaging Lanka had had no impact on Indrajit, which made Raavan proud.

The king of Lanka adored his son. He had picked the name himself: *Indrajit* meant *one who could defeat the king of the Gods, Indra.*

Indra was the legendary king of the Devas in the hoary past. The name had, over time, become a title for all who were considered the kings of the Gods. Raavan's high aspirations for his son were no secret.

'I agree with Kumbhakarna Uncle,' said Indrajit, speaking quietly so his voice wouldn't carry far. 'This is an important mission. I think we should be the ones to carry it out. We can't leave it to Uncle and Aunty, who are a hideous combination of arrogance and incompetence.'

Raavan regarded the man and the woman who stood at a respectful distance from him. Vibhishan and Shurpanakha—his half-siblings and Indrajit's 'uncle and aunty'. The two had volunteered for the job of kidnapping Sita. Raavan could barely keep his revulsion from showing on his face when he looked at them. They were born of a father he hated and a stepmother he despised, and if that wasn't enough, his rent-a-tear mother Kaikesi had adopted and nurtured them. She would go to any length to undermine him, he thought again.

'We'll take care of it, Dada,' said Vibhishan politely to his much older half-brother.

Vibhishan was of average height and unusually fair-skinned. His reed-thin physique was that of a runner. But he held his thin arms wide, as if to accommodate impressive biceps. His long, jet-black hair was tied in a knot at the back of his head. His full beard was neatly trimmed and dyed a deep brown. He wore a rich purple dhoti and a pink angvastram, with a lot of jewellery. He was a complete dandy and, according to Raavan, full of false politeness and humility.

'I am not your dada,' said Raavan firmly. 'I am your king.'

'Of course, my lord,' said Vibhishan, immediately correcting himself and holding his ears in respectful apology.

Raavan rolled his eyes.

'Our idea will work, my lord,' Vibhishan said.

Raavan's spies had informed him that Sita, Ram and Lakshman were camped in Panchavati, a peaceful spot along the Godavari River, with sixteen Malayaputra soldiers for their protection. Raavan was suspicious of the fact that only sixteen soldiers had been tasked with the security of someone as important as the Vishnu, but he was told that Sita was still angry with the Malayaputras for forcing Ram to fire the Asuraastra. She had refused their support. The soldiers with her were under the command of Jatayu, whom she considered her brother—which apparently was the only reason she had agreed to their presence.

Vibhishan proposed that they use Shurpanakha's beauty to distract Ram and Lakshman. An encounter with her would presumably lead to the two men letting their guard down. Shurpanakha would then find some pretext to lead Sita away from Ram and Lakshman, and kidnap her. The Ayodhya princes would be told that Sita had attacked Shurpanakha out of jealousy, and in the fight that ensued, she had accidentally drowned in the river. Since the Godavari was prone to swift currents, it was likely that her body would never be found.

This way, Vibhishan reasoned, they would be able to kidnap Sita without having the blame fall on Lanka.

'Why not just send in our soldiers and pick her up?' asked Kumbhakarna.

'What if Ram gets injured or hurt in the process?' Vibhishan responded with a question of his own.

What Vibhishan left unsaid was obvious to all. Ram was, technically, the king of Ayodhya, and the king of Ayodhya was considered to be the emperor of the Sapt Sindhu. If he died at the hands of a Lankan, treaty obligations would force all the kingdoms of the Sapt Sindhu to declare war on Lanka. And Lanka could not afford to fight a war right now. The army was too weak to go into a battle.

Kumbhakarna was still not convinced. 'I am sure we can find a better way to separate Ram and Sita without using our own sister as bait.'

'We fight with the weapons we have been blessed with, Dada,' said Vibhishan. 'And Shurpanakha has been blessed with extraordinary beauty.'

Shurpanakha smiled proudly, pleased with the compliment. She resembled Vibhishan, but unlike her sickly brother, she was bewitching in appearance. She had more of her Greek mother's genes than her Indian father's. Her skin was pearly white, and her eyes magnetic. She had a sharp, slightly upturned nose and high cheekbones. Her hair was blonde, a most unusual colour in India, and every strand of it was always in place. Everything about her petite frame was elegant.

She wore a classic, expensively dyed purple dhoti, which was tied fashionably low, exposing her slim, curvaceous waist. Her silken blouse was a tiny sliver of cloth, affording a generous view of her cleavage. Her angvastram, deliberately hanging loose from a shoulder, revealed more than it concealed. Extravagant jewellery completed the picture of excess.

Shurpanakha seemed convinced of her ability to pull off this plan. Kumbhakarna, however, was still sceptical. He turned to Indrajit for his opinion.

The confident young man spoke up immediately. 'Vibhishan Uncle, please don't think I am being rude, but I have honestly not heard a more stupid idea in my life. I don't see how this will work.'

Vibhishan tensed in anger, but controlled his tongue with superhuman effort. Being insulted by his elder brother was something he had learnt to live with. But to hear such words from this pup? It was intolerable!

'Do you think any man with a heart that beats can even think of resisting this?' asked Shurpanakha, pointing at herself.

'Good God, Shurpanakha! You are my sister. How can you say such things in my presence?' Kumbhakarna was appalled.

'You have turned celibate, Dada,' said Shurpanakha to Kumbhakarna, almost tauntingly. 'You will not understand.'

Kumbhakarna turned to Raavan. 'Dada, I don't approve of this. I say we go with our original plan.'

'Dada,' said Shurpanakha to Raavan—she had none of the diffidence that Vibhishan was saddled with—'I will handle this. You don't need to get your hands dirty. Allow us to earn your trust.'

Raavan thought about it. Kumbhakarna was already looking tired and sleepy. He would have to be given his medicines soon. Then there was Indrajit—his pride and joy. His heir. If there was a way to avoid putting these two at risk...

'Also, my lord,' said Vibhishan, 'many people believe that we are not close to you. So, even if we are caught out, in all likelihood, Sita's disappearance will not be linked to you. It will be like an independent act by relatives you don't like. Your hands will remain clean.'

Raavan narrowed his eyes. *That does make some kind of sense.*

'Dada,' Shurpanakha persisted, 'you have nothing to lose. If we fail, you can go to Panchavati with your soldiers in any case. What's the harm in giving us a chance?'

Yeah... What's the harm?

'All right,' said Raavan.

Shurpanakha whooped in delight, clapping her hands together.

Vibhishan went down on his knees ceremoniously and brought his head down to the floor, paying obeisance to Raavan. 'You will not regret this, my lord.'

Raavan looked at him. *Pretentious moron.*

Chapter 29

It had been many weeks since Vibhishan and Shurpanakha had sailed out of Lanka, to the port of Salsette, on the western coast of India. Located north of the ruined Mumbadevi port, the island was now the primary Lankan outpost in the area. It was also the port closest to Panchavati, where Ram, Sita and Lakshman were camped, along with sixteen Malayaputra soldiers.

Indrajit had accompanied his uncle and aunt to Salsette, but had been ordered to take no further part in the mission. Raavan did not want to put his son's life at risk. The brave young man had protested vociferously, but had finally submitted to his father's directive.

From Salsette, Vibhishan and Shurpanakha had marched with a company of soldiers to Panchavati, with the intention of kidnapping Sita.

But the mission had turned out to be a disaster.

'I am sorry,' Raavan said to Kumbhakarna. 'I should have listened to you.'

Raavan and Kumbhakarna were in the Pushpak Vimaan, accompanied by a hundred soldiers, flying towards Salsette.

Not only had Shurpanakha failed to kidnap Sita, she had been caught and bound by her. Sita had dragged the bleating

Lankan princess to the Panchavati camp, where the waiting Lankan soldiers had nearly come to blows with the followers of Ram and Sita. Worse, Shurpanakha had been accidentally injured on her nose by Lakshman.

Vibhishan had quickly ordered a retreat without offering a fight, thus keeping himself, his sister and their soldiers alive. They had rushed back to Salsette, and from there, led by Indrajit, had sailed back to Lanka, to appraise Raavan of their plight.

Raavan had responded by setting off from Lanka immediately, with as many soldiers as could be accommodated in the Pushpak Vimaan. While cosmetic surgeries would, over time, take away the physical marks of Shurpanakha's injury, the metaphorical loss of face could only be avenged with blood.

Raavan couldn't stop cursing his inept half-siblings all through the flight, but he also realised, with some prodding from Kumbhakarna, that he finally had a legitimate excuse to attack Ram's camp. After all, any outrage against a member of the Lankan royal family had to be responded to. It was a matter of honour, and any reasonable person would agree that it could not be construed as an act of war. And that would hopefully nullify the treaty obligations which bound other kingdoms within the Sapt Sindhu to come to Ayodhya's aid.

Kumbhakarna looked at his brother and smiled, waving the apology aside. 'It's all right, Dada. We've spoken about this already and cussed out our idiot half-siblings enough. Let's focus on what we have to do right now. We have to kidnap the Vishnu. That's it. Let's keep our minds clear.'

'True,' said Raavan, smiling. He stretched his arms over his head. 'You know what the most irritating part of an attack is?'

'What?'

'The waiting.'

'That is true.'

'It's excruciating to know we will be in the heat of battle soon, but till it starts, we have to sit around doing nothing. We have to talk and behave normally, keeping our heartrate in check and bloodlust high, but not so high that we lose control.'

Kumbhakarna laughed. 'But you will keep your bloodlust in check out there as well.'

Raavan glowered at Kumbhakarna.

'Dada, be realistic. You are not what you used to be. You are nearly sixty years old now. Your navel outgrowth and the continuous use of medicines have weakened you. You've fought enough battles. Let the soldiers do the fighting now.'

'Well, you're not exactly fighting fit either!' Raavan exclaimed petulantly.

Kumbhakarna glanced towards the pilots of the craft, who were within earshot.

'Which is why I will avoid fighting as well,' he said, keeping his voice low.

'They attacked our family. And you want us to not react?' Raavan spoke in an angry whisper.

'No, Dada. I want you to react intelligently.'

'I am not a coward!'

'I didn't say you are.'

'Then I must fight.'

'Absolutely not.'

'You don't have the right to order me around, Kumbhakarna.'

'You are right, I don't. But I do have the right to demand the first of the three boons you promised me.'

In a fit of guilt and remorse after the Battle of Mithila, where his mistake had caused permanent damage to Kumbhakarna's health, Raavan had told his younger brother that he could demand three boons from him, at any time in the course of their lives. And that those three demands would be met, come what may. Kumbhakarna had not asked for anything. Until now.

Raavan grunted angrily. He knew he had no choice. 'You are not playing fair, Kumbha!'

'We'll get the Vishnu, Dada. We'll kidnap her. But there is no need for you to put your life at risk.'

Raavan looked away, fuming.

Kumbhakarna laughed softly. 'Look at the bright side, Dada. I only have two boons left.'

—ॐ—

Raavan looked out of the porthole at the land of Salsette below him.

They had stopped briefly at the port, to pick up Samichi and her lover, Khara, who was also a captain in the Lankan armed forces. The vimaan had taken off once again, with its course set towards the Godavari River.

Ram, Sita, Lakshman and the Malayaputras with them had abandoned Panchavati soon after the botched encounter with Shurpanakha and Vibhishan. Lankan intelligence had lost track of them. But Samichi had managed to find the exact location of the Vishnu and her companions by brutally torturing a captive Malayaputra. It turned out that they were still close to the river, though much further down from Panchavati. As soon as Kumbhakarna was informed of this, he had ordered them to join his raiding party.

Raavan looked at Samichi, and then at his younger brother. 'Why do we need to take this woman along? I don't like having her around!'

'I know it troubles you, Dada,' said Kumbhakarna calmly. 'But she knows their exact location.'

'So what? We have the information now. We can go by ourselves.'

'Samichi knows Princess Sita better than any of us. She was in the service of the Vishnu for many years. Her advice may prove useful.'

'You could have debriefed her thoroughly before we left Salsette. I still don't see why she has to travel with us.'

'It's better to have her with us.'

'She was there during the Battle of Mithila. A fat lot of good that did us. She was useless!'

'But she is trying to make herself useful now. Let's give her the opportunity. What do we have to lose?'

Raavan took a deep breath and did not answer.

'Dada, trust me, please. It's important that we get the Vishnu; that we capture her alive. Let's put our emotions aside and focus on that.'

'You can be really infuriating, Kumbha! I don't know why I even painted you,' Raavan burst out suddenly.

'You've made a painting of me?' Kumbhakarna was genuinely surprised. He knew that every painting created by Raavan had only one constant character in it. 'You painted me with the Kanyakumari?'

Raavan nodded in the affirmative.

'When do I get to see it?' asked Kumbhakarna.

Raavan picked up a cloth bag lying next to him and pulled out a rolled-up canvas.

'What? You have it with you?' Kumbhakarna was delighted.

Raavan handed over the canvas to his brother.

Kumbhakarna unrolled it, shifting a little to make sure nobody else in the vimaan could see it. 'Wow!'

Raavan's eternal muse, the Kanyakumari, was at the centre of the painting. She looked older. Her hair was almost completely grey and her face was finely lined. She had a slight stoop. She looked at least sixty years old, if not more. But her face still had that angelic splendour—of grace, beauty and kindness.

She was helping a small child who was trying to climb a wall.

Kumbhakarna smiled. 'This child looks familiar!'

Raavan laughed softly, for the child was Kumbhakarna. Hairy, almost bear-like, with pot-like ears and two extra arms sticking out on top of his shoulders. Despite his oddities, the child looked adorable. Happy and huggable.

'Where am I going?' asked Kumbhakarna, his eyes fixed on the painting.

Raavan pointed to the fencing on top of the wall. A circular symbol in the shape of a wheel was repeated several times, to form a railing. Kumbhakarna recognised it only too well.

'The wheel of dharma.'

'Yes,' said Raavan. 'You will rise to achieve your dharma.'

'I don't see you in this painting. Where are you?'

Raavan didn't answer.

'Where do you see yourself, Dada?'

Raavan remained silent.

Kumbhakarna examined the painting closely. He then turned towards his elder brother, clearly unhappy. 'Dada—'

On the wall, visible only if one looked closely, were ten faces. Nine of them exhibited the *navrasas*, or *nine major emotions*, as described in the *Natyashastra*: love, laughter, sorrow, anger, courage, fear, disgust, wonder and tranquillity. The tenth face, in the centre, had no expression at all. A blank slate.

Kumbhakarna could see what Raavan had attempted in the painting. The king of Lanka was sometimes addressed as *Dashanan* by his subjects, for they said that he had the knowledge and power of *ten heads*. Raavan had sought to play on this name, and the symbolism that attaches to emotions in the Indian artistic tradition, to convey a much deeper meaning. Traditional wisdom says that true spiritual awakening is possible only when one transcends the wall of emotions that keeps one imprisoned in this illusory world. In the painting, Raavan had made himself the wall that the child Kumbhakarna was trying to scale.

'Climb over the wall of emotions you have for me, my brother,' said Raavan. 'Leave me, and find dharma. I am too far gone. There is no hope for me. But you are a good man. Rediscover your childhood and your innocence. Leave me and start from the beginning once again. Walk the path of dharma, for I know that is what your soul desires.'

Kumbhakarna rolled up the canvas tightly without a word, and slipped it back into Raavan's cloth bag.

'Kumbha… listen to me.'

'I am carrying out my dharma, Dada,' he said.

'Kumbha—'

'Enough now.'

—३७१—

An unseasonal storm had buffeted the Pushpak Vimaan as the Lankans approached the temporary campsite of the exiles. The pilots had somehow managed to land the craft without any damage. Dangerous as the storm was for the flying vehicle, it had inadvertently helped the Lankans. The howling winds had drowned out the sound of the vimaan's massive rotors. They had managed to disembark without being noticed and had successfully maintained the element of surprise as they attacked the temporary camp.

The battle had been short and sharp.

The Malayaputras were heavily outnumbered, so it was no surprise that there were no Lankan casualties. All the Malayaputras, save Captain Jatayu and two of his soldiers, were dead or critically injured.

But Ram, Lakshman and Sita were missing. Kumbhakarna had organised seven teams, of two soldiers each, to spread out and search for the trio.

At the same time, Captain Khara had been tasked with extracting information from the surviving Malayaputras, especially Captain Jatayu.

Raavan and Kumbhakarna stood at a distance, where they wouldn't have to get their hands dirty. Thirty soldiers stood close to them, ready to protect their royals at the first sign of trouble.

'This is taking too long,' muttered Raavan to Kumbhakarna.

'Should we go back and wait inside the vimaan?' asked Kumbhakarna.

Raavan shook his head. *No.*

Khara was still working on Jatayu, who was now on his knees, held by two Lankan soldiers. The Malayaputra's hands were tied behind his back. Jatayu had been brutalised; he was severely injured and bleeding, but he was not broken.

'Answer me,' said Khara, as he slid the knife along Jatayu's cheek, drawing some more blood. 'Where is she?'

Jatayu spat at him. 'Kill me quickly. Or kill me slowly. You will not get anything from me.'

Khara raised his knife in anger, about to strike at Jatayu's throat. Suddenly, an arrow whizzed in from behind the forest line and struck his hand. The knife fell to the ground as he yelped in surprise and pain.

Raavan and Kumbhakarna whirled around, startled. The Lankan soldiers close to them rushed in and formed a protective cordon around them. Kumbhakarna grabbed Raavan's arm to restrain his impulsive elder brother from charging into battle.

Other Lankan soldiers raised their bows in the direction that the enemy arrow had been fired from. They couldn't see anything. Somebody had shot the arrow from deep behind the forest line, behind the visually impenetrable line of trees.

'Don't shoot!' ordered Kumbhakarna loudly. He wanted the Vishnu alive.

The Lankan bows were swiftly lowered.

Khara broke the shaft, leaving the arrowhead buried in his hand. It would stem the blood for a while. He looked into the impenetrable line of trees. Into the darkness. And scoffed in disdain. 'Who shot that? The long-suffering prince? His oversized brother? Or the Vishnu herself?'

There was no response.

'Come out and fight like real warriors!' Khara shouted

There was no response to that taunt either.

Raavan and Kumbhakarna remained well protected by their soldiers, their shields raised high.

'Send the soldiers in,' said Raavan, pointing towards the part of the forest that the arrow had been shot from.

'No,' said Kumbhakarna. 'We should not thin out our force any further. There are three of them. They could have spread out. They can pick you off if our soldiers aren't with us.'

'Kumbha, I am not that important. Get those—'

Kumbhakarna interrupted his elder brother. 'Dada, you are the entire reason for this raid. We are kidnapping the Vishnu to keep you alive with the Malayaputra medicines. I will not put your life at risk.'

Before Raavan could argue any more, five more arrows were shot in a rapid-fire attack. In quick succession. Right where Raavan and Kumbhakarna were. But this was from a different direction. Far from where the first arrow had been shot.

The arrows hit the soldiers surrounding the brothers. Five Lankans went down. But the others did not budge. The cordon around Raavan remained resolute. Ready to fall for their king.

The bodyguards were showing the mettle they were made of.

'It looks like there are two of them in the forest,' whispered Kumbhakarna. 'I hope the Vishnu hasn't escaped.'

Raavan didn't say anything. He was getting suspicious. There was too much of a time lag between the first attack on Khara and the second five-arrow attack directed at himself and Kumbhakarna.

Some of the Lankan soldiers took off in the direction that the latest attack had come from.

Then came the sound of someone stepping on a twig. From another direction. Three soldiers rushed towards the sound.

Raavan was sure now. 'There is just one person. He is moving around quickly behind the forest line to confuse us.'

'Are you sure?' asked Kumbhakarna.

Before Raavan could respond, Khara moved. He stepped behind Jatayu, and using his uninjured left hand, held a knife to his throat.

One can chase hidden attackers in all directions. Or, one can draw them out with a well-targeted threat. Khara was smart. He did the smart thing.

'You could have escaped,' he said tauntingly. 'But you didn't. So I'm betting you are among those hiding behind the trees, great Vishnu. And you want to protect those who worship you. So inspiring… so touching…' Khara pretended to wipe away a tear.

Raavan, far in the distance, his view of Khara blocked by the many Lankan soldiers surrounding him, smiled. He turned to Kumbhakarna. 'I like this Khara.'

Khara continued aloud, 'So I have an offer. Step forward. Tell your husband and that giant brother-in-law of yours to also step forward. And we will let this captain live. We will even let the two sorry Ayodhya princes leave unharmed. All we want is your surrender.'

No response.

Khara grazed the knife slowly along Jatayu's neck, leaving behind a thin red line. He said in a sing-song voice, 'I don't have all day…'

Suddenly, Jatayu struck backwards with his head, hitting Khara in the groin. As the Lankan doubled up in pain, Jatayu screamed, 'Run! Run away, my lady! I am not worth your life!'

Three Lankan soldiers moved in and pushed Jatayu to the ground. Khara cursed loudly as he got back on his feet, still bent over to ease the pain. After a few moments, he inched towards the Malayaputra and kicked him hard. He surveyed the treeline, turning in every direction that the arrows had been fired from. All the while, he kept kicking Jatayu again and again. He bent and roughly pulled Jatayu to his feet.

This time Khara held Jatayu's head firmly with his injured right hand, to prevent any head-butting. The sneer was back on his face. He held the knife to the Malayaputra's throat. 'I can cut the jugular here and your precious captain will be dead in just a few moments, great Vishnu,' he said. He moved the knife to the Malayaputra's abdomen. 'Or, he can bleed to death slowly. All of you have some time to think about it.'

There was still no response.

'All we want is the Vishnu,' yelled Khara. 'Let her surrender and the rest of you can leave. You have my word. You have the word of a Lankan!'

A feminine voice was heard from behind the trees. 'Let him go!'

Kumbhakarna whispered to Raavan, 'It's her. It's the Vishnu.'

Khara shouted, still holding the knife to Jatayu's abdomen, 'Step forward and surrender. And we will let him go.'

And Sita, the princess of Mithila, the one recognised as the Vishnu by the Malayaputras, stepped out from behind the forest line. Holding a bow, with an arrow nocked on it. A quiver tied across her back.

The Lankan royals could not see the Vishnu. Raavan tried to push through the cordon surrounding him, to catch a glimpse of her. But he was pulled back by Kumbhakarna.

'Dada,' said Kumbhakarna, 'her husband and brother-in-law could still be hidden in the trees. We cannot risk you being in the open.'

'Dammit!'

'You promised me, Dada.'

Raavan remained where he was. Angry. But compliant.

'Great Vishnu,' sniggered Khara, letting go of Jatayu for a moment, and running his hand along an ancient scar at the back of his head. Stirring a not-quite-forgotten memory. 'So kind of you to join us. Where is your husband and his giant brother?'

Sita didn't answer. Some Lankan soldiers began moving slowly towards her. Their swords were sheathed. They were carrying *lathis, long bamboo sticks*, which were good enough to injure but not to kill. Their instructions were clear. The Vishnu had to be captured alive.

Sita stepped forward and lowered the bow, an arrow still nocked on it. 'I am surrendering. Let Captain Jatayu go.'

Khara laughed softly as he pushed the knife deep into Jatayu's abdomen. Gently. Slowly. He cut through the liver, a kidney, never stopping...

'Nooo!' screamed Sita. She raised her bow and shot an arrow into Khara's eye. It punctured the socket and lodged itself in his brain, killing him instantly.

'I want her alive!' screamed Kumbhakarna from behind the protective Lankan cordon.

More soldiers joined those already moving toward Sita, their bamboo lathis held high.

'Raaaam!' shouted Sita, as she pulled another arrow from her quiver, quickly nocked and shot it, bringing another Lankan down instantly.

It did not slow the pace of the others. They kept rushing forward.

Sita shot another arrow. Her last. One more Lankan sank to the ground. The others pressed on.

'Raaaam!'

The Lankans were almost upon her, their bamboo lathis raised.

'Raaam!' screamed Sita.

As a Lankan closed in, she lassoed her bow, entangling his lathi with the bowstring, snatching it from him. Sita hit back with the bamboo lathi, straight at the Lankan's head, knocking him off his feet. She swirled the lathi over her head, its menacing sound halting the suddenly wary soldiers. She stopped moving, holding her weapon steady.

Conserving her energy. Ready and alert. One hand held the stick in the middle, the end of it tucked under her armpit. The other arm was stretched forward. Her feet spread wide, in balance. She was surrounded by at least fifty Lankan soldiers. But they kept their distance.

'Raaaam!' shouted Sita, praying that her voice would somehow carry across the forest to her husband.

'We don't want to hurt you, Lady Vishnu,' said a Lankan, politely. 'Please surrender. You will not be harmed.'

Sita cast a quick glance at Jatayu.

'We have the equipment in our Pushpak Vimaan to save him,' said the Lankan. 'Don't force us to hurt you. Please.'

Sita filled her lungs with air and screamed yet again, 'Raaaam!'

She thought she heard a faint voice from a long distance away. 'Sitaaa…'

A soldier moved suddenly from her left, swinging his lathi low. Aiming for Sita's calves. She jumped high, tucking her feet in to avoid the blow. While in the air, she quickly released her right-handed grip on the lathi and swung it viciously with her left. The lathi hit the Lankan on the side of his head. Knocking him unconscious.

As she landed, she shouted again, 'Raaaam!'

She heard the voice of her husband. Soft, from a distance. 'Leave... her... alone...'

Kumbhakarna heard the faint voice too. He looked towards Raavan. And then shouted his order to the soldiers. 'Capture her now! Now!'

Ten Lankans charged in together. Sita swung her lathi ferociously in all directions, incapacitating many.

'Raaaam!'

She heard the voice again. Not so distant this time. 'Sitaaaa...'

The Lankan onslaught was steady and unrelenting now. Sita kept swinging rhythmically. Viciously. Alas, her enemies were one too many. A Lankan swung his lathi at her, from behind. Into her back.

'Raaa...'

Sita's knees buckled under her as she collapsed to the ground. Before she could recover, the soldiers ran in and held her tight. She struggled fiercely as a Lankan came forward, holding a neem leaf in his hand. It was smeared with a blue-coloured paste. He held the leaf tight against her nose. And Sita keeled over into unconsciousness.

'Carry her to the vimaan! Quickly!'

Kumbhakarna turned to his elder brother. 'Let's go, Dada.'

'Let me see Sita.'

'Dada, there's no time. King Ram and Prince Lakshman are close by, they might get here soon. I don't want to be forced to kill them. This is perfect. We've got the Vishnu and the king of Ayodhya has not been injured. You can see her once we are all in the vimaan. Let's go.'

Raavan and Kumbhakarna started walking towards the craft, still surrounded by their bodyguards. The Lankan soldiers followed, carrying Sita, unconscious on a stretcher.

—ॐ—

The Lankans began climbing in and taking their seats in the Pushpak Vimaan.

The last of the soldiers pressed a metallic button on the sidewall and the door began to slide shut with a hydraulic hiss.

As the brothers reached their seats, Kumbhakarna turned towards the pilots. 'Get us out of here quickly.'

While Raavan and Kumbhakarna braced for take-off, the unconscious Sita was being strapped on to a stretcher fixed on the floor of the Pushpak Vimaan.

'She's a fighter!' said Kumbhakarna, with an appreciative grin.

When the attack took place, Sita, accompanied by a Malayaputra soldier called Makrant, had gone to cut banana leaves for dinner. Ram and Lakshman were away hunting. They had all assumed that the Lankans had lost track of them.

The two Lankan soldiers who had discovered Sita had managed to kill Makrant but were, in turn, killed by Sita. She had then stolen to the devastated Malayaputra camp and had killed several Lankans from behind the tree line, using a bow and a quiver full of arrows very effectively from her hiding places. But her desire to save her loyal follower Jatayu had been her undoing.

'The Malayaputras believe she is the Vishnu,' said Raavan, laughing. 'She had better be a good fighter!'

Just then, the Lankans who were crowded around Sita left her and went to find their own seats in the vimaan.

Her unconscious body lay on a stretcher, some twenty feet away from where Raavan sat. She wore a cream dhoti and a white single-cloth blouse. Her saffron angvastram had been drawn over her entire body, with the straps of the stretcher tight across her. Her head was turned to the side, and her eyes were closed. Saliva drooled out of her mouth.

It was a large quantity of a very strong toxin that had been used to render her unconscious.

For the first time in their lives, Raavan and Kumbhakarna saw Sita.

The warrior princess of Mithila. The wife of Ram. The Vishnu.

Raavan stared at her.

Breath on hold. Heart immobile. Transfixed.

A shocked Kumbhakarna looked at his elder brother, and then at Sita. He couldn't believe his eyes.

The baby had survived. Thirty-eight years. She was a woman now.

Sita was unusually tall for a Mithilan woman. With her lean muscular physique, she looked like a warrior in the army of the Mother Goddess. There were proud battle-scars on her wheat-complexioned body.

But Raavan's eyes were glued to her face. One that he had seen before.

It was a shade lighter than the rest of her body, with high cheekbones and a sharp, small nose. Her lips were neither thin nor full. Her wide-set eyes were neither small nor large; strong brows arched in a perfect curve above creaseless eyelids. Her long, lustrous black hair had come undone and fell in a disorderly manner to the side of her face. She had the look of the mountain people from the Himalayas.

He knew this face well. It was a little thinner than the original. Tougher. Less tender. There was a faint birthmark on the right temple; perhaps a remnant of a childhood injury.

But there could be no doubt. Mother Nature had crafted this face from the same mould.

It was a face that Raavan could never forget. It was a face that he had seen grow old in his mind. It was a face that he loved.

The vimaan began to ascend as the mighty rotors roared to life, spinning powerfully.

Raavan could not breathe. He clutched his armrest tightly, trying to find a stable hold in a world spiralling out of control.

Perhaps the time had come, to finally settle an old karmic debt.

Ka... Ka...

The vimaan lurched, buffeted by a sudden gust of strong wind. But Raavan didn't notice.

He continued staring, wordlessly.

His breathing ragged.

His heart paralysed.

Time standing still.

It was obvious. It was obvious from her face.

Sita was the child of Prithvi.

Sita was the daughter of Vedavati.

—रोI—

'Guruji! Guruji!'

Arishtanemi rushed into the modest private chamber of his guru in Agastyakootam, the hidden capital of the Malayaputras.

Vishwamitra opened his eyes slowly, roused from his deep, meditative state. Normally, no one would dare to interrupt him at such a time. But this was an exception. He was expecting some news and had ordered Arishtanemi to inform him the moment it was received.

'Yes?' he asked now in his distinctive voice.

'It has happened, Guruji.'

'Tell me everything.'

'Raavan and Kumbhakarna received intelligence from Samichi about the whereabouts of Sita, Ram and Lakshman. They flew there in the Pushpak Vimaan and carried out a surprise raid.'

'And?'

'They have kidnapped Sita. Everyone in the camp was killed. I have been told that Ram and Lakshman survived only because they were out hunting at the time.'

Vishwamitra leaned back, a slight smile on his face. *We're back in the game.*

'Guruji, I don't know why we delayed sending more Malayaputras to their aid. We knew Raavan would seek vengeance for what happened with Shurpanakha. We could have saved—'

'Saved whom?'

'Jatayu and the other Malayaputras with them. They were all killed in the raid.'

'They sacrificed themselves for the greater good of Mother India. They are true martyrs. We will honour them. We will build temples to Jatayu and his band.'

'But what about Sita, Guruji? The Lankans have our Vishnu. From what I have heard, they captured her alive. But I don't know if Raavan can be trusted to not hurt her. Or, even worse, kill her.'

'He will not hurt her. Trust me.'

'Guruji, you and I both know he is a monster. Who can predict how a monster will behave?'

Vishwamitra looked at Arishtanemi thoughtfully. The time had come to reveal the secret.

'A monster, you say? Let me ask you then, do you know of any person this monster has been good to?'

Arishtanemi frowned at the strange question. 'I can only think of his brother, Kumbhakarna. And even he has been ill-treated at times.'

'Only his brother? Really? Nobody else?'

'Well, obviously, he is kind to his son. Oh yes! Also, his long-dead love, Vedavati.'

'Vedavati is the reason he will not hurt Sita,' said Vishwamitra.

Vishwamitra had long suspected that their earlier interpretation of the events at Todee had been off the mark. Many years ago, he had sent Arishtanemi and a few others, once again, to unearth more details. Arishtanemi had spoken to the men who had discovered the corpses at Todee and learned that a few bodies had been found tied to the trees close to Vedavati's house. Each of them bore clear signs of extreme torture. The bodies of the others who had died had been found strewn all around the village, suggesting that they had been chased and struck down while trying to escape. The corpses had been left to be eaten by wild animals. Arishtanemi had also ascertained that the only bodies that had been treated with respect and cremated with full Vedic honours were those of Vedavati and her husband Prithvi.

All this had caused Vishwamitra to revise his opinion on what had transpired. Perhaps Raavan had behaved honourably, contrary to what they had thought. Perhaps the men who had been tied to the trees and tortured were the ones who had killed Vedavati and her husband.

The conclusion was clear: Raavan had loved Vedavati deeply and had treated her well, till the end. The massacre was a result of his anguish at losing her. He must have ordered the killing of the villagers in a rage, after her death.

Vishwamitra was fairly certain that the tribe of the Mahadev, the Vayuputras, had reached the same conclusion. But he suspected they were unaware of what had happened after the massacre. They had not made that last crucial connection. That Vedavati's child had survived. Or they would have behaved differently towards Sita.

Arishtanemi was still looking puzzled. 'What connection can there be between Vedavati and Sita, Guruji? Why will Raavan not hurt her?'

'He will not hurt her because Sita is Vedavati's daughter.'

Arishtanemi was stunned. 'What?'

Vishwamitra nodded, the hint of a smile on his face. *Yes, we're definitely back in the game.*

'How long have you known this, Guruji? When did you find out?'

'Just before my decision to appoint Sita as the Vishnu. When she was about thirteen years of age.'

'By the great Lord Parshu Ram! That's nearly twenty-five years ago!'

'Yes. And it was the sound of a hill myna that helped me make the connection.'

'A hill myna? Really?'

'Yes. When I realised the connection, I became even more certain that my choice was right. Sita will be the perfect Vishnu, the ideal hero. Because the villain will never be able to bring himself to kill this hero.'

Arishtanemi bowed to his chief, in awe. 'You are truly worthy of being Lord Parshu Ram's torch-bearer, my lord.'

Vishwamitra acknowledged the compliment with a smile and said, 'Jai Parshu Ram.'

'Jai Parshu Ram,' repeated Arishtanemi. 'What now, Guruji?'

'Now, we use all our resources, our soldiers, our money— and Hanuman—to attack Lanka. Sita will destroy Raavan. And all of India will accept her as the Vishnu.'

'Why Hanuman? Considering he is close to...' Arishtanemi stopped himself just in time. He had been about to name his guru's arch-rival, Vashishtha.

'Many reasons,' said Vishwamitra. 'The most important one being that Hanuman loves Sita like a sister. And Sita trusts him like she would a brother.'

Arishtanemi smiled, shaking his head in wonder. 'There is nobody like you, Guruji. No one else could have planned this.'

'Wait and see. I have no doubt that Mother India will be saved. And she will be saved by our Vishnu. We will be remembered forever for this. Our ancestors will be proud of us,' Vishwamitra declared.

Arishtanemi put his hands together in respect and said, *Jai Shri Rudra. Jai Parshu Ram.*

Glory to Lord Rudra. Glory to Lord Parshu Ram.

Vishwamitra repeated the chant of the Malayaputras. 'Jai Shri Rudra. Jai Parshu Ram.'

— ऋषि —

'Divodas! Turn around and face me!'

Vashishtha, known as Divodas during his gurukul days, turned to face the man who had once been his closest friend: Vishwamitra.

'Kaushik...' said Vashishtha, through gritted teeth, using the gurukul name of Vishwamitra. 'This is all your fault.'

Vishwamitra looked at the cremation pyre and then back at Vashishtha. 'She's dead because of you. Because you simply couldn't do what had to be done! Sigiriya and Trishanku were supposed to be—'

Vashishtha stepped closer, interrupting Vishwamitra. 'Don't you dare! She died because of you, Kaushik! She died because you insisted on doing something that should never have been done. I told you! I warned you!'

Vashishtha was thin and lanky to a fault. His head was shaved bare but for a knotted tuft of hair at the top of his head, which announced that he was a Brahmin. His flowing black beard gave him the look of a philosopher. At the moment, though, he looked anything but gentle. He was shaking with fury, fists clenched tight. Rage poured out of his eyes.

As tall as Vashishtha was, he was dwarfed by the strapping Vishwamitra, who stood facing him. Almost seven feet in height, dark-skinned and barrel-chested, with a muscular torso and a rounded belly, Vishwamitra intimidated people just by his presence. His long black beard and knotted tuft of hair flew wild and free in the wind. He looked like he was fighting for control, to stop himself from wringing Vashishtha's neck.

'Get out of here,' snarled *Vishwamitra. 'I will not kill you in front of her.'*

Vashishtha stepped even closer and stared coldly at Vishwamitra. Their friendship was long dead. Its remains burned in the pyre that was consuming the woman they had both loved. From that same seething fire, a new enmity was being born. An enmity that would last more than a hundred years.

'You think I am scared of you? Bring it on! Let's battle! Say when!' Vashishtha proclaimed.

Vishwamitra raised his hand, then with great effort, controlled himself and stepped back. 'I will fulfil her dream. I will show her that I am better, better than you are.'

'You are nobody to do anything for her! She was mine. I will—'

'Guruji!'

Vashishtha opened his eyes, coming back to the present from the ancient, nearly-century-old memory.

He said a quick prayer in his mind and asked, 'What happened?' He had sent his friend Hanuman to save them, to save Sita and Ram. He could only hope Hanuman had reached in time.

'We received word from Lord Hanuman, Guruji. I am sorry, but Raavan has kidnapped Princess Sita.'

'And Ram?'

'The Lankans killed all the Malayaputras who were with Princess Sita. But from what we've been told, Prince Ram and Prince Lakshman are still alive. Our Vishnu is safe. The news is not as bad as it first seemed.'

The Vayuputras had supported Vashishtha's decision to recognise Ram as the Vishnu. They too believed that it would be good for India. Technically, though, as the tribe of the previous Mahadev, they only had the right to recognise the next Mahadev and not the next Vishnu.

'The news *is* bad, my friend,' said Vashishtha. 'The war has been triggered.'

'But… but I am not sure Raavan wants a war, Guruji. We know that Lanka is very weak.'

'It doesn't matter what Raavan wants. He's a mere puppet. He's not the one who is behind this.'

'Then who is?'

'Vishwamitra.'

'But—' The Vayuputra messenger held his tongue. He knew of the animus between Vashishtha and Vishwamitra. The worst enemy you can have is someone who was once a dear friend. He knew better than to get in the way of a battle as titanic and malignant as that between Vashishtha and Vishwamitra.

'What do we do now, Guruji?'

Vashishtha's fists were clenched tight, his muscles tense. His eyes, normally kind and gentle, burned with fury. His face was a picture of determination.

'Now… we fight!'

… to be continued.

Other Titles by Amish

The Shiva Trilogy

The fastest-selling book series in the history of Indian publishing

THE IMMORTALS OF MELUHA
(Book 1 of the Trilogy)

1900 BC. What modern Indians mistakenly call the Indus Valley Civilisation, the inhabitants of that period knew as the land of Meluha – a near perfect empire created many centuries earlier by Lord Ram. Now their primary river Saraswati is drying, and they face terrorist attacks from their enemies from the east. Will their prophesied hero, the Neelkanth, emerge to destroy evil?

THE SECRET OF THE NAGAS
(Book 2 of the Trilogy)

The sinister Naga warrior has killed his friend Brahaspati and now stalks his wife Sati. Shiva, who is the prophesied destroyer of evil, will not rest till he finds his demonic adversary. His thirst for revenge will lead him to the door of the Nagas, the serpent people. Fierce battles will be fought and unbelievable secrets revealed in the second part of the Shiva trilogy.

THE OATH OF THE VAYUPUTRAS
(Book 3 of the Trilogy)

Shiva reaches the Naga capital, Panchavati, and prepares for a holy war against his true enemy. The Neelkanth must not fail, no matter what the cost. In his desperation, he reaches out to the Vayuputras. Will he succeed? And what will be the real cost of battling Evil? Read the concluding part of this bestselling series to find out.

The Ram Chandra Series

The second-fastest-selling book series in the history of Indian publishing

RAM – SCION OF IKSHVAKU

(Book 1 of the Series)

He loves his country and he stands alone for the law. His band of brothers, his wife, Sita and the fight against the darkness of chaos. He is Prince Ram. Will he rise above the taint that others heap on him? Will his love for Sita sustain him through his struggle? Will he defeat the demon Raavan who destroyed his childhood? Will he fulfil the destiny of the Vishnu? Begin an epic journey with Amish's latest: the Ram Chandra Series.

SITA – WARRIOR OF MITHILA

(Book 2 of the Series)

An abandoned baby is found in a field. She is adopted by the ruler of Mithila, a powerless kingdom, ignored by all. Nobody believes this child will amount to much. But they are wrong. For she is no ordinary girl. She is Sita. Through an innovative multi-linear narrative, Amish takes you deeper into the epic world of the Ram Chandra Series.

WAR OF LANKA

(Book 4 of the Series)

As Raavan kidnaps Sita, Ram seethes with rage and grief. The war of Lanka is imminent; it's a war for Dharma, after all. Will Ram defeat the ruthless and seemingly invincible Raavan? Or will Lanka fight back like a cornered tiger? And, most importantly, will the real Vishnu rise? In this fourth book of the Ram Chandra Series, the narrative strands of Ram, Sita, and Ravana crash into each other and explode in a slaughterous war.

Indic Chronicles

LEGEND OF SUHELDEV

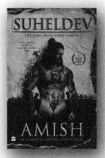

Repeated attacks by Mahmud of Ghazni have weakened India's northern regions. Then the Turks raid and destroy one of the holiest temples in the land: the magnificent Lord Shiva temple at Somnath. At this most desperate of times, a warrior rises to defend the nation. King Suheldev—fierce rebel, charismatic leader, inclusive patriot. Read this epic adventure of courage and heroism that recounts the story of that lionhearted warrior and the magnificent Battle of Bahraich.

Non-fiction

IMMORTAL INDIA

Explore India with the country's storyteller, Amish, who helps you understand it like never before, through a series of sharp articles, nuanced speeches and intelligent debates. In *Immortal India*, Amish lays out the vast landscape of an ancient culture with a fascinatingly modern outlook.

DHARMA – DECODING THE EPICS FOR A MEANINGFUL LIFE

In this genre-bending book, the first of a series, Amish and Bhavna dive into the priceless treasure trove of the ancient Indian epics, as well as the vast and complex universe of Amish's Meluha, to explore some of the key concepts of Indian philosophy. Within this book are answers to our many philosophical questions, offered through simple and wise interpretations of our favourite stories.

IDOLS: UNEARTHING THE POWER OF MURTI PUJA

A companion volume to the bestselling Dharma, this book brings back your favorite fictional characters, along with some new ones, to explore the essence and true meaning of murti puja. In this insightful book, Amish and Bhavna tackle burning questions about idol worship through simple, varied, and astute interpretations of myths and religious texts. In the process, they reveal the expansive philosophy behind the practice and how it can lead us to experience the Oneness of God through transformation, acceptance, and love.

30 Years *of*

 HarperCollins *Publishers* India

At HarperCollins, we believe in telling the best stories and finding the widest possible readership for our books in every format possible. We started publishing 30 years ago; a great deal has changed since then, but what has remained constant is the passion with which our authors write their books, the love with which readers receive them, and the sheer joy and excitement that we as publishers feel in being a part of the publishing process.

Over the years, we've had the pleasure of publishing some of the finest writing from the subcontinent and around the world, and some of the biggest bestsellers in India's publishing history. Our books and authors have won a phenomenal range of awards, and we ourselves have been named Publisher of the Year the greatest number of times. But nothing has meant more to us than the fact that millions of people have read the books we published, and somewhere, a book of ours might have made a difference.

As we step into our fourth decade, we go back to that one word – a word which has been a driving force for us all these years.

Read.

Harper
Collins

HARPER
PERENNIAL

HARPER
BUSINESS

HARPER
BLACK

हार्पर
हिन्दी

HarperCollins
Children'sBooks

HARPER
DESIGN

HARPER
VANTAGE

Harper
Sport